KELLY MORGAN

You Sound White

First published by Bright Headed Publishing, LLC 2025

This novel is entirely a work of fiction. The names, characters and incidents portrayed in it are the work of the author's imagination. Any resemblance to actual persons, living or dead, events or localities is entirely coincidental.

Kelly Morgan asserts the moral right to be identified as the author of this work.

Second edition

ISBN: 9781735753508

This book was professionally typeset on Reedsy.
Find out more at reedsy.com

Contents

Prologue

I have been told I sound white all my life.

At first, I didn't know what to make of it. Was it a compliment? An insult? A joke? I only knew that every time I heard it, something inside me shifted—an awareness that my voice, my way of speaking, carried meaning beyond my words.

I spent years trying to fit in, to be accepted. I adjusted my tone, softened my edges, measured every word. But no matter what I did, I was always *too much* of something. Too proper. Too different. Too 'white.'

The label followed me—through classrooms, friendships, romantic relationships, job interviews—making me question who I was and where I belonged. It made me wonder: *Why does the way I speak determine how people see me?*

This book is about that struggle. About identity, perception, and the unspoken rules of belonging. But most of all, it's about reclaiming the power of my own voice.

Because no matter what they say—**our voices belong to us.**

Chapter 1

The sun shone through the small kitchen window in Tallulah's 2nd-floor apartment. The open window let in a nice morning breeze. The apartment was small, but she liked to use the term "cozy" whenever her parents mentioned its size. The grayish, two-story building used to be a warehouse. They turned it into four apartments about fifteen years ago. The windows faced east, so there was always plenty of sunlight. Tallulah had found the apartment soon after she graduated college. The rent was cheap, and the neighborhood – though not the nicest in the city – was pretty safe.

Tallulah was a pretty girl. When she was in college, she was often referred to as "thick". Her skin was the color of brown sugar, and her brown eyes and thick lips accented her high cheekbones. She started growing dreadlocks at 15. One night, while watching TV, she saw a woman with long, beautiful dreadlocks. At that moment, she decided she wanted the same style. Her mother thought she was crazy. Her grandmother, however, liked the idea. She even helped her learn to grow and care for her locks. Once she'd transformed her hair into twist locs, there was no turning back.

Tallulah stood at a height of approximately 5'7", placing her above the average height. She was happy she was tall because it evened out her thick thighs and long torso. Her butt was round and full and poked out when she walked. When she was younger, she tried to hide it. Sometimes, she tied a sweater or hoodie around her waist to cover it up.

Her mother always said she was pretty. But it's tough to feel that way when the world defines beauty as skinny, blonde, blue-eyed, and milky white skin. Some of the white girls at her high school would make fun of her and call her "big lips" or "bubble butt". She only realized in college that men like women with big, round asses, thick lips, and soft but firm thighs.

When Tallulah first moved into her apartment, the walls were white. The landlord let her paint them a soft earth tone blue. This was great since it was the only paint on sale. She purchased all her furniture second hand and found her small kitchen set at a flea market. Chloe, one of her best friends, had mentioned her grandmother had the exact same set in her house. The two chairs were metal, painted yellow. The table was also metal and covered in big yellow painted flowers.

Tallulah had managed to find some old pictures at a thrift store. She had limited funds, so she chose the ocean beach setting. Then, she found a picture of a little Black girl running through a field. Chloe had donated the small sofa for her living room; it was just the right size for the space. Meanwhile, her downstairs neighbor, Mrs. Herrera, gave her a small coffee table. The only thing Tallulah moved in with was her bedroom set, a graduation present from her parents. Her queen-sized bed barely fit the bedroom, but it did allow enough room for a small dresser. The bathroom was equally small, with only enough room for a shower, sink, toilet, and small wall cabinet.

Tallulah sat in her living room, typing on her laptop. Her past and recent articles, poems, and unfinished short stories were scattered around her. She stopped typing long enough to glance at a piece of paper that read "Notice of rent increase". She frowned at the notice. The news of the increase made her panic. So, she quickly began searching for extra work. She spent the morning applying for various writing jobs. She sent samples to editors of magazines, newspapers, blogs, and online publications.Tallulah grabbed the coffee cup on the small table in front of her. She took a long sip, as she placed it down, her email notification chimed; it was a reply to a job she'd applied to. She felt a small flutter in her stomach. She guided her cursor and clicked on the email. Then, she suddenly frowned.

"Fuck!" she said out loud.

She then stood up and set down the laptop. "If I get one more rejection, I'm gonna kill myself!" she yelled. Her voice echoed throughout the apartment as she let out a huff and said, "Rejection is *not* cool."

She started pacing in the apartment. Then, she paused by two pictures on the kitchen window sill. The first one was in a silver metal frame, the second in a brown wooden frame. She picked up the picture in the metal frame, looked at it, and smiled; it was of her and her girls, Chloe and Zoe. They were smiling, holding up their diplomas, having graduated college. She set down the first picture and picked up the second one. In it was Michael, her best friend from high school, and her parents. Tallulah stood in the middle of the trio, her smile broadening. She and Michael had graduated high school and were holding up their diplomas.

She set the second picture back in its place and sighed. Everyone in her life was doing what they'd set out to do. Zoe and Chloe had their careers on an upward trajectory, and Michael had started his own paper. She stared at both pictures a moment longer, then said, "Y'all are doing great. Me...not so much."

Tallulah's circle of friends was small; she preferred it that way. She hadn't had many friends growing up. She felt different, as if she never fit in anywhere or with anyone. She grew up in a white neighborhood. The other kids often singled her out because she looked different. Over time, she learned to handle different situations. But most kids reminded her that she looked different. It wasn't until college that she began to feel comfortable in her own skin.

Chloe and Zoe had been her girls since the first day of college. The three of them were freshmen roommates and had clicked right away. As Tallulah looked at the pictures, her mind wandered to the first day she met them. Her parents drove her to school. She begged them not to come up. She didn't want anyone to think she needed her mommy and daddy to walk her to her dorm room. They agreed, but only after some hesitation. She kissed and hugged them, then grabbed a large box. They watched her struggle with it as she carried it up the stairs and disappeared from view.

As Tallulah carried the box into her dorm room, number 10, she spotted Zoe sitting cross-legged on a blue yoga mat. Her eyes closed, and she was chanting. Tallulah was afraid to speak; she didn't know what to make of the strange girl chanting. So, she scanned the room, spotted an empty bed, walked over to it, and set down the box. She didn't speak, she rather observed the girl sitting and chanting. She had no idea what she was doing and didn't want to interrupt. She thought about unpacking the box but didn't want to make any noise; so, she sat on the bed and didn't make a sound. Chloe, a second girl, walked into the room. She sang loudly and off-key. She didn't seem to notice the girl chanting, sitting on the floor.

Surprised to see Tallulah, she smiled and said, "You the new roommate?" As she brought a basket of clothes to her bed, she noticed Tallulah sitting on the floor. Tallulah was looking back at her. "Oh, don't worry about this bitch. She's bringing positive vibes into the room with her meditation stuff."

Tallulah smiled and shifted uncomfortably on the small twin-sized bed. As she looked down at her feet, she felt Chloe's eyes on her.

"Where you from? Don't you talk? You deaf?" Chloe said, pulling clothes out of the basket.

Caught off guard by this line of questioning, Tallulah stammered, "N-n-no, I'm not deaf."

"Well, that's good," said Chloe. "I thought I was gonna have to sign or some shit."

Tallulah noticed the girl on the blue yoga mat stirring. Finally, she opened her eyes. "Damn Chloe, you always say some dumb shit. What if she was deaf? She wouldn't have heard your dumbass anyway." The girl stood up, shook her head, and smiled at Tallulah.

"Hi, I'm Zoe. That mess over there is Chloe."

Tallulah said, "I'm Tallulah. Tallulah Brock."

Chloe stood up and said, "Tallulah?! Your parents gave you that name? How you spell it? Damn, girl, we need to shorten

6

that shit to T, just plain ol' T." Tallulah shook her head and replied, "I'm good with T. My parents call me Lula."

Zoe looked at Chloe, then turned to Tallulah. "I was meditating. Something I picked up a few years ago from my cousin. She's into the Universe and connecting. What's your major?"

Tallulah watched Zoe as she moved around the blue floor mat. She styled her hair in short twists, and her skin was a deep chocolate brown. The shortest of the three of them, Zoe was Coke bottle-shaped, with a small waist.

Tallulah answered, "Journalism."

"What do you write?" Zoe asked, going into a downward dog pose.

Tallulah watched her in amazement; she was so flexible. She answered, "Poems, articles, and short stories, stuff like that."

Zoe dropped down into a full plank and lowered herself to the floor. Tallulah found it intriguing how she flowed into each move.

"Really? I could never write. No good with words," Zoe said, taking her time to move into cobra pose.

Tallulah stammered, "W-well, I want to be a writer one day."

Zoe released her cobra pose and stood up. "I'm a business major," she said, smiling, then sat on the bed next Chloe. Tallulah looked to the floor and rubbed her hands together. She was nervous.

Chloe grabbed a bag of chips sitting on a small desk. "I'm a PR major," she said as she ripped open the bag and started eating.Zoe shot her a look of disapproval, like that of a mother scolding her child. "You know those'll kill you. Full of fat and grease."

Chloe looked at the bag and said, "Ah, no, they're potatoes, and potatoes are good for you." She looked at Tallulah. "Damn, girl, you all thick an' shit. You datin' anyone? You know there's a party tonight! We gotta show up and show out! Goddamn, the fellas are gonna love that ass!"

Tallulah twisted her head over her shoulder as if to look at her ass. *How could this girl know I have a fat ass? No one had ever called her "thick" before; she wasn't sure if it was a compliment.* Chloe then broke it down for her. She told her thick isn't fat; it's curves and softness in all the right places. From that moment on, Tallulah would always describe herself as "thick".

Chloe was tall and thin. Not an unhealthy thin, but a thick Black girl thin, as she described it. She took care of her body, although junk food was her weakness. Her nails had a flawless manicure and a light pink polish. Her hair was long, and she'd dyed it blonde. Her eyes were green, but that was because of the fake contacts. Her makeup, although light, was flawless. Chloe loved makeup and fashion. She said it was her calling.

Chloe's small closet was full of shoes. She had more shoes than Tallulah had ever seen one person own. She watched Chloe as she put down the bag of chips. She had a certain aura about her. She was full of confidence and spunk. Tallulah liked that.

Chloe noticed her looking at her collection of shoes and smiled. "As you can see, I love shoes. Now, if you decide you wanna borrow a pair, you ask me." She looked at Tallulah's feet and frowned. "I dunno, girl, your feet look kinda big. Maybe you'd better stick to those Skechers you got on."

Tallulah looked down at her feet. *What's wrong with Sketchers?*

8

Zoe lit an incense as she said, "My major is business." She sat down. "I'm gonna have my own restaurant before I'm 30. Cooking is my thing. I'm getting my degree to make my parents happy. I'm the first person in my family to go to college."

Chloe chimed in with, "But more importantly, this bitch can cook her ass off. If we had a kitchen, girllll, we'd all be big as houses. Now me? See, I'm gonna be a publicist for the most important people. I've got the people skills."

Zoe looked at her and rolled her eyes. "Don't worry about this one," she said to Tallulah. "She's harmless. I should know; I've been keeping her out of trouble since the 8th grade."

Chloe smirked. "You love me!" she shouted while throwing a pillow at Zoe. She then sat up and donned a serious look. "We do have a couple of rules in dorm room 10. Number one, I call everyone 'bitch'. It's a term of endearment, so don't get mad. Second rule, we need to stick together. Ain't too many of us around these parts!" she said in her best redneck voice. Tallulah laughed at this comment. "Third rule, no guys. The room is too small for all that. Follow these rules, and we'll have no problems." Chloe sounded like a grade school teacher.

Tallulah smiled at her new roommates. They weren't at all what she expected, but she liked both of them. The three stayed close in college. Tallulah smoked her first blunt, lost her virginity, and learned to handle her liquor. Chloe and Zoe made her feel like she belonged. They let her know she was a queen, not an outcast. Zoe told her it didn't matter what she sounded like; it only mattered what she felt like. Tallulah finally felt she belonged. She couldn't recall ever feeling that way before.

Making friends and getting through school had always been challenging for Tallulah. The academics came easy to her (she was smart), but the social aspect was where she'd always had problems. Her mom was always saying things like "You'll make friends, you'll see," or "Go outside and play with kids across the street."

Growing up in a white neighborhood had many challenges. When playing with kids, someone might comment on how Tallulah looked or talked. They'd make fun of her hair or nose. She heard a mom tell her little girl not to play with the colored girl. The mom said the girl might pick up bad habits. Tallulah had no idea she had bad habits.

When she would go to the corner market, Mr. Sabin, the store's owner, would always watch her like a hawk. He would say things like, "I know you people like to steal, so I gotta watch you." Tallulah had never stolen anything before. But now, she felt his gaze. He watched her and followed her around the store. She tried to be friendly, but Mr. Sabin would say, "You may sound like a little white girl, but you're black. If more of your kind moves in, the whole neighborhood will go to hell in a hand basket." She had no idea what he meant, but she didn't talk back. She'd just nod her head and put her money on the counter.

The neighborhood kids played with her now and then. Still, they often treated her like a science experiment. "Why are your lips so big?" one little girl asked once. Tallulah didn't think her lips were big. But when she saw the little white girl's lips, she noticed the difference. The little girl laughed and pointed at her lips. "They're so big, like a jungle person!"

Tallulah held back the tears and ran home. Her grandmother was in the kitchen making pies when she rushed in the back door.

"My word! What is the rush, Lula?" her grandmother said.

"Why are my lips so big?" Tallulah cried.

Her grandmother stared at her in shock. Then, she took Tallulah's hand and sat at the kitchen table. She gently lifted Tallulah's chin with her finger. "Who said you had big lips, baby?"

"The little girl across the street. She says I have big lips like a jungle person!" Tears flowed from her eyes. She didn't want to have big lips. "She said I was different," Tallulah said, looking up at her grandmother.

"Well, baby, you *are* different. Why do you want to be like everyone else? You're special," her grandmother said, hugging her. "Who's that little girl to you, Lula? Is she your friend?" Tallulah thought for a moment, then shook her head no. "Don't let anyone steal your light, Lula. People will try. They'll call you names or tell you you aren't good enough, but it isn't true. They see your light and want some of it, but they can't have it, so they try to dim it or put it out altogether. Do you understand?"

Tallulah smiled and said, "I do!" She liked talking to her grandmother; she always knew what to say to make her feel better.

As she grew older, the taunting by the white children became harsher. They'd tease her about her hair and told her it looked like steel wool. They'd tug at her braids and take her barrettes. They called her *Sambo, Jigaboo, Blackie, Darkie,* and of course *Nigger*.

The first time Tallulah heard the word "nigger", she was alone. It was a word they didn't use in her house, and her parents had forbidden her from ever using it. She rode her bike down the sidewalk. Then, she saw a small group of older white girls walking ahead. She didn't go around them. Instead, she slowed down, hopped off her bike, and walked behind them, hoping they wouldn't see her. One of the girls caught sight of her and motioned for the small crowd to stop walking.

She then grabbed the handlebars of Tallulah's bike, snarled at her, and said, "Why you following us, nigger?" The other girls laughed. "You probably stole this bike. All niggers steal; everyone knows that."

All the girls laughed. Tallulah thought their faces looked twisted and mean. She felt scared, so she pulled back her bike. The girl let go of the handlebars. "Leave me alone!" she shouted as she backed up, not taking her eyes off the girls.

The girl who'd grabbed the handlebars snickered at her and said, "Cross the street, nigger. This is *our* sidewalk!"

The girls howled with laughter and gave one another high-fives. Tallulah backed up on her bike until she stopped. She looked across the street and then back at the girls.

"Cross the street nigger!" they all yelled in unison.

Tallulah's eyes filled with tears as she turned and crossed the street. When she got home, she told her grandmother what had happened.

"Lula," her grandmother said, "some people will always hate and judge you. They may not appreciate your beautiful color, full lips, or lovely hair." I know the word is hateful, but remember what I said about your light? Your shine?" Tallulah shook her head yes, wiping tears from her cheeks. "Well, this is one of those times where they tried to steal it. It can be a little painful to hold on to your light, but it only makes it stronger and brighter." She hugged Tallulah. "I love you, baby. Those girls don't matter. But if one of them puts their hands on you, you kick their ass. Now don't tell your mom or dad I said so, okay baby?"

Tallulah hugged her grandmother tight. She could always make her feel better.

Her parents worked hard to provide for the family. Her dad was an accountant. He often gave her math story problems to solve. He said math is the universal language. She didn't like math, but she loved sitting and solving problems with him. By the time she was 6, she could do 9th-grade algebra. Her dad wanted her to be an accountant or controller. He hoped she would follow in his footsteps. But she loved stories and books.

Her mother was a librarian. Tallulah always loved going to work with her. She'd get lost in the stories she'd read, imagining being somewhere else. She could see the world from the library. She didn't have to be here; she could be someone else and go on great adventures. She began writing stories and poems after some time. Words came easy for her.

When she was older, her mother took her to the Black history section of the library. The section wasn't very big, but her mother had worked hard to get the library to recognize Black history. "Lula, in this section you can learn about people of color, our people. We didn't start out as slaves; we were teachers, musicians, builders, craftsmen, leaders. We were more than slaves. We were rulers, kings, and queens," her mother said with a smile.

Tallulah smiled back and looked around the small section of the library. "All these books are about people who look like me?"

Her mother nodded her head.

Tallulah would often spend hours in the Black history section. She learned about Madam C.J. Walker, the first black self-made millionaire. She also discovered John Mercer Langston, the first black attorney.

In 6th grade, Ms. Beal, her social studies teacher, asked the class to write an essay about a famous American. Tallulah felt excited about the assignment. She had read many stories about Black Americans and their achievements. Still, she struggled to decide who to write about.

After school, she ran to the library to tell her mother about the assignment. "Mama, we can write about any famous American we want!" She said while holding up the paper with the instructions, a smile of pride on her face.

Her mother smiled and said, "Well, you're in the right place. Who are you gonna write about? George Washington?"

Tallulah shook her head no. "I'm gonna write about Colonel Allen Allensworth."

Her mother looked at her and smiled. "And who is he?"

Tallulah sat down next to her mother behind the big reception desk at the library. "He was a colonel who founded a Black town in California in 1908. The town is the only town that was founded and fi...fi..."

"Financed," her mother said.

"Yeah, financed and run by black people. The town did real good for a little while, but then something happened to the water." She frowned a little. "But he was a good American, so I'm gonna write about him."

Her mother smiled and said, "Well, he sounds like a real smart man. He started a whole town. That's something. I can't wait to read your story, baby."

Tallulah smiled and took off for the Black history section of the library.

When she turned in her report weeks later, she felt excited. She was sure everyone would do their paper on George Washington or Abraham Lincoln. She was positive no one would write about Colonel Allensworth. When Ms. Beal returned the papers, Tallulah felt sure she'd get an A. She smiled as she watched Ms. Beal walk down the rows, handing back the graded work. Ms. Beal was a tall, thin white lady with gray hair. She didn't pay much attention to Tallulah like she did the other kids, but Tallulah didn't mind.

She listened as Ms. Beal said things like, "Great job, Tommy" or "Very nice work, Tina."

Finally, Ms. Beal stopped at her desk, and Tallulah looked up to see her frowning. She handed Tallulah the paper. "I will need to see you after class, Tallulah. You didn't do the assignment correctly."

Tallulah turned over her paper to see a giant 'F' in red ink. She frowned, then looked up at Ms. Beal and said, "I did it right. I wrote about a great American."

Ms. Beal looked at Tallulah disapprovingly. "Well, I don't think he is, and we'll discuss it after class."

Her voice was slightly raised, and the other children could hear her. They started to snicker and laugh. Tallulah looked around the room and saw the kids laughing and staring. She didn't want to make a scene, but she'd done the assignment. She stared at the F. She wanted to get up and run from the classroom, but she didn't. Her grandmother said there are times to run and times to stay and fight. She chose to fight.

When the bell rang, Tallulah stayed seated at her desk. Ms. Beal looked up from her notebook and said, "Okay Tallulah, we can talk now."

Tallulah grabbed her bookbag and paper, went to the front of the room, and stood next to Ms.

Beal's desk.

"Now, Tallulah, I'm very disappointed. You're always such a good student, but this paper, well...this colonel sounds made up. I don't want to fail you, but I don't think he exists. He isn't in any of the books we have in class. The assignment was to do an essay on a famous American. If I've never heard of him...well, then, dear, he isn't famous," Ms. Beal said with a scowl.

Tallulah pulled the library book out of her bookbag. The title was *Famous Black Americans*. She held up the book and said, "Colonel Allensworth is in this book. It's called *Famous Black Americans*. He's in the book, so he's famous." She held up the book so Ms. Beal could read it.

Ms. Beal was silent for a few moments, then shook her head and said, "Now Tallulah, you didn't follow the assignment."

Tallulah put the book down and said, "Yes, I did. He is famous. He's in a book titled *Famous Black Americans*. He started a town in California."

Ms. Beal stood up. "Now listen, young lady, I won't have you sassing me. I don't like your tone, young lady! Now I'm calling your parents about this."

Tallulah put the book back in her bag. She didn't speak; she stared at Ms. Beal. She didn't understand why she was so angry. After a few moments, Tallulah turned and left the classroom.

That evening, she had dinner with her parents and grandmother. She didn't bring up Ms. Beal or her paper. She sat at the table, moving the food around on her plate. She didn't feel like eating. She was sad and angry at the same time. She'd

16

worked hard on her paper. She even wrote it twice and doubled checked all her spelling.

Her mother spoke first. "Well, Lula, did you get the grade on your paper about the famous American?"

Tallulah looked up from her plate. "Yes, ma'am," she said, not moving.

Her mother waited, then said, "Can I see the paper?"

Tallulah frowned. "It's in my bookbag."

"Well, go get it, honey. We want to see it," her father said.

Tallulah sat for a moment. She'd never brought home a bad grade before. She got up and grabbed her bookbag. She pulled out her graded paper and saw the red F. Then, she turned and walked back to her mother, handing her the paper. Her mother frowned at it. She didn't speak; she passed the paper to Tallulah's father, who fixed his glasses and read it.

After a few moments of silence, he said, "Well, this Colonel Allensworth sounds a like a real smart man."

"He was," Tallulah said. Her voice was low. "He started a whole town in 1908, a town-owned by Black people. If you have a town named after you, doesn't that make you famous? she asked, trying not to cry.

Tallulah's father handed the graded paper to her mother. She looked it over again. Then she said to Tallulah, "I got a call today from Ms. Beal." She said you didn't do the assignment. She said you sassed her."

Tallulah's eyes widened. She was always taught to respect her elders. She wanted to call Ms. Beal a liar, but she didn't; instead, she said, "Can grownups be wrong?"

Of course, they can, baby," her grandmother said.

"Then Ms. Beal is wrong," Tallulah said.

"Let me see the paper," her grandmother said. Tallulah's

mother passed it to her, and she held it up. "Hmmm. Looks like you did real good on your spelling, Lula. Did you use the thesaurus like I taught you?" Tallulah shook her head yes, then walked over to her. Her grandmother smiled at her. "It's a good story, Lula. This man did things most of us never will. He was smart and courageous, like you. Don't ever let anyone dim your light."

* * *

The next day, Tallulah, her mother and grandmother went to Ms. Beal's classroom after school.

After they were all seated, Ms. Beal began.

"As you can see, Tallulah didn't do the assignment. Now, I never have any problems with Tallulah, but this colonel sounds made up. Besides, I can't find him in any of my textbooks."

Tallulah's mother spoke in a gentle tone and took her time with each word. "Ms. Beal, as I understand it, the assignment was to write about a famous American. Did you mean white American?"

Ms. Beal had a look of shock on her face. "Well...no. I had one student write about Christopher Columbus," she said, defending herself.

"Well," said Tallulah's mother, "did that student get a passing grade?"

"Of course," Ms. Beal said with a sense of pride.

"Well, then," Tallulah's mother continued, her tone soft and steady, "how could that student pass? Columbus wasn't American. He was Italian."

Tallulah's grandmother stood up and said, "You owe this

young lady an apology and passing grade. Ms. Beal, there are many famous Americans who aren't white. Many famous Americans might not be in your textbooks. Their contributions to America may seem unimportant, but they matter."

Ms. Beal didn't speak for a few moments, staring at Tallulah's mother and grandmother. "Well, I..." she started to say but Tallulah's mother interrupted her when she stood up next to her grandmother.

"I'll be expecting to see Tallulah's grade changed. Lula, give Ms. Beal back your paper."

Tallulah nodded her head and dug the paper out of her bookbag. She then handed it to Ms. Beal, who reluctantly took it. "Before I can change her grade, I'll need to verify that this colonel was a real man."

Tallulah adjusted her glasses and moved in her chair. Then, she pulled out a book called Famous Black Americans. "You can read my book, Ms. Beal. He's in here."

She smiled and offered the book to Ms. Beal. Ms. Beal glanced at Tallulah. After a moment of hesitation, she took the book from her hands.

The room was silent for a moment, then Tallulah's mother said, "Lula, please wait outside for me and Grandma. We want to speak with Ms. Beal."

Tallulah gathered her bookbag and went outside into the hall. After Tallulah left, her mother turned to Ms. Beal. In a harsh, steady tone, she said, "Don't ever fail my child again because of your ignorance." She did your assignment. Lula's failing grade shouldn't show your lack of knowledge about Black history. As a teacher, you failed her. I know she's the only child of color in your classroom, and that makes her special."

Ms. Beal didn't speak she had no words to defend herself. Tallulah's mother continued.

"Luckily, Lula has access to knowledge far beyond the reach of this classroom. She's a bright girl with a bright future, and I will not let you dim her light. Are you understanding me?" Ms. Beal nodded her head. "Good. Good day, Ms. Beal. Let's go, Mama."

Tallulah's grandmother said, "I marched with Dr. King. That's history. Teach that."

They both walked out of the classroom. Tallulah's mother walked up to her. "Lula," she said, "don't let anyone dim your light."

Tallulah nodded, then grabbed her mother's hand and skipped out of the school.

* * *

Tallulah spent most of her time at school alone. In high school, she worked hard to fit in with the white girls. But they always laughed at her hair and made fun of her curves and round ass. They told her boys don't like girls with giant asses or large, big lips. She wore long shirts or tied a jacket around her waist to hide her figure. Then, she would sit out of gym class or skip it altogether.

She knew she was different from the other girls. They never let her forget it. They always came at her with questions, and she always hated them: How do you wash your hair? Can I touch it? You can dance, right? You can sing, right? Do Black people tan? Do Black guys have bigger dicks? What are chitlins? Do you speak Ebonics? It was exhausting.

I'm not the authority on all things Black, she thought to

20

herself.

Her teachers would often say, "Tallulah, you are so well-spoken," or "You pronounce your words so well." It felt like they thought she was from a foreign country and that English wasn't her first language.

When her English class read *Tom Sawyer*, the teacher allowed her to leave the class. The first time the teacher, Mrs. Moore, said, "Nigger Jim," the entire class turned and looked at Tallulah. The words hung in the air like a thick fog. The other kids murmured, snickered, and laughed. She looked up to see the entire class staring at her. Mrs. Moore turned bright red and seemed hesitant to go on with the class reading.

After class, Mrs. Moore asked Tallulah to stay. She waited until the room was empty. "Now Tallulah, I don't want you to feel uncomfortable. So, I'll excuse you from reading *Tom Sawyer*.

Please know that I don't agree with the use of the n-word. I can give you an alternate book to read. You can go to the library during class."

Tallulah wanted to ask her if they would keep saying "Nigger Jim" after she left the room, but she knew the answer. It would be okay for the class to use the word *nigger* since it was a school approved book and she wasn't in the room.

"Okay," she said. She'd already read *Tom Sawyer*, and the idea of spending time in the library sounded better than sitting in class.

Mrs. Moore wrote out a pass and handed it to her. "Just check-in at the library desk. You can choose from this list." She handed Tallulah a list of books.

The next day, during English, she went to the school library. When she walked in, it was empty except for the library aide,

Michael Chang. Michael was the only Asian student in the school. She'd seen him around, and they had the same creative writing class. She'd heard he was supposed to be some kind of brainiac and have a black belt or something like that.

She handed Michael her pass. He looked up at her and grinned. "Seriously? *Tom Sawyer*?"

"Can I help it if Mrs. Moore has an issue with the word 'nigger'? I've read it anyway," she said, holding out her hand to receive her pass.

Michael passed it back and said, "Well, it's just you and me during this period."

She looked around the room, then walked over to a nearby table and sat down. On the table next to her was a chessboard. The pieces were set up as if someone was playing.

She turned toward Michael. "Do you play chess?"

He looked up and shook his head yes. "Why?" he said.

"Teach me?" she replied.

Michael smiled. "Don't you have a book to read?"

"I've read it. I've got 6 weeks of library time. I'm gonna be here every day. Don't you want someone to play chess with?"

Michael paused for a moment and walked toward the chessboard. "Okay," he said. "I'll teach you. I'm Michael."

She smiled. "I know who you are. We have creative writing. I'm Tallulah."

"I know who you are," he said.

Every day during English, Tallulah would go to the library. She looked forward to seeing Michael. Her chess skills were improving. She also learned that he shared her love of books and writing. He was going to college right after graduation. He had dreams of having his own newspaper. She was impressed. He was focused and seemed so sure of what he wanted to do with his life.

Michael was about her height, with short black hair and dark eyes. He wore John Lennon-style glasses and shiny silver braces. He was a nerd, but she didn't mind. He was probably one of the smartest people she'd ever met. He knew every inch of the library. He told her he spent most of his off periods in the library.

"I like sports," he said, "I'm just not good at them. So now I write about sports," he said, moving his queen into checkmate position.

Michael was the editor of the school paper. He had a great eye for editing and detail. He talked Tallulah into joining the paper. He told her it would boost her college application. This convinced her since she was serious about becoming a writer. Over the next 6 weeks, Michael became her best friend and confidant. He also convinced her to take AP English.

"It'll look good on your college application," he would say. Michael often talked about college. He told Tallulah she needed to get serious about applying herself.

When she got admitted into AP English, she discovered that Michael wouldn't be in the same class. "The reason I signed up is because you said we'd have the class together," she protested over a game of chess.

"Sorry, I don't make the schedule," he said as he studied the chessboard.

She impatiently tapped her foot. "I've got you – check-mate," she said.

Michael looked up at her and frowned. She'd beat him again.

* * *

Tallulah walked into her AP English class. She went directly to the seats in the back row and sat down. A syllabus was sitting on every desk in the room. She had always excelled in English. She felt even happier when she saw the list of books for the year. She quickly scanned the list and realized she'd read almost every book. The classroom filled up quickly, and the morning bell rung.

The teacher, Mr. Simon, was writing on the board. He turned around and said, "Okay class, settle down. The first book we'll be reading is *Canterbury Tales*, by Chaucer. Is anyone familiar with this book?" No one in the class moved. Tallulah slowly raised her hand. "Ah, a scholar in the back row." Mr. Simon looked pleased. "Can you please stand up and tell us about this literary gem?"

Tallulah looked around and saw everyone staring at her.

Damn, she thought to herself, *why the hell did I raise my hand? What the hell was I thinking?*

She slowly stood up. Her palms were sweating, and she felt flushed. She cleared her throat and said, "Well, it's a collection of 24 stories written from 1387 to 1400. I think it has something like 17,000 lines." The kids in the classroom snickered and laughed.

"Very good, Ms..." Mr. Simon trailed off.

"Brock," said Tallulah. "Well, Ms. Brock, you are 100% correct. Very good. Please be seated."

Tallulah sat down. She felt as if the entire class was staring at her.

One of the girls sitting beside her leaned over and whispered, "Quit tryin' to sound like a white girl."

Tallulah looked at her and opened her mouth to speak but decided to stay quiet.

After class, Tallulah went to the library. There, she saw Michael staring at the chessboard. He was deep in concentration. He didn't even notice her sit down.

"Do I sound white?" she asked.

He looked at her. "What?" he said, briefly looking up, then returning his eyes to the chessboard.

She pushed the chessboard out of the way. "Do I sound white!?" Her voice was cracking and raised.

"Hey!" he said. He looked at her and saw tears forming in her eyes. "What happened? What are you talking about?"

Tallulah was shaking and visibly upset. "A girl in my AP English class told me I was trying to sound white. Do I sound white? What does that mean?" Tears streamed down her cheeks, and she wiped them as quickly as they rolled down her face.

"Sound white?" he said, not knowing exactly what to say.

"I'm so sick of this bullshit. I mean, what the hell do I have to do, Michael? I work hard, I'm basically a straight-A student. I'm tired of people judging me by what I look like or what I sound like." Her voice cracked.

He sat in silence for a moment. "I know, Tallulah," he said quietly. "I'm not sure what it means either. It's a stereotype."

She was sitting across from him, wiping her tears. He understood how she felt. He knew about racism and stereotypes. He understood how tough it was to fit in. It was even harder when you looked different. Others made sure you never forgot that. Until he met Tallulah, he really thought he was the only one who felt this way.

With a look of defeat on her face, she wiped the last of her tears, then looked up at Michael. He'd been such a good friend to her. "Well, Michael," she said softly, "I don't care if it's a stereotype, it's bullshit and gettin' old. You know what I mean?"

He nodded his head. "I do," he said. "High school isn't real anyway. That's why you need to focus on college."

Tallulah shook her head. "Good ol' logical Michael." She smiled. "I guess I had a little breakdown." She looked at the knocked over chess pieces.

"Maybe just a little one," Michael said, grinning, showing off his braces.

She started picking up the chess pieces. "So, college is my window?" she said in a questioning tone.

Michael nodded his head. "Yep. Everything will change in college. Trust me."

* * *

Tallulah smiled as the memory faded away, then looked around at all the scattered papers. As she sighed and began to gather them up, her email chimed again. She quickly grabbed the laptop and checked it, holding her breath for a moment, then said, "Please let it be good news. Please...please...please..."

She put the cursor on the message and clicked. She read the two sentences.

Thank you for interest in Destination Magazine. We looked over your samples. We picked candidates who fit the position better.

Tallulah stopped reading and closed the laptop.

Chapter 2

Zoe's Soul Food Kitchen buzzed with the sounds of people eating, chatting, and laughing in the warm sun. The restaurant served delicious soul food. You could find ribs, chicken, greens, black-eyed peas, potato salad, catfish, and more. Her specialty: sweet potato pie.

The city housed the restaurant in an eclectic area. It sat on the corner, next to an art gallery and bookstore. The building had been empty for about a year before Zoe was finally able to lease it. The decor was more home-style than trendy. Lacy white tablecloths covered the tables. She said they reminded her of her grandmother's table. The chairs were brown with black leather. She'd decided on 20 tabletops. She would have added more, but the dining room was already a little crowded.

"Damn girl, how we supposed to walk to our table?" Chloe said, standing in the dining room. "It's too crowded, you gotta scale back a little. You know Black girls got those wide asses, and no one wants ass rubbing up against them when one of the big ass girls is trying to get to their table."

Zoe had an image of a woman trying to get through the dining room, her ass knocking over plates and cups. So, she scaled back to 15 tabletops.

On the walls were several soul food canvas prints. Zoe

didn't know who the artists were; she only knew she wanted the restaurant to have a certain vibe. There was a picture of a woman wearing an Aunt Jemima-style do-rag, holding a bushel of collard greens. She had of pictures of jazz singers - Duke Ellington, Count Basie, Ella Fitzgerald, and others. She'd installed a surround sound system and played jazz music in the dining room. The large windows allowed the sun to shine in and showered natural light into the building.

Zoe loved her dining room, but the kitchen was her place of worship. It was her temple.

- Three large ovens
- Ten top burners
- Four large sinks
- Two large walk-in refrigerators
- One large dishwasher
- One rinsing sink

The entire kitchen was stainless steel. She would spend all her time in the kitchen if she could. She would wipe down the stainless steel until it shined. The day she signed the lease, she blessed the kitchen and dining room with sage. She knew Chloe would make fun of her, so she did it alone.

Opening the restaurant had been more difficult than she imagined. She saved enough to lease the restaurant for a year. But, she didn't expect the high costs of food, supplies, and staff. She didn't want to take a loan from a bank, and honestly, she didn't think they would approve her. One thing about Zoe, she is resourceful. Because she'd already leased the space, she had to make it work. She began by selling takeout plates of food. She blocked off half the dining room and served from the front of the restaurant. She left 3 tables open so people could sit while waiting for their food. You could order your food and wait, but there was no dining in service.

Actually, Tallulah had come up with an idea. They were sitting in the empty dining room when she came up with it. "Why don't you just block off the dining room and do a to-go style thing? You don't need any wait staff, maybe just a person to take orders and ring up the sale.

You're the chef, so that's covered, then hire a helper to prep. Maybe do disposable dishes so you don't have to worry about washing and stuff. I read an article somewhere where a restaurant did this and it worked."

Zoe thought Tallulah was a fucking genius. She hugged her and ran with the idea. She'd never met someone who spent so much time reading and writing, but she was smart. Not street smart like Chloe, but a more polished, analytical smart.

On the first day she tried the to-go service, the business overwhelmed them. She hired a cook and cashier, and the business grew. After about 6 months, she was able to open the dining room. She hired Tallulah as a part-time waitress. Tallulah was having money problems while working for Michael's paper. She needed help.

Tallulah usually worked the lunch shift. The aroma of homecooked soul food filled the air. "Do you have my order yet?" she asked as she made 3 house salads.

"Yep, coming up, T. Hey, I thought you said you were taking the day off?" Zoe said as she passed her the 3 plates of ribs, collard greens, and mac and cheese.

"I know. But who can afford the luxury of taking days off? I need the money. I also have a deadline."

"Don't all artists starve before they make it?" Zoe asked

jokingly.

"Who's starving? I have all the sweet potato pie I can eat!" Tallulah smiled and grabbed her order.

When Tallulah completed her journalism degree, she expected many job offers. But that didn't happen. She loved working for Michael and his small paper. But the pay wasn't great. It was getting tough to make ends meet. She reluctantly took the waitressing job to help pay some bills. It was easy for the most part, and it was something she could do part-time. Besides, she got free meals when she worked.

Tallulah grabbed her order and delivered the food to her 3 customers. She then asked them if they needed anything else.

"Could we get some hot sauce?" the pudgy woman replied.

"Of course!"

Tallulah smiled, then dashed back to the kitchen. She grabbed the hot sauce and returned to the table. She then smiled and walked back to the kitchen. Zoe was directing her staff on various tasks. She was a champion in the kitchen; it was her true calling.

She walked over to Tallulah. "You got a deadline?"

Tallulah nodded her head while munching on a piece of Zoe's famous sweet potato pie. "Yes. Michael will kill me if I'm late again."

"Oh, he loves you. Take him some pie. He loves my pie. Besides, you're his best writer, T," Zoe said.

"I've been applying for other positions. I haven't told Michael yet." Tallulah felt guilty as if she was cheating on him.

Zoe smiled at her. "I'm sure if you found something, he would understand."

"I've sent out so many job inquiries, Zoe. I'm tired. I'm

30

getting desperate. I've applied everywhere. Why is this so hard for me? What's wrong with me?" she asked.

"There's nothing wrong with you. You'll find something," Zoe replied.

Tallulah put down the pie. "I have a degree in journalism, and I'm a part-time waitress...no offense."

Zoe smiled. "None taken."

A loud crash in the kitchen grabbed Zoe's attention. She quickly jumped back in, directing her staff and getting things under control.

"This is my life?" Tallulah said out loud as she turned and walked out of the kitchen. A few hours later, she was sitting at her small desk at the Big World office.

Big World was the small independent newspaper Michael owned. It was his dream. She was proud of him. He always said would have his own paper, and now he did. He'd taken a small inheritance he got from his grandfather and started Big World 5 years ago. He immediately gave her a job, and she'd been with him from the beginning.

Michael liked the idea of being independent. The office was small. The main room had enough space for 5 desks and chairs. He'd found them at an office liquidation sale. They were old, but they did the trick. He didn't worry about decor and didn't have pictures on the bare white walls. On each desk was an old 1980s office style phone. He didn't want to pay for cell phones and thought they gave the small office a vintage style look.

"Vintage? Tallulah said. "It's called cheap."

She loved working for Michael. He'd given her free rein on her topics and story choices most of the time. She would write about things she found interesting. It was the perfect job, but it didn't pay well.

About a year ago, Michael had cut her pay. The whole ordeal seemed to hurt him more than her. He'd taken her to dinner and broke the news. He tried to avoid it, but rising print costs and advertisers turning to social media left him no choice. Some of the staff left, but she stayed. The staff had dwindled from 10 to 5. Besides Tallulah, Michael had 2 other writers and an office person to help with other tasks. He sometimes wrote articles. But, he concentrated primarily on finding advertisers and designing the layout. He wanted to be a weekly paper, but due to the cost of printing, he settled on monthly.

The latest issue was released two days ago. Michael had given Tallulah the cover story, Women and Power. It had been his idea. He thought it would be good for the paper to write about more topics in the headlines daily.

He knew she didn't want to write the article. She'd pitched a story on the increasing homeless population.

"Michael, haven't you noticed the increase of homeless people lately? There was talk of building a new shelter, but it's gotten very quiet lately. Don't you think that's worth investigating?" she said one afternoon while playing a competitive game of chess.

Michael shook his head. "Sure, but not this edition. I think we should focus on what's hot, and women, power, sexual harassment or assault are hot topics. We have so many angles on this topic, Tallulah. Work with me, please," he said while moving his queen into checkmate position.

She reluctantly agreed. "Okay, fine. I'll write the article. But next time, I want to write about what I want to write about... agreed?" She extended her hand. Michael gave her a little smirk and shook her hand. She then moved her king and said,

"Checkmate."

Michael hurriedly walked over to her desk and held up the latest issue of BW. "Your story looks great. I told you it would create some buzz. My phone hasn't stopped ringing." As he sat on her desk so she'd have to speak to him, the desk made a series of creaking noises.

"Well, isn't that what you were going for?" she answered, not looking up.

"It is a good thing," he said. "The advertisers like the idea of more people reading the paper, and you know how I love advertisers." He smiled. She didn't look up at him. "Did you bring me something?" he asked, sounding impatient.

"I already pitched you my next story," she replied.

He looked at her and frowned. "That's not what I mean."

She paused for a second. Then, she reached into her backpack. She pulled out a Styrofoam container and said, "How could I forget?" Your pie."

Michael offered her a large grin and happily took the container. "I love the days you work for Zoe. Her pie is sooo good."

Tallulah pulled out a notebook and laptop and placed them on the desk. "How is Zoe?" Michael asked.

She looked up at him. "She's good," she replied in a nonchalant tone.

"That's good," he said, hoping for more information.

"Ah, you wanna give me a little room?"

She motioned for him to move off her desk. He stood up but didn't move. He watched as she opened her laptop and started to type.

He continued to make conversation. "The restaurant must be doing good business," he said, waiting for a reply. After a few moments of silence, he spoke again. "Well, I mean, she hired you, so that's a good sign, right? I mean..."

She stopped typing and looked up at him. "Zoe's fine, Michael. No, she isn't seeing anyone. Any other questions?" she asked impatiently. She immediately saw the hurt look on his face and felt guilty. "Michael, why don't you just ask her out?" she said. "It's not like she's a stranger. I don't get it. She's right around the corner. Go in there for lunch or dinner."

Michael didn't answer. He'd wanted to ask her out, but he just didn't have the courage. He'd thrown himself into his paper and rarely came up for air.

He met Zoe 5 years ago when she was roommates with Tallulah. Zoe was easygoing, funny, smart and beautiful. Michael would often make excuses to call Tallulah, hoping Zoe would be nearby. He'd then insert her into the conversation and always ask about her. He finally decided to accept an invite from Tallulah to a party. They didn't attend the same school, but he was willing to make the two-hour drive.

He was nervous. He was still socially awkward. Most of his time went to his dorm room, the library, or the college newspaper office. He spent most of his time in his room. Then his roommate, David, started a profitable business. He short-sold tests, term papers, theses, and other assignments from their dorm room. The room always had traffic. Michael complained, but David offered him 40% of the take, so he eventually agreed.

He parked his VW bug in front of a large white house. He could hear the bass vibrating against the windows as he turned off the ignition. He could see people on the porch. He looked at himself in the mirror. He ran his tongue over his straight white teeth. His braces had been off for 6 months. He pushed his fingers through his hair, smiled at himself in the rearview mirror, and opened the car door.

When Michael arrived inside the house, he was in a sea of people. He waded his way through the crowd, hoping to find an open area. He made his way to the kitchen and leaned up against the sink. He looked around but didn't see Tallulah.

A girl staggered up to him and handed him a cup. "Hold this," she slurred and vomited into the sink.

Michael, looking disgusted, put down the cup and moved to two large glass doors. He saw Tallulah by a table with two girls. They had to be Zoe and Chloe. He recognized them from Tallulah's lively phone descriptions.

"My two roommates are cool," she would say, "Chloe and Zoe."

He laughed. "Are they twins?"

"No. Chloe is crazy. She's got no filter. What comes into that head, comes out of her mouth. Zoe is relaxed. She meditates, chants does yoga. They're total opposites."

Chloe was the first to spot Michael. "Who's the fine ass Asian walkin' this way?"

Tallulah turned around. "Michael!" She ran over to him and hugged him. Zoe and Chloe watched.

"Did she say she was datin' a fine ass Asian dude? This bitch got secrets," Chloe said.

As Tallulah led Michael over to them, she was smiling. "Michael, this is Chloe and Zoe. Ladies, this is Michael."

Michael smiled. "Hey, ladies," he said in his sexiest voice. He'd been practicing on the drive down.

"Heyyyy," Chloe and Zoe said in unison. "T didn't tell us she was dating yo fine ass," Chloe said.

35

Tallulah felt herself blush a little. "We're not dating. We've known one another since high school. I thought it would be nice for him to come out," she replied.

Michael nodded his head. Zoe hadn't taken her eyes off Michael. She could feel herself staring and finally said, "You look thirsty." Everyone looked at her. "Not *thirsty* thirsty; you know, drink thirsty...parched, dry mouth..."

Chloe laughed. "Bitch, you thirsty, too."

Michael smiled. "A beer would be nice."

A moment of silence passed until Chloe nudged Zoe. "Oh, well, come on. I'll show you where the beer is," Zoe said as she motioned for Michael to follow her.

Tallulah watched them walked away. "I think someone likes Zoe," she said, giggling. Chloe watched for a moment. "Hmmmm. Like I said, that bitch thirsty."

* * *

Michael continued to stand at Tallulah's desk as she continued to type. She could feel his eyes on her, and she looked up and saw him grinning at her.

"What is it, Michael? I didn't bring more pie."

Michael slowly closed the laptop. "I really need to speak with you." She gave him a disappointed look, and he immediately understood her thoughts. "No, it's not about Zoe. It's about you and your future here with me."

Tallulah was caught off guard. "My future?" she said. "What do you mean, my future?"

He looked around the office and saw his assistant, Clara, sitting two desks over from them on the phone. "Come into my office."

Tallulah followed Michael into his office. It was small and cramped. He had stacks and stacks of past editions of *Big World* against all four walls. His desk was small and secondhand. It fit two chairs and three tall bookshelves. The shelves held old editions of Big World. There was also a personal computer, printer, phone, and lamp.

"You really need to clean this place," she remarked.

Michael sat down in his chair. His face was serious. "Have a seat," he said, motioning for her to sit.

Tallulah looked at him and sat. She was getting an uneasy feeling. "What is it, Michael?"

The last time he said "Come into my office", it was to tell her she couldn't have the cover story.

The time before that was to ask her to dinner to let her know he was cutting her pay.

"Are you cutting my pay again, Michael? You know I work for peanuts as it is. The only reason I stay is for you. Working two jobs is hard enough," she said with a huff and waited for him to respond.

Michael paused a moment and said, "No, I'm not cutting your pay." He stopped for a moment. His face turned serious. "I've been dealing with rising costs with the printer. I may have to cut back a little."

"Cut back? What do you mean?" She looked at him.

"I'm not sure what that means, to be honest," he said. "The paper isn't doing well. People aren't reading the paper anymore. Everyone is on some kind of device."

Tallulah studied his face. "Well, then go digital," she said.

"Well, that's what I was thinking. We go online, maybe develop an app or something. I dunno. I'm still working it out in my head. I just wanted you to know. Please don't say anything, okay?"

She nodded her head. "I'm sorry, Michael. I know you really wanted this. I know you like the feel of paper. I do, too."

"Sometimes I feel like I'm always playing a game of chess with my life. This move or that move.

I'm exhausted." As he leaned back into the chair, the wheels made a squeaking sound.

They sat in silence for several moments, then Tallulah slowly stood up. "I've got some research to do for the homeless story. You okay?"

He nodded his head. "Yeah, I'm good."

She walked back to her desk, looked at her laptop, and noticed she had a few new emails. She clicked on the email subject, "*Thank you for submitting,*

then read:

Dear Ms. Brock,

Thank you for your interest in Wow! Magazine. We looked at your writing samples. You have talent! However, we need someone with more magazine experience. Good luck in your job search.

Human Resources

Tallulah sighed heavily and deleted the message.

Chapter 3

"I never want to see this type of story for my magazine again!" Sylvia slammed the paper down on her desk. "We don't print shit like this!" she said, standing up.

She stared at the girl in front of her. Sylvia liked moments like this. Someone was cowering before her, eager for her next command. She enjoyed the look of helplessness on the girl's face.

She sat down and in a slow and controlled tone said, "Now Maria, I expect much more from you." Maria frowned but didn't speak. Sylvia continued. "I've worked very hard to raise the quality and standards of this magazine. There had better not be a next time." She paused for a moment. Maria stood motionless. "You can go."

Maria nodded her head and rushed out of the office. Sylvia then picked up her phone and dialed.

"Sharon, we need to talk. In my office...now!" She hung up the phone in a hurry. Moments later, Sharon Eckerson walked into the office.

"What is it, Sylvia?" She sounded annoyed.

"What the hell is this?" she said, handing Maria's article to Sharon.

Sharon took the article and scanned it. "What's wrong with

it?"

Sylvia shot Sharon a surprised look. "What's wrong with it? It's wrong for the magazine."

Sharon sighed. "I asked Maria to write a story about immigrant women who are separated from their children at the border." It's a relevant and very important issue, Sylvia."

Sylvia stared at Sharon, "Not in **my** magazine. I did not approve this. I don't want this sort of thing in my magazine. Our readers do not want to read about these types of people. It's depressing. Minorities are depressing, Sharon." Sharon bit her lip. Sylvia continued. "You may be the editor, but I'm the owner."

Sharon felt herself getting angry. "What do you mean, **these** types of people?"

Sylvia looked at her. "You know exactly what I'm talking about, Sharon. These stories on these illegal aliens are everywhere in the news. I'm supposed to feel sorry for them because they entered **my** country illegally? I don't think so. I don't want to read this, and neither do my readers."

Sharon started to speak, but Sylvia spoke first. "Fire Maria," she said dryly.

"Excuse me?" said Sharon.

"Fire her," Sylvia repeated. "She doesn't fit in, and I don't like her. She's always speaking that gibberish."

"You mean Spanish?" Sharon asked, still trying to comprehend what Sylvia had told her to do.

"Well, we speak English here, Sharon." Sylvia stood up. "Over the past 4 years, we haven't seen eye-to-eye on everything, Sharon, but you're a good editor. However, you were not my first choice. But here we are. You've done some good things, I will admit, but I'm the one who's pushed us to the top. Me. Not you. You work for me. Fire her." Sylvia sat down.

Sharon stood, not saying a word. She opened her mouth to speak but closed it in an instant. After a few moments, she spoke. "Sylvia, you're right, we haven't seen eye-to-eye on many things. I think adding diversity to the magazine would take it even farther. You're excluding millions of potential readers." Her voice was firm, but she kept her tone low. "I've put a lot of time and effort into growing this magazine. Don't you think your readers want to read more than trends, fluff, and gossip?"

Sylvia shot her a cold look. "I don't give a shit about diversity. That's what's wrong with this country; all this so-called diversity. Well, I for one am tired of hearing about it. If a woman is separated from her child because she enters a country illegally, that's her fault. If a Black man is arrested and beat up by the police, he was probably breaking the law; his fault. Now, if I see this shit again, Sharon, we'll have a problem. Now fire Maria. I want her gone. Her gibberish makes everyone uncomfortable." Sylvia watched as Sharon walked out of the office. "Unbelievable! Sylvia yelled.

Sylvia had been in charge of *You & Me* for the past 12 of the 15 years it had been in publication. She'd acquired it from her ex-husband, as part of the divorce settlement. The original name had been *Chatter*, but she changed it after the story on her mother was featured.

The magazine had always been profitable, which was all Sylvia cared about. She liked the idea of owning something and made it a point to tell everyone she was the new owner of *Chatter*. The magazine became popular by sharing celebrity gossip, fashion trends, exotic travel spots, makeup tips, and fun stories.

In the beginning, she didn't care what the magazine published. She was too busy and let her staff handle things. All she cared about was making the money and bragging to her fake friends. Two years after her divorce, her mother died from a drug overdose. She was found nude in a rundown hotel on the city's edge. A syringe was in her arm, and she had a lethal mix of heroin and cocaine in her system.

Sylvia was devastated, not because her mom had died, but because of the circumstances of her death. She didn't want to be the talk of her social circle, so she paid hundreds of thousands to keep the details quiet. Someone on her Chatter team obtained the toxicology report, police report, and scene photos. The magazine editor, Samantha Taller, chose to run the story anyway. It was an exclusive, and they were going to be the ones to break the story. She didn't bother to let Sylvia know. She said it just slipped her mind. She'd always thought Sylvia was a snobby bitch, and she was about to get her karma.

Sylvia, who had been out of the country since her mother's death, had recently returned to the states. She didn't mourn her mother's death but thought it would look good if people thought she was mourning. Upon her return to the states, she immediately booked a private cabana at her country club. It was the first time she'd been out in public since the funeral. She'd received several condolences and well wishes. Media coverage was limited. There was no mention of the details around her mother's death.

Finally, Sylvia decided 2 weeks of not being seen was long enough. She had to let people know she was back, so she decided to go to the country club to be seen.

She lay in her cabana on the upper deck, enjoying the sun. Suddenly, she felt annoyed when she saw Monica Dancy

42

walking toward her. Monica had been her rival since college, and she was everything Sylvia wasn't: Kind; caring, and pretty. She'd dated a boy in college whom Sylvia had eyes for. She hated Monica, and she decided she'd get revenge on her one day.

Just days before Monica's wedding, Sylvia slept with Monica's fiancé. Then, she made sure Monica would find them in bed together. When Monica did, Sylvia didn't care; instead, she laughed and told Monica she was a stupid bitch.

"Why would he want someone like you, Monica?" she said. "I mean, look at you, then look at me. Stupid bitch."

Monica married him anyway. Sylvia hated her and loved to degrade her every time they met. She took pleasure in Monica's misery.

As she watched Monica walk towards her, she thought she was fat and very plain looking. Monica was carrying a magazine. "Fat bitch," Sylvia whispered under her breath and then rolled over onto her stomach so she didn't have to see her.

"Knock, knock," Monica said. Her voice was high and shrill. "Why, Sylvia Blass, you snuck in here without saying hello to me. I'm so sorry for your loss. You're in everyone's thoughts and prayers."

Sylvia rolled her eyes in disgust. "Monica. I didn't even know you were here. I thought since your divorce you wouldn't want to show your face around here. It's one thing for your husband to leave you for another woman. We knew he had needs you couldn't meet. But it's different when that woman is Black. You are so brave," Sylvia said as she turned over; she had to see the look on Monica's face.

Monica didn't speak for a few moments. Her lips were

43

tightly pierced together, and she squinted her eyes.

She finally spoke. "Well, it can't be any more humiliating than what your magazine has published. I had no idea your mother was a drug whore!" She threw the magazine at Sylvia. "I wonder if the apple falls far from the tree." Monica hissed the words, then turned and left the cabana.

Sylvia looked at the magazine. On the cover was a picture of her mother. She was holding a champagne bottle and smoking a cigarette. The cover read: "*Rich socialist dies from a self-induced heroin-cocaine overdose. Found nude in a seedy motel.*"

Sylvia quickly turned the pages until she came to the cover story. There, in color, was her mother, spread out on the pages of her magazine. She'd been humiliated by own her magazine. She spent hundreds of thousands to keep this secret. Now, someone at her magazine has the information.

Sylvia continued to read in horror. How could she face her friends? Someone was going to pay for this.

She fired the entire staff that day. Everyone. She then became involved in every aspect of the magazine, and from then on it was what she wanted. Anyone who didn't agree, she fired. She changed the name to *You & Me*. She even graced the cover of the magazine whenever she felt like it.

Sylvia was a slender woman, with long, vulcanic blonde hair. Her long legs were toned, and her body, although not offering many curves, could rival that of a 30-year-old. Her skin was milky white, with just a hint of crow's feet around her eyes. Her cheekbones were high and round, with a hint of color. Her lips were thin. Her teeth were straight and copy paperwhite. She'd thought about plastic surgery but dreaded the idea of someone cutting into her face. So, she'd decided if she couldn't have beauty, her money would make up for it.

Sylvia was a no-nonsense type of woman. She didn't like indecision or those who can't focus or take charge. She didn't like foreigners, minorities, or those she thought were on a lower social class. She was raised in the south, and you could slightly hear the southern accent in certain words.

Although she hadn't lived in the south for several decades, she still held on to her southern beliefs. You didn't mix social classes or races. That had been her mother's way of life, and Sylvia followed suit. Her mother showed her that money could get you whatever you wanted.

Her mother wanted drugs, and she used most of her money to buy cocaine and heroin.

The poor were meant to be poor and serve the rich. She would never say this out loud, but her close friends knew how she really felt. Her attitude was that there's no shame in being poor, as long as you stay in your lane and do the things poor people do.

After she fired her staff, Sylvia decided to rebuild and rebrand *Chatter*, now called *You & Me*. She went through many interviews for an editor. Then, she decided to hire Monique Bastille. Monique was young, smart, and in high demand. Sylvia liked her style and thought she'd be perfect for *You & Me*.

When Sylvia met Monique at her downtown office, she thought they would just discuss money and finalize the deal. Sylvia had extended what she thought was a generous offer. Monique listened quietly to Sylvia's vision for the magazine and her role in it. After several minutes of Sylvia's talk, Monique raised her hand.

"Mrs. Blass, I don't mean to be rude, but I only agreed to meet with you in person so I could make sure we understand one another. Your magazine – if that's what you want to call it – is a disgrace to real journalism. You've printed lies, furthered rumors, and you even put your own mother on the front cover and sold her tragedy. I have no desire to be a part of your magazine, now or anytime." Monique stood up. "Thank you for seeing me." She turned and walked out of the office.

Sylvia felt dumbfounded. She wasn't sure what had just happened. "Disgrace?" she said out loud. She called her assistant on the intercom.

"Yes, Ms. Blass?"

"Get me, Sandra Grace, over at Travel Now!" she yelled into the phone.

When Sharon met Sylvia, she knew the stories. Sylvia had fired everyone after they ran the story on her mother. She knew it was known for tabloid journalism. *Chatter* had a reputation for printing stories based on half-truths, innuendo, and speculation. Sharon had heard when Sylvia showed up at the magazine's office, she had her editor thrown out into the street. So, when Sandra had told her about the opportunity, Sharon had no intention of meeting with Sylvia.

Sharon was sitting in Sandra's office when Sandra brought it up. "So, I just had an interesting call from Sylvia Blass," Sandra said. "You know she fired her entire staff, right?"

Sharon nodded. "I think everyone knows. The story they printed on her mother was tragic. How could she allow them to print those photos? Her own mother."

Sandra stood up, walked over to her office door, and closed it. "What I'm about to tell you is between me and you, OK?" Sharon turned around in her chair and saw Sandra staring at her. Sandra then lowered her voice. "She's shopping for a new editor." Sharon's eyes followed Sandra as she walked

46

back to her desk. "I recommended you," Sandra finished.

Sharon's eyes widened. "Me? Sandra, you know I don't do tabloid journalism. Too messy for me," she said, holding up both hands.

"I know, I know," Sandra replied, "but she's rebranding and revamping the whole magazine. It's called *You & Me*. I thought it might be a good opportunity for you."

Sharon smiled. "Thanks for the support, Sandra. I've heard scary stories about working with Sylvia Blass." I heard she eats small children and tortures puppies."

Sandra chuckled. "Well, that maybe, but it pays double what you make now, and you'd be the editor. I told her you were good. Maybe you can help her turn it around. Think of it as a challenge."

Sharon stood up. "Look Sandra, I appreciate you recommending me, but..."

Sandra interrupted, "She wants to meet with you. Dinner tomorrow at 6 pm. She's taking you to The Dome."

"The Dome? Too rich for my blood," Sharon said, then started walking toward the door.

"Sharon," Sandra called after her, "meet with her. Hear her out. You don't have to say yes."

Sharon stood at the door for a moment, then turned around. "It sounds like you already set this up," she said, sounding annoyed.

"Well, Sylvia doesn't take no for an answer," Sandra replied.

Sharon bit her lip. "Well Sandra, she may need to get used to hearing it. I'll go, but I'm not working for her."

As she opened the door, Sandra said, "One more thing: Don't take Keith."

Sharon spun around. "Why not?"

"Trust me on this one. Meet her alone. Close the door behind you."

Sharon walked out of the office and closed the door.

* * *

When Sharon arrived at the Dome the following evening, she had no idea of what to expect. She'd never been there before, but she'd heard it was overpriced and very exclusive. She arrived 30 minutes early; her journalist instinct had taught her always to be early. She told the hostess she was meeting Sylvia Blass and was immediately led to a table in the rear of the restaurant. The hostess told her it was Sylvia's private table. Sharon sat down. A waiter appeared, and she ordered a glass of house red wine. She sipped the wine slowly as she tried to blend into the room.

She looked at the table setting. It was formal, more than just a plate, cup, and flatware. She counted 23 pieces in front of her. Three forks were to the left of the plate, each one a little smaller. She decided the biggest fork was the salad fork. To the left of the plate were 3 knives, 2 spoons, and another fork. She was busy deciding which knife she'd use to cut the bread when she spotted Sylvia Blass. She was tall and thin, and her lips were a deep red, which matched the color of her high cheekbones. She wore a lime green dress and a black hat, and she held a small black clutch purse. When Sylvia and Sharon locked eyes, Sylvia smiled. Sharon thought it looked a bit sinister.

Sylvia waved and continued to walk towards her. Sharon took another sip of wine and stood up.

Sylvia spoke first. "Sharon!" she said. "Thank you for

meeting me."

Sylvia stretched out her hand but allowed Sharon to grab only her fingers. She then leaned over and kissed Sharon on both cheeks.

"Please sit," Sylvia said. She snapped her fingers, and the waiter presented himself. "Yes, I'll have a glass of red wine, not that awful house red." She paused for a moment. "As a matter of fact, bring a bottle of Chateau La Mission Haut Brion Pessac, 2010." The waiter's eyes widened.

"Very good!" he said and turned to retrieve the wine.

"This is an excellent wine," Sylvia said, looking at Sharon. "It's full-bodied and has a great palate of firm tannins." You'll love it!" She smiled and lightly touched Sharon's hand.

Sharon had no clue about wine. She smiled at Sylvia and shifted in her chair, hoping Sylvia wouldn't ask her opinion.

Sylvia smiled. "So Sharon, I'll get right to the point. I'm looking for a new editor. I've let my staff go, and I'm starting from scratch."

The waiter brought the wine. Sharon watched him cork the bottle and pour some into Sylvia's glass. Then, he let her taste it. Sylvia took her time, picking up the glass and holding it up in the light. She gently swirled the wine in the glass and slowly put the rim of the glass up to her nose. She took in a deep breath, taking in the aroma of the wine. She then put the glass to her lips and sipped.

After a moment of silence, she said, "Oh, it's simply amazing!" She motioned to the waiter to pour. He moved Sharon's house wine away from her and poured her a new glass of wine. She took a sip. "See," Sylvia said, "isn't it just wonderful?" Sharon nodded her head. Sylvia took another sip. "I want to move away from what the magazine has been doing. I'll be honest, I didn't even read it. I acquired it as part of my divorce settlement." She lowered her tone. "It wasn't until the unfortunate incident with my mother that I became...more vested in the content of *You & Me*."

Sylvia took a sip of her wine and waited for Sharon to speak.

After a few moments, Sharon cleared her throat. "Well, I'm flattered that you're considering me."

"Well, I've known Sandra for years. You come highly recommended. Shall we order?"

Sharon picked up the menu, and her eyes widened when she saw the prices.

"The chef is wonderful," Sylvia said. "I recommend the duck or veal porterhouse," she said, closing her menu.

The waiter quickly appeared, then took their order and left the table.

"Well, Sharon," Sylvia said, "are you ready to come on board? I'm fully involved in the magazine, but I know nothing about editing, layouts, or any of that. That's why I need a strong editor. I need to hire a writing staff and whatever else is needed. I have vision. You have the know-how."

Sharon shifted in her chair, then looked at Sylvia. "So, what's your vision?" she asked.

Sylvia smiled. "Fashion. High fashion. I want to target a certain type of woman."

"Fashion?" Sharon asked, sounding surprised. "Fashion. Make-up, trends, etc."

Sharon took a sip of her wine. She was stalling for time as she chose her words. "Well Sylvia, it sounds very exciting starting..."

Sylvia held up her hand. "Sharon, one thing you don't know about me is that I do not like bullshit. I am very blunt. I speak my mind. I always have; no need to stop now. I'm making you an offer. Probably the quickest offer you'll ever receive. I'll double your salary. You can start in a week or two; I don't want to leave Sandra in a bind." She finished her wine, then reached into her clutch purse, pulled out an envelope, and handed it to Sharon. "Here's my offer. I'm sure you'll find it more than generous."

Sharon hesitantly took the envelope, waited a few moments, then opened it. She tried to hide her facial expression. This was more money than she'd ever make as a writer. She'd be able to do many different things with this type of money.

She could feel Sylvia staring at her as she continued to read, then lay down the paper. "This is very generous, Sylvia. I'll need to speak with my husband before making any decisions."

Sylvia looked surprised. "Really? You mean, you need to ask your husband before you can take the opportunity of a lifetime?"

"We make all big decisions together," Sharon replied.

Sylvia cocked her head to one side. "I do exactly how I please. It's the only way to live. Family and marriage are definitely overrated. Do you have children, too?"

Before Sharon could answer, the waiter arrived with their food. Sharon watched as he carefully served. When he was finished, she replied, "We don't have any children. We're both focused on our careers."

Sylvia smiled. "I never had children. No time. And now with my magazine, I'm going to be busy, busy, busy. I do hope you'll join me, Sharon."

* * *

As Sharon sat in her office, the memories of her first meeting with Sylvia filled her head. She leaned back in the big leather chair. After a moment, she grabbed her office phone and called her husband, Keith.

"Hi, it's me," she said, her tone low.

"Hey, you. I was just thinking about you," he replied.

Sharon smiled; just hearing his voice would do that to her. "Remind me again why I took this job?"

"Sylvia issues?" he said.

"What else?!" she replied. "I don't think I can take much more, Keith. I've worked for this woman for 5 years, and –"

Keith interrupted him. "Quit."

Sharon paused. "I just might. Today may be the day," she said, sounding defiant.

Keith chuckled. "Okay, what happened?"

"She wants me to fire Maria."

"Why?" he asked.

"Well, she says it's because of a story she wrote. I told her to write it! But I think it's because she's Mexican. She called Spanish 'gibberish'. Can you believe that? This woman is unbelievable."

Keith was silent. He could hear the frustration in Sharon's voice. "I was serious when I said quit," he said.

She paused. "Remember that time we were in Costa Rica... the beach..." She smiled.

"I had sand everywhere." Keith laughed.

"I wish we were there now," Sharon said sadly.

"Hey, you don't have to do anything you don't want to do," he said. "I know. It's just; I thought this job would be different. I thought I'd be able to create something good. Not this bullshit we print."

"Your eyes were open, Sharon. You knew what kind of stuff the dragon lady wanted to do. Look, whatever you decide, I'll support you. I got you."

Sharon took a deep breath. "I know. One day..." She trailed off.

"Not today?" Keith asked.

"No, not today," she replied. "I gotta go, babe. I'll see you tonight." Sharon hung up the phone, and then quickly dialed her assistant. "Patty, please tell Maria I need to see her."

Chapter 4

"Come on, Michael, it's a good story."

Tallulah sat, folding her arms. She was sitting in his tiny office, trying to make a case for her story idea.

"I'm not saying it isn't, but it can't go in this issue, T. I've already completed the layout, and Tony wrote the cover story. You can't write all the covers, T," Michael replied.

She was frowning. "I know, but I was hoping since it's so prevalent in the media, you'd let me squeeze it in? Please? Pretty please?"

Michael looked at her. "Sorry, next issue."

"Come on, Michael."

"Next issue," he said.

Tallulah went back to her desk. Her 1980s phone was ringing, and she picked it up. "Tallulah Brock."

Chloe's voice came through the phone line. "Hey, girl. Let's meet up tonight. I've been workin' like a Hebrew slave in this motherfucker, and I need a motherfuckin' night out with my girls!"

Tallulah smiled. "Okay. Z's place, 11 pm."

Chloe said, "Cool, I gotta go."

Tallulah clicked off the phone, then laughed. "That girl has issues," she said out loud.

She opened her laptop and quickly scanned her emails. She opened three more "Thank you, but no thank you" emails and deleted all 3. She checked the time: 10 pm.

"I'm headed out. Be sure to lock up," Michael said, walking out of his office.

"I'm right behind you," she said, quickly closing her laptop. She grabbed her bag and purse and followed Michael.

"Thank Zoe for the pie," he said, locking the door.

"Is that all?" she said slyly, playfully poking at him.

"What?" Michael said, turning a little red.

"Are you blushing?" she asked.

"Look, just tell her thank you," he said, not sounding amused. He then looked around. "Do you need a ride?"

"Naw, I like the walk. I got mace."

She hugged him and watched him walk away, then pulled out her cell phone and texted Zoe:

I'm headed your way

Zoe:

I've got wine!

Tallulah smiled and texted:

I'll need a big glass. Is Chloe coming?

Zoe:

Yep, she is already here, eating of course

Tallulah:

Of course

She looked up to see Michael getting in his car, then turned and made the short walk to Zoe's Soul Food Kitchen. When she arrived, she softly knocked on the door of the restaurant. She heard laughter. Then, Chloe appeared. She smiled at her through the door, unlocked it, and opened it.

"Bout time your ass got here. Zoe makin' me hold the next bottle of wine till you got here!" Chloe said, grabbing her arm and pulling her inside.

Tallulah gave her a big hug. "Come on, girl. You know Zoe got us in the back."

Chloe turned and headed to the back of the restaurant. There, Zoe had a table ready. It was filled with ribs, collard greens, mac n cheese, cornbread, honey butter, and, of course, wine.

"You made it!" Zoe said, standing up and giving Tallulah a hug.

Tallulah looked at all the food on the table. "See, this is how you fatten us up, Zoe. Damn, girl, who you expecting?"

"Whatya mean?" Zoe said.

Tallulah laughed. "I mean all this food. There's enough to feed us, them, and then us again!"

Chloe sat down, handing Tallulah an empty wine glass. "Girl, stop complaining and dig in."

Chloe grabbed a rib and took a bite. "Mmmmm...I love your cooking, Zoe. I really do. These ribs are banging!"

"Pass me the wine," Tallulah said.

She poured herself a full glass, then set down the bottle and noticed both Zoe and Chloe staring at her.

"Uh oh...what's up?" Zoe said.

"What do you mean?" she said, taking a large sip of wine.

"I mean, what's with the full glass? What happened? You only drink like this when something's happened." Tallulah took another gulp of wine and set her glass on the table.

"I'm so tired of looking for a job. Every time I open my email, it's rejection, rejection, rejection." She took another drink of wine.

56

Chloe stopped eating. "You pregnant? Whose is it?"

Tallulah shot her a look of disapproval. "No, I'm not pregnant. What are you talking about? I'm serious, Chloe. You have a great job at a good firm. Zoe, you have your restaurant. I thought I'd be more established by now." She sank into the chair. "I'm tired of being rejected. One can only take so much." She finished her wine and poured another glass.

Chloe spoke first. "Bitch, you're a good writer. All these nos aren't rejection. It means something better is coming."

"Yeah? Well, it better come quick. My rent increased... again," she replied.

"How many publications did you contact?" Zoe ask.

"A lot. More than I want to admit," she replied.

The three friends sat in silence for a moment, then Tallulah looked at Zoe.

"I haven't told Michael yet that I'm looking for another job. I'm really hoping to freelance part-time. He's talkin' about cuttin' back on how often he prints. Right now the paper comes out monthly, but he may go to every other month."

Chloe looked up. "See, bitch? No one reads magazines anymore. Everything is online...everything. Hey look, I'm a PR rep. I'm constantly on social media. I rarely pick up a paper or magazine." She shrugged her shoulders and continued to eat.

Tallulah sighed. "What I am going to do?"

"Everything will work out. We got you. You know you ain't gonna be homeless," Zoe said.

"I'm willing to write about whatever at this point." Tallulah sighed. "Michael basically turned down my pitch for the homeless shelter."

Zoe poured the last of the wine into her glass. "The

homeless shelter?"

Tallulah nodded her head. "Am I the only one who noticed the new shelter was never built? Remember all the talk about a new building and an anonymous donor? Now nothing... crickets."

Chloe chimed in, "Girl, I can't even walk into my office without someone asking me for money. The other day, a lady sent her little girl up to me. How a bitch say no to a little kid?"

"I had an idea to write a story about the people who use and depend on the shelter. You know, talk with them, get their side of why they're homeless. Really, aren't we all a paycheck away from being homeless?" Tallulah asked.

"Hell no!" Chloe cried. "See, now you trippin'. I ain't ever gonna be homeless."

"You should volunteer at the shelter, T. It may give you some perspective. I started taking food to Marigold. They could really use the help. Besides, it's research," Zoe said.

"You're right," Tallulah said, pouring another glass of wine. "I should. No, I will."

"Well, let me tell you about my motherfuckin' day!" Chloe said.

"Oh, here we go," said Zoe.

"Let me start by saying I'm a professional Black woman. I keeps it moving, little time for games or bullshit, especially at the job."

"Why do we need a disclaimer for the story, Chloe?" Zoe asked.

"I'm just sayin'," Chloe said. "So they hired this new chick, right? Brenda, Tina...whatever the

fuck her name is. She all skinny, blonde, blue-eyed. But that's not the issue. I don't let the white girls at the job get me trippin', right? I know how good I am. My clients love me. So anyway, I

have to give a report to the team about upcoming stuff, junkets, press conference,

releases...whatever, right?" Zoe and Tallulah nodded. "So after the meeting, this bitch gonna come into my office and tell me I'm very articulate and speak very well."

"What?" Tallulah said.

"Yes, bitch. This bitch said I speak very well. So I said, 'Come again? What do you mean I speak very well?'"

"What did she say?" Zoe asked.

"Oh, you know I had to check a bitch. She was like, 'Oh, I mean in front of such a large group, you sounded so professional.' I went right in to check a bitch mode. I said, 'I'm not sure what you're trying to say, but I'm always professional with my colleagues and clients. That's why I'm the lead consultant.' Then she got all flustered, tryin' to backtrack. She was like, 'I'm sorry if I offended you.' I told that bitch she couldn't offend to get the fuck out of my office." She paused a moment. "Okay, well I didn't say that last part, but you get a bitch's point. I said that shit with my look."

"Wow. You know she scared now, right?" Zoe said.

"I don't give a fuck. That's some dumb shit to say. What, we aren't supposed to talk good? We ain't edumacated or some shit like that?" Chloe said.

"It's how the media portrays us, as Black women, and stuff." We're always supposed to be angry, on welfare, strung out, a bunch of bad ass kids, no job, no nigga," Tallulah said.

"Well, that's bullshit," Chloe said. She grabbed her purse and pulled out a blunt. "But we are going to smoke this." She slid the blunt across her nose and inhaled. "Now, this is some good shit. It'll help calm my nerves. I wanted to tell that bitch that contrary to popular belief, Black women are smart, educated, strong, and some of us even have a good grasp of the motherfucking English language. I can't stand that stupid shit."

Tallulah laughed. "Did she ask to touch your hair, too?"

Chloe laughed. "I wish a bitch would!"

Zoe jumped up. "Let me get some incense. I don't want this place smelling like weed."

Chloe looked at Tallulah. "You know, I can put my feelers out there and see what's available. "Stanley Roberts, my rich and attractive client, owns a publishing house," Chloe said as she lit the blunt.

She took a deep inhale and blew out the smoke. Tallulah watched as it danced in the air.

"Really, Chloe? That would be great. You know I would never ask."

Chloe took a deep breath and exhaled the smoke. She then handed the blunt to Tallulah. Tallulah inhaled, held the smoke for a moment, and finally blew it out.

"Bitch, I know. You my girl. I'll always help you. Besides, this'll give me a reason to call him."

"I told you to wait until I got some incense!" Zoe shouted as she walked towards them.

Tallulah passed the blunt to her. She took the blunt and inhaled.

"These are the best Friday nights. No club, no niggas - just us," Tallulah said.

Zoe nodded her head and passed the blunt to Chloe, then lit the incense.

They sat in silence for a while, smoking the blunt and

sipping wine. Jazz music played softly in the background.

"Hey, why don't you come with me Sunday to the shelter? I'm dropping off food and helping out with breakfast. You gotta come early like 7:30am," Zoe said

"Okay," said Tallulah. "I didn't know you dropped off food there."

Zoe nodded her head as she looked around at the smoke dancing over their heads. "I just started. This'll be my 3rd trip. I didn't want to throw food away." "How come you didn't ask me to go?" Chloe said.

"Because you, bitch, are not getting up on Sunday morning to go give food to the needy," Zoe said

"A bitch might," Chloe said.

Tallulah and Zoe looked at Chloe, and then they all started laughing.

Chapter 5

The Marigold Homeless Shelter was an old brick building in the heart of downtown. The building had seen many years of wear and tear. It needed a new roof, up to date electrical system, and the heater was making strange noises. Despite the issues with the building, the doors opened daily to feed and shelter the homeless. The shelter opened its doors to men, women, and families. It provided basic health care, shelter, and served meals 3 times a day. The main room served as a dining room during meal hours. Several long tables were lined up in rows that filled the entire room. At night, the long tables and chairs were cleared away and replaced with several cots.

Tallulah met Zoe at the homeless shelter on Sunday morning. People were lined up outside and around the block, waiting for a hot breakfast. Tallulah walked to the front of the line and gently pushed her way inside.

She spotted Zoe talking to an elderly Black woman. She watched as Zoe spoke to the woman, whose face looked somber and sad. Zoe was holding the woman's hand, comforting her.

Tallulah approached. "Hi. I'm sorry I'm late."

Zoe looked over at her, nodded her head, and continued to

speak with the elderly woman. "Now Lily, I'm going to be here all morning. I have to get the food ready for others. Why don't you sit here, and I'll bring you something to eat."

Lily, the elderly Black woman, nodded her head and sat down. Zoe then took Tallulah by the arm and led her away from the table. "So sad," she said. "Lily has mental issues. From what I'm told, she's been homeless for a long time. She's had the opportunity to get off the street, but she seems to want this life." Zoe shook her head. "She talks to herself a lot. But Tallulah, the woman can sing. The last time I came, she helped me in the kitchen. She has a beautiful voice. It's funny; you wouldn't think that voice would come from that frail old body."

Tallulah looked toward Lily. She didn't know what to say. A feeling of sadness came over her. "I guess some people want to live on the street," she finally managed to say.

Zoe looked at her. "Most of these people are mentally ill. The outcasts of society, T. I don't think they can function in the real world. Let's go to the kitchen."

She motioned for Tallulah to follow her. They walked through a large door into a large kitchen, which was full of volunteers. A young Hispanic woman walked over to them.

"Zoe, I'm so glad you're here. Thank you for bringing the food, we can really use it. We're going to have a full house this morning." She hugged Zoe and turned toward Tallulah. "I'm Anna. Zoe tells me you're here to help us today."

She extended her hand to Tallulah, who reached out and shook it. "I'm Tallulah. I'm here to help."

Anna smiled and released her hand. "Great. Zoe can show you what to do. You'll need a hair net and gloves."

"I'll show her, Anna," Zoe said. Anna smiled and walked

away. "Come on, T, let me show you what I do here."

Zoe led Tallulah over to the large stove, where she had several burners working all at once. "Today," she said proudly, "we have eggs, toast, oatmeal, Canadian bacon and some fresh fruit. I like to have fruit because they can take it with them." She reached over and pulled a pair of gloves out of a box. "When we serve, we use gloves. The hair nets are over there." She pointed to a box on the other counter. "You can serve. We usually make a line and have all the food on a table. We'll take everything from the kitchen and set up out in the dining room."

Tallulah nodded her head. She didn't know what to expect. She'd never volunteered at a shelter before. She didn't expect the rush of feelings when the woman and three kids came through the line. Then, an elderly white man with his scruffy dog asked for extra oatmeal. A young girl, maybe 17, smiled as she grabbed an orange and tucked it in her pocket. It was overwhelming, and she felt an air of hopelessness in each of their situations.

She noticed she was low on oatmeal and turned to Zoe. "I'm going back for another pot of oatmeal."

Zoe nodded her head. She was talking to a young boy who wanted a banana, and she smiled and handed it to him. Tallulah watched for a moment, then turned and walked into the kitchen. As she entered, she saw the elderly Black woman, Lily, standing next to the stove. She'd turned on a burner and was placing her hand over the fire.

"No!" Tallulah yelled and ran over to her. "Don't do that. You'll burn yourself."

Tallulah grabbed her hand and turned off the burner, then looked at Lily. Her face was dirty, and her brown eyes were sunken into her face. She looked lost. Her lips were chapped and dry.

She looked up at Tallulah. "I just wanted to see if I could still feel," she said softly.

"Just want to feel?" Tallulah led her away from the stove. "You could badly burn yourself."

Lily stared at her and said, "You are so pretty. I was pretty once. I had dresses and a lily in my hair." Tallulah didn't speak. Lily continued. "I had beautiful hair. Good hair, like my daddy."

"Let's go back into the dining room, okay?" Tallulah gently grabbed her hand, and Lily placed her other hand on Tallulah's.

"Okay. Soon it will be time. I'm not ready. I need my makeup and my dress. Can you help me find my dress? I think Amanda took it." Lily's lip began to quiver. Her eyes filled with tears, and she yanked her hand away from Tallulah

"You helped her take my dress! That's mine. Why did she take everything? Why did she take my dress?!"

Tallulah stepped back. She didn't know what to do, so she ran out of the kitchen and quickly returned with Zoe, who looked at Lily and slowly walked over to her.

"Lily," she said in a soft, low tone. Lily looked at Zoe, with tears running down her face.

"My dress. It's gone. It's all gone." Lily put both her hands to her face and sobbed.

Zoe wrapped her hands around her shoulders. "It's okay, Lily. Come on, let's go to the dining room."

She gently led Lily out of the kitchen and sat her at a table, then kneeled next to her. "Lily, it's okay. I know where we can get you a better dress, okay?"

Lily nodded. "You can't tell Amanda."

Zoe nodded.

As Lily sat and rocked back and forth, she muttered to herself. Zoe stood up and walked over to Tallulah, who looked flushed.

"She was trying to burn her hand. She said she wanted to feel," Tallulah said in a hushed voice.

"She's okay. She's always talking about Amanda and a dress. I'm not sure what she means," Zoe said, looking worried.

"Where does she come from?" Tallulah asked.

Zoe shrugged her shoulders. "I'm not sure. Anna would probably know." She looked around the room. "She's over at the front door. Let's finish serving, then we can talk to her."

Tallulah nodded and said, "Okay."

She then looked back at Lily, watching her rock back and forth. She watched her for a few more seconds, then joined Zoe in the serving line.

"We're getting more people," Anna said, sitting across from Tallulah and sipping her coffee. The dining hall was empty. A few volunteers were sweeping, but the dining hall had been cleared. "We rely on donations and volunteers," Anna said. "I'm glad you decided to join us today. As you see, we really need the help."

"You're really doing a good thing here, Anna. I write for Big World," Tallulah said.

"Big World?" Anna asked.

"It's a small independent newspaper. We write about the community, local events...stuff like that," Tallulah said. "I was thinking about running a story on the new homeless shelter. I remember hearing about it, but then things went silent. What happened?"

Anna's fingers circled the rim of her coffee cup. "We raised most of the money from private funding. Some came from government funds, but private funds did the heavy lifting."" She shifted in her chair. "We'd secured a large amount from an anonymous source. This person or persons pledged over $250,000."

Tallulah eyes widened. "That's great."

Anna said, "I thought so too, until I received a certified letter saying the funding had been taken back. The donor simply changed their mind. No explanation, no nothing."

"Did you ever find out who the donor was?" Tallulah asked.

Anna shook her head. "No. The money was just gone."

Zoe walked over, sat down, and pulled the hair net off her small twist. "I'm beat. I think it was busier than last Sunday."

Anna smiled. "You have been a godsend, Zoe. Bringing food, cooking food, serving food. I'm very thankful."

Zoe smiled. "I'm glad I reached out. It seems like such a waste to throw out food. Besides, I love to cook, and cooks love to see people eat their food...and like it. So when I see these people eat, they are truly grateful. It makes me feel good."

"So, I heard you had an encounter with Lily," Anna said, looking towards Tallulah.

"Yeah, she really scared me. She was trying to burn herself," she replied.

Anna's face looked serious. "We've had this problem with her before. I've tried to get her in housing, but she likes to be on the street. Sometimes she seems to be very aware. We talk about getting her off the street, her family. I know she has a brother, but that's all I know. Other times, like today, she just seems lost, incoherent, dazed.

Tallulah looked at Zoe, then back at Anna. "Anna," she said,

"I'd like to write a story about the shelter. Maybe generate some interest for donations. Maybe I could help Lily. Maybe I can find her family. Someone to help her."

Anna nodded. "That would great. We're doing okay for now, but as it gets colder, we'll begin to overflow...and then we'll have to turn people away."

"Where do they go?" Tallulah asked.

"Anywhere they can," Anna said.

Anna stood up. "Thank you for helping out today. Before you leave, be sure to get my card. We can set up a time to talk about the shelter." She walked over to Tallulah and hugged her.

Zoe stood up. "I have to grab a few things in the kitchen. I'll be right back."

Tallulah nodded and watched Zoe walk through the large doors into the kitchen. She then looked around the room and decided to walk around the place while waiting for Zoe. She found a hallway off the dining area. As she walked down the hall, she admired the children's artwork on the walls.

At the end of the hall was a door that led outside. Tallulah stepped through the threshold of the door into an alley. She felt a slight chill in the air, but not cold enough to see your breath. She looked around and turned to walk back in when she heard what she thought maybe singing.

She listened for a moment, not quite sure what she was hearing. She then turned around and slowly walked toward the sound. As she got closer, the sound became clearer: It was singing. She stopped next to a dumpster and peeked around the corner. Lily was sitting down, knees pressed up to her chest. She wore a blue and red ski hat and a large grey button down coat. Her black combat boots were covered in dirt. Her eyes were closed as she sang.

Tallulah listened to the sound; it was beautiful. Her voice filled the tiny area of the alley. It was cool and sultry. She listened, not making a sound.

She knelt next to Lily, who continued to sing, then opened her eyes and stared at Tallulah.

"Grandma," she said. "I wrote that a long time ago. I was so afraid the day we recorded it." She giggled. "I had on a blue dress. It was so beautiful. Blue was her favorite color." Lily swayed her head back and forth.

"Lily," Tallulah said, "it's getting cold. Let's go inside."

Lily looked at her. "No," she said. "I like the cold. I can feel the cold."

Tallulah stood up and shivered as a gust of wind passed by. "What were you singing? It was beautiful."

Lily looked up at her and giggled. "Grandma."

"Grandma," Tallulah echoed. "I've never heard it before."

"No one has," said Lily.

She was standing up, and as she prompted her body up from the ground, her voice sounded low and gruff. She slowly raised from the ground and was now standing directly in front of Tallulah.

"I wrote it. Well, I wrote the words. Owen did most of the music. He had a gift. Now, they say white men don't have soul, but Owen...now, he had soul." She turned and walked down the alley. Tallulah started to call after her, but Lily said, "I'll be back for dinner!"

She waved at Tallulah with her back to her. Tallulah watched her walk down the alley and out of sight.

Zoe sat on the small sofa in Tallulah's apartment and watched Tallulah pace back and forth. "T...T...sit down. I'm gettin' tired just from watching you."

Tallulah continued to pace. Suddenly, she looked up. "I can't help it. It helps me think," she said. "You should have heard her, Zoe. Well, wait, you have. I mean, she's good. Her voice." She continued to pace. "It just makes me wonder what happened to her. I mean, we all have a story, right?" Zoe nodded. "So, listening to her sing really made me want to help her. Find her family. I dunno." She stopped pacing. "My gut tells me there's a story here. I'm not sure what, but I'm sure of it. Maybe other papers or magazines would pick it up or something."

Zoe took a deep breath. "Sit down." Tallulah sighed and sat down. Zoe leaned forward. "T, I think it'll make a good story - about the shelter. You start prying into other people's business, their lives...well, that's something else. I'm just sayin'."

Tallulah leaned back into the sofa and thought for a moment. "My gut is saying something different. I gotta go with it."

Zoe shrugged her shoulders. "Okay, I can't compete with your gut. But you be careful. Remember that one time when you thought Chloe's boyfriend was cheating? Remember the 'I gotta go with my gut' speech you gave then? Remember, T? Do you remember what happened? You got all nosy in someone's business, and what happened?" Zoe put her hand up to her ear and cupped her fingers. "What?" she said. "I didn't hear you. Oh, you want me to say it? Okay. You convinced Chloe, remember? You told this girl her dude was cheating. And what did Chloe do? What, you don't remember? Oh, I remember. Oh, well she went the hell off. She tried to cut the nigga, T, remember? She tried to cut his dick off. His dick, T. And you know she would've. You know Chloe's ass crazy and unstable.

70

You're lucky he didn't press charges. That bitch still be locked up." Zoe shook her head. "So you just tread the fuck lightly on this one, T."

Tallulah's mouth was open as if she was going to speak, but no words came out.

Chapter 6

Chloe blew a kiss to herself in the bathroom mirror, then smiled, carefully put the lipstick back into her small purse, and checked her dress.

"Flawless!" she said and turned and walked out of the bathroom.

She headed back into her office and grabbed a folder. She was meeting with her boss, Brenda, this morning. She dreaded the meetings with her, who was always trying to relate to her on a level of color. She noticed Brenda never did this with her peers, but over time she'd gotten used to it.

Chloe scanned the folder and left her office. She walked down the hall, stopped at a door, and softly knocked. She heard a muffled voice say, "Come in."

As she opened the door, she noticed Brenda on the phone. She was speaking softly. Chloe stood in the threshold of the doorway, not sure if she should enter or wait. Brenda motioned for her to come in. Chloe shut the door behind her and sat in one of two large chairs in front of Brenda's large desk.

"Yes, I'm sure that will be fine," Brenda said as she nodded her head. "Okay, thank you." She hung up the phone and smiled at Chloe. "Chloe, what's up, girl?"

Here we go, Chloe thought to herself.

She managed to muster a smile and say, "Good morning, Brenda."

"I called you down here for a couple of reasons. First of all, our new client, Mr. Roberts, is looking to get into charities. He's been very pleased with your work and asked for you specifically on this project. He's looking around to partner with an organization. If you have any ideas, he's open."

Chloe nodded her head. "Okay. I have a few ideas. I'll run them by him."

"Great," said Brenda. "You know his account is big and very important to the firm. He seems to like you, your style. I don't know what you're doing, but girl, keep it up." Brenda smiled at Chloe. "I also wanted to ask you something else...non-work related," Brenda said.

Chloe raised her eyebrow. "Okay, sure. What can I help you with?"

Brenda stood up, walked over to Chloe, and sat down next to her. She then leaned in close to her. "I know I'm your boss and all, but I like to consider us friends. We have a certain vibe. You feel me?"

Did this woman just say "You feel me?" Chloe said to herself.

"I feel like I can confide in you. We're like sistas, or is it sisters? Anyway, I feel we have a bond." Brenda smiled.

It's "sistas", bitch, and where the fuck is this going? Chloe thought to herself. She cocked her head to one side, looking a little confused. "What do you need?" she asked.

Brenda hesitated a moment, then blurted out, "I'm dating a Black guy!"

Oh, HELL no! This bitch is too fucking much. Breathe, girl, breathe. What does she want me to do, throw a party? Alert the

73

media! Breathe, girl, breathe, Chloe said to herself

Brenda smiled widely and leaned back into her chair as if she'd just announced she cured cancer. Chloe didn't answer; she opened her mouth slightly, then closed it.

"I just wanted to talk to you and find out what I need to know about dating a Black guy. I mean, I never have, so any tips?" Brenda asked excitedly.

Chloe half-smiled. *Is this bitch for real? Tips? What the fuck?*

She took a deep breath and managed to say, "Well...a man is a man."

Brenda stood up. "Oh, I know that," she said, waving off Chloe's comment. "I just want to know what to expect. I mean, do Black men really...down there? What about cooking? I mean, I don't know the first thing about soul food. Hey, doesn't your friend own a soul food place?"

Chloe took another deep breath. "Brenda. I'm glad you're out there dating. As long as he treats you right and is kind, I don't think color really matters." She stood up. "And as far as your other question...well, I'm just gonna leave that right here."

Brenda frowned. "Oh, I hope I didn't offend you, Chloe."

Chloe smiled as she walked toward the door. "Of course not, Brenda," she said. "I'm going to reach out to Mr. Roberts."

She quickly opened the door and let herself out. She stood for a moment, then shook her head in disbelief. She walked to her office. She closed the door and called Tallulah. Tallulah picked up on the third ring.

"What's up, girl?" Tallulah said.

"Oh my motherfuckin' god! You will never guess what just happened to a bitch!" Chloe said.

"Someone tried to touch your hair?" replied Tallulah.

"Oh, you got jokes? No, bitch. Brenda, my boss, just asked me for tips 'cause she datin' a Black guy. She said that. Tips. Do you motherfuckin' hear me?? Tips!"

Tallulah laughed. "What? Are you serious right now?"

"Yes, girl. Then she gonna ask a bitch if all niggas have big dicks!"

"Wait, did she says 'niggas'?" Tallulah asked.

"T, no, if she would have said somethin' like 'niggas', I'd be callin' you from jail."

"Wait. Chloe, did you trip out on her?" Tallulah asked, sounding concerned.

"You know what? I do know how to control myself and communicate with people. So no, I didn't trip out. I kept my motherfuckin' cool. I actually got the fuck out of there before I did go the fuck off."

Tallulah laughed. "So, what tips did you give her? Should I be writing this down?"

"Girl, bye," Chloe said and hung up the phone.

She closed her eyes and took a deep breath, then decided to turn her attention to Stanley Roberts. She clicked on her computer, found the file on him, and opened it. She studied it for a moment, then called her assistant, April. April was a heavyset girl with brown hair. Her horned-rim glasses made her look older than she was. Chloe liked her. She was smart and very capable. She wanted to give her a complete makeover but never mentioned it to her.

"April, please set up an appointment with Stanley Roberts. Make it a few weeks from now," Chloe said to her as she stood in the doorway, quickly writing down the information.

"Is there anything else, Chloe?"

Chloe looked up. *Have you ever thought about contacts?* Chloe thought to herself.

"No, April, that's it."

April nodded and left the office.

"I wonder if she dates?" Chloe said out loud.

* * *

The lunchtime traffic at Zoe's place had thinned out. A few stragglers were still there, but the restaurant was mostly empty. Tallulah sat at an empty table and opened her laptop. She went to her email and quickly scanned her inbox, then stopped on a message that had "You & Me" in the heading. She clicked on it and read:

Dear Ms. Brock,

Thank you for submitting your writing samples. Your style is very unique. I would like to speak with you about an opportunity I have for a freelance writer. I would like to arrange a time to speak with you. Please call me. My office number is 555-887-9898. Speak with my assistant

Patty.

Thank you

Sharon Eckerson

Editor You & Me

She stared at the email. She read it again. She moved her mouth so as not to miss any words. She then smiled and said, *"Thank you, writing gods."*

Tallulah stood up and walked into the kitchen, where she found Zoe in her office, going over receipts. "I got one!" she said triumphantly.

Zoe looked up. "Got what?"

Tallulah sat down. "A job lead. I got a lead for a freelance writing gig."

Zoe smiled, put down the receipts, walked over to Tallulah, and hugged her. "Good job. I knew someone would recognize your talent."

"Well, I don't have the job yet. They just want to arrange an interview. But she did say my samples were unique."

"Who?" Zoe said.

"Sharon Eckerson, Editor of *You & Me*."

Zoe frowned. "Never heard of it. What do they write about?"

"Well," Tallulah began, "if I remember right, they're a glam magazine. You know, makeup, dieting stuff, fashion, and travel."

Zoe replied, "That doesn't sound like you. I've never known you to write about fashion or makeup."

She sighed. "It isn't me, but as long as it pays, I'll write about whatever they want."

"So, what's the next move?" Zoe asked.

"I need to call and arrange an interview," Tallulah said.

"Well, you can use the office phone if you want," Zoe said.

"No, I think I'll head home. I need to talk to Michael about my idea for the homeless shelter."

Zoe looked at her. "Your gut?

"I'm telling you, Zoe, there's a story there," Tallulah protested.

"Hey, did you hook up with Anna?"

"Tomorrow," Tallulah replied. "That's why I need to get with Michael today."

"Well, tread lightly, please, T. Don't go getting deep into someone else's business," Zoe said.

* * *

"If you continue to raise the price, I won't be able to print!
" Michael yelled into the phone. He listened to the voice on
the other end of the phone, and then abruptly hung up. "Fuck
you," he said to the phone, then leaned back into his chair.
"What I am going to do?" he said out loud.

He put his hands over his eyes and sat in silence for a
moment. When he heard a light knock on his office door,
he looked up to see Tallulah standing in the doorway.

"Is everything OK?" she said softly. He didn't answer. "I
overheard part of the conversation.

Didn't sound good," she said, sitting down.

"It wasn't. I can't keep up with the rising cost of printing,"
he said, frowning.

"I'm so sorry, Michael. I know this paper is your dream,"
she said softly.

"I know print is old fashioned. Everything's online now,
but the feel of a newspaper is something special. The way it
sounds when you unfold it. The smell of the ink. I know it
sounds corny," he said.

Tallulah didn't speak. She wasn't sure what to say.

"Well, maybe it's time to look at going online, a digital
platform," Michael said, perking up.

"Maybe," she replied. "Do you know how to do that?" she
asked.

He smiled. "Nope," he answered. "But I'm sure there's
plenty of info." He sat for a moment. "Okay, well, let's change
the mood in here. We're not out of business yet. What's up?"

Tallulah shifted in her chair. "Well," she started, "I want
to do the story on the homeless shelter. I volunteered with

Zoe last week. They lost their funding to open a bigger shelter. The anonymous donor backed out."

Michael raised an eyebrow. "So what are you thinking, you'll find out who the donor was?"

"I was thinking about highlighting people who need shelter to survive. We should also look at mental illness.""

Michael opened his desk drawer and pulled out a chess game box. "I'll tell you what. You beat me at chess, and you can work your angle. I win, you work the donor angle. Deal?" He smirked.

"Really?" she said, smiling. "You know you haven't beat me in years, right?" "I've been working on my moves," he replied.

"Okay," she agreed, "you have a deal."

Tallulah leaned forward and helped him set up the board, then watched him as he concentrated on the game.

"Remember when you taught me to play?" she said, not taking her eyes off him. Michael nodded and raised his finger to his lips. "Shhh...concentrating."

"It was the first time we ever met...formally. I was getting out of reading *Tom Sawyer*." She smiled. "Wow, that was like yesterday."

"Tallulah, please, you're messin' up my strategy," he scolded.

"It's going to be a long afternoon," she said.

The game lasted a little over 90 minutes. Michael took his time concentrating on his moves, studying the board.

She was texting on her phone when he said, "I never should have taught you this game." "Oh, is it my turn?" she said, not paying attention to the game.

"Seriously?" he asked.

79

"Sorry. You're just taking sooo long between moves. I got bored." She smiled. She looked at the board. "Oh, checkmate."

"What the fuck?" Michael stood up. "I hate you," he said. She smiled. "I love you, too. I guess it's my angle, right?"

"Yeah, yeah, whatever," Michael said, studying the board. "I really hate you."

"Well, your timing is perfect. I was just texting Anna, the shelter director. She can meet with me tomorrow.

Tallulah looked at the board, then at Michael. He was still studying the board. His hand was perched underneath his chin, and he had a scowl on his face. He muttered something.

"So..." said Tallulah. "I guess I'll be going." She stood up and backed towards the door. "It was fun...playin' you... again."

She stood for a moment longer and left the office. Michael continued to study the chessboard.

Chapter 7

Zoe stood in the kitchen of her restaurant. She saw the delivery driver roll in the week's food order. He carefully set down a pallet and then went back to his truck. She inspected the pallet and waited for him to return. He was grunting as he pushed the heavy dolly over the doorway threshold.

"Excuse me," she said as he rolled the dolly into the kitchen, "I don't think this pallet belongs to me. The label says 'The Eatery'."

The delivery driver stared at her, then walked over to the pallet and bent down. "So, you're right. Well, I already delivered it to them. You're the last stop of the day."

He stood back up, making a grunting noise on the way up. "I'm going home after this. Why don't you just keep it? Consider it a present." He winked at her and started for the door.

"Wait a minute," Zoe said. "I can't just keep their stuff. Can't you just put it back on your truck and take it to them tomorrow?"

The driver sighed. "Look lady, if I come in the morning with orders on my truck, I could get fired. I know you people know how to shuck and jive, so just give it to your homeboys to sell.

Whatever."

"Excuse me? 'Shuck and jive'? 'You people'? What the hell do you mean by that?" Zoe said angrily.

The delivery driver frowned. "Look, I don't care what you do with it. Sell it, keep it. As far as I'm concerned, I delivered it. Now, you wanna get rid of it? Well, do what you people do best. You know exactly what I'm talking about." He turned and rolled the dolly out of the kitchen, then out the back door of the restaurant.

Zoe watched in amazement as the delivery driver left. She looked at the door, then back at the pallet. She walked over to the pallet, bent down, pulled back some of the packagings, and readout, "Fruit cups. What the hell am I going to do with 200 fruit cups?"

Her phone rang. "Hello?"

"What's up, girl?" Chloe said.

"I just got 200 fruit cups."

"Fruit cups?"

"It's a long story. What's up?"

"So, I wanted to find out more about the shelter. I have a client who's lookin' to maybe donate or partner. Can you give me the director's name and number?"

Zoe walked into her office. "Sure. Who's the client? Yes, I'm being nosy," she said.

"That sexy, tall drink of Hennessy, Stanley Roberts," Chloe said.

Zoe laughed. "Why he gotta be Hennessey?"

Chloe laughed. "Because Hennessy is smooth and warm going down," she answered in a matter of fact tone.

"Well," said Zoe, "that explains everything."

Zoe provided Chloe with the information and clicked off her

cell phone. She decided to call The Eatery and let them know she had their order. She looked up the number and dialed.

"The Eatery," a voice answered.

"Hi, I believe I've received an order for you that was delivered to me," Zoe said.

"Please hold," the voice said.

After several moments, a voice came on the phone. "Can I help you?" the voice asked. Zoe explained the situation about the mix-up in orders and waited for a reply.

"Well, I show that order as being delivered."

"Well," Zoe said, "I have 200 fruit cups in my kitchen that say 'The Eatery'." A brief moment of silence followed.

"Well," the voice said, "I show we've received everything, so you can send them back or keep 'em, lady."

Zoe shook her head. "OK, I guess," she said, then clicked off the phone.

"What I am going to do with 200 fruit cups?" she said out loud.

Lily rubbed her hands together. The weather was getting chilly. She sat on the front step of the shelter. Her face was worn and chapped. She blew air into her hands to warm them, but it didn't seem to help. She rocked back and forth and started to sing. Her voice rose into the air, and she watched as her breath left her body, with sounds that came from deep within her. As she closed her eyes and continued singing, passersby would stop and listen. Some people left money. Others said, "Your voice is beautiful." But Lily didn't pay attention. She sat rocking back and forth with her eyes closed, singing.

Tallulah was walking toward the shelter when she heard that voice. She hurried her pace and found Lily singing on the steps of the shelter. She saw a few dollar bills and coins sitting in front of her.

As she watched Lily sing, she noticed she seemed to look different, at peace. Maybe even happy. She looked peaceful and alive at the same time. Tallulah watched the small crowd that had gathered in front of Lily. They listened as she sang, and Tallulah heard them make comments like "Beautiful" or "What a voice".

When Lily was done, she opened her eyes, surprised to see the small crowd that had gathered around her. She looked around and said, "I wrote that."

The crowd clapped and began to disperse. Tallulah waited until the crowd was gone, then walked up to Lily.

"Hi, Lily. That was a beautiful song," she said, sitting down next to her.

As soon as she sat down, she could smell the foul odor coming from Lily. She shook her head to try to overcome the stench, but it overtook the small area in which they sat.

"Is that your money?" Lily said, looking at the dollars and coins sitting at her feet.

Tallulah shook her head. "No, that's for you. The people left it while you were singing," she said.

Lily reached down, picked up the dollar bills and coins, and put them in her coat pocket. She turned at looked at Tallulah. "What do you want? You go get your own money," she said.

"I don't want your money, Lily. I like to listen to you sing," she said.

Lily smiled at Tallulah. "When I was a young girl, I would sing for my grandma. She loved to hear me sing. She made me join the choir and church. I was going to be famous. I was going to take me and Clyde."Tallulah raised an eyebrow.

84

"Who's Clyde?" she asked.

Lily looked at her and frowned. "Clyde is my twin brother. He couldn't sing, but he could write. He wrote stories and was going to be famous, too."

Tallulah shook her head and shivered a little. "Lily, let's go inside and get something warm to drink."

She stood up and reached out for Lily's hand. Lily looked at her hand and stood up without grabbing it.

"I don't know you. You want my money," she said.

"No. I don't want your money, Lily. I just want you to come inside with me. It's cold out here." She stared at Tallulah for a moment and said, "Okay, but this is my money. Ain't enough for two of us."

Once inside, Lily walked over to the table in the large dining room. She sat down, took the money out of her pocket, and began to count each coin. Tallulah watched her for a moment as Lily picked up each coin, held them in her hand, and smiled. She then took the coins and held them up to the light. She was talking to the coin, but Tallulah couldn't make out what she was saying. She was so caught up in watching Lily, she didn't even notice Anna standing next to her.

"Hi, Tallulah," Anna said.

Her words broke Tallulah's trance-like state. "Oh, you startled me," Tallulah said. "I didn't even notice you were standing next to me."

Anna smiled. "Come into my office," she said and motioned for Tallulah to follow her.

Tallulah watched Lily for a few more moments, then followed Anna to her office.

"Sit down," said Anna. Tallulah sat in a chair in front of Anna's desk. "So," Anna said, "you really seem fascinated by

Lily."

Tallulah was a little embarrassed. "I am. Her voice...it's so beautiful. She was singing when I walked up. She had a small crowd gathered around her. She even made a little money."

Anna nodded her head. "Yes, Lily showed up years ago, or at least since I've been here. She is a songbird."

Tallulah pulled out her notebook and tape recorder. "Do you mind if I tape our conversation?" Anna looked at the recorder. "No. Nothing here is a secret," she replied. "Great," said Tallulah.

"Okay, feel free to ask whatever you'd like," Anna said.

She spent the morning interviewing Anna about the shelter. She took notes, along with a recording. "So, tell me about Lily," she said. "I was thinking about highlighting some of the people who depend on the shelter. Lily seems to be a regular."

"Well," said Anna, "like I said, Lily has been coming around for years. She just showed up one day. I've talked to her about getting off the street. Some days she's open to the idea and will even start to fill out the paperwork, then other days she's incoherent. She mutters to herself. She insists on being on the street. She says it's her punishment."

Tallulah cocked her head to one side. "Punishment for what?" she asked.

"I have no idea," said Anna.

"Did you know she had a twin brother?" Tallulah asked.

"Clyde," said Anna. "Yes, she does talk about him. I think he was killed in an automobile accident, but I've never been able to confirm."

"She also mentioned someone named Amanda. Does that ring any bells for you?" Tallulah asked.

Anna sat for a moment. "Now that you say it, yes. She has mentioned Amanda before. I'm not sure who she is. She told me Amanda took everything from her. I'm not sure what that means." Tallulah nodded her head. "She told me the same thing."

Anna opened her bottom desk drawer and pulled out a file. "I started the application for housing a few years ago. I was never able to get her to finish filling it out. This is all I have."

She handed the file to Tallulah, who opened the file and began to read. "All the contact information is blank."

Anna nodded. "I know. I've also tried to get her to give me information so we can get her birth certificate and ID. When I mention it, she goes crazy. She says they'll find her." "Who will find her?" Tallulah asked.

"I don't know. Maybe Amanda. All I know is that Lily likes living off the grid. I think something happened. Something traumatic that made her walk away from her life."

Tallulah sat for a moment. "Okay, so let's talk about funding," she said, putting down Lily's file.

"Well," said Anna, "there isn't much to tell. We had a large donor who pledged a lot of money.

We were going to build a new shelter. It would be much bigger than this. I thought we'd be able to offer services, besides food and shelter."

"What kind of services?" Tallulah asked.

"Counseling, mental health, employment services, job training or school. Something to help these people reclaim their lives. I also wanted to have a school for the children. Just because you're homeless, doesn't mean you should stop learning.

Tallulah looked at Anna. "So, what happened to the funding?"

"I'm not sure," Anna answered. "One day we had it, and the next our money bags donor backed out. No explanation. I've had to put all the services I want to provide on hold. We can barely offer the 3 daily meals and shelter at night. Money is tight."

Tallulah shifted in her seat. "Did you ever find out who the donor was?" Anna shook her head. "Anonymous," she said. "So, what happens now?" asked Tallulah.

"We depend on volunteers, like your friend Zoe. We depend on donations." "How many volunteers do you have?" Tallulah asked.

"They come and go. I have my regulars who come in several times a week." She paused. "Wait, I think Marc is here. I should have you talk to him. He volunteers quite often. He's trying to start his own business, but he manages to come and help out. He's really bonded with Lily, too." Tallulah looked up. "Okay, he's here?"

Anna stood up. "I think he's in the kitchen. Let's see if we can find him."

Anna and Tallulah left the office and started for the kitchen. Tallulah could hear singing; it was faint, but as they got closer, she could hear two voices.

Anna looked at Tallulah. "Yes, he's in the kitchen with Lily."

They walked into the kitchen to find Marc and Lily singing. Lily was smiling and holding a spoon like a microphone. Marc was drumming on the counter. They didn't notice Anna and Tallulah standing in the doorway.

"Lovers come and then lovers go
That's what folks say
Don't they know

They're not there
When you love me
Hold me and say you care
And what we have is much more
Than they could see
What we have is much more
Than they could see..."

Marc noticed Anna and Tallulah standing in the door. He stopped the soft drumming and looked at Lily, who was holding her spoon microphone, as well as the last note. She noticed Marc was no longer drumming and stopped singing.

"Ah, sorry, Anna. Too loud?" Marc said.

Anna shook her head and walked over to him. "No, not at all. That's a beautiful song. I've heard it before," she said.

Tallulah and Marc said in unison, "LTD. Love Ballad."

Marc looked at Tallulah and smiled. "That's correct. A music lover," he said.

Tallulah smiled. Lily put down her spoon microphone, looked at Marc, then at Tallulah.

"I know lots of songs," Lily said. "I used to be a great singer. All gone now. Amanda took everything!" She started to scream. "SHE TOOK IT ALL! SHE TOOK CLYDE. SHE TOOK OWEN. EVERYTHING! THAT LYING BITCH. BITCH! BITCH!"

Marc grabbed Lily and wrapped his arms around her. "It's okay, Lily." He rocked her back and forth. "It's okay."

Lily buried her face into Marc's chest. She was sobbing.

Anna and Tallulah watched as Marc calmed Lily down. He hummed to her and rocked her back and forth. Finally, after several minutes, he released her.

"Lily," he said, "I've got you. It's okay. No one will hurt you here." He wiped her tears from her dirty face.

She smiled. "I used to be beautiful and young." He smiled at her. "You are beautiful and young."

Anna walked over to Lily. "Lily, how about you help me in the dining room? We need to set up for lunch." Lily nodded her head and took Anna's hand. "Marc, this is Tallulah Brock. She's doing a news story on the shelter. I thought you'd be a good person for her to speak with." She took Lily and led her out of the kitchen.

Tallulah watched them leave, then turned back toward Marc. He was smiling at her. She couldn't help but notice his striking good looks. He was tall, chocolate brown skin, and green eyes. His smile was white and wide. She stared at the gorgeous man. His chiseled features caught her eye. A quiver ran through her body.

"Hi," he said in a deep, soothing voice, "I'm Marc." He held out his hand.

She reached for it and managed to say, "I'm T...I mean Tallulah."

Marc smiled, and Tallulah thought she felt herself melt a little. "Nice to meet you. You doing a story?" he asked.

"Ah, yeah, on the shelter. I want to highlight some of the people who depend on the shelter. You know...tell their story," she said.

She was trying not to stare but found herself captivated by his smile. "Well," Marc said, "I've been a volunteer for about 3 years. I really like it. I found out by accident that Lily is a songbird. One day I was in the kitchen, singing with my headphones on. She wandered over to me and just started singing. We sing a lot. She's a great singer, as you heard." He walked over to the sink and began to rinse dishes. "I help out whenever I can. I like it. The giving back." He continued to

90

rinse the dishes. She walked over to him. She stood next to the sink and watched as he rinsed.

"Do you think I could interview you for my story?" Tallulah asked.

He continued to rinse. "Sure. I'm almost done here." He smiled.

She felt the melting sensation run through her body again. "Okay, I'll wait for you in the dining room," she said.

"Okay," he answered.

She watched him rinse the dishes.

A man who does the dishes and is fine, she thought to herself, then turned and left the kitchen.

Marc entered the dining room. Tallulah was waiting for him at a table. Her notebook and recorder sat in front of her.

He walked over to her. "Wow! A real interview, huh?"

She smiled. "I hope you don't mind if I record you," she said.

"No. I'm good," he answered as he sat across from her. "So, what do you want to know?" he said.

She turned on the voice recorder and looked up at Marc. "So Marc, what do you do here?" she asked.

He smiled. "Well, a little bit of everything. I mostly help out in the kitchen, clean, do laundry and help the people who come here."

She nodded her head. "What about Lily? You seem to really have a connection with her."

He leaned forward, interlocked his fingers, and placed them on the table. "I do. She reminds me of an auntie. She has troubles, but when it comes to singing...well, you heard her. I always look out for Lily. She just showed up one day. She was alone and lost. I try to keep her from drinking, but it hasn't really worked. She pretty much drinks every day." He stopped. "She drinks to forget," he added.

"Forget what?" Tallulah asked.

"Her life," he said.

A moment of silence passed between them, then Marc finally spoke. "From what I know, she's had it pretty hard."

Tallulah nodded. "I want to highlight her in my story. I was hoping to learn more about her. Her voice is sensational. She has one of those voices that's unforgettable. It resonates with you. I'm surprised she doesn't make a living singing."

Marc looked at her. "It's funny you say that. I said the same thing. I know she had a brother, but he died years ago."

Tallulah looked excited. "Yes, she told me she was a twin," she said.

Marc nodded his head. "She said that to me as well. I tried to find out more, but she doesn't talk about it. I get bits and pieces," he said. "I just listen to her. I tried to get her to get off the street, but she won't."

He looked at his watch. "Well, it's almost time to prep for lunch. Are you staying to help out?" he asked.

She looked at him. *I'd stay if you asked me to,* she thought to herself.

"I can...if you need the help," she said.

He smiled at her. "We can always use help," he said.

"Wait, so what do you do when you aren't here?" she asked. "Well," he said, "follow me to the kitchen, and I'll give you my life story." She stood up and followed Marc into the kitchen.

Chapter 8

When Tallulah left the shelter, it was after 2:00 pm. She spent the entire afternoon with Marc. She thought he was amazing. He owned a limo company and was a Lyft driver part-time. He told her he volunteered at the shelter as a way to give back.

"When I was a kid," he said, "me, my mom, sister, and brother stayed at a shelter. I know what it means not to know where you're going to sleep or when you're going to eat."

Those words resonated with her as she walked up the steps to her 2nd-floor apartment. She was deep in thought when she heard a voice call her name.

"Lula, mija, is that you?"

Mrs. Herrera was standing in the doorway of her apartment. She had immediately developed a fondness for Tallulah. She insisted on calling her Lula. Tallulah had told Mrs. Herrera her grandmother called her that. "Well, I'll call you Lula,too. "That's a lovely name," Mrs. Herrera said one day as she helped Tallulah paint her apartment.

"Yes, Mrs. Herrera, it's me."

"Home a little earlier today, huh?" Mrs. Herrera asked.

"Yeah, I was at the Marigold shelter. I'm doing a story," she answered.

She was always trying to feed Tallulah. "I have some tamales if you're interested?" Tallulah smelled the delicious scent of homecooked Mexican food from Mrs. Herrera's apartment. She was a great cook. Tallulah could eat her food anytime, but she had no appetite. She couldn't get the images of the people at the shelter out of her mind.

"No, thank you, I'm not hungry," she replied.

"Well, if you get hungry, come get some. I made extra for my grandchildren, but they haven't shown up yet."

"I will. Thank you, Mrs. H. I really appreciate it," Tallulah said and continued up the steps.

Once inside her apartment, she dropped her bag and took off her shoes. She then walked over to her laptop sitting on the kitchen table and opened it. She clicked on her email and found the message from *You & Me*. She took a deep breath, pulled out her cell phone, and dialed the number listed in the message.

The voice on the other end of the phone said, "Sharon Eckerson's office. This is Patty. How may I help you?"

Tallulah stammered, "Ah, ah, yes, my name is Tallulah Brock. I received an email from Mrs. Eckerson about freelancing." She paused.

"Hold, please, Ms. Brock," Patty replied.

After several moments of dead air, a voice came on the phone. "Hello, Tallulah, this is Sharon Eckerson. Thank you for calling me." She replied, "Thank you."

"I received your email," Sharon continued. Tallulah could hear paper shuffling in the background. "Yes, yes. Hold on, I have your information right here in front of me. Now, if I remember correctly, you write for a newspaper, correct?"

Tallulah was nodding her head. "Yes. It's a local small paper.

I've been with it since its beginnings." She could hear more paper shuffling in the background.

"Well, I've had the opportunity to read your samples. I think you're very talented, Tallulah. I'm looking for writers for freelance opportunities. Does this interest you?" Sharon asked.

"Very much. I love writing for the paper. But as I said, it's small. I have free time and could contribute to other publications."

"Great," said Sharon. "Why don't we set up a more formal interview? Most of my freelance writers live in other cities, so we can do this by Skype. Does that work for you?" Tallulah smiled. "Yes, Skype is fine."

"Perfect," said Sharon. "I'll have my assistant set every-thing up. It'll be myself and Sylvia Blass, the magazine's owner."

"That will be great," said Tallulah, smiling into the phone.

"I do have one more question. Do you read *You & Me*?" Sharon asked.

Tallulah thought for a moment. She could hear her grand-mother in her head.

If you start out honest, it's easier to stay honest.

"No, I don't read it on a regular basis. I am familiar with the format."

Sharon laughed. "Well, there's something to be said for honesty. It's okay. We're a fashion magazine, Tallulah. We didn't start out that way in our 15 years of being around. Actually, *You & Me* started out as a gossip magazine. Like *The Enquirer.* It was called *Chatter.* About 12 years ago, Sylvia came in and re-branded and changed the direction of the magazine. Don't worry. Reading it isn't a prerequisite for the job. I just really wanted to know."

Tallulah felt a wave of relief run through her body. "I want to be honest," she said.

"No worries. I'll have my assistant set up a Skype interview. I'm thinking next week, but my calendar isn't in front of me. I'll have her call you today or tomorrow for confirmation. It's been a pleasure, Tallulah," Sharon said.

"Thank you for the opportunity," Tallulah said and hung up.

She sat for a moment, then jumped up and danced around her apartment, still holding on to her cell phone.

"Yes yes yes yes!" she said.

She jumped on the sofa and danced around for a while, then she heard a knock at the door.

"Lula, are you okay?"

She stopped jumping.

"Yes, Mrs. Herrera. I'm fine," she answered as she walked toward the door. She unlocked it, opened it, and saw Mrs. Herrera standing in front of her with a plate covered in aluminum foil.

"I heard pounding and wondered if you were okay?" Mrs. Herrera said, sounding worried. Tallulah moved to the side and let her in. "I'm good, Mrs. H. I was just jumping around the apartment," she said.

"That's a strange way to behave," said Mrs. Herrera as she walked into the apartment. "I thought you might be hungry."

She handed Tallulah the plate. Tallulah took it and closed the door. "I was jumping around because I have an interview next week!"

Mrs. Herrera smiled. "That's so good, mija. All the more reason for you to eat. Tamales. Eat." Tallulah took the plate into the small kitchen and unwrapped the foil, then picked up a tamale and took a bite.

"Ohhh, so good, Mrs. H. You should sell these," she said while chewing the food.

Mrs. Herrera smiled. "It's nothing. Something to keep me busy. I get lonely in my apartment. I like to cook."

Tallulah smiled. "Well, I love to eat, so we're a match."

Mrs. Herrera nodded her head. "I'm going to go. I'll get the plate later."

She opened the door and let herself out. Tallulah watched as she walked down the stairs. When she heard the apartment door open and shut, she closed her door.

* * *

Chloe was in a shopping mood. She thought she might have a problem with shopping but shook the idea from her head. Was it her fault if she made great money and had a sense of fashion? She just couldn't help herself. She loved makeup, clothes, bags, and jewelry, but she loved shoes the most. She blamed her mother.

She remembered being little, going into her mother's closet, and seeing nothing but shoes. High shoes, low shoes, pointy shoes, round shoes, shoes of all colors. She would play in the closet for hours. She would put on one of her mother's dresses, then a pair of shoes to match. She would parade around the closet, looking at herself in the full-length mirror.

Chloe had called Tallulah and told her to meet her for a day of shoe shopping. She needed her to be on time and motivated. As she waited, she started to get cold and impatient, then finally spotted her walking toward her. She waved and

97

motioned for her to hurry up.

Shoe shopping with Chloe was a mission. She had so many shoes that her closet was full. So, she used her living room to display her heels, flats, pumps, sandals, and boots.

"I need power shoes for my meeting with Stanley Roberts," Chloe said, pulling Tallulah into the sixth shoe store of the day.

"All those shoes you have? Seriously?" Tallulah said, looking around the store.

"Yes. I need something that says, 'I can handle whatever you throw at me.' Feel me?"

Chloe smiled and turned and walked toward a display of Vivienne Westwood pumps. Tallulah sighed and followed her with reluctance. After what felt like hours, Chloe finally found a pair of Stuart Weitzman pumps. They cost her over $700.

It took everything in Tallulah's power not to say anything. To her, $700 was rent, food, and electricity. Definitely not a pair of shoes.

"These will set me apart from everyone else, T," Chloe gleefully said while putting the shoes on the counter.

"It should. They're as much as rent," Tallulah said.

"I'll look great, and the shoes definitely make the suit I just got," Chloe said with excitement.

"Can you afford $700 shoes?" Tallulah asked.

"Bitch, the question is, can I afford *not* to buy these shoes? The answer is, no, no, no. I must have them." Chloe smiled at her.

Tallulah smiled back and thought, *Shoes are her crack. She just can't help it.*

A young, stylish looking woman with long blonde hair was in front of them, speaking with a sales clerk. Tallulah caught herself listening to their conversation.

"You've got excellent taste in shoes," the clerk remarked to the blonde lady.

"I saw them and absolutely had to have them," the blonde replied back.

Tallulah watched the clerk and blonde go through the transaction.

"That will be $846.13. How do you wish to pay?" The clerk smiled at the blonde and gave her an approving look.

"I think I'll use a credit card," the blonde said. She began to search her wallet, choosing which one to pick. "Hmmm...I think it'll be AMEX today," she said and handed the card to the clerk.

Tallulah watched the clerk swipe the card and hand it back to the blonde. She then bagged up the shoes and handed them and the receipt to the blonde.

"Enjoy, and come back again." The blonde smiled and took her purchase.

The clerk looked at Chloe and Tallulah. She half-smiled and said, "Did you find something you like?"

Chloe pointed to the shoes on the counter, then turned to Tallulah. "I'm winning in these shoes, girl. Do you hear me? Winning." She then pulled out her wallet and handed the clerk her credit card.

Tallulah half-smiled and watched as the sales clerk took Chloe's credit card. She had a look of disapproval on her face.

"Ummm...do you have any ID?" the clerk asked, looking at both of them suspiciously. "We've had some issues with stolen credit cards, and I need to verify this card is valid." The clerk half-smiled and waited for Chloe to present her ID.

You didn't ask the lady in front of us for ID," Tallulah

responded.

"Oh...well, she's a regular customer, so no need. I know her. Do you have ID or not? It's for your protection as much as ours." The clerk looked intently at Tallulah. "Are you saying this card may be stolen?" Chloe ask.

"Oh, no, it's just...well...they are $700 shoes, and, well..." The clerk trailed off.

Tallulah glanced at Chloe, who had that "Not today, bitch" look. Before Chloe could say anything, Tallulah snatched the ID from her hand and gave it to the clerk. "See, they match," Tallulah remarked.

"Oh, so they do," replied the clerk.

She watched as the clerk swiped the card and bagged up her purchase.

"Enjoy, and just so you know, all sales are final, and we do not accept used merchandise." Chloe looked at the clerk, then Tallulah.

"You know what..." Chloe started.

Tallulah grabbed her arm and pulled her toward the exit. She didn't let go of Chloe until they were clear of the store.

"What the fuck just happened? That bitch just assumed I couldn't afford to buy the goddamn shoes!" Chloe yelled. "I'm so tired of this shit, fucking assumptions based on skin color," she continued. "Now, the old me would have just jumped over the counter and snatched her ass up!"

"Well, let's be glad the old you didn't show up. The last thing I need is to be bailing your crazy ass outta jail," Tallulah joked.

"I'm serious, T. That's bullshit. I'm tired of this shit. Damn." Chloe sat down on the bench and folded her arms. "What more do we need to do? What?"

Tallulah saw the seriousness in Chloe's face and walked slowly over to the bench and sat down.

She took a deep and breath and said, "Look, I know it's hard to be Black sometimes, but we can't be what they think we are. We're better than what they think. I know they expect us to act a certain way."

"You mean ghetto," Chloe interrupted.

"Okay, ghetto. But we know we're educated sistas out here, doing the damn thing. The minute we lower ourselves to their level, we've lost. Haven't we?"

They sat quietly on the bench.

"It may be subtle, but it's still racist," Chloe said, breaking the long silence.

"I know, girl, but look at it this way. That bitch is still going to work at a shoe store while we out killin' it. We gotta stay on our grind, right?" Tallulah smiled at Chloe.

"You're right, as always. The yin to my psycho yang. Let's go get us a taco." Chloe jumped up. "I'm buying. I got you."

"You'd better." Tallulah stood up, and they headed to the taco stand. "Better not tell Zoe we settled for tacos," she said with a smile.

"Can't nobody be eating that damn pie every day. I'll be as big as all outside," Chloe said.

They both laughed and walked toward the taco stand.

Sharon walked into Sylvia's office, carrying a folder with her. As she sat down on the small sofa located near the large window, Sylva looked and up. "Oh, is it that time?" she said. Sharon nodded her head. Sylvia walked over to the sofa and sat down. "So, what do you have for me?" she asked.

Sharon shifted on the sofa and cleared her throat. "Well, I've been interviewing freelance writers all week, and this is the cream of the crop." Sharon handed the folder to Sylvia, who looked through each applicant while humming. Sharon sat patiently, not wanting to interrupt her. Finally, she spoke. "Tallulah? You can't get more southern than that."

Sharon didn't speak. She wasn't sure if Sylvia expected an answer or was just commenting to herself. Sylvia continued going through the file, the finally put it down and looked at Sharon. "Well, all of these writers look pretty good. I mean, I'm no editor, but I like what you've brought me." She smiled an eerie smile.

Sharon answered, "I'm setting up Skype interviews for next week. Are you available?"

Sylvia frowned. "Probably not. I'm going to the Maldives for a friend's anniversary party. Didn't I mention that to you?" Sharon shook her head no. "Well, it doesn't matter. I trust you can handle things by yourself. I mean, you are the editor, for God's sake. I just want someone who'll do as they're told, write the way I think it should be written – and no foreigners this time, Sharon. I can't stand a thick accent. We need someone who can speak to our readers. You know, speak their language."

Sharon could feel herself getting warm all over. She bit her lip. Sylvia looked at her. "Yes, Sylvia. I understand what we're looking for," Sharon answered.

"Good. Now, did you fire Maria?" Sharon nodded her head yes. "Good. Her foreign gibberish was making me nauseous. I mean, my God, this is America; speak English. Is it really that difficult?"

Sharon took a deep breath before speaking. "Sylvia, Maria spoke three languages. She was a good writer and good employee. I hated to see her go."

Sylvia stood up. "Well, that's why I'm the owner. I have to make the tough decisions. If she speaks 3 languages, then English is what she should have spoken while she was here. Our readers want to know we hold ourselves to a certain... standard. Everyone in your file looks good. So, hire 1 or 2. We'll need them for the spring anniversary issue." Sylvia smiled. Her voice was condescending and demeaning. "You can go now."

She waved Sharon away as if she were a fly. Sharon stood up, picked up the file, and left the office.

"I love my job. I love my job. I love my job," Sharon repeated all the way to her office. She walked in and shut the door. "She is such a wicked old bitch!"

Chapter 9

"**G**et out of here!" the man yelled. His face was twisted from yelling and screaming. He was holding a wooden bat and waving it around. Lily stood at the counter and managed to duck his first couple of swings. She was staring at the loose dollars and coins she had spread out on the counter.

"I have enough money!" she yelled back.

The man waved his bat again, catching her on the side of her face. Lily screamed in pain and grabbed her face, then stumbled back into a display of potato chips. The display fell over and crashed to the ground. Lily screamed again and lunged toward the counter. The man held up the bat again. "You want more?!" he yelled.

Lily screamed and reached for the bat. The man swung and hit her on her shoulder. She screamed out in pain.

"Call the police!" the man yelled to a woman who'd just entered the small liquor store.

Lily could feel blood running down her cheek. She cried out in pain as she tried to grab the money she had on the counter. She missed the counter and fell to the floor. The woman rushed over to her, holding her cell phone. She looked at Lily's face.

"What are you doing?!" she yelled at the man.

"She's a dirty thief and liar. I don't want her in my store. She has a bottle underneath her coat!" the man yelled.

The woman shot him a cold look and turned her attention back to Lily. "You're bleeding. We need to get you some help." As the man got on the phone with the police, the woman helped Lily to her feet. "Here. Sit down," she said. She guided Lily to a floor display that served as a chair. Then, she focused on the store clerk. "Get me some fuckin' paper towels before she bleeds all over your floor, asshole!!" the woman yelled.

Lily felt dazed. She didn't know where she was. She looked at her hands and saw that blood covered them. She looked up at the woman, whose face began to distort before Lily's eyes. She tried to fix her vision by blinking her eyes, but the woman's face remained distorted. Lily closed her eyes and began to rock back and forth.

"I'm a good girl," she said. The woman held a paper towel to her face. "I'm a good girl," Lily repeated. The woman removed the blood-soaked paper towel, unrolled a new one, and placed it on Lily's face.

"You need your ass kicked!" she yelled at the man. "You don't go around hitting people with a bat, especially women. What the fuck is your problem?"

The woman waited with Lily until the police arrived. After she told them what she'd seen, the police questioned the liquor store owner. Lily watched as the man told his story. The policeman then nodded his head and walked over to Lily.

"Do you need medical attention?" he asked her.

Lily looked at him. "I don't need anything," she said. Her head hurt, and she felt dizzy. She tried to stand up but fell back down. The woman, who was standing next to Lily, stepped in.

"She needs a doctor! Can't you see she's bleeding? This man bashed her in the face with a bat! My God, am I the only one who sees this shit?"

The policeman called for an ambulance on his radio and walked back to the liquor store owner.

Lily began to sway back and forth. She felt herself slipping, then all was black.

Lily tried to open her eyes but couldn't. She had a terrible pain in her face and shoulder. She groaned a little. She tried to raise her hand, but someone gently pushed it away.

"Lily? Lily, it's Anna. Do you know who I am?"

Lily tried to open her eyes again and groaned.

"Where am I?" she said, not opening her eyes. "My head hurts."

"You're at the county hospital. "Someone has injured you," Anna said.

Lily tried to open her eyes. She managed to open her right eye slowly. Everything was blurry and distorted. She managed to focus, if only for a moment, on Anna.

"What are you doing here? Lily asked. Her voice was raspy, her breathing labored.

"They found my card in your pocket. They didn't have anyone to call, so they called me," Anna softly replied.

Lily reached her hand up to her face and felt a bandage on her left cheek. She tried to pull it off, but the tape made it difficult. She turned her head. Now able to open both eyes, she focused on Anna.

"Anna?" she asked.

Anna held her hand. "Yes. Lily, you're in the hospital. You were injured at the store. Do you remember anything?"

Lily turned her head and looked around the room. Her vision

would focus, then be distorted again. She blinked her eyes several times, trying focus. She tried to sit up, but a quick, sharp pain in her shoulder stopped her. She slowly lay back down.

"I was at the liquor store," Lily said. "The man. He had a bat." Anna said, "The doctor is releasing you, Lily." "Will you come with me, to the shelter?"

Lily looked at her. She trusted Anna. She gave her food and clothes. She was kind and would let her sing in the kitchen. So, she nodded her head yes.

"Okay, let me help you up. I brought you some clean clothes, shoes, socks, and underwear," Anna said.

"Okay," said Lily.

Lily sat in the wheelchair while Anna spoke to the doctors. She didn't like hospitals. She thought they smelled bad.

Anna walked over to her wheelchair and began to push her towards the large glass doors.

"My money," she said. "I don't have my money."

Anna continued pushing. "Let's get to the shelter, Lily. We can talk about your money then, OK?"

Lily tried to twist her neck around to look at Anna, but the pain in her shoulder stopped her. She nodded her head.

Lily smiled at herself in the mirror. She twirled around so the edge of the dress flared out. She giggled, then picked up a nearby hairbrush and used it for a microphone. She belted out "All of Me", by Billie Holiday. She twirled around again, and when she faced the mirror, she was on a stage.

The bright lights shone in her face. She couldn't see the audience, but she could hear them chanting her name. She walked up to her microphone and started singing "Grandma". The round tones of her voice carried throughout the room. She stopped singing and bowed.

She raised her face to look out at the crowd and was now facing an alley wall. She was sitting next to a garbage can. The microphone was now a large rat. She screamed and tried to stand. The rat looked at her and said, "Wake up...wake up...wake up..."

Lily jumped up and was immediately greeted with a sharp pain in her neck, shoulder, and face. She slowly lay back down. She'd been dreaming. She looked around the room. She was in an office. There was a desk and chair. She was lying on a cot next to the door. She blinked her eyes and focused on the room. She could hear people talking outside the door. She pulled herself around so both her feet were on the floor, then touched her face and felt the large Band-Aid. She braced her hands next to her and slowly raised herself up to a standing position. She used the desk to steady herself. She slowly walked to the door and opened it. She could hear talking down the hall in the dining room. She used the wall of the hallway to steady herself as she slowly walked.

When she entered the dining area, she saw people in line, getting food. When she felt steady on her feet, she pushed herself away from the wall and walked to a nearby table and sat down.

Marc, who was serving food, noticed Lily as she walked into the dining room. Her cheek was covered with a large bandage. He watched her walk over to a table and sit down.

He leaned over the person standing next to him and said, "Hey, can you take over for me? I'm going to grab Lily a cup of coffee."

He left the food line and walked over to the coffee cart, poured a cup of coffee, and took it to Lily.

"How are you feeling? I heard you had some night," he said as he handed her coffee. She tried to smile, but the pain was overwhelming.

Lily took the coffee and said, "Thank you." She took a small sip and sat the cup down. "Lily," he said, "what happened?"

She looked at him. She couldn't remember everything. She only had bits and pieces. She took another quick sip of coffee and said, "I don't remember. I was in the liquor store, and the man wouldn't take my money. He hit me with something. I don't know." She shook her head. "He has my money. I was trying to get my money," she whispered.

He looked at her cheek. "Yeah, I think you got roughed up pretty bad. I really think it's time you came off the street, Lily."

She looked at him. "All I need is a bottle to drown out the noise and a little food from time to time. Nobody cares about me, and I don't care about anybody," she replied.

"Now, you and I know that isn't true. You can't keep living like this. You could have really been seriously hurt a lot worse than a gash in the cheek. You could have been killed. Luckily, people like Anna do care about you. She went and got you last night. Brought you here. Put you to bed. She hasn't even been home. She stayed here with you all night." He paused for a moment. "She even got your money."

He dug into his pocket and pulled out a $20 bill. As Lily looked at the money, she could feel her bottom lip start to quiver. Her eyes filled with tears. She blinked, and they streamed down her face.

Anna walked over to Marc and Lily. Tallulah was with her. "Lily, how are you feeling? Would you like some lunch?" she said as she sat down.

"Lunch?" Lily echoed.

Tallulah sat down next to Lily. "Hi, Lily. Do you remember me?" she asked.

She nodded her head. "The alley," she replied. She looked at everyone around the table.

"I wasn't always on the street, you know," she said. "I had a family, my brother, my mama, and Owen." She put her hand up to her head.

"Do you want something for your head?" Anna asked.

Lily nodded yes. Anna stood up and walked toward her office.

"I was going to be a singer. I even made an album," Lily continued.

"What happened?" asked Tallulah.

She wiped a tear from her face. "Everything happened. I didn't have a say in who my daddy was. I didn't even know."

"I don't understand," Tallulah said, sounding confused.

"How could you?" Lily replied.

Tallulah didn't answer.

"Lily, do you have any family we can call? Anyone who can help you?" Marc asked. Lily frowned. "Family?" She paused. "I have no family, Marc. Not anymore."

Anna returned with two aspirin and handed them to Lily. She quickly put them into her mouth and washed them down with coffee.

"Lily, I'd like to find out more about your singing and your album. Would you be willing to let me interview you?"

Lily looked at Tallulah. "Interview me? What for?" she replied.

"I write for a small independent newspaper. "I'm writing a story about the shelter," Tallulah said. "I hope to raise awareness and get donations for the new shelter."

Lily didn't speak. She looked down into her coffee cup.

Tallulah continued. "You have the most beautiful singing voice, Lily. It's your voice that resonated with me. So hauntingly beautiful. People get paid millions and don't sound half as good as you. Your voice is really something special."

"Songbird. That's what Grandma and Owen called me, songbird," Lily replied. She had a faraway look, then suddenly spoke.

Her voice was rough and angry. "I had a chance. A shot. And then someone took it all away!

That selfish bitch. She had everything and wanted us to have nothing!" She quickly stood up.

The room started to spin, and she quickly sat back down.

"My head hurts. I want a drink. Not this shit coffee. I want a real drink!"

Tallulah looked at Marc. "I didn't mean to upset you. I just thought if people could hear you sing..." She trailed off.

Lily's face softened. She didn't feel well. She wanted to lie down. She wanted a drink.

"Can I lie down?" she asked, looking at Anna.

Anna nodded her head and replied, "You can use the cot in the office where you were. I wish I had something better. I know you don't feel well, Lily, and I understand. But I'll need to get some information from you for the hospital. We can talk about it tomorrow. Okay?" Lily nodded her head.

Marc stood up, then helped Lily to her feet. They slowly began to walk toward the hallway.

As Tallulah watched them walk away, Anna saw the look of disappointment on her face. "Don't worry, Tallulah. Lily will be okay. I know she has things she won't talk about. We all do. Secrets. I know I got mine." She smiled and walked toward her office.

As Tallulah sat in the dining room alone, she heard Zoe's voice in her head. *Tread the fuck lightly on this one.*

"Yeah, yeah," she said out loud.

She looked at her watch. She was doing the dinner service for Zoe. She grabbed her bag and

pulled out her cell phone.

She texted Zoe:

Omw. At shelter.

She waited a moment and didn't get a reply. She put her phone back in the bag and stood up to leave. Just as she started to walk toward the exit door, she heard Marc call her name. She stopped in her tracks and turned around.

"Where you running off to?" he said with a smile.

"Work. I wait tables for Zoe at her place. I'm doing dinner tonight. I told her I'd help prep today. I

gotta get going. It can be a fucked up bus ride."

"Bus?" Marc said, sounding surprised.

"There's nothing wrong with the bus. It's a perfectly fine mode of transportation," she replied. "Besides, I'm not in the market for a car at the moment."

Marc shook his head. "Do you listen?" he asked.

"Excuse me?" she said.

He grinned. "I'm a Lyft driver. I could give you a lift." "Oh," said Tallulah. "You did tell me that, didn't you?" "I just gotta grab my stuff. " "Okay," she said.

She watched him jog away, then quickly checked her breath by cupping her hands up to her face and blowing. She pulled out her phone, opened her camera app, and looked at herself:

Dreads – check; face – check. She closed the app and put the phone back in her purse.

Marc reappeared and casually jogged toward her. "Okay," he said. "Let's go." Tallulah smiled and followed him to the parking lot.

Chapter 10

Marc sang as he drove. Tallulah sat in the passenger seat, looking out the window. She watched as they passed buildings, people, and cars. She couldn't help thinking about Lily and the things she'd said.

Finally, after several blocks, she spoke. "I want to find Lily's album," she said, still looking out the window.

Marc stopped singing. "We don't even know if she really had one. It could just be her talking," he replied.

She turned her head towards him. "I don't think so. She said she wasn't always on the street. Her voice is so good, I don't think her being a professional singer is a stretch." "Well, we would need to find out more about her," he said.

She looked surprised. "We?"

He smiled. "I think I can help you solve the mystery. Besides, Lily trusts me. She may not be willing to tell you her secrets, but she may tell me."

She turned her head toward the window. "The reporter in me says there's something to her story. It's a vibe I get. I call it my gut instinct," she replied.

They drove a little while in silence. As Tallulah listened to the humming of the car, she thought about Lily.

"What's Lily's last name?" she asked.

Marc thought for a moment. "I think it's Duke."

"Lily Duke," she echoed.

He looked at her. She was beautiful. Her long dreadlocks flowed down her back. Her skin looked smooth and soft. He wondered if she was seeing anyone.

"Hey, what do you do for fun?"

She looked at him. *You* was the first thought that entered her mind.

"I dunno," she replied, "the usual stuff. You know, movies, hanging out, reading, and writing." "That sounds okay, but not really classified as fun. Sounds kinda boring," he replied. "I am not boring," she said, sounding a little insulted.

"I didn't say you were boring. I said your idea of fun sounds boring," he said.

She didn't want to admit he was right, maybe she was a little boring. She hadn't dated in a year. She had a bad breakup and decided she was going to donate time to herself. She didn't mind being alone. She spent most of her childhood alone, but it would be nice to have someone to hang out with.

"Okay, Mr. Fun. What do you do?" she said.

"Well, for starters, I love to travel. I don't get to very much, but it is something I try to do every year. I hit the gym and play in a basketball league. I enjoy eating and listening to live music. I like to hang out with friends, go to clubs, play some golf, BBQ, and play cards.

She stopped him. "Okay, so you have more fun than me. I get it."

He flashed his devastating smile at her. "I could show you some fun stuff. If you want."

She looked at him, trying not to look eager. "Okay," she said in her most noncommittal voice.

"Great. So give me your number, and we'll go have some fun," he replied.

She turned her head toward the window, mouthed, "Yes!", then turned back towards him.

"Okay," she said.

Marc pulled up to Zoe's Soul Food Kitchen. "Here you are!" he said cheerfully.

He put the car in park and pulled out his cell phone. She gave him her number, and he quickly put it into his phone. He then stopped for a moment and looked at her sheepishly.

"I'm not sure how to spell your name," he admitted.

"Well, my girls just shorten it to T, or some people call me Lula," she replied. "Lula," he said. "I like that."

He typed the letters into his phone and looked up at her. "Okay Lula, I'll be calling you very soon."

She smiled. "Great."

She opened the car door and let herself out. He waved goodbye, and she watched him drive away. She quickly walked into the restaurant. It was empty, with the expectation of a few customers having a late lunch.

The calm before the storm, she thought to herself.

She walked back into the kitchen and found Zoe in her office.

She danced into the office. Her eyes were bright, and she was grinning from ear to ear. Zoe watched her dancing around.

"You know you awkward, right?" she said.

She continued her awkward dancing and added words to her moves. "I have a date. I have a date. He is fine, so divine, I'll slowly sip him like a good glass of wine." On the last word, she sat down.

Zoe looked at her. "Okay, so I'll bite. Who's the lucky fine glass of wine?" "Marc from the shelter," Tallulah replied, smiling. Zoe looked surprised. "Fine ass Marc?" she said.

"Yes, girl. He's taking me out for fun!" She stood back up and started singing again. "I'm going out with fine ass Marc. It's not the end; it's only the start."

"Stop!" said Zoe. "You cannot sing, T. Please stop hurting me and anyone else who can hear you."

Tallulah smiled and awkwardly danced out of the office.

* * *

"Dinner tips are better than lunch tips," Robert said. He was sitting at a table with Tallulah. "I did good tonight," he said, standing up. "I'm out, T. Have a good night." "'Night, Robert," she replied, then watched him walk out the door.

She continued counting. She took the bills and put them in her wallet, then placed the wallet in her bag. Zoe came into the dining room, looking tired. She slowly sat next to Tallulah.

"I think this was the busiest night ever," she said, laying her head on the table. "I'm just gonna sleep right here."

"I did so good in tips, but my feet are killing me. You are really starting to get busy, Zoe."

Zoe groaned. "I know this is what I wanted, but it's a lot of work." She slowly sat up. "Anna from the shelter called me today. She asked me if I'd help with a fundraiser. She wanted to have, like, a dinner, but I suggested an open mic/poetry slam."

"What? Didn't I just hear you say you're exhausted? And now you want to do a fundraiser?"

Zoe laid her head back down on the table and groaned. "Yes. Okay, but hear me out." She lifted her head from the table.

"Okay. I could make some space over there; more in the

front of the dining room. We won't need a stage. Just a mic, maybe some speakers. I can run a modified menu. It could work. I would donate what we take at the door, and maybe half of the food receipts. What do ya think?" "It sounds like a lot of work. You have a good heart, Zoe. So, when are you trying to do this?"

"I was thinking a month to 6 weeks. Do you think Michael would donate some advertising space?"

"Nope. Not doing that," Tallulah said.

"Not doing what?" asked Zoe. "I'm not being y'all's go-between or mouthpiece. You and Michael are funny. He likes you, Zoe. He has since college. You like him. You have since college. Pull the fuckin' trigger already."

Zoe opened her mouth, but no words came out. She kept her head on the table.

"If you want Michael to give ad space for your fundraiser, you have to ask him yourself," Tallulah said.

Zoe groaned again. Her voice was low and serious. "Okay, I do like Michael. But both of us

have been really involved in our careers. Besides, he's shy. The one time he actually took me out,

he barely said anything."

"Really?" Tallulah said.

"Yes, really. But you're right. This is my deal. I'll call him. Besides, it's business."

"Okay. Well, if you need help, you should call Chloe. This is her thing. But don't let her turn it into a booty club."

Zoe raised her head off the table. "You know what? You're right. I should ask Chloe. She loves this shit."

"And she'll totally take over. Very little work for you," Tallulah added.

Zoe smiled. Her eyes lit up. "Again! You are a fuckin' genius!"

Tallulah bowed her head, as if standing in front of an audience. "Please, please, I already know.

Thank you. Thank you." They both laughed.

Zoe stood up. "Need a ride home?"

"You know I do."

* * *

"The last Skype interview is all set up, Sharon. We're scheduled for 3 pm," Patty said as she put the file on Sharon's desk.

Sharon rubbed her eyes. "I'm so tired of talking for one day. Interviewing is exhausting." Patty smiled. "Well, this is the last one. Tallulah Brock. All her information is in this file." Sharon nodded her head, picked up the file, and went through the pages. She then put the file down. "Thank you, Patty."

Patty nodded and left the office. Sharon checked the time. Her last interview was in 10 minutes. She picked up the file again and scanned the articles. She read the title "Women in Power" and smirked. It made her think of Sylvia. Sharon was glad she was gone.

Poor Maldives, she thought.

At 2:50 pm, Tallulah was sitting at her small kitchen table. She'd prepared for her interview. She did research on *You & Me*. She found out about the scandal involving Sylvia and her mom. The magazine also went through a rebranding phase. She'd also learned Sylvia Blass was a real bitch. She read several colorful stories about her. She'd been called a bitch, a racist, and dragon lady. She was the woman who sold out her own mother for headlines.

119

Tallulah readied herself. At precisely 3:00 pm, her computer chimed. She clicked the app, and a white woman appeared on the screen.

"Hi, Tallulah. I'm Sharon Eckerson."

Tallulah smiled. "Hi, Sharon. Nice to meet you."

They had a great conversation. Tallulah instantly took a liking to Sharon. She was down to Earth and easygoing. She learned Sharon had started out as a writer, then assistant editor, then editor.

Sharon learned about BW and how Tallulah came to write for the small paper. Toward the end of the interview, Sharon asked Tallulah about the types of stories she'd like to write.

"Well," said Tallulah, feeling relaxed, "I like to write about things that are real. Real issues, real people. I'm working on a story about a local homeless shelter. I've volunteered a couple of times. What appeals to me is that my story may help with funding and donations. I really want to help. I'm going to highlight some of the people who depend on the shelter."

Sharon smiled. "Wow, that sounds like a great project. I would like to read it when you're finished. I mean, it's nothing we would run in *You & Me*, but it sounds like a good cause."

"I'll let you know when I'm finished," Tallulah said.

"I've enjoyed speaking with you and would love for you to do some freelance stuff for me. We're preparing for our spring issue. Spring is always big for us. I can send over all the paperwork, and I have a list of topics for our smaller upcoming issues. You can choose 2-4 to write about."

Tallulah smiled. She felt the quiver in her stomach. "Sharon, that sounds great. I'm so excited to join you."

Sharon smiled and said, "Great. You'll hear from my assistant, Patty. She'll send over all the paperwork. Okay?"

"Okay," Tallulah replied.

"It was nice meeting you, Tallulah. We'll speak again soon."

Tallulah closed her laptop and sat for a moment. She then started jumping around the small apartment.

"I got a job! I got a job! Finally!" she yelled.

She continued to jump around until she heard a light knock at the door. "Lula, is everything OK?"

Tallulah stopped jumping and went to the door. She opened it to find Mrs. Herrera standing in front of her.

She smiled widely. "I just got a freelance job!"

Mrs. Herrera smiled and walked inside the apartment. "I am so happy for you. Now you don't have to worry about money."

Tallulah shut the door. "Yes. Wait – I didn't ask about what it pays." She had a worried look on her face.

"Don't worry. I'm sure it'll be enough. Are you hungry?"

Sharon leaned back in the large leather office chair and stretched and yawned. Patty came into the office, "So, how did it go?"

Sharon looked at her. "I really liked her. She had some great answers. She was down to Earth, smart, funny, and personable. I hired her."

Patty sat down in a chair facing the desk. "Great. Do you want me to send her the packet?" Sharon nodded. "Yes."

"Am I sending a packet to anyone else?" she asked.

Sharon thought for a moment. "No, not yet."

Patty nodded, stood up, and left the office.

Chapter 11

The large metal gates opened, allowing the black town car entrance into the large estate. The driver pulled in and slowly drove to the entrance of the house. He put the car in park and jumped out, then walked around the back of the car to open the door.

Sylvia sat impatiently in the back seat, waiting for the driver to open her door. When the door opened, she scowled at him.

"If you knew how to read English, we'd have been here at least 30 minutes ago! I swear you people come to this country, most of you illegally, then expect us to understand you." Sylvia stared at the driver as she got out of the car. She frowned and rolled her eyes, made a hmpf, noise and walked into the house.

Once inside, she was greeted by Shannon, her maid. "Welcome home, Mrs. Blass."

Sylvia handed Shannon her purse. "Find out who hired that driver!" she said. "I want him gone."

Shannon nodded her head. Sylvia looked at her. "Did you speak to the cook like I asked you?"

Shannon nodded. "English is not her first language, Mrs. Blass, but she said she understood.

She's a wonderful cook."

"I'm going upstairs to pack for my trip. I only hired her because of your recommendation, Shannon. If she can't understand English, then honestly, I have no use for her. "You speak perfect English," Sylvia said, pressing her lips together. She then waited for a response.

Shannon nodded and said, "Yes, Mrs. Blass," then walked out of the room.

The master bedroom was located on the upper level of the large mansion-like home. The room was bright, as the sunlight bounced off the yellow/tan walls. The oversized king bed was draped in white satin lace. A white bed bench was at the end of the bed. The eggshell white curtains hung open, letting sunlight stream through the big bay windows. On the bed were some clothes, a suitcase, her passport, and an itinerary for Naladu Private Island in the Maldives.

She walked over to the large walk-in closet and began to go through her clothes. She was happy to be leaving for a few weeks. She needed a break from the magazine and her annoying staff. Plus, Sharon was becoming more difficult.

Shannon entered the room. "Mrs. Blass, Dr. Wilson is downstairs to see you."

Sylvia walked out of the closet. "Here? Now? What the devil does he want?" she said, sounding annoyed. "Have him wait in the study. I'll be down in a moment."

The maid nodded and left the room. Sylvia walked into the bathroom and checked her hair. She thought she looked as young as sixty. She smiled at her reflection and walked out of the bathroom.

She stopped at the study door, cleared her throat, and walked in. "Dr. Wilson. What a surprise. I didn't know you made house calls."

Dr. Wilson stood up. He was a tall man, about 6 feet. His short black hair was graying. "Sylvia," he said, reaching his arms out to her. She took his hand and sat down on the large black overstuffed sofa. "I'm sorry I didn't call. I know you weren't expecting me," said Dr. Wilson.

"I was just packing for the Maldives. The Roberts. You know the Roberts, right? Jackson and Claudia Roberts. Anyway, it's their 40th anniversary in the Maldives. I'm so excited. I really need a vacation."

Dr. Wilson smiled and gently took Sylvia's hand. "Sylvia, I've been your physician for a long time. I looked after you and your mother. So, I wanted to bring this information to you in person." He caressed her hand a little harder.

"Is there something wrong? For Christ's sake, Peter, what is it?" she said, sounding worried.

"I received all the results back from your physical. I ran all the tests twice." He paused for a moment. "You have pancreatic cancer."

Sylvia didn't move. She couldn't move. She felt nauseous. She slowly pulled her hand away from him and sat motionless.

Dr. Wilson's voice was soft but reassuring. "Sylvia, there are treatments we can do, but we need to begin immediately. We need to consult with an oncologist and –"

Sylvia interrupted him. "What do you mean, treatments? Chemotherapy? So I can lose all my fucking hair?!" She glared at him. "I feel fine, Pete. Your tests must be wrong!"

He took her hand again and gave it a tight squeeze. He then looked at her and said, "Sylvia, the tests aren't wrong. We can beat this, but we need to start treatment immediately. Now, I've made you an appointment with the best oncologist in the state. I called in some favors, and he can see you tomorrow morning."

Sylvia quickly pulled away her hand. "Tomorrow? No, I'm going to the Maldives. I told you. You'll just have to reschedule."

He looked at her in disbelief. "Sylvia, this is your life we're talking about."

She stood up. "Exactly. Peter, it's my life. So, I'm going to do what I want. I will see him the moment I get back. Thank you for coming. I don't mean to be rude, but I need to finish packing. You can show yourself out." She quickly walked to the door and left the room.

By the time Sylvia entered her bedroom, she was nauseous. She ran into the bathroom and leaned over the white porcelain toilet. Her breathing was rapid. She could feel her stomach twisting and grinding. Her stomach muscles contracted. She inhaled, and the contents of her stomach spewed into the toilet bowl. She groaned and leaned back away from the toilet. She slowly inhaled, then exhaled. Tears streamed down her face. *Cancer?* She thought to herself.

She reached her hands up and grabbed onto the sink, then slowly pulled herself up. She turned on the cold faucet and drank. She looked at herself in the mirror; her makeup was smeared. Her face was wet from the tears. She picked up a bottle of perfume and threw it at the large bathroom room mirror, shattering the glass. She then slowly sat back down on the floor, surrounded by shards of glass. She didn't care. She didn't care about anything at the moment. She was dying. She buried her face in her hands and sobbed.

The old Ford truck rattled as it pulled up next to the G5 Learjet. The brakes of the old truck squeaked until it came to a complete stop. Stanley Roberts leaned his weight against the door and forcibly pushed it open. He grabbed his bags, jumped out of the truck, slammed the truck door, and walked toward the jet entrance.

He was met by the pilot. "Mr. Roberts, welcome aboard," he said, shaking Stanley's hand. Stanley smiled at the captain. He was a tall man with a muscular build. His green eyes and olive complexion enhanced his chiseled facial features. His thick black hair blew lightly in the breeze. He was casually dressed, wearing a pair of jeans, Nike shoes, and black T-shirt. He swung the big black bag over his shoulder and boarded the jet. He tossed his bag onto an empty seat and took a seat himself.

A flight attendant appeared with a bottled water and bowl of fresh fruit. "Welcome aboard, Mr. Roberts. Here's your water and fresh fruit."

She smiled and put the plate and bottle in front of him. He smiled at her and opened the water.

After a few large gulps, he felt his cell phone buzz. He pulled it out and answered.

"Hello. Chloe, so nice to hear from you," he said.

Chloe cleared her throat. "Mr. Roberts, sorry to bother you so early," she replied.

"It's never a bother," he replied. "I have a list of charities I'd like you to review. I've sent a file to your email. I think they're what you're looking for."

"Great. I'm on my way to my parents' anniversary party, but I'll be back in a few days. Get with my assistant and schedule a time for us to meet."

"Of course," Chloe replied.

Stanley clicked off the phone, pulled out his laptop, and went into his email.

The flight attendant returned with a pile of newspapers and magazines. "Would you care to do any reading, Mr. Roberts?" she said, holding the pile. "You can just set them down," he said.

As he pulled out his headphones and put them on, the flight attendant nodded and walked away. He opened a music app on his phone and selected jazz. The music flooded his ears. He turned his attention back to his email and opened the file Chloe sent him.

Sylvia Blass sat in the first-class section of the large Boeing 357. Her laptop was open, but she wasn't working. She was staring out the small plane window. She watched as they glided through clouds. She turned back to her computer and typed in the words *pancreatic cancer treatment*. She was overwhelmed with the search results. She scanned the search results and sighed out loud.

Let's not do this now, said the voice in her head. *You're headed to the Maldives. You're due for a vacation, Sylvia,* the voice continued.

Sylvia nodded her head and closed the laptop, then leaned back into her seat and closed her eyes.

The flight attendant awakened her. "Excuse me. Would you care for lunch?"

Sylvia opened eyes and shook her head no. She didn't feel like eating. She pushed the button on the seat to raise herself forward. She opened her laptop and keyed in the words *pancreatic cancer treatments. She looked at the search results. She noticed words like "incurable," "alternative treatment," and "survival."* She slowly closed and opened her eyes, then stared at the screen. After several moments, she clicked on "alternative treatments".

Chapter 12

Tallulah ripped open the package from *You & Me*. It was bigger than she expected. Inside, she found the last two issues of You & Me. There was also a letter from Sharon, a job offer, and a list of articles she needed to write and submit. She looked at her article list. It included beauty tips, fashion trends, weight loss programs, and healthy eating.

She frowned. "What do I know about makeup?" she said out loud. She sat for a moment, then pulled out her cell phone and quickly dialed.

After two rings, Chloe answered, "What's up, T?"

"I need you," Tallulah said.

"What do you need? I got you. What's up?"

She told Chloe about the articles. "I mean, I don't even wear makeup, Chloe...well, not really. I need an expert, and that's you."

"Okay, it sounds like you need a full beauty by Chloe boot camp. I've been waiting for this moment!" Chloe announced. "I'll bring the beauty supplies. I have a closet full of stuff some of our makeup clients gave us. You're responsible for wine and party favors. When's the masterpiece due?"

Tallulah laughed. "I have two weeks from today."

"Good, we have enough time. Saturday, your place. And please have some real food, T. A bitch gotta eat. Maybe your fabulous neighbor can whip up something!"

Tallulah smiled. "Mrs. H? All she does is cook. I'll see what I can do. Thanks, girl. Love you." She clicked off the phone.

The silver-blue Lexus pulled up to the gray apartment building. Chloe put the car in park and turned off the ignition. She glanced at the several boxes in the back seat, then pulled out her cell phone and dialed Tallulah.

"I need help bringing this stuff up!" she said.

"We're coming down," Tallulah said and clicked off the phone.

Moments later, Tallulah and Zoe walked through the apartment door. Chloe smiled and opened the rear door.

"Beauty boot camp!" she said as she opened the door.

Tallulah and Zoe looked in the back seat. Their eyes widened.

"What beauty supply store did you rob?" Zoe laughed.

"Wow, you weren't lying when you said had a lot of stuff," Tallulah added.

Chloe reached into the back seat, grabbed several bags, and handed them to Zoe and Tallulah. She did this two more times until the back seat was empty. They walked into the apartment building, each with several beauty bags in hand. Once inside, they put all the bags on the sofa in the small living room. Zoe pushed the bags to both sides, sat in the middle of the sofa, and started looking through the bags. Tallulah sat on the floor with her back up against the sofa and motioned for Zoe to hand her a bag. Meanwhile, Chloe turned, walked into the kitchen, and smiled. On the counter was a plate of catfish, collards greens, mac n cheese, and a biscuit. "Thank you, Zoe!" she shouted from the kitchen. "Of course," Zoe replied.

As she went through the bag, Tallulah pulled out a Tom Ford Eye Quad box. "Isn't Tom Ford high as hell?" she asked.

"Yes!" Chloe said, with a mouth full of food.

"Where did all of this stuff come from?" Zoe asked.

Chloe walked into the kitchen, holding her plate and chewing. "It's from one of the firm's clients. This was in my closet. Now, most of this stuff isn't for Black skin, but a bitch love free stuff, so I took it."

A few hours later, the three friends were in the small apartment's living room, doing makeup on each other. Tallulah was finishing applying bright blue eye shadow to Chloe's eyes. "There you go. You look great. I think I missed my true calling as a makeup artist," she said. She cocked her head to one side, admiring her work.

"You mean a clown makeup artist." Zoe laughed.

Chloe reached out for a mirror, and Zoe handed it to her. She then flipped her hair and blew kisses into the mirror.

"It doesn't matter; clowns need love, too."

They all laughed. She passed the mirror to Tallulah, bright blood-red lipstick partially on her teeth. Tallulah smiled into the mirror and rubbed off the lipstick.

"Okay, now out of all of these products, what should I write about?"

A long silence passed in the room, then Zoe finally said, "So most of this is for white skin, right?" Tallulah and Zoe shook their heads yes. "So why not find makeup for darker skin? Whatdoya think?"

Tallulah looked at Zoe. "You're a fuckin' genius!" She leaned over and held up her hand for a high-five from Zoe.

"Actually, you can write about makeup for every bitch. That

way, you got your bases covered," Chloe said.

Tallulah looked at her and smiled. "You're a fucking genius, too."

Chloe took a bow. "Now, you can't do all makeup, so I'd start with base and concealers. This way, you can talk about the various shades. It gives you more to write about."

Tallulah stared at Chloe. "Who the fuck are you?" she said, shaking her head.

Chloe winked at her. "I'm the bitch who just wrote your first freelance article for *You & Me*."

Tallulah walked back up the steps to her apartment, entered, and closed the door. The makeup, package wrappings, and bags covered the small room. She smiled and waded through the bags and sat on the small sofa. She could hear her cell phone vibrating and found it under a pile of bags, then glanced at the number. She didn't recognize it but answered anyway. "Hello?" she said.

"Lula?" the deep voice asked.

"Yes, who's this?

"Hi, it's Marc. Remember me from the shelter? Gave you a ride to work?" he replied.

Tallulah smiled wide. "Yes, I remember you," she said.

"So, how ya been?" he said.

"I've been good," she replied.

"I was wondering if you wanted to get together tomorrow? Maybe we can do lunch or dinner?" Marc said.

She stood up. "Ah, yeah, tomorrow is great. We can do either one. I'm good." She started dancing among the bags and makeup.

"Great. I can either meet you or pick you up?"

She stopped dancing and looked around her small apartment. "Well, I can meet you," she said. "What do you have in mind?"

She pushed her way through the bags and went directly to her closet.

"Well," said Marc, "how about lunch and maybe catch a movie or something?"

She rearranged her clothes in the closet. Then, she tossed dresses, skirts, shirts, jeans, slacks, and sweaters onto the bed.

"Yeah, that sounds great. Where do you want to meet?"

"How about in front of the museum downtown? You know, the one with the giant fountain in front?" he replied.

She turned the phone to speaker mode and put it on the bed, then started sorting through her small wardrobe.

"Casual?" she asked while staring at a very short miniskirt. "Yes, casual. I'll see you tomorrow. Eleven-thirty okay?" he said. "Eleven-thirty is perfect. Bye, Marc." "Bye, Lula," he said.

She pressed the end call button. Then, she looked at the pile of clothes on her bed. A smile spread across her face as she danced around the small bedroom. She halted her dancing without warning.

Wait a minute, she thought. *He called me Lula.* She smiled and continued dancing around the bedroom.

Marc stood in front of the large fountain, watching the people as they walked by. He checked his watch; he was early. He sat down on the edge of the foundation and continued to watch the people. After several moments, he saw Tallulah walking toward him in the distance. He stood up and took a deep breath.

"Hi," she said. "Am I late?"

He shook his head no. "I'm always early. I blame my mom. She couldn't stand to be late," he replied.

Tallulah smiled and looked around. "So," she said, "what should we do?"

Marc looked at her. She pulled her long dreads up on top of her head in a bun. She wore a pair of jeans and black shirt. He noticed she wore little makeup; he liked that. Other women he'd dated were more materialistic than she appeared to be.

"Well, I thought we could grab some lunch, then maybe we could go for a walk or go inside the museum or catch a movie. Your choice," he said, smiling. She nodded her head. "Sounds good."

They ate at a small cafe near the museum. He told her about his dream to have a large fleet of cars for his limo service. She told him all about her friends and her work as a writer for a small paper. She watched him as he spoke to the waitress and got the check.

"So, what would you like to do now?" he said.

She looked around. "Well," she said, "I'm not really in the mood for a movie."

He smiled. "We could walk and talk. There are some great shops around here if you like to shop."

She looked surprised. "You like shopping?"

He laughed. "I was raised in a house full of women, just me and my brother. Shopping was one of those things I had to do."

As they walked down the sidewalk, they saw a homeless man sitting, his back up against a wall. His clothes were black from dirt and dust. His hair was matted and snarled. His face was dirty, worn, and tired. Next to him was a shopping cart. It was full of tin cans, old worn blankets, shoes, and newspapers.

Two cups were hanging from the cart, attached by a small piece of wire.

Marc walked over to him. He pulled out his wallet and gave the man $10.

"I know it isn't much, but it'll get you something to eat," he said.

The homeless man looked at Marc, then at the $10 he was holding in his hands. He didn't take the money; he just stared. Marc pushed the money into his hand.

"Take it," he said.

The man took the money and said. "Thank you. Thank you so very much."

"There's a shelter not far from here," Marc said. "You could get a hot meal and bed for the night."

The man shook his head. "It's always full, so I sleep on the street."

Marc pulled out his wallet again, this time producing a business card. "Here, take this. When you go to the shelter, show them this card. It should help you get a bed tonight."

The man took the card and looked at it, then put it in the pocket of his coat. "Thank you. You are a kind man," he said.

Marc nodded his head. "Now, you be sure to show them the card, okay?" The man nodded.

Marc and Tallulah continued to walk. "What was that card you gave him?" she asked.

"The shelter has emergency cards for those who are in dire need. It's like a go to the head of the line kind of thing," he replied.

"Oh, so what does that mean?" she asked.

He stopped walking. "It means he'll be able to get a bed and some food tonight."

They continued to walk in silence for a while, then she stopped and said, "I'm writing my story on the shelter."

He looked at her and said, "I hope it helps. If they don't get some funding soon, they'll need to cut back or shut their doors altogether."

"That can't happen," Tallulah said. "I know there's a stigma with being homeless, but sometimes bad things happen to good people."

He nodded his head. "I really worry about Lily. She's had a rough time lately. "

They continued walking, looking at the shops as they passed. Tallulah suddenly stopped in front of a record store. She grabbed Marc by the arm.

"Let's go in here and see if they have her record!" she said excitedly.

"You know, it could all be bullshit," he said.

Tallulah looked into the window of the record store. "It could be, but we could at least check it out. I think we should go into this store and see if they have her record."

As she smiled and opened the door to the store, a little bell that hung from the top of the door chimed. She turned and looked at Marc and went inside. He stood on the sidewalk for a moment, then shook his head and followed her into the store.

Tallulah spotted a man sitting behind a large counter. Behind him, high up on the wall was a neon sign that read *Back in the Day Records.* The man flipped slowly through his newspaper. He fixed his glasses and cleared his throat when he spotted Tallulah walking towards him. As she got closer, she realized he was reading a copy of *Big World*. She smiled to herself. He looked up from his paper and smiled.

"Can I help you?"

She walked over to the counter. "Hi. Yes. I'm looking for a singer. An artist by the name of Lily Duke."

The man sat up and raised an eyebrow. "Lily Duke?" he asked.

"Yes, I was told she made an album. I don't know the name," she said.

Marc walked up next to her. The man put down his paper.

"Well," he said, "I've never heard of her, but that doesn't necessarily mean anything. I can check the store database, and there are a few other databases I can check for you. Do you know her genre of music?" he asked.

Marc and Tallulah looked at one another. "Maybe jazz or R & B," Marc said.

The man walked over a computer terminal behind the counter and began typing. He looked up at Tallulah and Marc.

"This might take a bit. You can look around the store while you wait. I've got the largest selection of vinyl in the city," he said cheerfully and turned back to the computer.

Marc and Tallulah moved around the store. They saw rows and rows of albums. All genres. She wandered over to the jazz section and began flipping through the albums. Ella Fitzgerald, Sarah Vaughan, Etta James, Aretha Franklin, Nina Simone, and Billie Holiday.

These are some great Black women jazz singers, she thought to herself.

She was deep in thought when she heard the man behind the counter call out to her.

"Miss!" he called.

She looked over her shoulder to see the man gesturing for her to come over to him. She scanned the store for Marc; he was on the other side of the store, looking at albums. She walked over to the man. "Did you find something?" she asked.

He shifted in his chair and fixed his glasses. "I may have. Now, I checked about 4 databases I use. The first 3 didn't have anything, but the last one, I got a hit. Now, I'm not sure if it's what you're looking for, but I can order it. It's gonna take some time to get here, and there ain't no digital copies. So, it has to be the album."

"Okay," she said. "Does it show you a picture of the record?"

He looked at the computer screen and shook his head no. He turned the screen toward her so she could see it. "No picture, but there is some information. The producer was Owen Katz. It was recorded at Twilight Studios in 1961. That's really all that's here."

Tallulah looked at the screen, took a small notepad out of her bag, and wrote down the information.

"How much is it?" she asked.

The man hummed cheerfully as he checked the computer. "Well, it would come to about 18 bucks. If I order it, you need to pay for the shipping now, and that's another $12. So, an even $30 total."

"Okay, how long until it gets here?" she asked.

"Well, for about 2 weeks. I can call you when it gets here. You can leave your name and number."

Tallulah nodded her head and started searching her bag for her wallet.

"I got this," Marc said and handed the man $30. He looked at her and whispered, "Remember, we're doing this together."

The man took the money and opened the register. "Okay," he said, "it'll probably take a couple of weeks." He handed

Tallulah a piece of paper and a pen. "Write your info down here. I'll call you when it comes in."

He watched as she wrote down her name and number. He then picked up the paper and read it. He raised an eyebrow and said, "Tallulah. That's a different kinda name. I've heard it somewhere before. I just can't remember."

Tallulah smiled and pointed to the newspaper lying on the counter. He looked at her, then turned his attention to the paper. "The paper?" he said, sounding confused.

"Yes, I'm a writer for *Big World*. Maybe that's where you saw my name," she said.

He looked at the paper again, then picked it up, opened the pages, and started turning each one. Tallulah and Marc waited patiently as the man carefully inspected each page. "Ah!" he said. "Here you are, Tallulah Brock. Nice story. I like this one."

She smiled and replied, "Thank you."

"I'm Pete," he said, extending his hand. She shook his hand, then he extended his hand toward Marc.

"Are you a writer, too?" he asked.

"No," said Marc.

"Oh, well that's okay. We all can't be writers, now can we? If we were, who would read what was written?"

Marc gave a half-laugh and said, "Well, that's true. I'm Marc." "Pete. I own this place."

"Well, Pete," she said, "please let me know when the record comes in. You've been very helpful."

Pete smiled. "My pleasure."

They left the record store and walked quietly for a bit. Then Marc asked, "What if you find her record?" What then?"

She looked at him and thought for a moment. "Well, maybe

we can reboot her career? I don't know. All I know is that there's a story here. I can feel it. I think I can do some good."

He nodded his head. "I'd like to see her off the street. Sometimes when she talks, she has a faraway look in her eyes. I don't know what happened to her, but whatever it was, it sent her into a depression. She drinks to forget."

They continued to walk until they were in front of the fountain. Tallulah spotted a bench, walked over to it, and sat down. Marc followed and sat next to her.

"I had fun today," he said.

"Me, too," she replied.

He reached over, gently held her hand, and smiled at her. She felt a warmness flow through her body. She smiled and gently squeezed his hand. They sat in silence, listening to the rushing water of the fountain.

"Hey," said she suddenly, "did you know Zoe was going to host a fundraising event for the shelter? She's going to host an open mic."

"Really? I knew Anna was trying to put something together. An open mic is a good idea. When is it?"

"I'm not sure," she replied, "but what if we could get Lily to sing? She would be great." He cocked his head to one side, like a curious puppy. "I don't know about that."

She had a look of excitement on her face. "Yes, why not? We both know she can sing, and it's for the shelter."

"Hmm," he said. "She did say she wanted to sing again. But we would need to get her ready." "I've got just the person who can fix her up, with hair, makeup...the works!" Tallulah said.

"That's not what I meant," he said. "I mean ready to sing for a crowd on a stage. Have her sober."

Tallulah's face turned serious. "Oh, I didn't think about that." She paused for a moment. "Okay, that's your area. You said you wanted to help, and this'll help."

Marc nodded his head. "Hold up a minute. What do you mean, my area?" he said.

"Well, she trusts you, so maybe you can start to put the idea in her head. Practice singing. I don't know."

"Okay. We just need to find out when it is, then slowly introduce the idea to her," he said. She smiled at him. "See, we make a great team!"

Chapter 13

The large reception room featured sophisticated decorations. Crystal chandeliers hung from the high ceiling. They glittered and twinkled in the light. They hung a large banner from the ceiling that read, HAPPY 40TH ANNIVERSARY. White tables dotted the large room. The catering staff busily set up tables, chairs, china, food, and cutlery for each one.

Sylvia scanned the room and spotted Claudia Roberts talking to a young woman. She was smiling and make grand gestures with her hands. The woman was nodding her head in agreement and walked away. Sylvia began to walk towards Claudia, admiring the room decorated with elegance. The walls were draped in white and black curtains that went from the ceiling to the floor. On each table was a glass angel centerpiece, with large white and black roses. She looked up and noticed large silver stars hanging from the ceiling. The stars sparkled when they caught the light bouncing off the chandeliers. Sylvia slowed her stride and stood in the middle of the room and looked around.

It's so beautiful, she thought to herself. *I'm sure Claudia spared no expense.*

A waiter walked up to her and offered her a glass of champagne. She looked confused, and he pointed to Claudia, who was waving at her. Sylvia took the champagne and walked toward her. She'd known Claudia for several years, having met her while dating her now ex-husband. Their husbands were business partners. Together, they made several million dollars.

The only thing they had in common was money and how to spend it. They'd gone to great lengths to one-up each other over the years. This continued for a few years. Then, Chatter published an unflattering story about Jackson Roberts and his harem of mistresses. When Claudia confronted Sylvia about the story, she shrugged it off. She really didn't care if it embarrassed or humiliated her. That magazine sold more copies than any other previous issue, and Sylvia made a fortune. Claudia and Sylvia hadn't talked for a while. But when Claudia realized she didn't have an invite to the Met Gala, she had to reach out to Sylvia.

Sylvia had rebranded her magazine and was making her presence known in the world of fashion. Her magazine launched the careers of many famous designers and fashion models. Claudia chose to set aside her pride and call Sylvia. Sylvia had made her nearly beg for the invite and enjoyed every second of it. They decided to move on from the magazine incident. Claudia then attended the Met Gala, the world's most exclusive party.

Claudia then became indebted to Sylvia. Sylvia used the Met Gala incident to control Claudia. She pretended their "friendship" was still strong. Claudia acted like she was friends with Sylvia. She invited Sylvia to parties, dinners, and other events. Meanwhile, Sylvia used Claudia to learn about their husbands' business deals. She planned to use this information as leverage in court. By the end of her divorce, she gained a lot of information from Claudia. She walked away with more than half of his business and personal assets.

"Sylvia, so I'm glad you made it, and thank you for coming early. I was hoping to catch up with you. You know once the party starts, I'll be in hosting mode."

She kissed Sylvia on both cheeks and briefly hugged her. Claudia was wearing an all-white Zuhair Murad's embellished fishtail gown.

Sylvia smiled. "Your gown is divine, Claudia. Simply divine. Is it Murad's?"

Claudia smiled and turned around. "Yes. You like it? I saw it and knew it would be perfect for tonight."

"Yes, I think that maybe a few years old, but still lovely all the same."

Claudia half-smiled and said, "I have a moment. Come, let's sit, and tell me all the gossip!" She took Sylvia's hand and led her to a nearby table. Sylvia put down her glass and sat down. "So," Claudia began, "how is the world of fashion and trends?"

Sylvia half-smiled and said, "Oh, we're gearing up for the spring issue. Very exciting." Claudia smiled. "I'm glad you could make it. I'm so excited. Stanley is coming. I made him promise to take a day off from saving the world's poor and join his parents. You know, he's really not at all what I and his father expected. I thought he'd be married by now and me with grandchildren to spoil. But no, he's always in some remote country or working for some goddamn charity. I swear, Sylvia, every time I turn around, he's donating money to some organization. I mean, it's okay to give back, but don't give it all away."

"Well, you can't take it with you, now can you?" Sylvia said.

"What's the matter, dear? You don't seem to be yourself today," Claudia said. "Oh, I'm fine. Just a little tired from the flight."

Claudia frowned. "Did you fly commercial? Oh dear, no wonder you're tired. Next time, you need to fly with us on Jackson's new plane. I tell you, bypassing all the lines and people in the airport is great. I couldn't fly commercial again. I don't know how people do it."

Sylvia shifted in her seat. She frowned a little but allowed Claudia to continue talking.

"I just can't understand what Stanley gets out of it. I mean, yes, people are poor, but that isn't our fault. I thought after college he'd go into business with his father, not give away his money.

Claudia looked at Sylvia. "Are you okay, dear? You look a little flushed." Sylvia managed to smile and say, "Yes, Claudia. I'm fine."

Claudia motioned for a waiter. "There are going to be so many people here. I decided to wear my dress now. It's just so beautiful." Claudia admired the sparkles in her dress, then continued. "Oh, you remember Constance Worthington?" Sylvia nodded her head yes. "I heard she has stage 4 breast cancer. Poor dear. She lost her hair and simply looks a fright. I just don't know what I would say to her. I mean, I wanted to invite her, but...well, you know. Cancer. I heard she had a double mastectomy. Oh, could you imagine? Poor dear. I'll send her some flowers when I get home."

"What about treatment?" Sylvia asked. Claudia leaned closer to her. "I heard she had the best doctors money could buy. You know her husband is head deep in oil, so money wasn't a problem. I heard she tried everything, even experimental treatments. You know, it's a shame. All the money in the world and they still can't save her. I heard she tried everything. Stephanie Dell told me she saw her at a dinner party. She had on some kind of turban head wrap thing. Why would you even think about going out and making everyone uncomfortable?"

"So what, Constance gets cancer, and she's supposed to stay inside?" Sylvia said. "I didn't say that," Claudia protested. "Are you sure you're okay?"

"You said her cancer made everyone uncomfortable. Do you think Constance is comfortable, Claudia?"

"Well, no, of course not. I just wouldn't know what to say." "I see," said Sylvia.

"I have so much to finish. Now, Sylvia, you go back to your room and get some rest. I want you looking fabulous. I put you at our table, next to Stanley, for dinner. There will be music and dancing." Claudia's voice was upbeat. "You'll have a wonderful time."

Sylvia stood up. "I can't wait."

Claudia stood up carefully, making sure not to snag her gown. "Yes. We'll have a wonderful time. Now, what happened to that waiter? I'm sorry, Sylvia, I really must go. See you tonight." Claudia turned and walked toward a group of catering staff. Sylvia stood and watched her. She felt tired. She wanted to tell Claudia what was going on, but she knew Claudia wasn't a friend. She would tell everyone she had cancer, and they'd talk about her the same way Claudia talked about Constance. She turned and walked out of the ballroom.

"Stanley, you simply must stay for the week. I insist," Claudia said, scolding her son.

Stanley gently grabbed his mother's hand. "Mom. This is time for you and Dad. You don't need me hanging around. Besides, I have meetings set up that I must attend."

She sat on the large sofa in Stanley's villa, careful not to snag her dress.

"Meetings on how to give your money away."

He looked at her and smiled. "I enjoy helping others, Mom. It's probably one of my best qualities, next to my good looks – which I get mostly from you."

She smiled at her son. It was so difficult for her to stay angry with him. "I'll let your father talk some sense into you. Oh, by the way, you're sitting next to Sylvia Blass tonight."

Stanley frowned. "Really, Mom? Sylvia Blass? Out of all the people who are attending, you sat me next to her?

Claudia slightly inhaled. "What's wrong with Sylvia? She's one of my closest and dearest friends."

Stanley raised an eyebrow. "She's a bitch, and you know it. It wasn't that long ago that she published that story on Dad and..." He stopped.

Claudia smiled. "Water under the bridge. We mended that incident a long time ago. Sylvia can be a little much, but she's still a friend."

Stanley stood up. "Okay, Mom, I'll sit next to her and be nice. But I'm not staying the week. I leave tomorrow night."

She looked up at him. "Fine, Stanley. Why are you rushing off anyway?" He held out his hand and helped her stand up. "I have a new charity I want to check out. It's a homeless shelter. They do a lot of good and are in need of funding."

She sighed. "A homeless shelter?"

He walked her to the door. "Yes, a homeless shelter."

She stood in front of the door, blocking him from reaching

for the doorknob. "Why can't you find a nice girl, Stanley? Really? A homeless shelter? You could be working for your father right now."

Stanley gently pushed his mother to one side and opened the door. "Now Mom, the last girl I brought home, you hated."

"I didn't hate her. She just wasn't one of us."

"You mean white, rich, and privileged?" he said sarcastically.

"Exactly," she said. "I don't have a problem with Black people, but you dating a Black woman?" "Well Mom, I'm the one doing the dating, so you don't have to do anything. We've been through this before. I date who I like, end of story."

She sighed, reached out, and kissed him. "I know, I know. Bye, darling."

He watched as his mother walked down the beachfront walkway and closed the door.

Sylvia sat alone at the table in the reception hall. The rest of the table guests were dancing. The air was full of energy and laughter. She watched people as they danced and laughed. She tugged at her white and gold dress and wished she were at home. She watched as Claudia and her husband, Jackson, worked the room. They smiled, shook hands, and posed for pictures with their guests. She was just about to get up to leave when Stanley appeared. He was wearing a tuxedo.

"Sylvia Blass, don't you look wonderful? Are you leaving?" Stanley said, startling her.

She looked up at him. He was so much older than the last time she saw him.

He sat next to her. "It's so nice to see you, Sylvia. I'm sure my parents are pleased you're here." He smiled at her.

She nodded her head. "It's so nice to see you, Stanley. You

look very nice in your tuxedo." She leaned into him and gave him a slight hug.

"You look nice as well," he said, adjusting his tux. "Mom really knows how to throw a party," he said, looking around the room. "I'm sure she spared no expense."

Sylvia smiled. "Well, it has been 40 years, darling. That's a lifetime for some." She stared out into the crowd.

She turned back to Stanley. "So, I hear you've been doing a lot of charity work," she said.

He nodded. "Yes, I'm actually looking at helping out a homeless shelter. They lost their funding to buy a new building, and I think I can help."

"Really? A homeless shelter? Such a noble cause. So what, you just give them a check, and off they go?"

He looked at her disapprovingly. "It's more than just money," he said.

She turned toward him. "So then what is it if not money? I mean, yes, it does feel good to give back, but you can't give away all your money, darling," she said.

He smiled. "I enjoy helping people. If I'm able to help, then I will. I just happen to be rich, but rich or poor, my attitude would be the same. They're people. Less fortunate, but still people. Some suffer from mental illness, others just need a break. This shelter wants to help those who are sick, too. They'd like to have a small clinic. They had an uptick in those suffering from cancer and other terminal diseases. Those who could no longer pay for treatment lost everything. They still need care."

Her eyes widened. "Cancer?" she said.

Stanley nodded. "Yes, cancer. The shelter can provide access to health care, like hospice and other services. It's a great organization."

She sat for a moment and didn't speak.

"I know this might not interest you much. You run a successful fashion magazine, after all. Trends and celebrities probably catch your eye more," he said.

"I donate once a year to several organizations, Stanley," she said, defending herself.

"There are several organizations that need money and time. They need volunteers. People to get involved. I don't doubt you donate. It's a great tax write off. Look, I don't mean to be insulting, I don't, but there's more to life than being rich, white, and privileged." He looked at her and continued. "While my parents are out making money, I'm out helping those who are less fortunate. I enjoy what I do. The opportunity to help people."

She took a sip of her wine, and it moved down her throat into her stomach. She felt a little queasy but continued to smile. "How many charities do you work with?" she asked.

Stanley leaned forward. "Well, I just finished a big campaign with the American Cancer Society. I think with my connection with them, I can maybe bring some much-needed help to the shelter." Sylvia noticed Claudia and Jackson coming toward them. Stanley stood up and hugged his mother and father, then turned to Sylvia. "Hey, I was just talking to Sylvia. Mom, the room looks great. You really outdid yourself this time."

Claudia smiled and took her son's hand. "Well dear, after 40 years, what did you expect?" "I told her money was no object for this one. When we hit the 50-year mark, that'll be even bigger!" Jackson Roberts announced.

Sylvia smiled and chuckled. She wasn't feeling well. She

wasn't sure if it was the cancer or anxiety. Either way, she didn't feel like herself.

"Stanley was just telling me about his charity work," Sylvia said.

Jackson frowned a little and said, "My son, the charity boss. I swear, Stanley if you put that energy toward my company, we'll double, triple our profits."

Sylvia gently touched Stanley on the arm. "Dance, Stanley?" she said.

He looked a little confused. "Sure. Mom, Dad, I'm going to take Sylvia out on the dance floor. Care to join us?"

"Oh, I need to check on the cake," Claudia said.

"Well then, that gives me time to make a call," Jackson said.

"You promised no work tonight, Jackson," Claudia protested.

"It'll only take a moment. Excuse me," he said and walked away.

Claudia watched him walk away. "That man. I swear," she exclaimed and headed toward a waiter.

"Shall we?" said Stanley to Sylvia.

She smiled and walked with him to the dance floor. He slid his hand around her waist and started moving slowly from side to side.

"You know," he said, "I was a little surprised to see you here. You know, with everything that happened."

"That was a long time ago. Me and Claudia have made amends."

Stanley continued to lead her as they danced. "You've made quite a reputation for yourself, Sylvia. I mean, you start off printing smut and gossip, and now you print fashion tips."

She glared at him. "I mean, even after the article you ran on my parents, you did nothing. Well, not until you ran a story on your own mother."

Sylvia stopped dancing and looked at him. "People change, Stanley," she said in a huff and walked away.

Stanley stood alone on the dance floor, smiling. He watched her a moment longer, then headed toward the table.

Chapter 14

Zoe walked into the shelter carrying a large box. "A little help?" she announced and looked around the room. She spotted Anna coming toward her. "You're early!" Anna said, walking quickly up to her.

Anna helped her carry the box to the table. "Wow, this is heavy. What's in here?" she asked. "Fruit cups," Zoe answered. "I have more at the restaurant."

Anna looked at her curiously, then opened the box and looked inside. "Why do you have all these fruit cups?" she asked.

"Long story," Zoe said.

They both sat down at the table. "Okay Anna, I've given it a lot of thought, and I want to move forward on the fundraiser. I think we should do an open mic. We can bring in local talent and have them perform. We could charge at the door; maybe. But I'd be willing to give part of the night's receipts to the shelter."

Anna didn't speak; instead, she just reached out and hugged her. "Thank you, Zoe. I really mean it."

Zoe hugged her back. "It's my pleasure, Anna. You do good work here. I love helping out. I thought we could do some initial planning today. My girl does PR, so I'm hoping for free marketing. Tallulah...well, she writes for *Big World*. I'm going to ask them to donate some ad space."

"You are amazing," Anna said, then stood up. "I have some stuff in my office that may be of use. I'll be right back." She left the table and walked to her office. Zoe sat patiently, waiting for her to return when she suddenly heard singing.

"Must be Lily," she said out loud.

She stood up and followed the sound of the singing, which led her to a small room next to the kitchen. Lily was sitting in a chair, staring out the window. Her voice was melancholy and soft. Zoe listened to the words as she stood in the doorway of the room.

When Lily was done, she spoke to her. "Lily, that was so pretty. What was that song?"

Lily didn't turn around; she just continued to stare out the window. "It's just something I wrote a long time ago," she replied.

Zoe walked over to where she was sitting. "You sing so beautifully. I'm having a fundraiser for the shelter. It's going to be an open mic."

"Open mic?" Lily said, turning her head towards her.

"Yes. An open mic is where different artists, like singers or musicians or poets, come and perform. It's called an open mic because anyone can do really whatever they'd like."

Lily looked back out the window and hummed the song she was singing. "Would you like to sing, Lily?" Zoe asked.

She stopped humming. "Sing?" she replied.

"Yes, sing. Everything we raise goes to help out here at the shelter."

Lily had a vacant look on her face. She faced Zoe and spoke. "Amanda stopped me from singing."

Zoe looked confused. "Who's Amanda, Lily? And why would she stop you?" she asked. "She found out what he'd done, so she punished us, Mama, me, and Clyde."

Zoe looked around the room and found a chair. She pulled the chair next to Lily and sat down.

"Who's he?" she asked.

"My father. I didn't know. We didn't know. No one told us. I didn't take the money. I left it there. Clyde, now he took the money. He said we were due. That we should benefit from our father's name."

Anna walked into the room. "There you are. I have some information that should help us. Lily, are you okay?"

Lily nodded her head and went back to staring out the window.

"We were just talking. I asked Lily if she'd like to sing at our fundraiser," Zoe said. "That's a wonderful idea. What do you think, Lily?"

Lily didn't answer. She just hummed and looked at the window.

"Lily," Zoe said, "would you sing at the fundraiser?"

Lily stopped humming. "I don't know. I don't know if I can."

Suddenly, she stood up. She was shaking and had a wild look her in eyes. She backed away from Zoe and Anna.

"Why are you doing this? I already told you!"

Anna reached out for her and hugged her tightly. "It's okay, Lily. You don't have to sing. We want to help you." Anna released her and stepped back. Lily stared at them. "I want to sing, but I can't," she said.

She put her head down and walked out of the room, leaving Zoe and Anna standing there, speechless.

"What just happened?" Zoe asked.

"She's becoming more agitated," Anna said sadly. "She's been drinking more. Ever since the liquor store thing, she hasn't been coming around much."

Zoe sighed. "Well, all the more reason to get this fundraiser going." She touched Anna on the shoulder and smiled.

"Let me show you the information I have," Anna said.

They both walked out of the room.

* * *

Tallulah sat in front of her laptop at the kitchen table. She fixed her long dreadlocks and patiently waited. Her laptop chimed, and she clicks on the video chat.

"Hi, Tallulah," said Sharon. "Is this still a good time?" Tallulah shifted in her chair and smiled. "Yes, this is great."

Sharon held up her article. "I read your article. It'll run in the next issue. We're doing a whole makeup series, so this will go nicely with what we have."

Tallulah smiled and replied. "Thank you. It was a change from what I normally write about. But it was good. No worries."

Sharon shuffled papers around. "Okay, so next time I'd like to see something on weight loss. There are a lot of new fads out there, maybe you can pick 5 or 6 and do some research?"

Tallulah nodded her head as she wrote down Sharon's request. Sharon continued. "Oh, by the way, how's your shelter article going?"

"Well," Tallulah said, "slower than I thought. But my friend is doing a fundraiser at her restaurant, so I'll be able to include that in my piece."

Sharon smiled. "Sometimes a good article takes time, Tallulah. I'm sure it'll be good." Tallulah nodded. "Thanks.

"Okay, so weight loss, 5-6 diets or fads. You've got some breathing room on this, so not due for 40 days."

"Great. I'll send you a rough draft in about 2-3 weeks. Thank you for the opportunity, Sharon." Sharon smiled and clicked off.

Tallulah closed the laptop and sighed. She grabbed her bag and pulled out her small notebook. Then, she flipped through the pages. Finally, she found what she had written at the record store. She read the name out loud, "Owen Katz, producer." She opened a new browser. Then, she searched his name and scanned the results. She decided to try Twilight Records. It yielded one promising article.

She found a small announcement on an archive newspaper website. She clicked the link and started to read out loud.

"Twilight Records studio, owned by Owen Katz, burned yesterday in a fire. Police suspect arson, but they have made no arrests. Mr. Katz was not available for questioning."

"A fire?" she said. She continued. "The studio was home to several negro musical artists."

She conducted another search but didn't find anything. She pulled out her cell phone and called Marc. He picked up on the third ring.

"Hey, it's Tallulah. You got a second?"

"Sure," said Marc. "What's up?"

"So, I did a search on the producer of Lily's record and didn't find anything. Then I did a search

on Twilight Records and found a small announcement saying it burned in a fire and was home

to several negro artists."

"Is there more?" he asked.

"No, that's it," she said. He could hear the frustration in her voice. "I was hoping for more. But I do have a location of where the studio was. Maybe I can access the public record," she said.

"Maybe," he said. "Hey, what are you doing now?" he asked.

"I gotta go to work at the restaurant."

"Oh," he said, sounding disappointed.

"We usually hang out when it closes. I know it's late, but you can come by. We usually have some wine, food, and talk," she said as her voice quivered a little.

She liked him. She hadn't had the best luck with relationships. The last guy she dated just disappeared, ghosted, stop calling. She felt hurt, but not in the sense that she was in love or anything. She felt hurt that she didn't know why he stopped calling.

She'd sent a few texts and left some messages, but Chloe had put an end to that.

"Stop chasing niggas, T. You deserve better. If that man can't see and appreciate you, then fuck him. What you want from him? You wanna have his babies? Marry him? Girl, please. No more texting. Definitely no more calling." She then took Tallulah's phone and deleted his information.

She waited for Marc to reply to her. She thought, for a moment, that maybe she shouldn't have mentioned it to him, but then he answered her.

"Sure. That sounds nice. Do I need to bring anything?"

She felt a quiver in her stomach. "Just yourself. It'll be after closing. We close around 10, so is 11 pm okay?"

"It works. See you then," he said.

"Bye," she said and clicked off the phone.

"So, how did you do tonight?" Zoe asked Tallulah

She was counting her tips at a table in the back of the restaurant. Zoe was sitting across from her, sipping a glass of much-needed wine.

"You know you how they say Black people don't tip?" she said while counting the dollar bills. Zoe nodded her head. "Well, they're wrong. I did really good tonight. This will pay the electric bill, and then some."

Zoe smiled and replied, "Well, they aren't always right."

Tallulah continued counting her money. "Hey," she said, "I invited Marc to stop by around 11pm. I forgot to say something to you. I hope it's okay."

Zoe smiled and raised her eyebrow. "Marc from the shelter?"

Tallulah smiled and nodded her head. "We went out the other day. It was fun. No pressure. Causal. We talked and walked. Oh shit, I forgot to tell you. We stopped at a record store, and I think we found Lily's record. I had the guy at the store order it for me. And Marc paid for it." She carefully folded the stack of bills and put them in her wallet.

Zoe looked at her curiously. "You know, I was at the shelter, talking to Anna about the fundraiser, and I saw Lily. She was singing some song she said she wrote. I asked her if she wanted to sing, and she said Amanda wouldn't let her."

Tallulah reached for Zoe's glass of wine. She handed it to her and continued. "Then she said Amanda is punishing her for what her father did."

Tallulah stopped drinking. "Wait, what?"

Zoe nodded her head. "She said she didn't know and she didn't take the money. She said Clyde took the money, but she

158

didn't. She said Clyde said they should enjoy their father's name. Whatever that means."

There was a loud knock on the restaurant door. Zoe looked at her watch. "It's probably Chloe. I'll go let her in. Oh, by the way, I asked Michael to stop by."

Tallulah choked on her sip of wine as Zoe quickly walked to the door and let Chloe in. She could hear from all the way in the back of the restaurant, "Queens and bitches, I've arrived!"

Zoe followed Chloe to the back of the restaurant.

"What up, girl?" Tallulah said, handing her an empty wine glass.

Chloe smiled. "See, that's why I love you. You always looking out for a bitch."

Tallulah watched as she poured a glass of wine and took a large sip. Zoe sat next to her. Tallulah looked at her and said, "Okay Zoe, spill it. When did you talk to Michael?"

Zoe smiled and poured wine into the empty glass on the table. She poured slowly, smiling, making Tallulah wait for her answer.

Chloe looked at both of them and said, "Wait, can you catch me up? What are we talkin' about?" Tallulah looked at Zoe and folded her arms. Zoe finished pouring the wine and took a long sip, then exhaled and put down the glass.

"Zoe!" they both shouted.

"Okay," Zoe laughed, "I went to *Big World* to ask Michael if he'd donate ad space for the fundraiser. We got to talkin', and, well...he's coming here tonight."

Chloe threw up her hands. "Just pull the fuckin' trigger and fuck him. Y'all been mind fuckin' since college. The first time you met him, you mind fucked him. Not in a bad way, not like playin' head games. I mean, you literally fucked him in your mind. Mind fuck. Y'all do the cute, flirty thing, but damn, I'm tired of watching this show."

They looked at her. After a brief moment of silence, they broke out laughing.

"I'm serious," Chloe said, with a laugh.

"Are you blushing?" Tallulah asked.

Zoe turned her head away. "No", she said, smiling.

Chloe took a sip of her wine and said, "You're going to love me even more than you do now, Zoe." She smiled. "So my very cool, young, good looking, sexy client – the Stanley Roberts – is looking for a new charity to give his money to. He asked me to put together a list of charities he could partner with. I added your shelter to the list and did a fabulous write-up." Chloe stopped and took a sip of wine. She shifted in her seat and leaned forward. "I emailed all the info, and he got back with me. He's interested in...wait for it...the shelter!"

"What?!" Zoe shouted, "No shit?"

"No shit," replied Chloe.

"Do you know what this means?" said Zoe excitedly. "This is means a new building, more resources!"

"Okay, now don't get ahead of yourself. He's interested. I thought I'd invite him to the fundraiser, tour the center, meet Anna and the staff."

"When do you think this'll happen? You know, the tour and stuff?" Tallulah asked.

Chloe looked at Zoe. "When is the open mic? You may need to move the date."

Zoe thought for a moment. "Well, we were thinking 30-45 days. We want to get the word out. Anna said they don't really have a marketing budget, but we could put out a press release. I think the local stations would pick it up. Michael said he'd advertise for us for free."

Chloe thought for a moment. "I'm sure I can with PR, even if Stanley doesn't come through. He was headed out of the country and said he'd be back soon. So, I'll probably know more next week."

There was a light knock at the door. Zoe and Tallulah looked at one another.

Chloe looked puzzled. "What? I –"

"It's probably just Michael," Tallulah said.

"Or Marc," Zoe added.

"Who's Marc?" asked Chloe.

Zoe stood up and started walking toward the door. "Ask T," she said.

Chloe looked at Tallulah. "Okay bitch, who's Marc?"

Tallulah smiled but didn't answer her. She could hear them talking but couldn't make out was what was being said. She waited. Chloe reached over and lightly hit her. "Who the fuck is Marc?!"

"Shh," she said, waving Chloe off.

Zoe appeared, with Michael walking behind her.

"It's Michael, y'all," Zoe announced.

Chloe looked at Tallulah. "It's Michael," she said. Tallulah motioned for him to sit down. "Hi, Michael." "Hey," he said.

Chloe passed him an empty wine glass.

"Wine?" she said.

Michael nodded, and she poured a glass. She set the glass down and pushed it over to him.

"Hi, Michael," she said.

Michael sat next to Tallulah and took off his jacket. He smiled and took a sip of wine.

Zoe stood for a moment and then said, "Okay, I have food

in the kitchen. Chloe, I know you're hungry. So, I have some catfish and chicken that was leftover from dinner. Everything else is on the counter in containers. Help yourself."

Chloe stood up. "Good looking out." She smiled and walked toward the kitchen.

Zoe sat down and poured herself a glass of wine. "This bottle is done. I'll go get another one." She stood up and walked toward the kitchen.

Tallulah watched her walk away, and when she went into the kitchen, she said, "So, I didn't expect to see you here."

She smiled at Michael slyly and winked.

He fidgeted in his chair. "Well, she came by the office, we talked, and here I am."

She held up her glass and motioned for Michael to do the same. The glasses clicked together, and they both took a long sip.

Zoe emerged from the kitchen with two bottles of wine. As she started walking toward the table, she heard a light knock.

She said, "T, I think your guest is here."

Tallulah stood up and fixed her shirt. She pulled her dreads back behind her ears and walked toward the door. She passed Zoe, who winked at her.

She unlocked the door to find Marc standing here.

He always looks so good, she thought.

"Hi, come on in," she said.

"Thanks," he replied.

He was wearing a pair of jeans, black form-fitting T-shirt, leather jacket, and Kangol hat. As he passed by, she inhaled his cologne. It was perfect; not too strong or flowery.

"So it's me, Zoe, Chloe, and Michael. I'm glad you could make it," she said. She led him to the back of the restaurant.

Zoe and Michael were talking and laughing when they walked up to the table. "Zoe, you know Marc, from the shelter. Michael, this is my...friend, Marc."

Michael stood up and extended his hand. "Nice to meet you, man."

Marc smiled and shook his hand. He looked at Zoe and nodded his head and waved.

"Wine?" Tallulah asked. "Well, I'm more of a beer guy," he said.

"There's some beer in the large fridge in the kitchen," Zoe said, Sit down, Marc."

He looked around the restaurant. "It's strange being here when you're closed," he commented. Zoe smiled at him. "There's food in the kitchen. Now, I know it's late, but it's kind of a tradition that we meet here, eat, and drink. So welcome. Come on, I'll show you to the kitchen."

Zoe stood up and motioned for Marc to follow her. She smiled widely as she passed Tallulah.

"Ahem hem," Michael said, looking at Tallulah.

She looked at him. "What?"

"Come on. Who's Marc?" he asked.

She quickly sat in the chair next to him and whispered, "Okay, okay. I met him at the shelter. We've had one date. It was nice. I like him so far. That's it."

Chloe emerged from the kitchen, carrying a plate full of food. "What y'all all huddled up for?" she asked as she put the plate down on the table.

"Work," Tallulah answered quickly.

"Hmm," said Chloe, then she sat down and started eating.

"Wow, that's a lot of food," said Michael.

She didn't answer; just continued eating. Soon, Marc and

163

Zoe came out of the kitchen and joined them at the table. Zoe handed a plate to Michael.

Zoe looked around and said, "So, how's the food?" Chloe looked at her and said, "Stop playin'."

The group ate in silence. Finally, Zoe spoke again.

"So Marc, have you been to the shelter lately?"

He looked up from his plate, nodded his head, and swallowed the food he had in his mouth. "I was there yesterday. I helped fix the back door. Someone broke the lock, and Anna said the quotes from the locksmith were really high."

Zoe nodded her head. "I was over there today. You know we're planning a fundraiser here at the restaurant. An open mic. I'm hoping to get a good turnout. I even asked Lily if she would sing."

His eyes widened. "What did she say?" he asked.

Zoe frowned. "She said she can't sing. Amanda won't let her sing. She also mentioned something about her father..."

Tallulah and Marc looked at one another.

"Well, we," Tallulah said, pointing to Marc, "found a record store, and I think we found Lily's record. I ordered it. Should be a few weeks before I get it." "A record?" Michael asked.

Tallulah poured herself another glass of wine and told the story about Lily and her record. "I have the name of the producer and the location where they recorded it, but that's about all.'"

Chloe pushed her glass toward Tallulah and gestured for her to pour. "Y'all should hire a private investigator. Someone who could dig into her past, find things out. Maybe she's famous," Chloe said.

"Sounds good, but PIs take money," Marc said.

Tallulah agreed. "Yeah, Chloe, money – and last I checked,

I don't have any."

"Should you really be digging into someone's past?" Zoe asked. "I mean, yes, she needs help, but like she said, she wasn't always on the street."

Chloe said, "Hmmm, well, I know digging into someone's past can be bad business." She looked at Tallulah.

Tallulah half-smiled. "Okay, okay. I'm going to speak with Lily before I write anything. I don't have any money for a PI, so there's the end of that," she said.

Michael cleared his throat. "I know a guy who does that kind of thing...you know, find people. My college roommate. He seems to be pretty good at it from what he says. Not sure what he charges."

"You mean Crazy Dave? Term Paper Dave?" Tallulah asked.

Michael nodded his head. "I can call him if you want. It's worth a try," Michael said.

"What about money?" Tallulah asked. "We can figure that out later. Besides, this story is for BW; maybe I can figure a way to write it off."

Chloe took a sip of her wine and said, "Can this Lily really sing? What's her story? Why is she at the shelter?"

Marc answered, "I'm not sure where she came from. She's been on the street for years, so she says. I've tried to get her off, but she says it's where she belongs. She once told me she was trash, and you throw trash away."

Michael said, "Well, I've donated ad space for your event. I'll call Crazy Dave tomorrow." Zoe smiled. "And if we can get Mr. Roberts to jump on board, we should have enough blessings for everyone here."

"So, Chloe tell us about Stanley Roberts. I hear he's loaded," said Michael.

Chloe smiled. "Yes, Stanley does have money, but he's a really nice guy. Very down to Earth. A bitch was lucky to get his account. All the chicks in the office swoon over him when he comes in. I keep it professional."

Michael smiled. "Professional?"

Chloe shot him a look. "Actually, yes, professional. See, they already expect a bitch to act some kinda way. So I flip the script, keep it professional. I'm the opposite of what they expect."

"And what do they expect?" Marc asked.

"Well," Chloe said, "they expect the loud, angry Black woman. The one with attitude, and the one who is unapproachable."

Zoe chimed in, "I think we've all experienced that at one time or another."

Tallulah nodded her head. "I know I have. When I was in high school, the white girls would expect me to be the expert on all things Black."

"Well, race is a funny thing," Michael said. "I get it. As an Asian, I usually get stereotyped, too." "How so?" Marc asked. "Well," he began, "I'm supposed to be very smart. Which is true. But I'm also supposed to be a bad driver and eat dogs."

"I think we've all experienced some form of discrimination," Zoe said.

"I had someone tell me I sounded white the other day," Michael said.

Tallulah turned toward him. "What?" she said.

Michael nodded his head. "I was out getting some new advertisers, and I went into this Korean restaurant. I guess it's new. Anyway, I asked to speak with the owner, Mr. Kim. He was happy to see me at first until I spoke. He told me I sounded like a white man." "What did you say?" asked Tallulah.

"I told him I was born in America and my parents immigrated from Japan. He didn't seem to care. He then asked me if I spoke Japanese. I know a little, but my parents wanted me to learn

English, so we didn't speak much Japanese in my house. Needless to say, Mr. Kim was very disappointed. I didn't get his business."

"Because of how you sound?" Chloe asked.

Michael nodded his head.

"That's just fuckin' stupid," Chloe said.

"Yeah, well, Mr. Kim didn't think so," Michael said.

Marc said, "I had the opposite happen to me. I own a very small fleet of cars. I'm starting a limo business."

"How small a fleet?" Zoe asked.

Marc smiled. "Okay, I own two cars. Anyway, I picked up a white man at the airport. He was heading to the financial district. At first the ride was quiet, just some small talk. Then he asked me where he could get some weed n' shit. At first I thought he was joking. But he kept on. He finally said, and I quote, *I know you people know where to get the drugs.* Now, at first, I let it slide. But when he said it again, I finally had to let him know all Black folks don't do drugs. He laughed it off."

"Well, hell, since we're telling stories, I got a good one for ya," said Chloe. "My boss, who is a white woman, asked me to come to her office. It was our weekly meeting. So I go, we talk. She says, "I want to ask you a question, non-work related." You know when your white boss says that, it's probably about race. So anyway, I say, 'Sure, what's up?' Then this bitch tells me she's dating a Black man and wanted to know if I could spare my Black Man Manual. You know, the book on how to handle a Black man. She also wanted tips." Everyone laughed. "True story," said Chloe.

"See, we all have stories," Tallulah said.

"We do," Zoe added.

The group sat and talked for a few more hours. Michael was the first to leave.

"Well, I really appreciate the food and drink, but I gotta get going. I've got a layout to finish, and I'm waiting for a so-called reporter of mine to finish her article." Michael looked at Tallulah and smiled.

"I'll walk you out," Zoe said as she got up.

"I really like your place," Michael said. "My favorite is the pie." Zoe smiled. "Yes, my pie is good."

When they reached the door, they both were silent. Michael broke the silence.

"Hey, I know you're busy with your business, and now this open mic, but there's a jazz festival this weekend. Do you want to go?"

Zoe blushed and looked down at the floor. "Ah...sure, I'd love to go. I'm not sure if I can get away. I'm training a new cook, and he's pretty good, but..."

Michael laughed. "You're not ready to give up the reins. I get it. No pressure, Zoe."

Zoe looked up at him and smiled. "Thank you. I really want to go. I can meet you there, say later in the evening."

Michael nodded. "Sure, whatever works for you."

As she leaned past him and unlocked the door, Michael gently kissed her on the cheek, then walked out. She watched him walk down the sidewalk until he turned the corner. She could hear laughter coming from the back of the restaurant and went to join her friends.

Zoe sat down, listened for a moment, then said, "So Marc, how did you get involved with the shelter?"

Marc's face turned serious. "Well, when I was a kid, we lived at a shelter for a little while. Not that shelter, but a shelter. They really helped my mom. I felt embarrassed when kids at school asked why I wore the same clothes or didn't have new Nikes. But the people at the shelter were always kind. I always said I'd give back when I was able. I don't have a lot of money, but I have time, and I cook a little...well, until you came. She puts my shit to shame."

"A bitch can cook," Chloe said.

"I like it," he continued. "Besides, the limo business is a little slow, so I try to keep myself busy. I've been doing a lot of small repairs for Anna."

Chloe sat up. "Hey, if you need a limo gig, I can help. I plan on taking Mr. Roberts to tour the shelter. He drives like a madman, so I could use a driver. Got a business card?"

Marc smiled. "Hell ya, I got a business card!"

He pulled out his wallet and passed the card to Chloe. She took it and smiled. "Great. I'll be in touch. Soon." Marc nodded his head. "You got it."

Tallulah, Zoe, Chloe, and Marc ended the night around 2:00 a.m. when Marc drove Tallulah home. She wanted to ask him up, but she hesitated. Instead, she kissed him lightly on the cheek and told him goodnight. Marc smiled and watched her enter her building, then drove away.

Chapter 19

Tallulah sat in the dining room of the Marigold Shelter. She'd been there most of the morning, waiting for Lily to appear. She'd about given up hope when Lily walked through the shelter doors. She was shivering and holding a small bottle of vodka. She looked around the dining hall and walked over to the coffee station. She tried pouring a cup but spilled most of it on the floor.

Tallulah got up to help Lily, handing her some paper towels and to clean up the spilled coffee. Lily looked and her and said, "I've got coffee all over me. Fuck it." She slurred her words.

She turned and headed for the nearest table. Tallulah finished cleaning up the coffee and joined her at the table. Lily hummed to herself, taking big swigs of the bottle. When the bottle was empty, she set into the table.

"Barkeep!" she yelled. "Another round for me and my friend here!" She stood up and started to wobble back and forth.

"Lily, why don't you sit down?" Tallulah said.

Lily looked and her and smiled. "You know, you're right. I should sit down." She sat and started humming again.

Tallulah said in a gentle voice, "Do you want some coffee?""

Lily looked at her. "I spilled some all over me."

Tallulah smiled and said, "I'll bring you a cup."

She returned to the coffee station. She poured coffee for herself and Lily. Then, she took some cream and sugar packets. Finally, she walked back to the table. "Here you go, Lily. Coffee."

Lily took the coffee, wrapped her fingers around the cup, and closed her eyes and put the cup to her mouth. She then took a drink and exhaled.

"Lily, I was hoping to see you today," Tallulah said. "I'm writing an article about the shelter and would like to interview you if that's okay."

Lily stared at her. "You've been hanging here a lot lately, haven't ya?" she asked.

Tallulah nodded her head. "I have. I'm writing a story," she said.

"What do you want?" Lily asked. "Why are you always being so nice to me?"

She took a breath and said, "I found your record, Lily. I have it with me."

Lily stared at her. She opened her mouth, but no words came out. Tallulah grabbed her bag, pulled out the record, and handed it to Lily.

Lily took the record and held it up to her face. She then turned it over and read the list of songs.

"My songs," she whispered.

She turned the record back over, moved her fingers softly across the cover, and looked at Tallulah.

Tallulah smiled and said, "I got it from a record dealer. Do you want to listen to it?"

Lily's eyes lit up. "Listen to it?" she echoed.

"Yes, I brought a record player, too," she said. She pulled

out the briefcase-looking record player and opened it on the table. She spun around and found an outlet near the table, then plugged in the player with great care.

Lily was still holding the record. Tallulah took it from her with care, slid out the record, and handed the jacket back to Lily. She put the record on the player and placed the needle on it. The first note played, and Lily gasped. She turned toward the record player. She froze. She didn't move. She listened.

After several moments, Lily's eyes filled up with tears. She couldn't control herself. She moved closer to the player and listened. She moved back and forth to the music. She didn't even realize she was singing along.

Tallulah watched her. Lily looked completely different. It was as if a fog had lifted from around her.

She's glowing, Tallulah thought.

Anna walked into the dining room and touched Tallulah on the shoulder. Tallulah turned around and put her finger to her lips, then motioned for Anna to follow her. They stepped into a hallway. Tallulah was smiling.

"I found Lily's record! She really made one!"

"What?!"

Tallulah nodded her head excitedly. "She's listening to it right now. That's Lily you're hearing!" Anna turned toward Lily and started walking toward her. She was singing along with her record, standing next to the table, her eyes closed, gently rocking back and forth. It was hard to tell her voice from the recorded voice. Anna walked over to the table, picked up the album jacket cover, looked at both sides, and turned around toward Tallulah, who nodded her head and walked towards her.

"She really made an album?" Anna said.

"Yes," said Tallulah.

They stood together, watching Lily sing and move with her songs. She looked so peaceful, so happy. She continued to sing along until the album ended.

When the record ended, Lily sat down. Her face was wet from tears as she stared at the record player. The album was spinning around on the record player. Tallulah walked over and turned it off.

Lily looked up at her. "This is my record. I recorded this over 20 years ago. It was my first and only record," she said.

"I found it at a record store. I thought you'd like it."

Lily felt clear. The fog in her head was gone. "Owen Katz was my producer, my mentor, and my friend. He was more excited about the record than I was," she said.

Tallulah sat next to her and said, "I...I...read about the studio, Twilight Records...it burned down."

"Yes, they never found out who did it. He didn't even get the insurance money. I know Amanda had something to do with it."

Tallulah took the record and put in back in the jacket cover. "Lily," she said, "I want to do a story on you, but I need your help. I think you sing beautifully. What happened? What happened to you, your career, Owen, and Clyde?"

"It was such a long time ago. A lifetime ago," Lily said. "I don't know you."

"That's true. You don't know me. But I truly want to help you. This record, it's beautiful. You have the most amazing voice. I think others deserve to hear your gift. Now, I don't know why you stopped singing, but with a little digging, I could probably find out. I'm a reporter, Lily." She stopped for a moment. "I don't want to tell your story without you.

Whatever happened, it was a long time ago. Maybe this is your time," Tallulah said.

Lily didn't speak. She stared at the record player and held the album in her lap.

Tallulah looked around the shelter. "Lily, did you know the shelter is having a hard time keeping their doors open?"

Lily looked at her. Tallulah continued.

"My friend Zoe owns a restaurant. She comes in and cooks. You remember Zoe, don't you?" she asked. Lily nodded. "She's having a fundraiser at her restaurant, an open mic." "I think she told me. My memory isn't so good," Lily said.

"I thought you may like to sing for us," Tallulah said.

Lily sighed. "You can never run from your demons, can you?" she asked.

Tallulah looked confused. Lily continued.

"My demons have been chasing me my entire life. I'm done. I don't want to run anymore. I'm tired." She looked toward Tallulah. "This story...what do you want to know?"

Tallulah felt a quiver in her stomach. "I want to know what happened to your career. Why only one record? Where's Owen? And who's Amanda? Why are you here at the shelter? And what would it mean to you if the shelter went away?" she said.

Lily sat for a moment, then placed the record on the table with care. "So many questions. Funny, I have to ask myself some of those same questions. Okay, Tallulah. You want my story? I began singing before I could walk. My grandmother was always singing, and I picked it up from her. She watched me and my brother Clyde. My mother was always working. When she was home, she was sad and mean at the same time."

Tallulah stopped her. "Do you mind if I record you?" she

174

asked.

Lily shrugged her shoulders. Tallulah pulled out a small recorder and set it on the table. She then nodded her head for Lily to continue.

"I sung in the choir. I loved to sing. My grandmother called me Songbird. I would listen to Ella and Billie on the radio. I wanted to be them. I wanted to be a famous singer and travel the world. Clyde, he wanted to be a writer. Like you." Lily smiled at her. "He was always telling stories. He had such a way with words."

"When I turned 16, there was a big party at the park. Not for me, but it was the annual church picnic. I was singing the solo, as I always did when I noticed a white man watching me.

At first, he made me a little nervous, but he had such a kind face. He was smiling at me, clapping to the music. After the song, he came over to me. He said he was a record producer." Lily smiled. "At first my grandmother wasn't having it. She shooed that man away so many times." She started laughing as tears rolled down her face. "My grandmother was the glue in my family. Every family has glue. Who's the glue in your family?" she asked.

Tallulah thought for a moment and said, "My grandmother. She lived with me my entire childhood. She helped me start my dreadlocks and taught me how to use a thesaurus and told me never to let anyone steal my shine. She died about 2 years ago." "Grandmas are glue," Lily said.

"So this white man, this producer, he's Owen Katz, right?"

Lily's face softened, "Yes, Owen was my producer. He paid a lot of money to make the record." "His studio burned down," Tallulah said.

"Yes, it burned down. And the music stopped."

"So, what happened? How do you go from upcoming singer to living in the street?" Tallulah asked.

"I chose the street," said Lily. "Or it chose me; I forget. One day I'm living in a small apartment. I've buried my brother and mother. Amanda had taken everything from me. She made sure I never sung again. She made sure Owen didn't make a dime or sell a record."

"Who's Amanda?" Tallulah asked.

Lily sighed and looked at her record. "Where did you find this?" she asked.

"I went into a record store. They ordered it for me," Tallulah said.

Lily turned over the jacket cover. "I wrote some, a little. I wrote 'Grandma'."

She looked around the shelter. "I like this place. They're good to people," she said. "Lily, who's Amanda?"

Lily laughed. "If I tell you, you won't believe me." "Why wouldn't I believe you?" "Amanda Worthington-Blass," Lily said.

Tallulah paused for a moment. "Amanda Worthington-Blass stopped your career?" she asked. Lily nodded her head, then stood up and put the album on the table. "I don't feel like talking anymore," she said.

Tallulah turned off the recorder. "Wait, Lily, it doesn't make any sense. Why would Amanda Worthington-Blass want to stop you from singing?" Lily lowered her head. "Why do you care?"

Tallulah stood up. "Because I do. Amanda Worthington-Blass was a rich socialite who died a long time ago. She had nothing, at least to my knowledge, to do with the record business. Besides, she's been gone for years. What could she possibly do to you now?"

"Amanda took my life, she took my brother's life, she took my mother's life, and she took Owen's livelihood!" Lily yelled. "She took everything from me!" "Why?" Tallulah said.

Lily was shaking. She sat down and rocked back and forth. Tallulah sat next to her.

"My mama fell in love with a white man. I seen him once or twice, but I didn't know who he was. I knew he was rich. I knew he helped a lot of people in the neighborhood. I knew he gave my mama a job. When I turned 18, I got a certified letter in the mail. I thought it was the papers for the tour Owen was planning. I'd been singing at nightclubs, parties, and dinner houses. We'd just finished recording the album, and Owen was planning to send it to the radio stations."

Tallulah reached over, grabbed her recorder, and turned it on. She showed it to Lily, who nodded her okay, then continued.

"The certified letter was from a lawyer. My father had left something for me and Clyde. Mama didn't get a letter, and we didn't show it to her either. We went to see the lawyer."

"What happened?" Tallulah said.

"Oh, we went into his office. White man. He gave us a copy of a will. He said it was from our father. I remember feeling afraid, but not Clyde. He read the will to us. Cliff Blass was a wealthy man. He was well-known for his business dealings and generosity. He was our father. Amanda Worthington married Cliff Blass. However, he loved my mama and had been with her for years. He died about 5 years before we turned 18."

Tallulah gasped "What? Cliff Blass is your father?" She looked at Lily and said, "You're the half-sister of Sylvia Blass? The fashion magazine mogul?"

Lily nodded her head. "We were kids. Sylvia never knew about me or Clyde, but we knew about her."

Tallulah turned off the recorder. "I'm so sorry, Lily. I can't imagine how you felt when you found out."

"I haven't been able to talk about it for so long. I don't know why I'm talking to you. I need more coffee," she said.

Lily walked over to the coffee station and poured another cup of coffee. She poured in some creamer and slowly stirred it into the coffee. "The only thing I remember is feeling afraid," she said.

She held on to the coffee cup with both hands and sat next to Tallulah. "I felt scared. When the man told us about our father and the money, he left us. I felt scared. Clyde was happy. He said we deserved that money."

"What did you do?" Tallulah asked.

"At first I didn't do anything. Clyde and Mama got in a terrible argument when Clyde confronted her."

Lily sat motionless, her mind faded to that day. The fight between her brother and mother. The fight that changed everything.

We pulled up to the small blue house. Clyde turned off the jalopy and looked at me. "Mama was wrong. She's been selfish all these years, punishing us for her mistakes," he said. He was angry. I've never seen him so angry. He said, "I'm going in there and tell her we know everything."

He jumped out of the car. I called after him. I begged him to come back, but he wouldn't. He walked in the front door and started screaming for Mama. I waited in the car until I heard her call out, "Land sakes, Clyde! What the devil is wrong with you?"

Then it was quiet. I got out of the car and walked up the steps to the porch. When I opened the screen door, Mama was sitting

178

on the sofa, holding the letter the lawyer gave us. She was crying and shaking her head no.

The tears didn't stop as Clyde was tearing into Mama. "You knew who my daddy was all this time and didn't tell me. You made me think I was a mistake, I was worthless. Every time you looked at me, you saw pain and hurt. Well, now I know who my daddy is. I'm taking his name and his money. I'm leaving today, and if Lily were smart, she'd come with me."

She looked up at him. She looked afraid. "No, Clyde," she said. "You can't do this. You can't take your father's name. What I did was protect you."

But Clyde wouldn't hear any of it. He walked into his bedroom and started packing. Mama looked at me. "Lily, listen to me. I've always loved you and Clyde. What I did was protect you. If she finds out you're Cliff's children..." She trailed off.

"Who, Mama?" I asked. I was still standing in the doorway.

"Amanda," she replied.

Lily's gaze fell to the floor. "When Amanda Worthington found out about the will, the affair, the money, and us, she flew into a rage. Mama was trying to protect us. She blackballed Owen and me from the industry. No tour, no record sales, and Owen's studio burns down. My brother dies in a car accident. My mama loses her job. She'd worked the same job for 15 years, and all a sudden they have to let her go. No one would hire her. She fell into a deep depression. I tried to be strong. I did. I tried to keep my career going, but no one would work with us. No one. Then Clyde died. That was it for me. My mama went crazy. She checked out. I tried to live life, I left, got a job, and tried to move forward. One day, it became too much. So, I left my apartment, my job, and I checked out. Now you know how I got here. You know all my secrets. I also drink a lot, too. It helps keep me numb." Lily stood up. "Tell your friend I'll sing at her open mic. Thank you for bringing me the record."

She walked down the hall and out the door that led to the alley. Tallulah watched her walk out the door, then packed up the record player and put the recorder in her bag. She pulled out her cell phone and called Michael.

"Hey, you at the paper?" she said.

"Yeah, what's up?" he asked.

"I need you to hear something," she said. "I'm on my way."

Chapter 15

Stanley casually walked into Chloe's office. He was wearing a pair of jeans and red T-shirt. Chloe thought he was the most casual man she'd ever met, especially one with millions in the bank. She stood up and walked around her desk to greet him. She was dressed in a black form-fitting dress, with black heels.

She extended her hand. "Stanley, I'm so glad you could make it. Please have a seat." Stanley smiled and sat down.

"Chloe, it's always a pleasure."

"How was your trip?" she asked, sitting down next to him. He leaned forward. "Do you vacation with your parents?" Chloe looked confused. "Ah, not since I was a kid. Why?"

"That's what my trip was. Vacation with my parents. It was their anniversary."

"Sounds nice," Chloe said.

"It was okay. I managed to hide out in my villa and get some work done. Which brings me to your email. I really like the shelter, and it sounds like they could use a lot of help."

Chloe grabbed a folder and opened it. "Yes, they've been struggling for quite some time. They received a large donation about a year ago. For some reason, the donor took the money back. No explanation. The money was just gone."

She handed Stanley the folder. He opened it and started going through the information. "So, tell me about this fundraiser. You briefly mentioned it in your email. Is it a dinner/dance thing or what?"

"Actually, no. It's an open mic." Stanley looked confused. "An open mic is where you just open the mic. People can get up and do whatever they'd like, sing, poetry, play instruments. Mostly you get poets, spoken word artists," Chloe said.

Stanley looked intrigued. "I like this idea. Where is it?" he asked.

Chloe smiled. "Actually, my good friend Zoe owns a restaurant called Zoe's Soul Food Kitchen, and it'll be there. She'll have an amazing menu and will be giving part of the receipts to the shelter, and they take everything at the door. They're going to charge a few dollars to get in. The performers won't get paid, so 100% of the door receipts will go to the shelter."

"How much are you planning to raise?" Stanley asked.

"Well, we don't have a set amount. Whatever we raise, it'll definitely help the shelter. Now, I can arrange a tour of the shelter this week or next week, whatever works for you. We can have media there and really play it up."

Stanley frowned. "No media yet. I want to talk more about this open mic. Who performs?" "Whoever has the courage to go up to the mic," she said. "So I could perform?" he asked.

Chloe had a look of shock on her face. "What do you do?"

Stanley raised his eyebrows. "I play a mean guitar. I was going to start my own rock band when I was a kid, but my parents wouldn't hear of it."

"Sure, call the guys. Tell them the band is getting back together," Chloe joked.

Stanley laughed. "That's good, Chloe." He leaned forward,

rubbing his hands together. "Okay, I'd like to see the shelter, and I'd like to donate to the open mic. What do you need?"

Chloe smiled. "I suggest we speak with Anna Gomez. She's the director of the shelter. She can provide a lot more detail. As for the open mic, how about lunch or dinner? You can taste the food, meet Zoe, see the restaurant, and we can see what happens."

"Perfect. Set it up!" Stanley said.

Chloe grabbed a notepad and jotted down some notes. She felt Stanley's eyes on her. She looked up and saw he was grinning at her.

She continued writing, then said, "So, I'm not sure of the date of the open mic. The marketing budget is a little tight. I know Anna and Zoe have been asking for newspapers for free ad space and were going to ask the local media to pick it up."

Stanley frowned. "I own a media company, Chloe. I think I can help spread the word." Chloe smiled. "Great. Let's say next week for the tour of both the shelter and the restaurant." "Sounds good," he said. He sat quietly for a moment, then continued. "Chloe, would you like to attend the open mic with me? As my guest?"

Chloe stopped writing. "Stanley, I'm flattered, but I don't date my clients."

"It's not a date. I need you there. You're my PR guru. Come as my guest, which isn't the same as a date." He smiled at her.

She sighed and said, "Okay, Stanley, as your guest. It should make for a fun night." "You have no idea," he said.

Sharon rolled over in bed. It was early. She reached for Keith, but he wasn't there. She sat up in bed and saw a note on the table that said, *Gone running.*

"Of course he's running. What else do you do at 6 am on a Saturday morning?"

She lay back down and pulled the covers over her head. They had been a couple for 10 years. They met when she was doing a cover story on Doctors without Borders. Keith was a very successful surgeon and was a partner in a large surgical practice. They'd decided not to have children, as both of their careers were demanding.

Saturday morning, Keith woke up first. He stretched and looked over at his sleeping wife. She looked so peaceful, and he decided not to wake her. He slowly got out of bed and grabbed his jogging clothes. He ran almost every day, or when time allowed. He walked into the bathroom, changed his clothes, and headed downstairs. He grabbed his headphones, beeper, cell phone, fitbit, and headed out the door.

The morning was quiet. He checked his watch: 6:10 am. The neighborhood was still. He breathed in the morning air and stretched, then walked down the driveway and began his run. He passed several large mansion-style houses, like his own. He smiled to himself. He'd done well for a kid who grew up poor. He worked hard to get into college, then medical school. He was the first person in his family to go to college. He worked his way through medical school and his surgical residency. Now, he was set on being successful.

As he jogged, the sounds of Al Green played in his ears. He didn't even notice the police car he passed.

As he continued to jog, he thought about what Sharon had told him about Sylvia. He would support her in whatever she decided; he knew she'd be successful wherever she landed. She was a great editor. He didn't get why she worked for a racist bitch like Sylvia. Still, he knew her job mattered to her.

He was about a mile into his run when he noticed flashing lights behind him. He looked over his shoulder to see a police car behind him, flashing its lights. He took off his headphones and stopped jogging. He wasn't sure if the car was going to pass him or the officers inside wanted to speak with him. It wasn't until the car stopped that he realized they wanted to speak with him. The police cruiser pulled up beside him and stopped, then the window of the driver's side door rolled down.

Keith spoke first. "Good morning, Officer, can I help you?" He was a little out of breath.

"What are you doing here?" the police officer asked.

"Jogging. I live nearby," Keith said.

The officer gave him a look of suspicion and continued. "Well, we've gotten some calls that a suspicious man is in the area. I'm going to need to see your ID." The officer put the cruiser in park and stepped out of the car. Keith looked at him and smiled.

"Well, I don't have any ID on me. Like I said, I'm jogging and didn't bring it with me. I live about a mile up the street." Keith pointed in the direction of his house.

"You live in this area? I doubt that. Put your hands on the car and spread your legs." Keith hesitated and said, "Look, I live just a mile down the road."

The police officer lunged at Keith and threw him onto the hood of the cruiser. He grabbed the back of his head and forced it down so his cheek was pressing hard on the hood. Keith began to struggle.

"Now stop resisting! I said stop!" the officer yelled.

Keith tried to speak but struggled with his words. "I...told... you..."

"There ain't nothin' you can tell me, boy. You in the wrong neighborhood. You out here
intimidating these good people."

"I live here!" Keith yelled.

The police officer didn't speak. Instead, he pressed his elbow hard into Keith's back. He then began to pat Keith down, searching him. He took the cell phone and beeper out of his pocket and placed them on the car.

"You have any weapons on you? I know y'all usually do." The officer threw the cell phone and pager on the hood of the car.

"What's the pager for? You a fuckin' drug dealer?"

Keith cried out in pain, but the officer didn't stop. He pushed down on Keith's back even harder.

Keith could feel the officer's breath on his neck.

"You move again, and we're gonna have us a problem. Now, what are you doing in this neighborhood?"

"I told you, I live just a mile down the road. I'm a surgeon." Keith was struggling with the words but managed to get them out.

"Shut the fuck up. Goddamn niggers. Y'all make me sick."

The officer grabbed his radio and called for backup. Keith tried to turn his head, but the officer applied more pressure to his back with his elbow.

"I doubt this is your 'hood, boy. You in the wrong place. You ain't no doctor either. Now, what are you doing in this neighborhood?"

Keith didn't answer. A second police cruiser arrived and parked behind them. The officer stepped out and walked over to Keith and the first officer. The first officer was out of breath.

He looked at the second officer and said, "Hey Bill, I found this guy running in the neighborhood. He says he lives here. He doesn't have any ID."

The second officer walked over to Keith. They made eye contact. Keith struggled a little trying to get the officer to ease up off his back. The second officer reacted and pulled his weapon. "Don't move. If you continue to resist, I'll shoot your monkey ass!"

Keith couldn't believe what was happening to him. He'd lived in his neighborhood for 5 years and never had any issues. All his neighbors seemed friendly, and there were never any disturbances. He took part in a police seminar on handling fractures and trauma.

Keith didn't move; he froze. His heart was pounding in his chest, and his back and head hurt. A third cruiser pulled up, and the officer got out and approached.

The first officer said, "Sergeant, I found this boy running. He matches the description of the call that came out this morning."

The sergeant walked over to Keith. He looked at him, then spoke. "Dr. Eckerson?"

Keith looked at the sergeant. He recognized him from the seminar he'd given a few months earlier.

"Yes," Keith said.

The sergeant looked at both the officers and frowned. "Why have you pulled your service revolver on Dr. Eckerson, Officer Bennett? Holster it," he snapped. "Release him." The officer hesitated.

"I said let him go!" the sergeant yelled. The officer backed up and removed his elbow from

Keith's back. Keith stood up. He was in pain.

"Dr. Eckerson, I'm very sorry," the sergeant said.

"What the fuck? I was just jogging," Keith said. He was angry but controlled his voice. "I told the officer I lived about a mile down the road and was out jogging, but I guess niggers don't jog or live in good neighborhoods."

"Again, I'm sorry. Would you like to file a formal complaint?" the sergeant asked.

Keith stared at the first officer. He wanted to punch him, but he didn't. Instead, he slowly took his cell phone and beeper off the hood of the car. He made eye contact with the first officer but spoke to the sergeant.

"I've lived in this neighborhood for 5 years," Keith said.

"I'm very, very sorry, Dr. Eckerson. Officers Jones and Bennett are new to the force." "Well, you might want to better train your officers, Sergeant!" Keith said angrily. "I understand. I can write up a formal complaint."

"What the fuck good is that gonna do?" Keith yelled. "Can I go?"

"Yes, Dr. Eckerson, you're free to go," said the sergeant. "I really enjoyed the seminar you had a few months ago. The information came in handy. Again, I'm very sorry for any trouble this may have caused you."

"Your force is a fucking joke, Sergeant," Keith said. He stared at the first officer and began to jog toward his house.

By the time Keith got to the house, he was angry. He decided he wouldn't share the morning's events with Sharon. She was in the kitchen, making coffee.

"Nice run?"

"Yeah, it was okay."

"That's good. I'm making coffee. Do you want any breakfast?"

"No, I've lost my appetite."

"You okay, Keith?"

"Yeah, I'm good. I'm just going to jump in the shower."
"You look pissed."

"No, I'm good. Are you sure you want to continue working for Sylvia? Especially now that you know how she feels toward people of color. Does she even know I'm Black?"

She thought for a moment. Sylvia had never met Keith and really didn't seem to care about any of her employees' families.

"No, she doesn't, Keith. I never mentioned it."

"So what, you're keeping it a secret?"

"No," she replied. "She never asked or seemed to care about her employees or their families." "Well, everyone in my practice knows you. They know my wife is white." He could feel the anger boiling up again.

"Do you want me to tell her?" Sharon replied, sensing Keith was getting angry. "You never cared before."

"I care now," he snapped back. "Are you afraid she'd fire you or look at you differently if she knew your husband was Black?"

"Do you think I give a fuck what she thinks? Seriously, Keith? What is this about? Are you trying to start an argument?" she said.

"I'm tired of racist motherfuckers. I'm tired of seeing it in the news and reading about it in the paper. At what time do we just simply get over this bullshit?" Keith was yelling.

His reaction surprised her. "Keith, where is this coming from? What happened?"

He looked at her. He knew everything that happened wasn't her fault. He took a deep breath and sat down at the kitchen table.

189

"At what point is race no longer the issue, Sharon?" he said, lowering his tone. "Why must Black men, women, and people of color face judgment each day based only on their skin color?"" It's I guess the issue you have with Sylvia really bothered me more than I let on. I just want you, us, to be happy and live our lives. I knew when we got married that people would look at us, judge us, no matter what we did. Rich or poor, smart or dumb. I knew most people would just see black and white." He lowered his head. His back arched, and his head was pounding. "It's your decision, but I just had to let you know how I really feel."

Sharon walked over to him and kneeled in front of him, then put her hands on her face. "When I married you, it was because I love you. I didn't care about the race thing. I know it hasn't been easy for us. I know we get it from both sides, but I didn't care about any of that. I know we get looks from both Blacks and whites. Right now, I just need time to think. All I know is that I love you very much. If my staying with her makes you this upset, I'll give her my notice when she returns in a few weeks."

She gently kissed his lips. He looked at her. He loved her. He didn't mean to take out his frustrations on her.

"No. I know you'll make the right decision. That's why I married you. Sharon, you know I love you." He kissed her passionately and looked into her eyes, holding his gaze a long moment. "You want some company in that shower?" She smiled. "Always." He took her and led her upstairs.

Saturday morning, Tallulah slept in. She felt exhausted from the back-to-back shifts on Friday. It was afternoon when she finally rose out of bed. She went into the kitchen and started to make coffee. Her phone buzzed. She looked at the number and didn't recognize it, but she answered anyway.

"Hello?"

"Hello, Tallulah?" the unfamiliar voice said.

"Yes, this is Tallulah. Who's this?"

"Hi, this is Pete from the record store. I told you I'd call about the Lily Duke record." "Yes, hi, Pete."

"I've got your record. It came in sooner than I thought. You can pick it up anytime. Now, I do have a question. Do you own a record player?"

She laughed. "I don't."

"Well," said Pete, "I can sell you one fairly cheap. It's not like they're flying off the shelves." "Great. Thank you, Pete. I'll come down today," she said.

"I'll be in the store until closing. We close at 9 pm," Pete replied.

"I can come by and get it in a few hours. Thank you for calling," Tallulah said.

"No problem. I'll be looking out for you," Pete said, then clicked off.

She walked into the bedroom, undressed, and hopped in the shower. She then stepped out and quickly dressed. Once dressed, she called Michael. He answered on the first ring.

"Hey T, what's up?"

"Just checking in. Did you finish the layout?"

"Late last night. I still think it's missing something. I was thinking of covering the jazz festival. Whatya think?"

"Yeah, you could do that. Cutting it a little close to the deadline, aren't you?" she remarked.

"Oh, look who's worried about deadlines." He laughed.

"So, I need a favor?"

"What's up?"

"Can I borrow your car? I'll bring it back tonight and put gas in it." "Yeah, I can meet you at the office in about an hour. Does that work?" "Yes. Thank you, Michael. I really appreciate it."

"Anytime. Besides, I know where you live and work." "Right. Okay, an hour. Do you want me to take you home?" "No, I got some other stuff to do," he said.

"Are you sure?" she asked, not wanting to leave him stranded.

"Yeah, yeah, it's fine," he said.

"Thank you. See you in an hour." She hung up.

She drove to the record store. When she entered, Pete was helping a customer. She wandered over to the hip-hop section and began to flip through the albums. Nas, Jay-Z, The Fat Boys, Big Daddy Kane, and Sugarhill Gang.

"Tallulah, I'll be right with you."

She turned and saw Pete go behind the counter and into the back. She turned back to the albums and kept browsing. She looked at Slick Rick, The Beastie Boys, Run DMC, Wu-Tang Clan, and LL Cool J.

She turned to see Pete walking toward her with the Lily Duke album.

"Here you go," he said, smiling. "I've also got that old record player. I figured you could just take it, seeing as how you only own one album. It's really not worth selling." He handed her the record. "I've got it over here on the counter."

"Thanks, Pete," she said and followed him to the counter. He pulled out a very old record player. "Now, I know she ain't much to look at, but I've gotten years off her."

It looked like a briefcase. Pete unhooked the locks on each side and opened the lid. She was surprised to see the record player.

"Wow," she said, "it is old."

"They don't make them like this anymore," Pete said. "The lid is the speaker. Just plug it in, and you're ready to go. I also changed the needle for you."

"Are you sure you want to give it away? Isn't it an antique or something?" she asked.

"It's yours." Pete smiled. "Consider it a gift." He closed the case.

"Thanks, Pete. Hey, I noticed you've got some great albums; jazz, hip hop," she said.

"I've got the best selection in town," Pete said with pride.

"Yes, you do."

"Now, this Lily Duke. I've never heard of her," he said.

"I don't think anyone has," she replied.

Tallulah grabbed the record and player and walked out of the store. She put the items in the car and called Marc.

"King and Queen Limo Service."

"Marc, it's me. I just picked up Lily's record. I'm heading home to listen to it. Do you want to come over?"

"Really? Yes, I'd like to hear it," he said.

"Okay, meet me in about an hour," she said and hung up the phone.

She drove the car back to the office, parked the car in the back, and walked around to the front door. She tried to open the door, but it was locked. She knocked; no answer. She dug through her purse and found her keys, unlocked the door, and let herself in. The office was quiet. She walked to Michael's office; the door was shut. Michael's door was never shut. She knocked. "Michael?" She knocked again. "Michael?"

She slowly opened the door and was surprised to see Michael

sleeping on a cot.

"Michael?"

He slowly stirred, rolling over. He lay for a moment, then opened his eyes. "Oh shit, what time is it?"

"It's about 3:30. Okay, I have two questions. Why is there a cot in your office? And why are you asleep during the day? I wasn't even gone that long."

He sat up, rubbing his eyes. "Yeah. Can you give me a moment?"

"Sure." She left the office and walked over to her desk. She set down her bag, then sat on the desk.

"Okay," she heard him yell.

She walked back into the office. He'd put on a shirt and a pair of jeans.

"So, you're sleeping here now?" she asked.

He looked at her. "Well, I kinda live here now."

"What? What do you mean, live here?"

"Tallulah, I just woke up. Give me a minute, okay? I need coffee." He walked out of the office and headed to the restroom. She followed.

"You still haven't answered my question." She stopped at the restroom door and waited until he came out.

"Well?" she said.

"Okay, okay. I couldn't afford to pay rent on the office and my apartment, so I gave up my
apartment about a month ago."

"A month ago?"

"Yes, Tallulah, a month ago."

"Michael, why didn't you say anything to me?" She followed him back into the office.

"And say what? The paper is barely holding on. Costs are

up, and advertising down. I had to make a choice, so I did." He yawned and sat at his desk. "Oh Michael, I'm sorry. I didn't know it was this bad."

"I know, no one does. I'm trying to figure out what to do. It seems more people aren't reading the paper; they're online, getting their news from social media. It's hard to compete." She sat down. He continued. "You know this is my dream, so I'm trying to figure out a way to hold on to it." He frowned.

Tallulah could see the sadness in his face.

"You hungry? Let me buy you a late lunch."

"That would be good," he said. He opened his desk drawer and took out a washcloth, soap, toothbrush, and toothpaste. "Let me go wash up. I'll meet you outside."

He stood up and walked out of the office. As Tallulah stood outside to wait for Michael, she texted Marc.

T: *Hey change of plan can we meet at 7 pm?*

M: *Sure, everything okay?*

T: *Yes. Something came up.*

M: *Okay. 7 pm*

T: *Bye*

She took Michael to a small cafe not far from the newspaper offices. He ordered eggs, bacon, toast, pancakes, breakfast potatoes and coffee. They talked while they waited for their food. "So, what does this mean for the paper, Michael? I say this as a friend, not an employee." "Honestly, I don't know. I've been trying to figure that out."

The waitress came over, brought two coffee cups and a pot of coffee. Michael poured a cup. "Well, how can I help?"

"Tallulah, there's nothing you can do, unless you have a large stash of money I can have?"

"No", she said, pouring her coffee. "But so many people

read *BW*. I don't understand."

"Well," he said slowly, "the printer increased their prices again, and over the past few months,

I've lost advertisers. Like I said, social media."

"I'm sorry."

"Not your fault. You've been with me from the beginning, T. It's okay." He stirred his coffee, not looking up.

After a brief silence, she spoke. "I found Lily's record. You know, the homeless lady we were talking about?"

Michael looked interested. "Really? How does she sound?"

"I don't know yet. I'm meeting Marc at my place at 7 to listen to it."

He looked at her and grinned.

"It's not a date," she said sternly.

"Okay, whatever, not a date." He laughed. "But you and him alone, listening to some record, sittin' in front of the fireplace, drinking wine."

"Ha ha. I don't have a fireplace, so the joke is on you."

"I have 1500 in my savings. "It's yours," Tallulah said with genuine sincerity.

He looked at her and smiled. "No, I don't need your money... yet. I'm still working with the printer on his cost."

"Hey Michael, have you ever thought of going digital? You know, a *BW* app?" she asked. "Funny you'd say that because it did cross my mind. That may be my next move. It's too bad. Who would've ever thought that paper would become a dinosaur?" "What about the offer you got from the major paper?"

"No, I would never sell to them." Michael took a drink of his coffee. "At least not then, but I don't think the offer still stands. Some giant publisher acquired them, so who knows what'll happen to them?"

"Oh. Well, just a thought. If you lose the paper, what'll you do?" she asked. "Well, that's a good question. I try not to think about it. I guess I could write," he said.

"You're a good writer, Michael, but your skill is editing. You're one of the best editors I know." "Know many editors, do you?" he said.

"Well, a few, but you have a gift. I love working with you. You know that. I'm not trying to gas you up."

"I know," he said.

The waitress brought their food, and the two friends talked the late afternoon away.

"I'm stuffed," Michael said. "Thanks for letting me use your car. You know you can always crash at my place. It's small, but it's cozy."

"Well, the way my back feels, I may take you up on that. Are you serious?" "Of course. Mi casa es tu casa," she said. "Gracias," he replied.

"Well, I guess I'd better get back to the office – or rather, home."

"Michael, get your stuff and come crash with me. Not tonight, because of my no date, but tomorrow. At least there will be coffee in the morning." "Let me think about it. Okay?" he said.

The waitress brought the check. She reached in her bag to grab her wallet, then handed her credit card to the waitress. She looked over at Michael. He was staring out the window. He looked like a lost puppy.

"Go get your stuff and come to my apartment whenever you're ready. But not tonight, because I have no date. You can't keep living at the office," she said.

"I know, I know. I thank you for the offer. I would even think of crashing a no date. Let me give it some serious thought," he said.

Tallulah rushed around her apartment. She wanted to tidy up before Marc got there. She went into the bathroom and pulled her dreadlocks up on top of her hair, then smiled at herself in the mirror. She heard a knock at the door, which startled her.

She looked at her reflection and said, "Okay, stay cool. You don't have to sleep with him. Stay cool."

She took some deep breaths and walked toward the door. He wore a pair of jeans and a blue T-shirt. He held a pizza in his hands.

"I wasn't sure if you'd eaten or not," he said, walking over the threshold of the door. She smiled and closed the door behind him.

"Thanks! Just put it on the table," she said, pointing to the small kitchen table. He put the pizza down and looked around the small apartment.

"Nice place," he said.

"Thank you," she said.

Tallulah stood for a moment, watching his face as he surveyed her apartment. He seemed to look pleased.

"Have a seat," she said.

Marc walked over to the sofa and sat down. She sat next to him and pulled out a bag. "Okay, here's her record. It's strange. The cover is plain. Just a white lily, but there are 10 songs."

He took the record. The cover was black, with a single white lily. The title read "Lily". He turned it over. The back cover listed 10 songs. In the bottom right corner, it said, Recorded at Twilight Studio/Producer Owen Katz.

"Wow. She really recorded a record."

He looked around and laughed. "How are we going to play it?"

"Luckily, Pete looked out and gave me an old player. It's right beside you on the floor." He looked down to see a briefcase. He picked it up and set it on the coffee table.

"My uncle had one of these." He unlocked the latches and opened the case. "Now, this is old

school. We need to plug it in," he said.

"Behind the sofa," she said.

He plugged in the player, carefully removed the record from its jacket, and placed it on the turntable. He pushed "on", and the turntable spun around, then he gently picked up the needle and placed it on the record.

A soothing sound of horns played, gentle and easy. A piano joined, adding to the horns. Lily's voice came through the small record player. Her sound was sad and somber. She joined perfectly with the piano. It was beautiful. Her soulful tones reminded Tallulah of Anita Baker. Marc turned to her and said, "She was good."

Lily's voice filled the apartment. They listened, only speaking to comment on a song or her voice. As they reached the final song of the record, Tallulah got up and brought the pizza into the living room. She opened the box and grabbed a slice. He followed suit and grabbed a slice, too. As they ate, the song "Grandma" played on the record.

Tallulah listened for a moment and said, "I've heard this before. She was singing this song!" Marc listened for a moment and said, "I think I have, too." When the song ended, he carefully put the record back into the jacket cover.

199

"She really did it. She recorded a record, and she's good. Really good. What happened that she would stop singing? I mean, she could have been famous," Tallulah said. Her voice was full of frustration. She pierced her lips and sat back on the sofa. "I just don't get it. It doesn't make sense. And if you add in what Zoe said about her father and this Amanda person who stopped her from singing, it just doesn't add up."

"Did you ever stop to think maybe she's running from someone or something and doesn't want to be found?" Marc asked.

"Look, I know you're a reporter. A writer. You write stories about people. I get it. I just wonder if digging into Lily's life is a good idea."

She looked at him. "Wait, at first you all wanted to get involved, and now you're saying I'm digging into her life?" Okay. What if we ask Lily if she'll tell her story? What if we can help her reboot her career?"

"So what now? You know someone in the music business?"

"No, but with social media and Chloe's help, we could create some buzz. I dunno, Marc. I'm not trying to hurt Lily. I want to help her. What if she agrees? We can show her the album. Play it for her. See what happens," she said.

He remained silent while examining her with deep contemplation.

"Okay. Show her the record, see what she does," he said.

Michael sat in his office. He was watching Netflix on his laptop, drinking a beer. He sat back in his chair and closed his eyes.

"How long can I really fucking live here?" he said out loud.

He sat up and looked at the papers scattered around his desk. The ad for the benefit for the shelter caught his attention. He pulled out his cell phone and called Crazy Dave, his old college roommate.

Crazy Dave had done many things since leaving college. He was a skydiving instructor. He worked on a fishing boat in Alaska. He taught English as a second language. Now, he is a private investigator. Also, he didn't go by "Crazy Dave" anymore; he just wanted to be called "David".

Michael dialed David's number. He picked up on the 3rd ring.

"Mike, what's up, man!" Crazy Dave yelled into the phone.

"David, man, what's going on? I just thought I'd call to see what's up," he said. "I'm good. Business has been good, too."

"The private eye thing?" he said. "What's that's like?"

"It's never a dull fucking moment," Crazy Dave replied. They both laughed

"Hey, what do you charge?" he asked.

"You need someone investigated, Michael? Personal shit?" David asked.

"No, nothing like that. It's for a story. I need to find out some history. Can you do it?" David laughed. "Good. I thought maybe something was up. Sure, I can do it." "What'll it cost me?" Michael asked.

David thought for a moment. "You just looking for some background info? I don't have to chase anyone down?" he asked.

Michael replied, "Just background. All I have is a name. I don't have anything else." "Give it to me," David said.

"Lily Duke. I do know she made a record, probably in the sixties. I know where she is. I don't need you to find her or anything like that," he said. "So why not just ask her?" David said.

"David, isn't this what you do?" he said.

"Okay, okay. So if you just want info, I can do it as a favor to you. But if I gotta start chasing
people, that's something else. Deal?"

"Deal," Michael said.

"Text me if you get anything."

"You got it." David hung up.

Chapter 16

Sharon met with Sylvia in her office. She sat on the large, overstuffed white couch as Sylvia was finishing a phone call.

Sharon listened as Sylvia finished speaking. Sylvia hung up the phone and joined Sharon on the couch. Her eyes had large bags underneath them. She looked tired. Sharon watched her as she sat next to her. She put a folder on the table and spoke.

"Sharon, how have things been?"

The question confused Sharon. Sylvia never asks her how things have been; she tells her how things are.

"Things are good, Sylvia. We're on schedule to go to print on the next issue. We should be ready by tomorrow."

Sylvia smiled weakly. "Good. Very good. Did you hire the extra staff you needed?" Sharon opened her mouth but nodded her head instead of speaking.

"Good," said Sylvia. "I saw the layout this morning. It really looks good, Sharon." "Ah, well, thank you, Sylvia. I'm glad you approve. No changes?" she asked.

"No changes."

Sylvia looked at Sharon, then cleared her throat and said, "What do you think of me, Sharon?" Sharon's eyes widened. She sat up and said, "Excuse me?" "What do you think about me?" Sylvia asked again.

"In what way?" Sharon asked.

"It's a simple question, Sharon. What do you think about me? You can be honest. I won't get mad or lash out. Just tell me. I want to know."

"Well," Sharon started, "I have to ask first, why do you care what I think? You've never really asked for my opinion before."

Sylvia sighed. "Yes, that's true, but I'm asking now. Do you believe people can change?"

Sharon paused. "Well, Sylvia. I like to think people can change. To be perfectly honest, I don't think you're a nice person. I mean, you had me fire someone because they spoke Spanish. You rarely allow me to make any real changes or impact to the magazine. You've turned down the majority of my ideas or suggestions. And now you want to know what I think about you?"

Sylvia frowned. "You know, when I was a little girl, I got everything I wanted. All I had to do was go to my daddy. When my mother said no, I'd go to my daddy. I was his little girl. When I got a little older, he passed away. His funeral was a sight. So many people. I thought my daddy was the most well-known man in the county. What I didn't realize until I was a little older is that everyone he came in contact with loved him. He loved to help people. Make them better. He was very different from my mother. She was mean and cruel. She hated everything. She used alcohol and drugs to numb her from everything...including me. She never was happy."

Sylvia wiped a tear from her eye and continued. "When my mother passed, we were barely talking. She was a drunk and drug addict. She was an embarrassment. I felt ashamed. She embarrassed me at my high school graduation and wedding. I swore then that I was finished with her. But somewhere along the way, I picked up the meanness. I'm more like her than I care to admit."

Sharon didn't speak. She handed Sylvia a box of Kleenex on the table. Sylvia took the tissue and wiped her tears. "My father was a kind, gentle soul. He believed in all people. We lived in the South. Jim Crow times. My mother hated anyone who didn't look like her. Who didn't look like us? She hated the Blacks, the Mexicans, the Jews, anyone. She used her money for hate. My father tried to change her heart, but he couldn't. When he died, a part of me died, too. I started to hate, too. It was easy. I exchanged pain for hate. My mother chose alcohol and drugs to numb her pain. When she died, it was a scandal." Sylvia chuckled. "But you know the story. I sold her out for a story. For magazine sales. I leaked the pictures to *Chatter*, knowing the editor at the time would run the story. It was so perfect. I would play the victim and sell more magazines. My plan was perfect. I put on the performance of a lifetime. I fired everyone and then rebranded. I wanted to humiliate her, even in death. Why should I cover up her bullshit?"

Tears poured from her eyes. She wiped them, but it didn't stop the flow. Her voice cracked, but she continued to speak.

"After my mother passed, I went to the reading of the will and found out my father had another will. He had another family. He had an affair that produced a set of twins."

Sharon gasped. "Sylvia, why are you telling me all this?"

Sylvia looked at her. "Because I need to tell someone," she answered.

"Anyway, my father had two other children. He left them

money in a separate will and wanted to give them his name. I was never told. My mother was most likely furious. She tried hard to stop the children from getting their inheritance and my father's name. I understood her embarrassment, but she did everything to hurt these children."

"Why?" Sharon asked.

"Because they were Black. My father had an affair with a Black woman. She gave him twins. A boy and a girl. My mother used all her power and money to destroy them. They would never see a dime of that money. We didn't need it. But she didn't want them to have it. She hated them and my father."

"What did she do?" asked Sharon.

"From what I found out, and what the attorneys told me, she used her money to stop their lives. I don't know what happened to them. I do know part of the money was held in trust for years, no movement. I had a hell of a time gaining access. It took years. The money was to be donated to a homeless shelter. All of it. It had accrued interest over the years, and it was well over $500,000. I stopped the payment to the shelter. I don't know why, but I did. Part of me was hoping someone would come forward and protest, but no one did."

Sharon looked at Sylvia. "Did you stop the donation of the money?" Sylvia, why?" Sylvia sobbed. "I don't know. I just did."

She wiped her tears and looked at Sharon. "I'm dying, Sharon. I have pancreatic cancer. It's in the final stages. Over the past few weeks, I've been reflecting on my life, my friends, and my choices. I fired my maid because she spoke another language. Not because she wasn't good. She was a good maid, but I fired her anyway. I knew she was trying to build a better life for her family, but I didn't care. I fired her because I could."

"So, the twins. You don't know who they were?" Sharon asked.

"My mother saw to that," she said.

"But they know who I am. My father's attorney told me the will for his other children revealed who he was. They knew when they turned 18. My father was rich, and my mother richer. My mother comes from old money. "My father was new money. It had some weight, but money and the Worthington name meant more.""

Sharon said, "Okay, so give the money back to the shelter. Simple."

Sylvia shook her head. "I can't. I shouldn't even have access to the money. It's complicated. Believe me when I tell you that I cannot just give it back. At least not right now."

"Okay Sylvia, so what is it you want from me? Why tell me all this?" Sharon asked.

"I want you to help me find the children. Well, they aren't children anymore. I have a brother and sister somewhere. I'd like to know who they are. I can give you all the information I have, but I'd like you to handle it. I trust you, Sharon. I know you think I don't, but I do. I've come to realize that I don't have anyone in my life."

Sharon had a look of surprise on her face. "You want me to find the twins? Sylvia, I'm not a private investigator."

Sylvia laughed weakly. "I know, Sharon, but I want you to hire one and find them if you can. I want you to...represent me..."

"You have attorneys who can do this kind of thing for you, don't you?" Sharon asked. Sylvia nodded. "Yes, I do. I'm asking you for your help, Sharon. I know it's a lot. I do." "Can I think about it?"

Sylvia nodded. "Of course. I know it's a lot. Know that I told you this in confidence. I really just needed a friend."

Sharon stood up and walked toward the door. "We aren't friends, Sylvia, but I do understand discretion."

She opened the door and walked out of the office.

Michael made his way to the second floor and knocked on the apartment door. He waited; no answer.

He heard a voice from downstairs. "If you're looking for Tallulah, she's not home."

Michael walked down the steps to the first floor. "Are you Mrs. Herrera?"

"Sí. You must be Michael. Tallulah left me the key for you. Come in, come in."

Michael followed her inside. The smell of homemade tortillas and chili verde filled the room. "Something smells good."

"Oh, I was just making tortillas for my grandchildren. I always make too much." She smiled. "Are you hungry?"

Before Michael could answer, she walked into the kitchen. She was still talking.

"Tallulah is such a nice girl. She told me about you staying with her."

Michael slowly walked toward the kitchen. On the stove were two large silver pots. The oven door was open, and Michael could see a plate full of homemade tortillas. The smell was welcoming. His stomach growled.

She was busy fixing him a plate of tortillas, beans, rice and chili verde.

"Come, sit." She set the plate down on the table. He did as

he was told and sat at the table. She handed him a paper towel and fork. "Eat, eat before it gets cold."

Michael took the fork and napkin. "Thank you."

"Eat, eat. When you're done, I'll give you the key. You need to eat. Too skinny." She smiled and sat down. He began to eat. She watched him happily.

"This is great, Mrs. Herrera," he said with a mouth full of food.

She smiled and nodded. "I always make too much. You young people don't eat the way you should. My grandchildren are the same way. No time to eat. You need to sit, eat, enjoy your food. Savor the flavor. Every flavor is a labor of love to be shared with others." She smiled, then continued. "I'll make tamales tonight. You and Tallulah will have them for dinner. She loves my tamales, so I make them for her. Do you like tamales?"

Michael shook his head yes, then continued eating and listening.

"Good. I'll bring it upstairs. You must eat."

He finally took a breath. "This is really good." He leaned back into the chair.

"More?" she asked.

He raised his hand in a stop gesture. "No, I'm stuffed." He happily rubbed his stomach.

Mrs. Herrera looked pleased and reached into her apron pocket. "Here's the key." He took it from her and said, "Thank you for the food." "My pleasure. No one should go hungry."

He stood up and smiled. "You're a good cook."

"Oh, it's what I do." She walked him to the door. "Now, if you ever get hungry, you come downstairs and see me, okay?"

He nodded and walked out the door, then thanked her again

and went up the steps. Mrs. Herrera watched him make his way up the steps. When she heard the door open and shut, she went back inside and closed her door.

Once inside, Michael texted Tallulah to let her know he was at her apartment. He set his bags down and went directly to the sofa, where he slowly sat down and sighed. For the last several weeks, he'd been trying to negotiate with the printer on costs, but he wasn't getting anywhere.

Some of his advertisers were exploring new ways to reach customers. They turned to social media and tech-driven marketing platforms. He was finding it difficult to compete.

He lay his head back on the sofa and closed his eyes. He had no idea what his next move would be, and he never saw himself sleeping on Tallulah's sofa. As he lay there, his thoughts were about Zoe. How could he tell her he was sleeping on Tallulah's sofa?

She'll probably make up some excuse about being busy, he thought.

He went into his text message contacts and found Zoe's number. He sighed and put away the phone. He was looking forward to seeing her. He wanted to text her, but he didn't know how to explain his situation. He felt embarrassed. He thought about canceling the date altogether. He picked up the phone again and scrolled to her name, then started texting:

Hey Zoe its Mich –

Suddenly, the door opened, and Tallulah walked in. She was carrying a bag of groceries. She set the bag down on the table, closed the door, and walked over to him and sat down.

"You look like shit," she said.

"I feel like shit."

"Well, you can stay as long as you need. My place is small,

but you're welcome." Michael half-smiled.

"You hungry?" she asked. "I'm not the greatest cook, but I've got some chicken." "No, I met Mrs. Herrera. She's bringing tamales later," he replied.

"Yes, good ol' Mrs. H. She's saved my ass on more than one occasion. She loves to cook and feeds me often. She makes the best homemade tortillas."

"I found out. She wouldn't give me the key until I ate." "That's Mrs. H. She's sweet. I think she's lonely."

Michael looked around. "You know, I've never been here before."

"Really? Well, let me give you the tour. No need to get up. The living room and your bedroom are here. My room is through there. The bathroom is behind the door on the left; it has only a shower, not a tub. The kitchen is to the right. Tour over."

"I like it. But this is temporary," he said. "I'll be looking for a cheaper place and be out before you know it. So, how was your first article for the magazine?"

Tallulah smiled. "Oh, it was thrilling. I wrote all about makeup, specifically concealer and base. It was like nothing I've ever written before."

He could detect the sarcasm in her voice. "It's a job, T," he said.

"I know. Next up is diets. I've been researching the topic. I never knew there were so many diets out there. The article is due in a few weeks."

"Are you going to try any of them?" he asked.

"With Mrs. H livin' downstairs? Are you crazy?" she said.

He grabbed his bag and handed her a folder.

"What's this?" she asked.

211

"It's from Crazy Dave," he said. "I called him. Ask him to find out some info on your friend Lily." She took the folder from his hands and scanned through the pages. He watched her read and waited for her to reply. After several moments, she put down the folder and looked at him.

"So, this is what he found?" she said.

"Yes, it would seem Lily had a very promising career. Lived at home with her mother and twin brother Clyde, who was killed in an auto accident." "She has two last names. Duke and Blass," she said.

"Yes. Crazy thought it was strange, so he's doing some more checking."

"Do you think he can find out about the record label? All I know is that the studio burned to the ground years ago," she said.

"I'm sure he can. Right now, he's just helping us out. No fees. But if he has to start chasing people, then we pay."

She turned her attention back to the pages in the folder. She pulled out a page and held it up. "So, Lily recorded a record, lived like a hermit, and then just disappeared? Only to turn up homeless? It doesn't make sense," she said.

"I agree. Crazy Dave said he was trying to get some sealed court documents. He noted that it might take time, or he may not get them at all."

She frowned. "Do you think we're doing the right thing? Snooping into her life? Now a PI is involved. I know there's a story here; I just want Lily to tell it to me. I don't want to find out bits and pieces. Marc said I was digging in her business and I should talk to her before writing anything."

Michael smiled. "Well, you're a reporter, and a good one. Of course, the story would be better if she told it. A good reporter goes to the source. She's the source. The story will come, T. Besides, Marc has a point, but I'm biased. I like to get stories about people who are willing to tell them; less speculation."

"Well I'm going to talk to her," Tallulah said.

"So, how 'bout a game of chess to get the strategy juices flowing?" he said.

"Really. You sure you want to play?" she said.

"I'm sure," he said.

Mrs. Herrera hummed as she piled a plate full of tamales. She was so happy to be cooking for someone other than herself. She placed two big bowls of beans and rice into a basket and covered the tamales with aluminum foil. She put on her apron and carefully put the tamales in the basket, along with the beans and rice. She then picked up the basket and walked toward the door. As she opened it, her phone rang. She thought about answering it but thought it may be Connie asking her to cover for her again.

The answering machine will pick it up, she thought and walked out the door, closing it behind her.

She continued to hum as she walked up the stairs to the second floor. She knocked on the door and smiled when Michael appeared. He smiled and motioned for her to come in.

"Hola, Michael," she said as she walked in. "I hope you're hungry!" "If it's anything like earlier today, you have no worries," he replied.

She set the basket on the small kitchen table. Tallulah came out of the bedroom. "Hi, Mrs. H. Something smells delicious."

"It's just a little beans and rice, and of course tamales. I know how you love them." Tallulah walked over to her and gave her a hug. "You know I love your tamales."

213

"You're why I make them. Well, I'll let you eat your dinner. I'll get the dishes later." She turned to leave.

"You aren't eating with us?" Michael asked, looking surprised.

"Of course she's eating with us," Tallulah remarked as she walked into the kitchen cabinet and took out 3 plates.

Mrs. Herrera smiled at the two of them. She was all too happy to have someone to eat with.

"Yes, I'll stay."

"Good," said Michael.

Tallulah took the plate and bowls out of the basket and dished up the food. Once she had the plates full of food, she handed one each to Michael and Mrs. Herrera.

"Okay, let's eat!" she said.

They sat on the tiny sofa in the small living room and talked, ate, and laughed. Mrs. Herrera told them stories of her childhood in Mexico and how she came to the states. She told them about her five grandchildren and how she loved to cook for them.

"When they were little, I saw them a lot. Now that they're grown, they're busy. They never seem to have time to visit an old lady." I was so happy when Tallulah moved in, it gave me someone to cook for."

Michael took another bite of his tamale and said, "These are so good, you should sell them." "Oh my god, that's what I said," announced Tallulah.

"I love to cook. I was a cook and maid for many years. I'm retired now. I clean every once in a while. I cleaned a big house the other day. It was so big. Too big for one person. Sometimes I get very bored or lonely, so when they call me to help out, I sometimes do."

"Well, you can cook for me anytime," Michael said, finishing the last of the tamales.

Mrs. Herrera smiled. She liked being around them. They made her feel at home and welcome. For the first time in months, Mrs. Herrera didn't eat alone.

Chapter 17

Zoe stood in front of the mirror, examining her body. She slightly turned to the left and right, moving her hands over her curves.

"I wish I had bigger breasts," she said out loud.

As she looked at herself, she thought about Michael. It had been a while since she'd dated anyone. After college, she put all her time and energy into her restaurant. Even if she wanted to date, she had so little time. Men were a distraction. She wished she could be more like Chloe. "Date and dump," she called it. Chloe rarely had 3 dates with the same man. She said she liked to keep things fresh and moving.

"But what if you have a real connection with someone?" Zoe asked her one night during one of their after-hour get togethers.

"Connection? Girl, please. I'm not looking for a connection. I want to have fun. No strings, no emotional bullshit."

"You sound like a dude," Zoe said.

"What the fuck ever. I just know what I want, that's all. Don't label a bitch a dude because she can hit it and quit it. I don't need you to hold me or cuddle. You don't need to call or text me. Just keep it movin'."

She heard Chloe's words in her head. "I want a connection,"

she said.

She had no clue of what to wear. She went through her closet and pulled out several pairs of jeans, dresses, miniskirts, and shorts. She finally decided on a pair of jeans and a tunic top. She wore a pair of long silver earrings, bracelets on both wrists, and a simple silver chain with a small black onyx. She touched up her twist and put on nice, low black boots. She liked Michael, and she hoped their date – or kinda date – would go well. It had been so long since she had anyone in her life.

She walked out of the bedroom and into the kitchen. There was a large picnic basket on the table. She filled it with cold fried chicken, a green salad, forks, napkins, two bottles of wine, and two wine glasses. Plus, there were two mini sweet potato pies. She covered the basket with a large cloth and closed the top. Then, she grabbed her phone and set up a Lyft ride. She'd told him she'd meet him there.

When Tallulah told her Michael had given up his apartment, she wanted to call him but didn't know what to say. She felt some hesitation about going on the date because he was essentially homeless. She didn't want to add any pressure to his situation, so when he called to confirm, she decided she'd bring food and wine. She grabbed her keys, basket, purse, and cell phone and headed outside to catch her ride.

Michael had finally found a place to park. He'd used his press pass, but parking was still crowded and not very plentiful. He'd arrived a couple of hours before he was supposed to meet Zoe. After parking, he strolled through the jazz festival. He chatted with vendors, musicians, and event organizers. He wanted to spend as much time with Zoe as he could, despite his work obligations.

He was sitting at a table, rewriting his notes when he looked and saw Zoe walking toward him. He felt a little nervous. He'd never spent any time with her alone, except for their one date. It was a disaster. He was so nervous; he could hardly put two sentences together. He was so embarrassed; he never asked her out again and threw himself into his paper.

He couldn't believe how beautiful she was. She was carrying a basket and smiling brightly. He waved to her and stood up. She waved back and continued to walk toward him. "Hey!" he yelled as he walked toward her.

"You made it!" Michael was now standing in front of her. He wasn't sure what to do next, so he reached out to hug her. "I'm so glad to see you," he said.

She was surprised by the hug greeting, but she liked it and hugged him back. "I'm happy to see you, too." She released him. "I brought food. I thought we could have dinner and a little wine." "Great," he said. "I was just finishing some notes. Let's go sit down."

They walked over to the table. She put the basket on the table and sat down.

"This is nice. I'm glad we did this."

"Me, too," Michael said.

"Whatcha writing?" she asked.

"Oh, well I decided to cover the festival for the paper. I've been here for a while. I wanted to get that out of the way so I could spend time with you."

Zoe smiled and blushed a little. *That's some thoughtful shit,* she thought to herself.

"That's so thoughtful, Michael, but I wouldn't have minded hanging out while you talk to people." "Well, I did talk to a lot of musicians and can get us some VIP passes. I didn't know if you wanted to sit on the lawn or the seats."

"Ya know, VIP sounds good, but I like the lawn. Plus, I brought a blanket and basket. I thought
we could sit on the lawn and eat."

"You got it."

He quickly finished his notes and put them into his backpack. "You wanna find a place on the lawn?" he said.

"Sure," she replied.

He reached for the basket and her hand. She hesitated for a moment but then decided to extend her hand. He gently wrapped his hand around hers and led her to the lawn. She was shocked that he wanted to hold her hand, but now, in the moment, it just felt right. Her hand was soft yet strong. She squeezed a little tighter as they walked, happily allowing him to lead. They waded their way through the crowd and found a large empty space in the back.

"How's this?" Zoe asked.

"Perfect," he said, setting down the basket.

She opened the basket and pulled out a large cloth and fanned it out.

"Sit," she said.

Once sitting, she pulled out the chicken, green salad, plates, forks, and napkins. "Wow!" he exclaimed. "You didn't have to go to all this trouble." "Hey, I cook for a living. I can't help myself," she joked.

She pulled out a bottle of wine and two wine glasses. She rushed to dish up the food and handed him a plate. It couldn't have been more perfect.

They ate, laughed, and drank. She felt completely at ease with him. He was easy to talk to, a great listener, and he had her same quirky sense of humor. Horns, guitars, and drums filled the air. She watched as crowds danced and swayed to the music. She'd often find herself looking at him. He was smiling, watching the band, enjoying the music. She tapped him on the arm and offered him one of the mini pies.

He laughed. "You know, I was secretly wishing for pie." "I thought so. I know T brings you pie when she works."

Michael took the pie from her, picked up his fork, and dug it into the pie.

"Ya know, I've never had sweet potato pie until I met T. You might as well call it crack. I love it." He took a huge bite and groaned with delight.

"I'm glad you like it. So how are things, the paper?"

He swallowed. "Well, I guess you know I'm crashing on T's couch," he said.

"She told me, Michael. I'm sorry."

"Don't be. I'm not sure what'll happen, but I know things will be okay. The printer has been increasing costs, and now it's to a point where I can no longer afford it. People don't read the paper anymore. Everything is online. You can get your news in a moment."

Zoe frowned. "So, what are you going to do?"

He sighed. "Well, I don't know yet. I guess I'll have to eventually shut down the paper. I can probably keep it afloat for a few more months. I guess I could find a job writing or editing. I've never worked for anyone, so I'm not sure what that's like."

"Well, I've worked for someone, and there's nothing like owning your own thing. I love running the restaurant. I'm not getting rich, but I'm doing pretty good."

"I think you're doing great. You're doing what you love. What could be better than that?"

She nodded her head. "Ya know, T's a good friend. I know y'all are cool and close. She cares about you. You've been a good friend to her; more like a brother. Now she's paying it forward." "I just want to make sure you know. I never thought I'd be sleeping on her couch. I don't want things to be awkward between us. On the bright side, her neighbor, Mrs. Herrera, has been feeding me the best homemade Mexican food."

"Well, I guess you ain't starving. You know T can't cook, right?" She laughed.

"I know. I got Mrs. Herrera," he joked.

As the night continued, the air becomes cold and chilly. The cold nip of the night air was enough for them to pack up the food and leave.

"Where did you park?" Michael asked, grabbing her hand.

"I took a Lyft," Zoe said.

"Can I drive you home?" he asked.

"Sure. That would be nice."

There was no hesitation in her answer. She didn't want the night to end. She'd learned so much about him and wanted to learn more. She liked him. He was so different than any other guy she'd ever dated.

They walked to his car. He unlocked and opened the passenger door for her.

Damn! He opens doors, too?! He walked around to the driver's side, opened the rear door, and placed the basket inside. He then climbed into the driver's seat and started the ignition.

As he went to put the car in reverse, she gently turned toward him and put her hand on his arm. "Wait."

Michael looked surprised and put the car back in park. "What's wrong?" he asked.

"Nothing's wrong. I just wanted to say that I really had a great time with you. I mean, I've known you for a while, but this was different. I feel like I know you better. I really didn't know how the night would go. I mean, the last date we had, you didn't say much."

Michael smiled. "I know. I was just so nervous. I had a good time, too. I really enjoy spending time with you."

She leaned over and kissed him. The warm, wet kiss caught him off guard. He felt her soft, gentle lips press up against his, and closed his eyes and kissed her back. She gently pulled away and looked into his eyes. He was staring at her. He started to speak, but she leaned in and kissed him again.

She leaned back and said, "Okay, I'm ready now." "You're full of surprises. I like surprises."

He put the car in reverse, and they drove off.

She was giving him directions. Then, they saw a homeless woman with four kids. They were sitting on the curb by a convenience store. The woman had a few jugs of water and a few small plastic cups. She was sitting in a lawn chair, with her children sitting around her. She held a sign that read, "*Please help, hungry. Need money for a hotel room. Anything helps.*"

The woman wore a small jacket and hat. The children sat on big cardboard pieces, huddled close for warmth. He noticed that they didn't seem to have coats and that they were wrapped in small blankets.

Zoe and Michael both looked at the woman as the car passed. As they came to a stop at the stoplight, he looked in the rearview mirror. He watched her as she put down the sign and began pouring water from one of the jugs into a small cup. She handed the cup to the littlest child. Michael thought he must have been about 4 years old. He heard Mrs. Herrera's voice in his head: "*No one should go hungry.*"

He continued to watch the woman when he heard Zoe's voice. "Greenlight," she said.

He started to move forward. As he passed through the light, he turned into a small grocery store parking lot.

"What are you doing?" she asked.

"I'll be right back."

Michael put the car in park and went inside the store. Several minutes later, he emerged from

the store with several bags, blankets, and a cooler. Zoe jumped out of car, ran around to the

driver's side, and opened the rear door.

"What's all this?" she said, surprised.

"It's for the lady and her kids," he said. "No one should go hungry."

He loaded everything inside the car and drove back to the corner, where the woman was sitting. He got out of the car and walked up to her. "I have some food, cups, and blankets for you in the car."

Before the woman could speak, Michael walked back to the car and opened the rear door. He pulled out a cooler, blankets, and several bags.

Zoe jumped out of the car to help. He placed the cooler in front of the woman and opened it. It was full of ready-made sandwiches, juice, water, and Gatorade.

"Wwwwhat?" the woman stammered.

"For you and the kids," he said.

He turned toward the 4 kids. The oldest couldn't have been older than 10.

Zoe carried the bags of food and set them next to the cooler.

"There's fruit, crackers, chips, and snacks in the bags," she said.

Michael said, "I found some hats and gloves, too. I hope they fit."

The woman stared at him. She tried to speak, but she had no words. Tears began to flow from her eyes, and she reached out and hugged him.

"Thank you," she whispered. "Oh my God, Jesus is good. Thank you, sir. Thank you!" "You're welcome. Do you have a place to stay?"

The oldest child, who was a little girl, walked up to him and said, "We don't have no place to stay."

The woman was still crying, staring at Michael.

She nodded her head and managed to say, "I lost my job and have no money for a hotel room. The shelter is full."

"How much is the hotel?"

"I have a voucher, so it's only $40 per night. I start a new job on Tuesday."

He pulled out his wallet and looked inside. He had exactly eighty-five dollars. He handed her the money.

"Go get the room. This is enough for two nights. I wish I had more. I just want to help." Zoe looked at Michael. This had caught her completely off guard.

The woman started crying again and held up her hand. "You've done enough," she said. "Take it, please." He took her hand, put the $85 into her palm, and wrapped her fingers around it. "Do you need a ride?" he asked

"No," the woman managed to say. She was still crying. She hugged him again. "I prayed for some help. Just a little help. God is good."

She hugged him a little harder and released him. Zoe

watched in amazement as the woman hugged Michael. She then turned toward Zoe and hugged her, too.

"Thank you," she whispered. "Thank you so much."

"Are you okay? Do you need a ride?" Michael asked again.

"No, the hotel is across the street." The woman looked at her 4-year-old daughter and gently said, "We don't have to sleep outside tonight. These nice people are helping us. They're angels."

The little girl walked over to Michael and said, "Are you really an angel?"

Michael looked at the woman, who spoke for him. "You don't ask an angel if they're an angel; you just know. He is an angel."

The little girl wrapped her arms around Michael's waist and gave him a firm hug. "Thank you, Mr.

Angel," she whispered, then smiled and ran over to her siblings.

The woman turned toward Michael. "I can pay you back. If you give me your name –"

He held up his hand. "No, angels don't need money." He winked at her. "If you're okay, we'll be going now."

The woman started crying again and nodded her head. Michael walked over the driver's side and got in the car. He watched the woman hug Zoe again. "Bye," Zoe said, then got in the car.

She turned toward Michael. "Michael, what you just did... I..."

"I just wanted to help. Pay it forward. Sometimes everyone needs a little help, a little saving," he said

"Wow. I'm speechless. You gave that lady $85, bought her food and water, and I'm the one full of surprises?"

He smiled and put the car in drive.

"Something just hit me." She grabbed his hand and squeezed it. "You're gonna get your blessings, Michael. You have a good heart," she said, with a smile. He gently pressed on the gas, and they drove away.

Chapter 18

Chloe's office intercom buzzed. "Chloe, I have Stanley Roberts on line one." Chloe smiled. "Put him through."

On the second ring, she picked up. "Stanley, I'm surprised to hear from you," she said in her most professional voice.

"Not disappointed, I hope."

"No, not at all. I have the tour all scheduled for Tuesday. Where should I send the car?" she asked.

"Oh, I can drive myself," he said.

"No, Stanley, not this time. I'm not getting in that truck. Do you want to meet me here at the office?" she asked.

"What's wrong with my truck?" he asked, chuckling.

"Nothing. I'm not getting in," she said.

"Okay, I'll meet you. What time?"

"Let's meet at 10 am."

"Very good. 10 am, it is. I look forward to seeing you again, Chloe."

Chloe felt herself get a little flushed. "I'm sure this charity is just the thing for you. See you Tuesday."

She quickly went through her purse and found Marc's card. She dialed.

"King and Queen," the voice said.

"Yes, I'm looking for Marc," she said.

"You found him. What can I do for you?" he said.

"Marc, hi, it's Chloe, Tallulah's friend. We met the other night."

"Oh yes, the subject matter expert. What can I do for you?" he said.

"I need to hire a car for Tuesday. I'll have a very important client with me."

"Mr. Roberts?" he said.

"The one and only. Now, he isn't the fancy type, but I'd like to keep it professional," she said.

"Of course," Marc said.

"Great, I'll have my assistant reach out to you with details. Thanks, Marc," Chloe said. "No, thank you. I appreciate the business."

Chloe hung up the phone.

Michael sat at the small kitchen table, eating a bowl of cereal while flipping through a copy of *You & Me.*

"Fashion," he said out loud.

He heard a buzzing noise from the sofa. He walked over and dug through the cushions. Finally, he found the cell phone.

"David! What's up, man," he said as he walked back to the table.

"I wanna know who the lady is I've been investigating for you. She's got a strange background," David said.

"What do you mean?" asked Michael.

"Well, first of all, it's like she just disappeared without a trace. I could find some information on her family. Her mother passed away some years ago, and I already told you about the brother. She rented a small apartment for a while years ago, then nothing. I even called the apartment building.

The landlord said she was quiet and distant. One day he went to collect the rent, and she was gone. She left everything in the apartment," David said.

"That's strange," Michael said.

"I also found out she, at one time, had a shit ton of money, over $250,000. Someone held it in an account. There was one for her, and one for her brother. Now, the authorities have closed the brother's account for years. But here's...well, this is the strange thing: The money was never touched. I actually reached out to the bank, who pointed me to an attorney. I called the dude. He's retired, and his memory's not very good. He said someone told him to put the money in a trust and it would be donated at a later time."

"Donated?" Michael echoed.

"Yes, now this is where it gets even stranger. Someone contacted the bank about 2 years ago and told them to donate it to charity. But the money was never given to the charity. Instead, someone emptied out the account and closed it. The bank wouldn't provide me with any information. I'm thinking about banking practices that are highly irregular. So, are you gonna tell me who this lady is or what?" David asked.

Michael paused. "Well, I don't know her. A reporter of mine is doing a story on the homeless shelter. She met this lady, Lily, and wanted to include her in the story. I guess she was a singer or something."

"Hmmm...so, you mean to tell me this lady I've been investigating is homeless?" David asked.

"It would seem so," Michael said.

"Isn't it funny that someone planned to donate money to a shelter, and now it's gone?" David asked.

"Yeah, that is strange. She's homeless." "Good point,"

David said.

They both sat in silence for a moment, then Michael said, "Hey, can you do me another favor?" "Shoot," David said.

"Okay, same lady. Now, my reporter found out she recorded a record back in the sixties, and she even found the record. The studio burned to the ground way, way back, but can you see if the producer is still alive?" Michael asked.

David laughed. "Sure, but if I have to get on a plane or drive somewhere –" "I know," Michael said, "it's gonna cost me." "Okay, give me the info," David said.

"I'll take a picture of the album and send it," Michael said.

"Even better. I'll be in touch," David said, then hung up.

Michael looked around the apartment and found the record sitting on top of the old record player. He snapped a photo of the front and back and sent it to David.

Praises of Hope is a small nursing home. The outside of the building is in bad need of paint, and the grass could use a little water. Dust covers the windows, making them look as if someone hasn't cleaned them for years. The halls are cold, and the white walls, now turning an off-yellow color, are bare. It's a somber place to be.

Owen Katz was sitting in his wheelchair, looking out the window. The small room consisted of a bed, small end table, sink, small bathroom, two chairs, and TV mounted on the wall. He watched the cars drive by and every so often would mumble to himself. When the day nurse walked in, he didn't turn around; rather, he just kept staring out the window. She was a pudgy lady, with long black hair and long fingernails.

"Owen," she said, "it's time for your pills."

He looked up at her and snarled. "I don't want to take any more fucking pills. Just let me die already! Didn't I tell you to stay the fuck out of my goddamn room?!"

The nurse shook her head. "Now Owen, what have I said about your language?"

"I don't give two shits about what you think, you overweight pile of shit. Get the hell out of my room!"

The nurse set the pills on a small table next to the bed. "Owen, if you don't take your pills, I'll have to call the doctor," she said.

"Do whatever you want, you old bitch. Get out of here!"

She stood for a moment, then turned and walked out of the room. He waited a moment, making sure she didn't come back. When he felt she was gone for good, he wheeled himself over to the small dresser. He turned his chair sideways, opened the bottom drawer, and pulled out a large photo album. He put the album on his lap, closed the drawer, and wheeled himself back to the window. He slowly opened the album and stared at the first picture. It was a picture of a building, with 4 people standing in front, smiling. He slowly took his hand and moved it over the picture and smiled. The words on the building read *Twilight Studios.* He looked at the next picture. It was of a young Black girl holding a microphone. She was sitting on a piano. Her dress was white, and she had a single white lily in her hair.

As he stared at the picture, he didn't hear the footsteps enter his room.

"Owen?" the voice said softly. He looked up to see an older woman with white hair. She placed it in a bun that stood high on top of her head. She wore horn-rimmed glasses, her face was kind, and she smiled warmly at him. She pulled a chair next to him and sat down.

"Owen, I've heard you cussed out the nurse. Is that true?"

He looked at her, then back toward the window. "What if I did? Ya gonna kick me out? Put an old man out on the street? I just want to be left alone. And she smells funny. I don't like her," he grumbled.

The woman laughed. "Why would I kick out my best patient? But you do need to be nicer to the staff. They're here to help you." She placed her hand over his and looked out the window. "See anything good out there today?"

He turned his head toward her and grinned. "I like you, Doc. You're the only one in this godforsaken place. But where's an old man to go when he gets old? My daughter has a family of her own, my wife is gone, my business is gone, my dreams are gone..." He stopped talking. The doctor squeezed his hand and noticed the photo album on his lap. "You're looking at pictures today, Owen?"

He looked down at the photo album. "This was the happiest time in my life. You know, I was going to be a famous record producer. I had a studio and the singers and musicians to make it happen. I had one singer; she was special."

"Lily?" the doctor asked.

His eyes widened. "Yes, Lily. She had a set of pipes on her that would put Lena Horne to shame. She was soulful and sultry. Her voice was like velvet. It was smooth..." He drifted off.

"She sounds wonderful, Owen. What happened?" the doctor asked.

He frowned. "Well Doc, back in those days, white folks and Black folks were knee-deep in segregation. It was a horrible time. The majority of my singers were Black, musicians, too. I was the only place they could go and record. So much talent not heard or recognized because of color. Lily, well...

she was a victim of circumstances. Things that weren't in her control. Her career ended overnight. *Poof.* Gone That goddamn Amanda. She just had it out for Lily and her brother. I did what I could to help, but well, when you have money, you make things happen. People disappear. Erased from the world." His eyes saddened, and he looked down at the photo album.

The doctor patted Owen's hand. "What do you mean, 'erased'?" she asked.

"I mean take all the money in the world and use it to destroy someone. Lily was innocent. Oh, back in those days, interracial relations weren't welcome. Well, Lily was the product of just such a union. But that wasn't the problem. The problem was, her mama and daddy weren't married to one another, but her daddy was married to a white woman. So, scandal erupts, and Lily goes away."

The doctor shook her head. "I'm very sorry, Owen. I wish I could have heard her sing, this Lily." He half-smiled. "We did one record. I sank every penny into that recording. Then I was blackballed from the industry. No one would work with me or have anything to do with me. I couldn't give the records away. One night, I got a call that my studio was on fire. I lost everything. All the records, too. And Lily, well, she was strong for a little while, but after Clyde died, she just checked out. I haven't seen her for over 20 years. She'd be in her 50s or 60s by now. I don't know if she's even alive. She would call or write, but then one day it just stopped."

The doctor gently rubbed his arm. "Owen, I need you to take the pills. They're for your heart. I want to see you stick around a while. What would I do without my best patient?" she said softly. He looked at her and nodded his head. She handed him a small cup with pills inside and a glass of water. He popped the pills in his mouth and drank the water.

The doctor smiled at him and checked her watch. "I have some time. Will you show me the pictures in your album?"

He looked at her and smiled. No one ever asked him about his life. His voice brightened. "I can tell you stories, too, Doc. I got some of the best goddamn stories you've ever heard. I knew the jazz greats!" He smiled at her and turned the page in the photo album.

Chapter 20

Sharon took her time sipping her Sangria. It was her third one in the past hour, and they were tasting better with every sip. She leaned back into the sofa and put her feet up on the table.

"I'm so fucking mad right now!" she yelled. "That bitch wants my help. She never needed my help before!"

Keith walked into the living room. He held two plates in his hands. "Sit up," he said.

Sharon sat up and took one of the plates from his hand. He sat next to her. She put the plate down and continued to inhale her drink.

"You better slow down on those," he said.

She took a big sip and set the glass down. "Keith, I thought I'd seen a lot. I thought I knew a lot, but then she said she stopped a payment to charity. The money wasn't even hers; it belonged to her mysterious half-sister. What the fuck?"

He chuckled. "Yeah, it sounds like a bad soap opera. Drama."

"'Drama' is fucking right. I didn't lay the big bomb on you," she said.

"Wait, there's more. I know she's dying, right? Cue the dramatic music." He laughed. She was quiet. He stopped laughing. "Wait...seriously...she's dying?"

She nodded.

"Yeah, she has cancer."

"I'm sorry, baby, I had no idea," he said

"I know. It's so much. So now she wants me to find out where her siblings are and who they are. She told me to hire a private investigator. You'd be proud of me. I told her we weren't friends."

He raised an eyebrow. "Really? What did she say?"

"I don't know. I left the room in dramatic fashion. I didn't give her the chance to reply."

"Good for you!" he said, then raised his glass and took a drink. "So now what? What are you gonna do?"

She shook her head. "I don't know. Tell me what to do. What would you do?" "Honestly?" he said.

She nodded.

"I'd do it," he said. "I'd find out everything I could about her." "Why?" Sharon asked.

Keith shrugged his shoulders. "I'd want to know how she became such a bitch." She laughed. "She was born a bitch. Her mom was just as bad, if not worse."

He had a serious look on his face. "So, what are you going to do about you? Are you staying with the magazine or what?"

She frowned. "I don't know." She took the last sip of her Sangria.

She leaned her head all the way back, so as not to waste any of the cocktails, then looked at the empty glass and frowned.

"I need another one. Will you get me another one?" she said.

He looked at her. "You don't need another one."

"This isn't about need, babe; it's about want. I want another one."

Keith looked at her and shook his head, then took her empty glass and left the room.

She shouted out to him, "Thank you! Okay, I'm going to find out this info for her, then I'm gone."

He walked back into the room with a full glass of Sangria and handed it to her.

"Are you sure?" he said.

"Yes, I'm sure. Besides, I'm married to a rich doctor. Maybe I'll stay home and raise our children," she said, looking into his eyes.

He smiled. "You promise to get fat?"

She leaned forward and pulled him down on top of her. "I promise to get so fat, you can go out and bring me whatever I crave."

He pushed his lips down on hers. He could feel her warmth as her body started to move underneath him.

"Let's go upstairs," he whispered.

She nodded. He stood up and reached out his hand for her. They embraced and kissed, then he grabbed her by the hand and led her up the stairs.

The next morning, Sharon sat at her desk. Her head was pounding. She took the four aspirin sitting on her desk and washed them down with a large glass of water. She then rubbed her head and groaned.

"I shouldn't have had that 4th Sangria," she said out loud.

Her line buzzed, and her assistant came over the intercom. "Sharon, I have a Barry Proctor on line 3."

"Okay, put him through."

She picked up the phone. "Mr. Proctor, thank you for calling me back. Yes, I need to hire a private investigator. I need someone who understands discretion."

Tallulah and Michael listened to the recording of Lily's story in his small office. "You were right, T. There is a story here."

She looked at him with a serious face. "I don't think I feel comfortable telling the world Lily is Sylvia Blass's half-sister. I work for Sylvia Blass!" "Well, that explains the two birth certificates," he said.

"What should I do?" she asked.

He thought for a moment. "Take it to your editor and write the story. You're a good writer. Write the story."

She stood up. "I'm going home. I need to figure this out. Plus, I have my diet article due in a few days."

"I'll be here a while. I'll see you later," he said.

She waved goodbye and left the office.

Michael sighed and leaned back in his chair. He heard his cell buzz and dug the phone out of his pocket and clicked it on.

"Hello?"

"Mike!" Crazy Dave yelled into the phone.

"David, what's up?"

"Your homeless lady, I found the record producer. He's living in a rundown nursing home outside of Atlanta," David said.

"He's alive?" Michael said.

"Yes. I called the nursing home. He's there. He really doesn't have visitors."

Michael pulled out a piece of paper. "Give me the info," he said.

He quickly wrote down the information and thanked Crazy Dave, then called Tallulah.

"Hey, Michael," she said.

"So, I just hung up with Crazy Dave. Lily's producer is alive. He's in a small nursing home outside of Atlanta. I have all the info. I'll text it to you."

She gasped. "Wait...what?"

"Owen Katz is alive and living in Atlanta," he said. "Texting you now."

He quickly texted her the information, then texted Zoe:

I'm on way.

He stood up, grabbed his jacket, and walked out of the office.

Michael arrived at Zoe's restaurant around midnight. He knocked on the door. After several minutes, he saw her walking towards it. He waved and smiled, then watched her unlock the door and push it open.

"Hey, come on in." She smiled.

He was standing in front of her. She looked so beautiful. He wrapped his arms around her waist and pulled her close. He leaned in and kissed her. She was warm and soft. He melted into her, then released her with care.

"Hi," he said.

"Hi back," she said.

They held the gaze for a few more seconds, then she grabbed his hand and led him to the back table. "I thought we could sit and talk unless you're too tired." "No. I'm good to sit and talk."

He pulled out her chair. She smiled and sat down.

On the table was a bottle of Montoya Cabernet. "So far, you've liked every wine I've picked, so tonight I picked this." She held up the bottle.

"I don't know much about wine, but I'm guessing this is the good shit," he said. "If you like cabernet, yes, this is the good shit."

"I like everything you serve me," he said, giving her a sly look.

She poured his glass, then hers. They clinked glasses and both took a drink. "So, how was your day?" she said, sounding excited. "How's the layout coming?"

"Well, actually, pretty good," he replied, taking another drink of wine. "This is really good."

"What about you? Business good today?" he asked.

"Yes, as a matter of fact. We're experiencing consistent growth. I like it, but I didn't know how much work it would be. But I love it, so it isn't really work, right?" she replied.

"I'm like that with the paper. When I get in the editing zone and I'm putting together the layout, I tune everything out. I usually turn my ringer off and put on a pair of headphones so I get no distractions."

"You enjoy what you do, don't you?" she said.

"Yes, I do. I've wanted to be a journalist and/or editor since I was a kid. I put every dime I had into the paper. For a while, things were good. We've been around for 5 years, and I'm proud of that."

"You should. I do read your paper. Tallulah would kill me if I didn't." She laughed.

"Well, I think I can maybe publish 3 more editions. I plan on speaking to my staff next week. Most of them know, but we're family, so they should hear it from me."

He finished his wine, and she poured him another glass. "Isn't there some way you can keep the paper going?" He shook his head, "I'm tapped out, Zoe."

She frowned, then finished her wine and poured herself another glass.

"But on a good note, Tallulah got Lily to talk to her. She told her about her record and how she chose a life on the streets. I listened to most of the interview earlier," he said. "Wow," she said. "How did she do it?"

"She played her record for her."

"Smart," said Zoe.

"Okay, so I haven't told you the good part," he said.

"I love the good part of a story," she said.

"So, Lily had this singing career. It was just taking off. When she was 18, she found out Cliff Blass, the millionaire was her real father. His wife, Amanda Worthington-Blass, went nuts and stopped Lily's career," he said.

Zoe's eyes got wide. "So that's the Amanda she was talking about. But wait. Who's Amanda Worthington-Blass?"

He pulled out his phone and searched the Internet for Amanda Worthington-Blass. When he found what he was looking for, he handed the phone to her.

He watched her read and drank his wine. When she finished reading, she put down the phone.

"Wow," she said.

"Wow is right."

She took a drink of her wine. "So, Lily is a Blass. She's related to Sylvia Blass."

Michael nodded. "Yes. I don't think in today's world it would really be such a scandal. But back in the 60s? An interracial relationship led to children, and the husband came from a wealthy family. it was a big deal then," he said.

"Do you think Lily will sing at the open mic?" she said.

"Well, according to T, she said she would do it. But I dunno. She seems a little unpredictable to me," he said.

"She is," she said.

Chapter 21

Lily walked down the sidewalk at a leisurely pace, humming to herself. She stopped in front of a large bank, peered in the windows, and cupped her hands around her eyes so she could see in. She counted out loud, looking at the people in line. "One, two, three..." Then, she stepped back from the window and walked into the bank.

The tall security guard gave her a suspicious look. She wore an old overcoat, large black combat boots, gloves, and a bright pink crochet hat. Her face was dirty, and her lips chapped. She managed to smile at the guard and walked past him. A woman sitting at a desk noticed her and rushed over.

"Yes, hello, may I help you?" She gave her a look of disapproval and frowned.

"I need to see Mr. Franklin," Lily said, her voice steady. She stood up straight as if her appearance didn't matter.

"Mr. Franklin is in a meeting," the woman replied. "Can you tell me your business here?" Lily looked around the bank and spotted Mr. Franklin's office in the back. She began walking toward the office.

The woman's face turned to horror as she reached for Lily. "Excuse me!"

Lily slipped her grip and rushed toward the office. The

security guard saw Lily and the woman talking. He jumped out of his chair and ran to them. Lily turned to see him running toward her and quickened her pace.

"Hey!" he shouted.

She was about 5 feet from Mr. Franklin's office door when the security guard grabbed her by the shoulder. She yelled out in pain as he spun her around.

"You need to leave!" he shouted.

She spun around in a hurry and cried out, "Mr. Franklin." It's Lily Blass!"

The security guard grabbed her arm and pulled her away from the office door. Mr. Franklin, hearing the commotion, walked to his office door. "It's okay, Bill. "Please let Ms. Blass go," he said in a calm voice.

The security guard released her and shot Mr. Franklin a confused look.

"It's okay. Come in my office, Ms. Blass."

She turned toward the security guard and flipped him her middle finger. He squinted his eyes and turned around in a hurry before leaving. Lily looked around the bank and saw everyone staring at her. She adjusted her large overcoat and walked into Mr. Franklin's office.

Mr. Franklin closed the door behind her, then gestured for her to sit down. She looked around the office and chose a chair closest to the door. Mr. Franklin smiled and pulled a chair around so he was sitting next to her. He frowned a little at the lingering smell coming from Lily but did his best to hide his discomfort.

"Ms. Blass, it's been a long time. I must say, I'm surprised to see you," he said. She looked around the office and said, "I'm here about the money."

Mr. Franklin nodded. "Okay," he said. "Let me pull up your account. Do you have your ID or any identifying information?"

He watched as she opened her large overcoat and dug into an inside pocket. She took out a bottle of vodka and placed it on his desk. Then, she dug into her large pocket and pulled out a worn ID card. He took the card from her, walked over to his desk, and began typing on the computer. After several moments, he spoke.

"Ms. Blass, we decided several years ago that you would donate the money to a charity of your choice." At that time, you chose the Marigold homeless shelter. Is that correct?"

She nodded.

He continued to type, then stopped abruptly and stared at the computer. He wasn't sure what to make of what he was seeing. The money was gone. Someone stopped the transfer and drained the money from the account. He cleared his throat and continued typing.

Lily sensed something was wrong. "Mr. Franklin," she said, "what's taking so long? I want to know if someone transferred the money. The shelter is in need of the money. I signed all the papers."

Mr. Franklin was silent. "Lily, there seems to be a problem. It's going to take a little while to figure out."

"What do you mean, 'problem'?" She asked with a trem-bling voice.

"Like I said, I need a little time to figure this out. I'm happy to contact you in a few days. How can I reach you?" he asked.

Lily felt herself getting anxious. She grabbed the bottle of vodka from the desk, screwed off the lid, and held the bottle in her hand. She was shaking. She put the bottle down and began pacing around the office.

Mr. Franklin watched her pace around. She started mumbling to herself and rubbing her hands together. She was starting to make Mr. Franklin nervous.

"Ms. Blass, I found some irregularities, and I need to investigate," he said. She stopped pacing and looked at him. Her eyes looked sunken and sad.

"Where's the money?" she whispered.

Mr. Franklin didn't answer; instead, he stood up and walked over to her.

"Ms. Blass, I need a little time. Please sit down. I can call you a cab to take you wherever you want to go. When you come back in a few days, I should have some information." She didn't sit. "I trusted you, Mr. Franklin. You said you would help me."

She walked toward the door. "I know that money will help the shelter. I'm not crazy. I know what's happening around me. I may seem like I'm out of it, but I'm not. I'm not crazy." She placed her hand on the doorknob. "I'll be back to get my money."

She opened the door and walked out. As she made her way through the bank, she spotted the security guard. He was watching her. She flipped him her middle finger again and walked out of the bank.

Chapter 22

A week had passed since Tallulah played the album for Lily. She'd been to the shelter to speak with her again, but no one had seen her. It was as if she'd disappeared. She was at Marigold daily, waiting for Lily to show up, but she never did.

She'd started the article at least 10 times but found herself stuck. She needed to tell Sharon. She sat in front of her computer, waiting for Sharon to contact her. Michael had left early that morning to finish the layout. She took a sip of her coffee and waited. After several moments of silence, her computer chimed. She clicked it on, and Sharon appeared on her screen.

"Hi, Tallulah," she said.

She smiled back. "Hi, Sharon. How did you like the article on diet fads? Who knew there were so many?" she said.

Sharon laughed. "Yes, we love to find new ways to lose weight. I read it. It's good. I like how you did the pros and cons."

"You look down today, Tallulah," she said. "I mean, the last few times we connected, you seemed in better spirits. Anything I can do?"

She sighed. "Well, it's my homeless shelter article. It's

been more difficult than I expected." "Well, sometimes those hard stories are the best stories. Is the article done?"

"No, not yet. I seem to have a block or something. It's complicated. I have a great story, but..."

Sharon cocked her head to one side. "What is it?"

"Well, the shelter I'm writing about is in financial trouble. They had a large donation, but for whatever reason, someone took the donation back. My editor wanted me to go with that angle, but I went with something a little different. I thought I'd focus on the people who use the shelter, depend on it. Maybe highlight their stories. So anyway, I kinda took to one lady, Lily. Sharon, she has the most beautiful singing voice. But...well, there's a problem."

Sharon's face changed when she heard about the donation and homeless shelter.

"Are you okay, Sharon? You look...flushed."

She shook her head. "I'm okay. Tallulah, what's the name of the shelter?" "Marigold," she replied.

"And this donation, do you know where it came from or who was donating?" "No, but...well, I do have something I want to tell you."

Sharon sat up in her chair. She felt her stomach quiver. "Tallulah, can you hold on a moment? I want to shut my door."

Sharon came back to her desk and pulled out a large folder.

"Okay, what do you need to tell me?"

"Well, the homeless lady, Lily...well, I think...well, she says she's Sylvia Blass's half-sister."

Sharon sat speechless for a moment. Her jaw dropped in surprise. She looked down at her folder and shuffled through some papers.

"I think she may be," said Sharon.

"What? Wait, how do you know?"

"We need to speak in person," Sharon said.

"Wait, what?" Tallulah said.

"It's a long story, and I'd prefer we meet. I can come to you. It's important, Tallulah."

"Wait, if you're going to let me go because of Sylvia Blass…" Tallulah started, but Sharon interrupted her.

"No, that's not it. It's a long story, but we can help one another. I can be there in two days."

Tallulah felt confused. "I was trying to figure out how to let you know about what I'd found, which is one of the reasons the article isn't one. I mean, I work for Sylvia Blass."

"Don't worry, Tallulah. I'll explain everything when I arrive. I need to go. I'll see you in two days. We can arrange a place to meet. I'll have my assistant reach out to you."

"Okay, but I don't understand, Sharon."

"I know. I'll explain everything when I see you. Thank you, Tallulah. I'll see you in a few days." With that, Sharon clicked off, and Tallulah's screen went blank.

She sat there, looking at the screen. "Oh, shit," she said out loud.

Sharon clicked off the computer and looked at the folder on her desk. She opened it and scanned the first page. The private investigator had found most of the information she requested in a short period. He was able to get birth records and copies of Cliff Blass's wills.

She turned to the pages of the will and stopped where it talked about children. It read as follows:

I do attest that I have 3 children. My children are Sylvia Blass, Clyde Duke, and Lillian (Lily) Duke. My estate will provide funds to all three children when they reach the legal age of 18 years old.

To Clyde and Lily: I know you may not understand, but I always loved you. I loved your mother. I know I was not there for you, but I always wanted to be in your life. Now that I am gone, I want you to know who your father was. I have signed each of your birth certificates. We will provide you with copies of the birth certificates. I have provided a check for $500,000, payable immediately on your 18th birthday. You two will split these monies.

She set the page aside and flipped through until she found the article about Clyde Duke's death.

September 15, 1962

One Black male is dead after he slid off the road at the Forest Junction. Authorities identified the man as Clyde Duke, 22, who was killed immediately and pronounced dead at the scene. Police are investigating rumors of foul play, but they have not made any arrests.

She sighed heavily and put down the article. She shuffled to a few more papers until she found the birth certificates of Lily Duke and Lily Blass. The private investigator told her that Lily Duke had been moving around since her brother died. A car hit her mother, causing her death in 1965. He told her again that the police thought there was foul play. The investigation was short, and no arrests happened.

He then told her the last known address for Lily Duke was about six years ago; after that, nothing. The money the twins had inherited had disappeared as well. All Clyde's accounts were closed, and he couldn't find an account for Lily Duke. Sharon had asked him to search under Lily Blass, but she hadn't received any information yet.

She picked up her phone and called her assistant.

"Yes, Mrs. Eckerson?" Patty said through the phone.

"Patty, I need you to make some travel arrangements for

me. I'll be out of the office for the next week."

Sylvia Blass sat in the large leather chair. Light from the large windows on her right side filled the room. She shifted in the chair and crossed her legs. She was growing impatient. Then, the door opened behind her, and she heard a woman's voice. "Sylvia, I'm so sorry to keep you waiting."

She turned in her chair to see a short Black woman walking toward her.

She gasped. "Oh, who the hell are you? I'm waiting to speak with Mr. Meyers, my attorney, if you don't mind. If you're the paralegal, then you're wasting both of our time!" she huffed at the woman.

The Black woman smiled at her and sat behind a very large oak desk. She looked at her and placed a black folder on the desk.

"Mrs. Blass, Mr. Meyers requested me to see you. He had some urgent business out of town and will not be back for several weeks. Now, you can wait for his return, but from what I heard, you said that you find the matter urgent. My name is Carla. Carla Avery. I handle all Mr. Meyers's...special clients, like yourself, when he's away."

Sylvia scowled at Carla. "Do you know why I'm here?"

"I do. It seems you had some connections involving the illegal access of a trust fund. This, as you know, is a crime. It would seem you used resources outside of this firm to gain access, and now you want us to fix it. Is that correct?"

Sylvia nodded her head.

"It would also seem this trust fund actually belongs to your half-sister, Lillian Blass. This is the name on the fund, correct?" Carla asked.

Sylvia again nodded her head.

"Now Mrs. Blass, the firm is willing to assist you in this matter, as you and Mr. Meyers have made an arrangement. I'm here to reestablish the trust. I don't care to know about anything beyond that. Do you understand?"

"Yes, I completely understand. Did you go to law school, or are you a paralegal? I mean, anyone cannot handle matters such as these. "I mean, you people are known for being loud and lazy," she said as she sat up straight in her chair to show she was in control.

Carla made direct eye contact with her. "Mrs. Blass. Please know that I am a Yale Law graduate, top of my class. I've practiced law for 10 years, only with Mr. Meyers and his firm. Your comment only reveals the ignorance you have toward men and women of color. I am more than happy to let Mr. Meyers know you chose to go a different way. As I said, he won't be available for the next few weeks. How would you like to proceed?" Her voice was cool and calm. She sat back and waited for an answer.

Sylvia was speechless. She stared at Carla as she shifted in her chair.

"Okay, Ms. Avery, you said? Well, this matter is of great importance to me. I don't want to see any delay. My comments were...were...short-sighted."

"Fine, Ms. Blass. Once I have all the needed information, I will start rebuilding trust. I'll also need to know where the money went. Your full cooperation is necessary in this process. I will not tolerate someone lying to me. I assure you, I am not loud or lazy and will not tolerate any further remarks about my ethnicity. Any stereotypes you have playing out in your head...well, you need to keep them there. I am a professional, and others will treat me as such. If you feel you cannot speak with me with respect, then we need to end our discussions now. Do you understand, Mrs. Blass?"

Sylvia nodded her head, then sighed and said. "Yes, yes, I will cooperate. I need this to go away."

"Great," Carla said. "Let's begin."

* * *

Lily walked into the bank. Unlike the previous bank she'd entered, no one stopped her. She approached the counter and spoke in a gentle voice to the teller.

"I need to get into my safety deposit box," she said.

The teller looked up. She was smiling until she saw Lily, then her smile transformed into a frown.

"Ah, OK. I'll need to see your ID and the key."

Lily dug deep into her pocket, pulled out her worn ID, and laid it on the counter. She then took a chain from around her neck. On the chain was a key. She laid that on the counter, too.

The teller looked at the ID and key and told Lily to wait there. She came around the counter and escorted them to the room that held the boxes. She found Lily's box and placed it on a table, then nodded and left the room.

When Lily was alone, she sat down and unlocked the box. Inside were documents, newspaper clippings, jewelry, and money.

She stared at the money and glided her hand over the top of the bills. They were all hundreds. She picked up a stack and counted out 10 one hundred dollar bills, then placed the stack back in the box and closed it. She locked the box and left the room.

Once outside the bank, she walked a few blocks to a small motel, where she rented a room for the week.

"Do you know where I can find a cheap clothing store?" she asked the motel clerk.

He looked at her and said, "Ain't no mall around here, but there is a thrift store 'bout 3 blocks west."

She thanked him and left the motel, then walked to the thrift store and went inside. She looked through the clothing racks. She found some dresses, jeans, shirts, a coat, a new pack of socks, panties, and a bra. She decided to get a pair of sneakers, too. She purchased her clothes and walked back to the motel.

The room was small, but it had a bed, phone, TV, and small microwave. She wandered into the bathroom and found clean towels and soap. She went back into the main room and began to undress. She wanted to shower; it had been over a week since she was able to change her clothes. She put the dirty clothes into one of the shopping bags she got from the thrift store, then threw it in the trash.

The shower was hot. She let the water run over her body. Then, she rubbed soap everywhere. She watched as the suds and dirt washed down the drain. She took the soap and washed her hair. When she finished, she stepped out and wrapped a towel around herself. Then, she wiped her hand across the steamed mirror until she could see her reflection.

She struggled to recognize the face staring back at her in the mirror. She moved her hands through her hair, rubbed her face, and pushed out her lips. As she stared at herself, she had the desire to sing. So, she filled the entire room with her voice.

Praise Him

Praise Him
Praise Him
Praise Him
Jesus, blessed Savior,
He's worthy to be praised.
From the rising of the sun,
Until the going down of the same;
He's worthy, Jesus is worthy,
He's worthy to be praised
She stopped singing and looked at herself in the mirror.

Chapter 23

The black Town Car pulled into the parking lot. Marc arrived at Chloe's office at precisely 10 am. He adjusted the rearview mirror and glanced at the back seat. Then, he turned down the radio and waited.

The office door opened, and he spotted Chloe, who was dressed nicely, along with a tall white man. He assumed he must be Stanley Roberts. Marc was surprised at how casually he dressed for a millionaire. He opened the door and walked to the passenger side. Then, he greeted his two passengers.

"Good morning!" He said with a cheerful tone.

Chloe smiled and him and replied, "Good morning, Marc. Thank you for being on time. This is Stanley Roberts. Stanley, this is Marc. He'll be our driver today."

Stanley extended his hand. "Good to meet you, man." Stanley shook his hand with a strong grip. Marc shook his hand back and said, "Nice to meet you, Mr. Roberts." "Please, call me Stanley," he said.

"Okay, Stanley. Please get in," he said.

Chloe smiled and slid in the back seat. Stanley smiled and climbed in behind her. Marc shut the door and walked around to the driver's side and got in the car.

"Marc, we'll be visiting the Marigold shelter, and then we're going to Zoe's Soul Food Kitchen," Chloe said.

"Very good," he said and put the car in drive.

Anna greeted Chloe and Stanley as they entered the shelter. She gave them a tour of the shelter and introduced Stanley to the staff. When the tour was over, Stanley asked to speak with Anna in her office.

"You're doing good work here, Anna. I'm very impressed with what you've accomplished with little money," he said.

"We really depend a lot on donations. We get 40% of our food donated. We have groups that will help us with blankets, bedding, hygiene supplies, clothes, shoes, and first aid supplies. I have volunteers who help in the kitchen. They donate time and supplies for maintenance, upkeep, and cleaning of the building. As you can see, we do a lot of laundry here, so having a working washer and dryer and other supplies is a priority. For most of the people we help, this is the only place they can take a hot shower or get clean clothes."

"You do more than offer shelter," he said.

"Yes, we do," replied Anna.

"I like what you're doing, and I'd like to help. Chloe tells me you have a fundraising event coming up," he said.

"Yes, one of our volunteers has allowed us to use her restaurant to have an open mic. She's been planning. We're very excited," Anna said.

"Yes, Chloe mentioned your marketing budget was a little tight. I'd like to contribute some money to help you spread the word. I can also help with social media. I can make a few phone calls and have a campaign put together in a few hours," he said.

Anna's eyes lit up. "I don't know what to say. Thank you."

"I also heard you had a large donor back out," he said.

"Yes," said Anna. "Our plan is to buy a new building. The facility would be larger and be able to accommodate more people. There are times when we're at capacity and have to turn people away."

"I'll be honest. I can donate to any charity, several charities. But I'm looking to partner with an organization and develop a long-term relationship. An organization that can grow and expand. Your shelter is such an organization. You have tremendous room for growth, and you help hundreds of people a day. I like what I'm seeing. I want to be a part of it." "Mr. Roberts –"

"Stanley," he interrupted.

"Stanley," she said, "I'm at a total loss for words. I've never had such a generous offer. I don't know what to say."

"Say yes, and let's get started!" he said.

"Anna, if you give me info for the fundraiser, I'll send it to the marketing team," Chloe said.

"Of course," she said.

She sifted through the papers on the desk. Then, she found a flyer with the event details. Chloe took it from her hands.

"Yes, this will do. Is it okay if we come up with a logo and spice it up a bit? It'll look better on the social media platforms."

"Sure, do whatever you'd like," Anna said.

"Great," said Chloe. "Stanley, we're due at the restaurant for lunch."

"I'm going to have my assistant call you today, Anna. We need to get things in order. For starters, I want to give a small donation today. Use it on what you need, but know that more help is coming. I want to talk about the new space you were looking to buy." He pulled out his wallet and handed Anna

$1,000.

She stared at the money. "Take it," he said.

She took the money, ran around her desk, and hugged him.

"Thank you, Stanley." She had tears in her eyes.

"It's my pleasure to help you and your wonderful organization. My assistant will be in touch today," he said while hugging her back.

Marc was waiting for them as they emerged from the shelter. He opened the passenger door and let his passengers in. Then, he hopped into the driver's seat and drove to Zoe's Soul Food Kitchen.

"Marc, have you been inside the Marigold Shelter?" Stanley asked.

Marc looked into the rearview mirror. "I actually volunteer in the kitchen and help out with some maintenance."

So you know Anna?" Stanley asked.

"Anna is great. She cares about the people. I mean, she spends her own money if something the shelter needs supplies. I've worked with her for a while," Marc said.

"So, you volunteer and drive?" Stanley asked.

"Well, I volunteer because I have some spare time and I enjoy giving back. I'm working to expand my business. You know, buy more cars, hire more drivers, that kind of thing. So when things are slow, I drive Lyft or Uber and volunteer at the shelter."

"Wow," said Stanley. "An entrepreneur and a volunteer. I'm impressed, man."

"Thanks," said Marc. He caught Chloe's reflection in the rearview mirror, and she winked at him.

He smiled and continued driving.

Chloe sent a group text to Tallulah and Zoe:

C: We're on our way -"A" game bitches

The town car pulled in front of Zoe's Soul Food Kitchen. Marc put the car in drive and jumped out of the driver's seat. Stanley had already opened the door and was climbing out of the car before Marc could get to the passenger's side of it. Stanley then held out his hand for Chloe and helped her out of the car.

He turned toward Marc and said, "Come on, man, you gotta eat, too," motioning for him to come inside.

A tall hostess greeted the trio. Chloe said, "Hi Simone, is our table ready?" "Yes, Ms. Chloe, this way," she replied.

She led them to a table toward the back of the restaurant. It was Zoe's favorite table. Close to the kitchen, but not too close.

Tallulah walked up to the table. She felt surprised to see Marc.

"Welcome. My name in Tallulah, and I'll be your server. Can I start you off with something to drink?"

Stanley spoke first. "It's customary to let the lady order first. Chloe?"

"I'll have some water and a sweet tea, please."

Tallulah nodded her head and wrote down her request. Stanley looked at Marc. "Too early for a beer?"

Marc held up his hand. "I'm driving. I'll have water, and that sweet tea sounds good."

Stanley smiled. "Well, I'm not driving, so I'll have a beer."

Tallulah smiled and said, "Great, I'll bring those right out." She then turned and walked toward the kitchen.

Stanley opened the menu. "Chloe, what do you recommend? It all sounds great."

She didn't even bother to open the menu. Zoe makes

amazing ribs, catfish, oxtails, brisket, and chicken. She also prepares collards, mac and cheese, potato salad, and more. What do you feel like, Stanley?" she said.

"I haven't had ribs in so long...ribs," he said.

Marc nodded. "They're good. The catfish be on point, too."

Tallulah returned with the waters, beer, and sweet teas. She was carrying a large tray and a small folding table. She unfolded the table with care and set the tray on top.

"Okay, for the lady, water and sweet tea. For the gentleman, water and another sweet tea. And for the other gentleman, beer, and I also brought you a water."

"Are you ready to order?" she asked.

Chloe looked at her and said, "T, you know what I want. Gentlemen?" "T?" Stanley questioned.

"Stanley, this is my best friend, Tallulah Brock. She's the writer I told you about." "It's nice to meet you, Mr. Roberts," Tallulah said.

"Tallulah, it's nice to meet you. I hear you're a very talented writer. We should talk," he said, extending his hand.

She shook his hand. "Really? That would be great."

"Great, what are you doing now?" he said.

"Well, I'm doing this, helping out Zoe. I also write for a small local paper called *Big World*, and I'm freelancing for *You & Me*," she said.

"*You & Me*?" he said. "That's the glam mag...Sylvia's thing, right?"

"Yes, but I've never met her. I work with the editor, Sharon Eckerson. Now, I know what Chloe's having. What about you gentlemen?" she said.

"Ribs, with all the works!" said Stanley.

"I'm going with the oxtails," said Marc.

"Great. I'll put this order in right away," she said, then turned to walk back to the kitchen.

"What's the name of the paper you write for? I'd like to read your stuff," Stanley said.

She spun around. "*Big World*. I have a copy. I can bring it to you."

She walked into the kitchen and immediately started jumping around. "Hell yeah!" she yelled.

"What's that about?" Zoe asked.

Tallulah continued to dance around. In a singsong voice, she said, "Stanley Roberts wants to read my stuff. He's a media mogul!" She danced around and handed Zoe their order. "He wants your ribs, with all the fixins!"

"Stop. Please stop." Zoe laughed.

After lunch, Zoe joined the group at the table. She introduced herself and sat down. Her restaurant impressed Stanley. He complimented her several times during their talk. Tallulah walked up to the table and handed Stanley an old copy of *Big World*. "Thank you," he replied. "Please, sit down, join us."

She looked around, then looked at Zoe. "As much as I'd love to sit and talk with you, I have other tables. It was a pleasure meeting you."

Stanley stood up. "It was great to meet you. We'll talk again, I'm sure," he said.

"So, Stanley," Zoe started, "what did you think about the shelter?"

"I'm impressed with Anna. I also like the way she works with the volunteers. People like you and Marc. I can definitely see the potential to reach a lot more people. I like the idea for your fundraiser. It's unique and different. I'm going to partner with Marigold," he said, looking at Chloe. She opened her mouth, but he held up his hand. "I'll make the announcement next week, in time for the fundraiser. That also gives us time to put together a social media blitz." Chloe shook her head and pulled out her note. She jotted down some notes and looked at her watch.

"Well, Stanley, this is all I had planned for today. Marc can take us back to the office, and we can put something together there," she said.

Marc stood up. "Thank you so much for lunch, Stanley."

Stanley stood and smiled. "My pleasure. I like entrepreneurs. I think you'll do well. Any referrals I can push your way, I'm happy to do so."

Marc smiled. "Thank you, that's very generous. I'll be in the car," he said.

He thanked Zoe for lunch and headed toward the main door of the restaurant. On the way, he caught sight of Tallulah. They made eye contact, and he winked at her. She smiled back, then turned her attention back to her customers.

"So, you and Chloe went to college together?" Stanley asked.

"Yes, Tallulah, too. We were roommates," she replied.

Chloe stood up and hugged Zoe. "Thank you so much for lunch. I'll call you later."

Zoe shook Stanley's hand, and they walked toward the door.

"So, what do you think about this place for the open mic?" she asked.

He looked around. "Good food, welcoming atmosphere...I like it. I'll admit, I've never been to an open mic, so it'll be a first for me," he said.

Zoe stopped at the door and watched Marc open the door for Chloe, then turned to Stanley. "I'm glad you enjoyed lunch. I look forward to seeing you soon," she said.

Stanley nodded and waved goodbye. She watched him climb into the black Town Car and drive away.

* * *

Tallulah unlocked her apartment door. She felt exhausted. As she stepped inside, the first thing she did was take off her shoes. She then closed the door behind her and went straight into her bedroom. She usually would have gone to the couch, but that was Michael's bed, and she tried to give him ample space.

She threw herself across the bed and rolled over onto her back. She closed her eyes and groaned out loud, lay there for a few moments longer, and decided to take a shower. When she finally stepped out of the shower, she could hear Michael on the phone. She couldn't make out what he was saying, but she could hear him. She dried herself off and dressed in a pair of old sweat pants and an oversized T-shirt. She then put up her hair and went out into the living room.

Michael was ending his call. "Thanks, Dave. No, it's next week. I expect to see you...okay...later."

He hung up, and she sat next to him on the couch. "Hey, how was your day?" she asked.

"I just hung up with Crazy Dave."

"Okay, and...?"

"Well, he said he spoke with Owen Katz today. Lily's old producer."

"And?" she said, sounding anxious.

"Well, Dave said the man is a talker. It took forever for him to explain who he was and why he was calling. But he said the old man has a memory like a steel trap. He told him all about his time with Lily. How he met Lily, when they recorded the album and his studio burning to the ground. To this day, he believes it was Sylvia's mother, Amanda Worthington-Blass."

Tallulah's eyes were wide, and she was sitting up. Her mouth was open a little. "He talked to him?"

"For over an hour. He recorded the call, so he's sending the record over via email. I should have it in an hour or so."

"So, Owen Katz...huh. Well, I've got some news," she said. "What a day I had. So first of all, let me say, the article for the shelter is almost done. I took your advice and told my editor."

Michael looked at her.

"For fuck's sake, Michael, you told me to tell her. I work for the lady. So anyway, I tell her. Next thing I know, she says she's coming here in two days. Wants to talk in person."

"What's that about?" he said.

She shrugged her shoulders. "I have no fucking idea. Would you hop on a plane to fire someone?"

He laughed. "No. I she could do that over the phone."

"Oh, and I met Stanley Roberts today. I gave him a copy of *BW*."

Michael looked shocked. "He asked for a copy?"

"Yes, so I had an old copy and gave it to him. He's going to partner with the shelter."

"I never thought someone like Stanley Roberts would pick up a copy of *BW*, Michael said.

"And why not? It's a good paper," she replied in a matter of fact tone.

Michael leaned back on the couch. "I've been looking at apartments. I found a few I'm going to check out next week.

Zoe offered to have me stay with her, too," he said.

Tallulah's smile stretched across her face. "And?"

He shook his head. "No, I'm going to get a place soon. It would be awkward. I like her. I don't want to live with her; not like this."

"I get it," she said.

There was a light knock at the door. They looked at one another. The knock came again. "Tallulah, are you home?"

Tallulah smiled. "Mrs. H." She stood up and walked over to the door.

Mrs. Herrera stood in front of her door, holding a large basket. "I brought some food. I was cooking today and thought you and Michael might be hungry."

Tallulah stood to the side and let her in.

Chapter 24

Sylvia sat on the cold examination table. She tugged at her gown, trying to cover her backside. She tried to get comfortable on the small table, but it was cold. She sighed and mumbled to herself.

After a few minutes, a nurse came into the room and said, "You can get dressed now Mrs.

Blass. Dr. Callan will meet you in his office."

"It's about time!" Sylvia huffed.

Sylvia walked into Dr. Callan's office. She felt frightened but told herself to put on a stern face.

Dr. Callan was the oncologist her doctor had sent her to.

"He's the best oncologist in the state," he said.

He was a tall man with white hair. His glasses sat on the edge of his nose as he looked at the file in front of him. He stood up as she walked through the door. His skin was alabaster white, and his voice was calm and soothing.

He spoke, using layman's terms to better help Sylvia understand the treatment. He continued to speak, but she didn't hear him. She could see his mouth moving, but instead of words, she heard a high-pitched noise. She would pick up words such as "aggressive," "spreading," and "pain." Then she'd hear "treatments," "hair loss," and finally "death."

She would nod her head from time to time, showing her understanding, but she didn't care anymore.

It was as if she was watching herself in the room speaking to Dr. Callan. She could see herself sitting and nodding.

"Mrs. Blass...Mrs. Blass..." Dr. Callan said.

She felt as if she'd woke up. She managed to focus her eyes on his face. "Oh, I'm sorry, what were you saying?"

"I said we can start chemo and radiation treatment immediately. The cancer is aggressive, but so is the treatment. We can start tomorrow. I can have the nurse make an appointment."

"What happens if I choose not to do the treatment?" she asked.

Dr. Callan looked at her with concern. "It's your right to choose not to do the treatment. Chemo has its pros and cons, but I recommend we start treatment."

"Will I die quicker without treatment?" she asked.

He looked up at her, paused for a moment, and said, "The cancer will run its course. It's difficult to predict how long you'd have without treatment."

Sylvia stood up, thanked him, and walked out of his office. He ran after her.

"Wait, we need to schedule the appointment!"

She continued walking down the hall to the elevator. She didn't turn around or look back.

When Sylvia arrived home, she felt exhausted. The new maid, Tina, greeted her.

She'd fired Shannon over the dispute with the cook.

"Welcome home, Mrs. Blass," Tina said as she stepped into the large white marble foyer. She handed her Tina her coat. "Hot tea, please, Tina," she said with a serious expression. "I'll be upstairs."

She tossed her purse on the bed and sat down. She buried her hands in her face and began sobbing. The tears rolled down her face, and she wiped them away, then went into the bathroom. She stared at her reflection, turned on the water, and splashed it over her face. She then grabbed a small hand towel and pressed it softly against her face.

Tina entered the room with her tea and set it down on a small table. Sylvia walked out of the bathroom.

"Thank you, Tina. Any calls or messages?"

"No, Mrs. Blass."

"You may go home, Tina. I will not need you tonight."

Tina nodded her head and left the room. Sylvia poured her tea and sat on the edge of the bed. She was alone. She felt alone. She set the teacup down and walked downstairs. She wandered through the house, going from room to room. She moved her hand across a large picture of her mother and father. They were standing in front of a large chapel. Her mother wore a long white wedding dress. The dress flowed behind her like a wave of clouds. She held a large bouquet of large red roses. Her father stood tall and regal next to his wife. He wore a black tuxedo with a red rose.

She picked up the picture and moved her hand over the silver picture frame. She put down the picture and continued to wander through the house. She made her way to her study. It was her favorite room. She admired the various pictures she'd purchased over the years.

The doorbell rang.

"Tina!" she shouted, forgetting she'd told her to go home.

She shouted for Tina again, then got up and walked to the door. She felt surprised to see Sharon standing in front of her.

"Sharon," she said. "What are you doing here?"

Sharon cleared her throat. She held a black folder in her hands.

"I have information from the private investigator I hired. I thought we should talk here, not at the office. Can I come in?"

"Yes, come in." She gestured for Sharon to come in and closed the door behind her. "Let's go into the study." Sharon nodded and followed her. "There's no one here but us," Sylvia said. "You live in this huge house all by yourself?" Sharon asked.

Sylvia nodded her head and sat down. "So, what do you have for me?" she said.

Sharon handed her the folder and sat down. "It's all in here," she replied.

She watched Sylvia go through the pages in the folder. Sylvia took her time to read each page. After she finished a page, she would lay it down on the table. She worked for a while. Finally, she reached the last page. She placed all the papers in the folder with great care. She laid the folder on the table.

"Thank you, Sharon. I appreciate you doing this for me. I know I haven't been the easiest person to work for. I know this."

Sharon cleared her throat. "Well, there's more that isn't in the folder."

"Oh?" Sylvia said. "And what would that be?"

"I know where Lily is living. It's a long story, and I'm going there the day after tomorrow. I don't have a lot of information. "It's a strong hunch, perhaps a coincidence," said Sharon.

"I see. So, you're telling me you're playing a hunch and leaving in two days?"

Sharon nodded. "I wanted you to know I was leaving."

Sylvia sat for a moment, then said, "And if you find out this person is Lily?"

"I'll call you and let you decide what you want to do, Sylvia. I said I would help," Sharon said.

Sylvia nodded, then placed her hand on Sharon's hand and looked down. "I saw the oncologist today. I debating on whether I'll do the chemo/radiation treatments. I'm supposed to start tomorrow. I'm scared, Sharon. I realized today I have no friends. I have no one to help me. I'm alone." Sylvia felt her bottom lip quiver. Her eyes filled with tears that rolled down her face.

Sharon felt sorry for Sylvia. She looked around the room and spotted a box of Kleenex, then got up and gave the box to Sylvia. She watched her wipe her tears and face.

"Sylvia, why would you not do the treatments?"

"Over the years, I've hurt many people. When you confront your death, you start to see things in a different light. I always thought I'd have people around me, taking care of me. But look around, Sharon, I'm here alone. No friends, no family, no one. People are here because I pay them to be here. I went and saw my lawyer about this trust business. My personal attorney is out, so I met his associate. She was a Black woman."

"Okay, what was wrong with that?"

"Nothing," she replied. "Nothing but my attitude. I told her that her kind of people are loud and lazy. I don't know why I said it. But she didn't let me get by with anything. She was direct and professional. I felt ashamed. I don't like what I see when I look in the mirror. I used to think I had it all, but I realize now that I don't. I've alienated people by treating them poorly due to their appearance or manner of speaking. I never realized how much hate I've carried inside. And now, when facing the end of my life, I can't even tell you why. My mother died with so much hate and anger. I don't want to do the same." She bowed her head, and tears flowed down her cheeks.

Sharon sat a moment, listening to her words. "It's never too late to make changes in your life, Sylvia."

"If this woman, Lily, is my half-sister, I'd like to meet her."

Sharon nodded her head and stood up. "I'd better get going. My husband is waiting for me."

Sylvia looked up at her. "Yes, your husband. Sharon, I don't know that much about you in all the years we've worked together."

"You never ask," Sharon said, then walked toward the study door. "I'll call you when I get some more information. Have a good night, Sylvia."

She walked out of the room and to the front door. Sylvia watched her leave. She wanted her to stay. She wished she had someone to talk to. A friend. She realized at that moment she needed to make changes before it was too late.

Stanley walked into his office, threw down his backpack on a large sofa, and sat down. He then pulled out his cell phone and dialed.

"Charlie, Stanley. Hey man, how's it going? Great. Well, I want to put together a partnership with a homeless shelter. Yes, I need the team working on this. You bet. I'm here all day. Catch up with me on my cell. Right. Later."

He hung up the phone and walked over to his desk. He wasn't in his office often. His assistant had opened stacks of mail, and he had several messages and a full cup of cold coffee. He picked up the cup and looked inside, frowned, and put it down. He was going through the messages on his desk when his assistant Tonya walked in.

"Stanley, so nice of you to come in today. I thought you'd be out saving the world," she joked.

"Well, I am kinda like a superhero," he said.

"I picked up the copies of *Big World* you asked for. They're under that stack of mail. Chloe called to say they've started the social media campaign for your fundraiser." He stopped her. "It's not my event, Tonya. I'm just helping," he said.

She looked at him. "Right," she said. "Your father called several times, and so has your mother."

He sighed. "My parents. You'd think they'd call me on my cell," he said. "They do, but you don't answer," she said. "Do you need anything else?" He thought for a moment. "What's your favorite flower, Tonya?"

"Well, I like sunflowers, but if you're trying to impress a lady, then roses are always a good choice."

"Roses, of course. Please send two – no, three dozen white and yellow roses to Chloe's office." Tonya raised an eyebrow. "What should the card read?"

"Thank you for everything. Looking forward to having you as my guest at the open mic.'" He leaned back into his chair and smiled.

She frowned. "That doesn't sound very romantic."

"She doesn't date clients."

"Smart girl," she commented, then left the office.

Stanley moved the pile of mail until he reached the copies of *Big World*. He then opened the paper and started to read.

Chapter 25

Sharon picked up her rental car and drove straight to her hotel. She didn't sleep well the night before, and she hadn't felt like herself over the past couple of weeks. She unlocked the door to her hotel room and went inside. She immediately took off her shoes, sat down on the bed, waited for a moment, then pulled out her cell phone.

"I don't even know why I'm here. This goes way beyond my job description," she said into the phone.

"I know," Keith said. "But you said you were done after this.""

"I am done. This is crazy. Who does this for their boss? A boss who doesn't even give a shit about anyone but themselves?"

Keith laughed. "Well, it's obvious you do."

"Ha ha," she replied. "Okay," she said, "I should only be a few days."

"Hey, what if this homeless woman is Sylvia's half-sister? Then what?" he asked.

"I have no idea," she said, sighing. "She says she wants to meet her. My thing isn't the sister; it's the money. This woman took money out of the mouths of homeless people. I work for a heartless bitch."

He chuckled. "Well, not for long. I'll call you tomorrow. I have surgeries scheduled for the morning," he said.

"I love you," she said.

"I love you, too," Keith replied, then hung up the phone.

* * *

On the other side of town, Lily walked into the Marigold Shelter. For the first time in years, she felt clear and sober. She was clear as if a fog had lifted. She'd spent several days in the motel. She was sick, but she knew it was the detox; she'd been through it before. After a few days, she felt better. Finally, she left the motel and checked into a day treatment program. She was getting sober.

She called the hospital that treated her after the liquor store incident. She knew that Anna might be responsible, and she didn't want that to happen. She made arrangements to pay the bill in full.

She spotted Anna hanging a poster and walked over to her.

"Anna," she said.

Anna turned around and could hardly believe what she was seeing. Lily's hair was combed and put up in a bun. Her face was clean, and her eyes were gentle and warm.

Anna smiled. "Lily?"

Lily nodded her head. "I wanted to come by and find out how to sign up for the open mic."

Anna's eyes widened. "That's wonderful! I have a signup sheet in my office. I'm so glad you decided to sing, Lily. I just need to finish hanging this poster, then we can sign you up."

After she finished hanging the poster, they walked into her

office. She sat behind her desk and gestured for Lily to sit down.

"Lily, you look wonderful. Where have you been?"

Lily shifted in her chair. "I...I...decided to stop drinking. I got into a program. It's time to stop running."

"I'm so happy for you. You look so good. Is there anything I can do to help?" Anna asked. Lily shook her head no, then said, "No. I'm okay. I'd like to sign up."

Anna passed her the signup sheet and a pen, then watched as Lily wrote her name on the sheet. When she was done, she handed the sheet back to Anna, who glanced at it and smiled.

"What will you be singing?" she asked.

Lily shrugged her shoulders. "I don't know," she replied.

"Oh, before I forget: I need your help with some information for your hospital bill. I'd been meaning to speak with you, but you hadn't been around," Anna said. She reached for a file as Lily stood up.

"She said, 'I have paid the bill.'"

Anna stopped searching for the file and looked up at Lily. "What?" she said.

"The hospital bill. Someone has paid it."

"But how can that be? It was almost $5,000."

Lily didn't speak; she turned and left the office. Anna called out for her, but she didn't reply or come back.

Anna jumped up and ran out of the office after Lily, who was walking out of the door to the shelter. Anna called her name again and watched the door close. She turned around and walked back to her office. There, she took the medical form file on Lily and put it in the drawer. That's when she heard her name and looked up to see Lily standing in the doorway. "Anna, I'm sorry. I told myself I was going to stop running away."

Anna smiled. "Thank you, Lily. Sit down."

Lily sat in one of the chairs in front of Anna's desk and rubbed her hands together. She kept her eyes down, looking at the floor.

"It's okay, Lily," Anna said.

Lily looked up at her and said, "I paid the hospital bill. I didn't forget. I want to get my life back together. Stop running. I've been running for so long." A tear rolled down her cheek.

"How did you pay for it?" Anna asked.

Lily wiped the tear from her cheek and shifted in her chair. "I...I...I had some money. It was my brother's money. He left it to me when he passed. I put it in the bank and left it there. I never wanted the money." She stopped and took a deep breath. "The girl, Tallulah. She played my record for me. She actually found my record. It brought back so many memories. It woke up something in me. Something that's been asleep. Something I pushed down deep. I want to do good. I owe them."

Anna listened to her, then nodded her head and said, "Lily, that's wonderful. Can I help you in any way?"

Lily thought a moment. "The girl, Tallulah. Can you help me reach her?"

Anna nodded and pulled out her cell phone. "I have her number. I don't think she'd mind if I gave it to you." Anna wrote down the number for Lily and handed her a small piece of paper. "She works at Zoe's Soul Food Kitchen. The open mic is going to be held there."

"Thank you, Anna."

Anna stood up, walked around the desk, and hugged Lily. "You're welcome, Lily." She released her and watched her walk out of her office.

Tallulah sat in the small coffee shop, her hands trembling slightly as she drank her coffee. She was meeting Sharon in a few moments. She'd gone over every scenario in her head.

Why's Sharon coming to meet with me?

She sighed and took another sip of her coffee, and that's when she noticed Sharon walking through the door.

Tallulah waved at her, and she walked over, sat down, and smiled at Tallulah. "Hi. I hope I'm not late."

Tallulah smiled back and replied, "No, I was a little early. Do you want some coffee or something?"

Sharon shook her head no. "I've been up for a while. I've had my limit of coffee for one day."

An awkward moment of silence passed between them, then Sharon said, "I know you're wondering why I'm here. I'm just going to lay it out for you." She pulled out a large file folder and set it on the table. "Okay, what I'm about to share with you is confidential. It's a long story, so bear with me. As you know, Sylvia Blass owns *You & Me*. You know the history, right?"

Tallulah nodded her head. "So, Sylvia came to me a few weeks ago and told me a very troubling story. She's searching for her half-sister. Same father. She asked me to hire a PI to help her find this woman. Her name is Lily Duke or Lily Blass. I think the woman you're writing about is the same woman. Tallulah, Sylvia is dying. She has cancer. No one knows. This is why she wants to find her sister."

Tallulah sighed. "I know Lily is her half-sister. My editor also hired a PI, and he found out for us. Even produced two birth certificates, one with Blass, and the other with Duke. Lily told me the story. I was trying to figure out a way to tell you before I moved forward with my article."

Sharon opened the file folder. "This is a picture of Lily when she was younger." She handed the picture to Tallulah, who nodded.

"Yes, this is her. Lily's been homeless for a while. After learning about her father, Amanda Worthington-Blass decided to use her money and power to end her singing career. She checked out after she lost her brother, Clyde. He died in an automobile accident. She said Amanda was furious when she found out about Lily and them. All this time, she knew Sylva was her sister."

"So, do you know where Lily is now?" Sharon asked.

Tallulah shook her head. "I don't. I saw her a few weeks ago. She had a promising career as a singer. Before Amanda could stop her, she recorded an album. I found it, went to the shelter, and played it for her. I haven't seen her since."

"Okay," said Sharon. "I need to find her."

"What's Sylvia going to do?" Tallulah asked.

"I have no idea," Sharon said.

"Are you going to fire me?" Tallulah asked.

Sharon chuckled. "Of course not. I'd like for you to wait before you publish your article."

"I thought you'd say that. I can take you to the shelter. We may be able to find Lily."

"I'm only here for a few days. I leave the day after tomorrow."

"Okay, we can get going now."

They left the coffee shop and started out for the shelter.

* * *

Zoe opened the oven with caution and inspected her five sweet potato pies. She then smiled and closed the oven.

"Pies almost done, Robert," she said. He looked at her and nodded. "I'll be in my office. If you need me, come get me."

Zoe walked into her office and sat at her desk. She was going over inventory when Simone, the hostess, appeared at her door.

"Zoe, sorry to bother you. There's a woman looking for you." Zoe looked up. "Who is it?" she asked.

Simone shrugged her shoulders. "I don't know. Do you want me to send her back?"

"No, I'll come out."

As she walked to the front of the restaurant, she spotted a woman waiting by the front door. She didn't recognize her. The woman had her back slightly turned toward her, so it was hard for Zoe to make out her face.

She walked up to her and said, "Hello. I'm Zoe. May I help you?"

The woman turned around. "Hi, Zoe," Lily said.

Zoe was amazed to see how much Lily had changed. How good she looked.

"Lily?" Zoe said. "Lily, is that you?"

She smiled and nodded her head.

"Hi, Zoe. I...I...I'm looking for Tallulah. She's your friend, right? Anna said she works here."

Zoe's mouth was ajar. She was trying to process what she was seeing in front of her. "Lily...I'm so surprised to see you. Ah...come into my office."

Lily walked behind Zoe. They went through the restaurant, into the kitchen, and then into Zoe's office. There, Zoe signaled for Lily to take a seat. She watched Lily as she looked around the office.

"You own this place?"

Zoe nodded her head. "Yes, I do."

She smiled and turned towards Zoe. "I know you're surprised to see me. I...I...well, I'd like to find your friend Tallulah. I want to speak with her. She played my record for me."

"I know. Lily, you have a beautiful voice. Tallulah will be here for dinner, or we can call her."

Lily pulled out the small piece of paper Anna gave her. "I have this," she said as she handed the paper to Zoe.

"Yes, this is her number. Do you want to call her now?" she asked.

"I want to thank her for finding my record. I'm getting sober. I got into a program. I've been off the street for a little while. The music woke me up. I need to stop running. I see you and the others at the shelter, helping us, and I just want to...do better. I gave up. But hearing my voice on my record...I'm not crazy."

Zoe sat for a moment, not saying anything.

Lily then said, "Thank you."

Zoe smiled. "What are you thanking me for?"

Lily smiled at her and said, "For being a kind face on a hard day."

Zoe's laughter was gentle. "Stop. You're gonna make me cry."

"Can we call your friend?"

"Of course," Zoe said and pulled out her cell phone.

Chapter 26

Sharon turned down the radio as she drove down the busy street. "Thanks for trying," she said. "I wish Anna would have been there. Maybe she's seen her," Tallulah said. "I don't know where she would go." She felt her cell phone vibrate, pulled it out of her purse, and clicked on.

"Hey, Zoe," she said. "I'm with Sharon Eckerson. Do you think I can call you back?"

"Ah...well, I have Lily in my office, and she wants to speak with you.

"Lily's there?" Tallulah said.

"Yep. She's looking for you," Zoe said.

"Okay. Tell her I'm on my way. I should be about 20 minutes."

"Okay," said Zoe, then she clicked off the phone and looked at Sharon. "I know where Lily is. Make a U-turn at the next light."

Twenty minutes later, Sharon parked in front of Zoe's Soul Food Kitchen. She put the car in park and looked at Tallulah.

"Can we sit a moment? I'm not feeling well," she said.

"Sure. Are you okay?" Tallulah asked.

"I'm good. Maybe too much coffee this morning," she said.

They sat for a few moments. A wave of nausea passed over Sharon. She thought she was going to vomit, but the feeling passed in an instant.

She took a few deep breaths and said, "Okay, I'm feeling better now. Let's go inside."

They entered the restaurant. Patrons were talking, smiling, and eating. The aroma of home-cooked soul food floated through the air. Sharon's stomach growled, and she stood next to Tallulah.

Tallulah looked around the dining room and said, "Let's go to Zoe's office." She motioned for Sharon to follow her.

"It smells wonderful in here," Sharon said.

"Zoe is quite the chef."

She led Sharon through the kitchen and into Zoe's office. She stopped short of walking through the door and stared at the woman sitting in one of the chairs in front of Zoe's desk. Her mouth was ajar, and she gasped with a sharp intake of breath.

"Lily?" she said.

Lily turned towards her and stood up. She nodded her head with a gentle motion and smiled.

"I can't believe it. You look...good," Tallulah said.

She walked over to her and gave her a hug. Sharon stood in the doorway, watching the exchange. She glanced at the woman sitting behind the desk and noticed she was smiling.

Tallulah released Lily and said, "What are you doing here?"

She turned her glance towards Zoe, who was staring at the two of them, smiling.

"Why don't you sit down, T, and let Lily explain," Zoe said in her most reassuring voice.

"I brought someone with me. Someone who wants to meet

you." Tallulah turned toward Sharon. "Lily, this is Sharon Eckerson. Sharon, this is Lily Duke."

Sharon crossed the doorway threshold and extended her hand. "It's nice to meet you, Lily." Lily looked at her hand and then shook it.

Zoe stood up. "I'll go grab another chair. Sharon, please take my seat."

She walked past Lily and Tallulah and left the office. Sharon sat in Zoe's chair. Lily and Tallulah sat as well.

"I...I...wanted to find you to thank you. Ever since you played my record, my brain has been all over the place. It woke up something in me. I'm in a program and have been staying at a small motel. I bought some clothes, too."

"That's great, Lily. Sharon has been looking for you. She works for Sylvia Blass. She sent her here to find you," said Tallulah.

Lily looked at Sharon, and a wave of fear rushed over her. Her first instinct was to run, but she didn't.

Instead, she said, "What do you want?"

Sharon cleared her throat. "It's a long story, Lily, so I'll start from the beginning."

Sharon, Lily, and Tallulah talked in Zoe's office for over an hour. Zoe would come in from time to time but never interrupted them. Sharon told Lily about Sylvia and how she'd asked her to find her. She handed Lily the file from the private investigator. Lily flipped through each page. Then, she set it down on Zoe's desk and sighed.

"Sharon, you don't know me, and I don't know you, but we have something in common: Sylvia. I've been running from the Blass name since the day I turned 18. I knew about Sylvia. I wanted to approach her after the death of her mother, but

I was dealing with my own demons. I also knew she would never accept me."

"Sylvia wants to meet you, Lily," Sharon said.

"Why?" she asked.

Sharon shook her head. "I don't know. I think she's trying to right her wrongs before it's too late."

"Right her wrongs?" Lily said, sounding surprised.

"I know this is a lot to take in, Lily. I'm here because I told Sylvia I would help her. I've worked for Sylvia as Editor-in-Chief for *You & Me* magazine. I think I'm the only person she could turn to. I have no idea what she wants from you. It's all quite strange. I hired Tallulah to freelance for the magazine. We'd never met before that. She told me about the story she's doing on you and the shelter. We put two and two together, and it led me to you."

Lily glanced at Tallulah, who sat in silence, listening. Lily thought her face was kind, and she reminded her of herself when she was younger.

"Sharon, I've been running from my past for a very long time. A place where Amanda Worthington-Blass couldn't find me. A place where I could drown myself. I don't know if I'm ready to meet Sylvia or what she wants from me. You see, I'm still bitter because of what her mother did to me. I'm not saying Sylvia can make it better or even make it up to me. A lot of things I did or didn't do were my choice, and I accept that. But meeting her..." Lily's voice trailed off. She had tears in her eyes.

Sharon looked at Tallulah, then at Lily. She then took a deep breath and said, "Lily, I'm not here to cause you any trouble. I'm here as a messenger. I'm not here to force you into doing anything. I'm also not here as an editor or reporter. I'll do

284

whatever you like, but she does want to meet you."

Lily looked at Tallulah. "Do you still have my record?" Tallulah nodded her head. "I'd like to hear it again," Lily said. She then looked at Sharon. "You can tell Sylvia you met me, but that's as far as I'll go. I don't want to meet her."

Sharon nodded her head. "Okay, Lily. I understand. I do have one question for you."

"Okay," Lily said.

"A donor was set to donate a large amount of money to a shelter." Someone had held the money in a trust for years. Is it yours?" Sharon asked.

Lily's facial expression shifted in an instant. She squinted her eyes together and licked her lips. She looked at them, then the floor.

"When I turned eighteen, me and Clyde received an inheritance from Cliff Blass. Clyde took his money, moved out, bought a hot rod, and forgot about writing. You'd think he had all the money in the world. I didn't want anything to do with the money. I contacted a lawyer, and he helped me put the money in a trust. When Clyde passed away, I got what was left of his money. I didn't want it, so I put it in a bank. The money in the trust is gone. Someone took it. I found out a little while ago. I decided to give the money to the shelter, but someone took it."

Sharon sighed. "Thank you, Lily."

Tallulah looked surprised. "Lily, you donated your inheritance to the shelter?"

Lily nodded her head yes.

Tallulah looked at Sharon, then at Lily. "So, what happened to the money?"

Lily didn't answer. She looked at Sharon, who shifted in

her chair. She knew what happened to the money but felt this wasn't the time to divulge that information.

She sat for a moment longer, then said, "The private investigator I hired found your old producer, Owen Katz."

Lily's demeanor perked up. "You mean Owen is alive?"

Sharon nodded her head, "Yes, he's living in a nursing home in Georgia. I can give you the information. I didn't reach out to him because I found you."

Lily smiled. "Owen is alive."

Sharon took a page out of the folder and handed it to Lily. "This is his address and contact number. I didn't call him," Sharon said.

Lily took the paper. She stared at the name and number, then smiled. "Owen was my friend. He was like the father I never had. He was kind to me and my family. He lost everything. I used to write to him but stopped after a while." She folded the paper and put it in her pocket, then took a deep breath. "Tallulah, can you play my record again?"

"I don't have it with me. You can come to my apartment, and I can play it for you," she said. Lily smiled. "I would like that." She turned towards Sharon. "Tell Sylvia I don't want to meet her. I'm trying to get my life back. I want to sing again, even if it's just for a little while."

Sharon nodded. "I understand. I'll tell Sylvia. I do wish you well, Lily. I've heard you have a beautiful voice."

Tallulah grabbed a piece of paper on Zoe's desk, then wrote down her address and handed the paper to Lily. "This is my address. If you want to come by tomorrow evening, I'll be home. I'm working here tonight."

"Thank you," Lily replied. She stood up. "I'll see you tomorrow, Tallulah. Goodbye, Sharon." They watched her walk out of the office, then out of sight.

"You work here, too, Tallulah?" Sharon ask.

Tallulah nodded. "Yeah, I usually work the dinner shift, sometimes lunch, too. The tips are good."

Sharon smiled. "You remind me of myself when I was starting out. My writing career was off to a slow start. I didn't wait tables; I worked at a bakery and was a dog bather."

"Zoe is good to me. Between this, *Big World*, and freelancing, I do okay."

Sharon smiled. "Well, this has been an interesting day. I never thought I'd be doing this." She grabbed the folder from Zoe's desk. After a moment, she said, "I think you should write your article with the whole story." Your story is about Lily. I want to run it in *You & Me*. I want it to be the cover story. A real story."

Tallulah was speechless.

"I'll talk to Sylvia. It won't be a scandal like her mother. Lily doesn't want anything but her life back. It's a good story, and it'll break. Why not do an exclusive?"

"You want to run my story in *You & Me*?"

"Yes, and I want it to be the cover," Sharon said.

"The cover?" Tallulah gasped.

Chapter 27

Lily sat on the bed in the small hotel room. She was looking at the paper Sharon had given her. She picked up the phone and dialed the number. The phone trilled into her ear. She was nervous. She licked her lips and waited with nervous anticipation for someone to answer.

After the 4th ring, a voice came over the phone. "Praises of Hope. May I help you?" Lily stammered. "I...I'd like to speak with Owen Katz, please." "I can ring his room," the voice said

There was a series of clicks, then the phone was silent. She waited, her body rocking back and forth.

"Hello?" Owen's voice came on the line. "Who the hell is this?" he barked.

Lily smiled. "Owen? Owen Katz?"

"Yes, it's me. Who the hell is this?"

Lily hung up the phone.

* * *

Sharon walked into Sylvia's office and closed the door behind her. Sylvia was sitting on the large, overstuffed sofa. Sharon sat next to her, holding a file in her hand. She handed her the file.

Sylvia looked at her and said, "You found her?"

She nodded. "I met with her and spoke to her. I asked her if she wanted to meet you. I'm sorry, Sylvia, she doesn't."

Sylvia looked at her with a sorrowful expression. "What do you mean?"

"She doesn't want to meet you, Sylvia. From what I can tell, Lily's life hasn't been all that easy. She lost her career, her brother, her mother, and her mentor. She checked out. She's been living on the street for a while."

"Why doesn't she want to meet me?" Sylvia asked.

"I don't know, Sylvia. I don't think she's ready," Sharon said.

Sylvia frowned and put down the file.

"She knows about the missing money," said Sharon.

Sylvia had a look of worry on her face. Sharon continued.

"She knows the money is gone, but she doesn't know who took it."

Sylvia sighed. "I'm working on giving it back. I don't even know why I took it."

Sharon cleared her throat. "Sylvia, there's something I wanted to speak with you about. I found Lily through one of my freelance writers. She's doing a story on the shelter. In doing her story, she found Lily. She knows about her being your sister. She's running the story in a small local paper. We should run the story in *You & Me*."

Sylvia shot Sharon a cold look. Sharon held up her hands.

"Now, I know what you're thinking, Sylvia, but the story is coming out regardless. It's a small paper, but someone else could pick it up. Why not make it positive? Okay, she may not want to meet you, but you can reach out to her by doing a wonderful story. Maybe the coverage would help her reboot her career. Maybe this can be a way to give back what your mother took."

Sylvia's mouth was agape, but she didn't speak. Her face softened, and she closed her eyes and slumped back into the overstuffed couch.

She took a few deep breaths. Then she said, "I've never given you full control over editing, have I? I've always done things my way, even if it wasn't the best. My life has been a cliché. A rich girl, white and spoiled, becomes a privileged, judgmental woman."

She opened her eyes. Sharon was staring at her, not saying a word. She continued. "Oh, for fuck's sake, don't look at me like that. Do your story. Do your job and edit the magazine to your liking. I'm too tired to fight you, and frankly, I'd rather spend my time doing something else. I haven't started treatments, and I'm not going to. I'll lose my hair. I'll be goddamned if I let myself die bald.'"

"But if it could save your life..." Sharon said.

Sylvia turned her head toward Sharon. "I'm surprised you care. It wouldn't save my life; only prolong it. I've got just enough time to finish my business. I've been nothing short of awful to you, and yet here you are."

Sharon half-smiled. "Yes, here I am. Thank you for letting me run the story. I'd like to have a photographer take pictures of Lily. I'd like to speak with her producer, Owen Katz. He's still living. I'd also like to include you as well."

She thought Sylvia might react to her request, but she didn't. She shook her head yes and said, "Do whatever you need. I'll make myself available to you when you're ready."

"What about the money, Sylvia?"

"I plan on using my own money to give to the shelter, and I'm working on re-establishing the trust. If such a thing is possible. I'm going to donate the money in Lily's name. I've already put things in motion, Sharon," she replied.

"Thank you, Sylvia," she said. She stood up and walked toward the door.

"You're welcome, Sharon."

Sharon smiled. Sylvia had never thanked her for anything.

Maybe there's hope for her, she thought to herself and headed toward her office.

Chapter 28

Lily stepped off the Greyhound bus and stretched. The ride was long, and she was happy to finally get off and walk around. She waited as they unloaded the bags and found her small brown suitcase. She walked into the small bus depot and found a man sitting at the ticket counter. She approached him and spoke.

"Excuse me, I'm looking for Praises of Hope nursing home."

The man was reading a paper. His eyes moved until they met hers.

He folded his paper and said, "Praises of Hope? Don't you have a cell phone or GPS or something?"

Lily didn't have a cell phone. She didn't have anyone to call. She shook her head no.

The man smiled and said, "Well, I got maps for sale. Ain't sold a map in years, but I got 'em."

He grabbed a map and opened it. "Now see here, we're here, and the home is...well, down here." He pointed at both locations. "You could take a bus or cab. Hell, you could even walk if your feet are up to it," he said.

She smiled and watched the man point with his finger. "No, I think I'll take a cab. Can you show me where I can find a motel?"

She took a cab to an old, rundown motel at the edge of town, where she rented a small room for 3 nights. When she entered the room, the first thing she noticed was the smell. The room smelled musty as if no one had stayed in it for years. She set down her suitcase and opened the large window facing the parking lot. As she stared out the window, she thought about Owen and how kind he'd been to her. Her thoughts wandered to the day they finished recording her record. Owen had purchased a cheap bottle of champagne and wanted to celebrate.

"We did it!" Owen exclaimed. "You're gonna be a star, Lily. We've both put our blood, sweat, and tears into this record. Now it's time to celebrate!" He picked up the bottle and poured some champagne into a small plastic cup.

"Now don't you go tellin' anyone I gave you champagne. It's our little secret," he said, winking at her. "We're on our way!"

Lily smiled and walked away from the window. She decided to go see Owen in the morning. She didn't know what would happen, but she knew she had to see him.

The sound of a large crash awakened her. She felt disoriented and for a moment didn't remember where she was. She then looked around the room and began to focus her eyes.

She heard the loud noise again and went to the large window. A dump truck was emptying a large trash dumpster. She paused to watch, then closed the curtain. After that, she went to the bathroom and splashed cold water on her face. As she gazed at her reflection in the mirror, she wondered if Owen would recognize her. It had been so many years.

Lily showered and dressed, then called the cab company and waited for her ride. After what seemed like an eternity, she saw the cab pull into the motel parking lot. She grabbed her large purse, walked outside to the cab, and got inside.

When she arrived, the lady at the front desk gave her directions to Owen's room. He was lying in bed. Eyes closed. She tapped lightly on the door.

"Go away! Let an old man be!" he yelled, not opening his eyes. "I told you I don't feel well. Leave me alone."

She walked over to the bed. "Owen," she said in a gentle tone.

He fluttered his eyes open to see Lily standing over him. He opened his mouth to speak, but no words came out.

"Owen, it's me. It's Lily." She grabbed his hand and squeezed it with gentle pressure.

"Lily?" he whispered.

She nodded. "It's me."

They both had tears in their eyes. She leaned down and hugged him. He hugged her back. She released him and wiped the tears from her eyes.

"Lily, where have you been?" he asked, sitting up in bed. "You stopped writing and calling."

She grabbed a chair and sat it next to the bed.

"I'm so sorry, Owen. I couldn't do it anymore. I felt so lost and alone. It was hard out there alone. I walked away one day. I didn't want the money. I never did. I took what Clyde had left and put it in a safety deposit box. I took my money and held it in a trust. Things were okay for a while. I had an apartment and a job. That's when I was writing to you."

She wiped more tears from her eyes. He smiled at her and reached for her hand.

"I started drinking to numb the pain. It took hold of me. I started not to care. Thought maybe Amanda was right. Maybe I wasn't good enough. So, one day I left my apartment and never came back. I'm so sorry, Owen."

"It's okay. You're here now," he said. He let go of her hand, then swung his legs over the side of the bed and placed his feet on the floor with deliberate care. He reached for the wheelchair sitting next to the bed, swung himself over, and landed in the chair. "I've gotten pretty good at gettin' around." He was now sitting in front of her.

"I tried to call once," Lily said, "but the number was out of service."

He frowned. "My no-good daughter put me in a home years ago. Once I lost the use of my legs, she had no need for me. We never got along anyway. One day she told me she was done, and she put me in a home. Not this home. I've been kicked out of 6 so far. This one is okay. The doc is a nice old bird."

"Six nursing homes?" Lily said.

He smiled. "Yes, six. I guess I'm a crotchety old man with a foul mouth who doesn't want anyone to bother me." He wheeled his chair over to the small dresser and opened the bottom drawer. He pulled out the photo album and wheeled back over to Lily.

"I've kept this all these years. I look at this every day."

He handed the album to her. She set it on her lap and opened it. She smiled as she looked through the old photos, sometimes looking up at him to see him smiling. She came to the picture of her sitting on a black baby grand piano. She had a white lily in her hair. He beamed with joy. "Remember when we took this?" He said with excitement.

She shook her head yes. "We'd finished recording Grandma'," she said.

"Yes. I knew it was going to be a hit," he said. "But then all that bullshit with fucking Amanda Worthington-Blass. She

295

had no right, Lily. No right. You didn't ask to be his daughter. She was an evil, vengeful bitch, and I'm glad she's dead."

She looked at Owen and frowned. "Owen, don't say that. She died a horrible death."

"She got what she deserved," he said in a tone devoid of emotion. "She could have used her money for something good. Instead, she used it to hurt people. She hurt you, me, Clyde, and your mom." He saw a tear fall from her eye.

"I'm sorry, Songbird. It's just that you're something special, and I tried to make things right. I did."

"I know, Owen," she said. "But that's all past. I've been staying at a shelter on and off. The people are nice. They were always trying to help me. Make sure I had food, warm clothes, or a place to sleep. I donated my trust to the shelter. All of it."

Owen's eyes widened. "All of it?"

"Yes," she said, nodding. "I thought the money would be better spent helping others. I set it up so that the donation would occur, but it didn't happen. Someone took the money."

"What are you talking about, took it?" he said. "You can't take a trust."

"I know, " she said staring at him.

"Unless you have the money and the means," he growled. "If it wasn't Amanda, then it was her bitchy daughter, Sally, or whatever the fuck her name was," he snarled.

"Sylvia," she replied.

"Yeah, Sylvia. She was a piece of work. That bitch sold out her own mother. She was a racist piece of shit."

"Same ol' Owen," Lily said, smiling.

He smiled back.

"So anyway, I got into a program. Went and took some of Clyde's money out of the bank and got a small room. It's so funny how things work, Owen. This girl, a reporter, was doing a story on the shelter. She heard me sing. I told her about the record, and she found it. She played it for me. She actually found it."

He smiled. "She played it for you?"

"Yes. It was wonderful, Owen. I just got swept up in it. It made me want to get clean. Sing again. The shelter is having a fundraiser in a few weeks. I'm going to sing, Owen," Lily said, sounding excited.

"Finally!" he shouted. "You should have been singing all along, you nitwit!" He chuckled.

"It's only a fundraiser, but I'm going to do it," she said.

"I'm happy for you, Songbird. You deserve happiness. I love you," he said. "I wish I could be there to hear you."

She smiled. "Me, too." She paused a moment. "There's something else."

"What?" he asked.

"Well, the girl, the one who's writing the story. Her name is Tallulah. Anyway, she's a part-time writer for a magazine. *You & Me.* Sylvia owns the magazine. Anyway, she introduced me to another lady, Sharon, who works for Sylvia. She said Sylvia hired a private investigator to find me. She said she wants to meet me. She's dying, Owen. She has cancer."

"Cancer?" he echoed.

"I said I didn't want to meet her. I don't think I want to," she said.

"That understandable. So, she knows you're her sister?" he asked.

"I don't know. Maybe. I told Tallulah the whole story. How we made the record and I was singing in small nightclubs. I told her about how you put every dime into that record. I told

297

her about Amanda and Sylvia. The lawyer and the inheritance. Clyde. I told her everything," she said.

"And why shouldn't you?!" he exclaimed. "I mean, hell, why not tell your story? Why not be who you are? You shouldn't have to hide in the shadows or feel ashamed. I'm glad you finally came to your senses. I told you a long time ago, you were special"

"I know, I know," she said softly. "I wanted you to know. I'll have an address, too. Maybe you can come and visit me. Once I get on my feet, maybe live with me. I don't want to leave you here, Owen."

He smiled. "If I died today, I'd die a happy man. Knowing you're going to sing again. That you're getting your life together. You've still got time to make a good life, Lily."

Chapter 29

Tallulah sat at her kitchen table. She was busy typing when her laptop chimed; it was her Skype app. She clicked on it, and Sharon's face appeared on her screen.

"Hi, Tallulah!" She expressed her excitement. "I hope I'm not interrupting you."

"No, not at all. I'm working on my article."

"Great. I want you to know I talked with Sylvia and we're going to run your article. I want it to be our cover story, as I told you. I want to get some pictures of Lily for the story. Also pictures of the shelter and so on. I was thinking we could shoot Lily at the open mic. What do you think?"

Tallulah found it hard to hide her excitement. "That's great. I'm honored that you'd give me the cover."

"It's a compelling story, and one people would enjoy reading. Besides, *You & Me* should run it before someone else does," Sharon said.

"I agree. I haven't been able to find Lily since that day you met with her. I'm sure she'll turn up," Tallulah said.

"I talked to Sylvia and explained the situation to her. She agreed. So, no scandal or behind the back bullshit. I just wanted you to know," Sharon said. "I'll be in touch with the info on the photographer. You may want to tell Lily when you see her. If you have any problems, let me know."

Tallulah nodded, and Sharon clicked off. She then jumped up from her seat and started dancing around the room. "I have arrived!"

* * *

Lily was deep in thought. She'd spent the last 2 days with Owen. She retrieved her bag and waited at the cab stand, then climbed into the back of the cab and closed her eyes.

She must have fallen asleep because the next sound she heard was that of the cab driver talking. "Hey lady, we're here. Lady, you asleep? Wake up."

Lily opened her eyes to see the cab driver looking at her. She paid the fare, climbed out of the cab, walked to her motel, and used her key to open the door. She then walked into the small room, set down her suitcase, and closed the door behind her.

She couldn't help thinking about what Owen had said about Sylvia taking the trust money. She couldn't figure out how she could have taken it. But someone did take it. She knew that for certain.

She opened her suitcase and looked at the photo album Owen had given her. She placed the album on the bed with caution and opened it, then moved her hand gently across the photos and smiled.

She turned the pages of the album until she came to the announcement of Clyde's death. In the announcement was a picture of the mangled car. She frowned and closed the album.

She dug in her coat pocket, pulled out a folded piece of

paper, and unfolded it with great care. She stared at Tallulah's number, hesitated for a moment, then picked up the phone and dialed. She listened to the trill of each ring until she heard a voice say, "Hello?"

"Is this Tallulah?" she asked.

"Yes. Is this Lily?"

"Hi, it's me. I was calling to see if you could meet me tomorrow and bring the record."

"You can meet me in my newspaper office. I can give you the address. It's not far from Zoe's restaurant. I'm glad you called, Lily. I was getting worried," she said.

"I'm okay. I've been...busy." She turned over the piece of paper and grabbed a pen. "I'm ready for the address," she said.

Tallulah gave her the information. "I'll be there tomorrow by 11 am," Lily said.

"Great. See you tomorrow, Lily."

Lily hung up the phone, then decided she'd visit Mr. Franklin at the bank. She had to find out what happened to the trust money.

* * *

Michael walked up the old stairs to the 3rd-floor apartment. He had searched for a place for weeks. But everything was either too expensive or about to be condemned.

The stairs creaked with every step he took. When he finally reached the 3rd floor, he was a little out of breath. He checked the apartment number on his phone. Then, he walked down the dim hallway to apartment 3F. He tapped lightly on the door.

"It's open!" he heard a voice shout.

Michael applied gentle pressure to the door, opening it.

The room was bigger than he imagined. Two windows in the kitchen allowed light to flow into the room. He was surprised that someone had furnished it.

"Come on in," the voice said. "I'll be with you in a moment."

He stood in the main room and looked around.

Must be the living room, he thought to himself.

The furniture was old but clean. He smiled while looking at the couch. It was long and green.

Bigger than Tallulah's, he thought to himself.

A young-looking woman entered the room.

"Oh," she said, "are you here to look at the apartment?" He nodded and said, "Yes, is it still available?"

"Yes. My dad lived here until he passed away about 2 weeks ago." She noticed the look of concern on Michael's face. "Oh, he didn't pass here. He'd been in the hospital. I've been trying to clean up and get the place ready to rent. My name is Cindy. My uncle owns the building, so there's been no rush to rent the place. I was hoping to have everything moved out of here by now."

He shook Cindy's hand. "I'm Michael Chang," he said. "Nice to meet you, Cindy."

She looked around the room. "The place won't be ready for a while. I've got to figure out what I'm gonna do with my dad's furniture and stuff."

"Can I look around?"

"Sure, have at it," she said.

Michael wandered around the apartment. He opened and closed doors, looked into cabinets, turned on faucets, and opened and shut windows. When he finished his inspection, he found Cindy in the kitchen. She was taking some dishes out of the cabinet.

"I never realized how much stuff my dad had," she said, reaching for another plate.

He reached over her and grabbed the plate. "How much is the rent?" he asked while handing her the plate.

"Well," she started, "I'm not sure. My uncle owns this building and rarely comes around. Most of the apartments are empty due to repairs. To be honest with you, I don't think he cares. He said he's giving me this place, but I don't think I can handle it. I mean, I do work and have a family. He said he'd repair the apartments and I could be the manager, but I don't even live near here." She looked at him. "I'm sorry. I shouldn't be laying all this on you. I'd say the rent would be about $800-$1000."

"So, there isn't a manager for the building?" he asked.

"Well, there's me, and I'm not much of a manager," she said.

Michael thought for a moment. "What if I managed it for you? You know, collect the rent, deal with the tenants."

"You? Well, do you have any experience managing a building?"

"Well, no, but I do run my own paper. It's called *Big World*, so I have management experience."

"Your own paper, huh?" she said. "I've never met anyone who owned their own paper."

"It's not as exciting as it sounds." He chuckled.

"Well, you seem like a level-headed guy, but I'll need some references." She walked over to the kitchen table and picked up a notebook. "Leave your information here. I'll need to do some checking before I say yes, OK?"

"Okay," he said, taking the notebook from her hand.

She sat down in a chair and gestured for him to sit. "So you own a newspaper? What's that like?"

He picked up a pen that was sitting on the table and sat down. "Well," he said, "it's fun and challenging at the same time. It's a small paper, but I've been doing it for 5 years." He stopped writing and looked up at her. "The cost of print is rising, so I may not be able to keep it afloat. I make money with people who by ad space. Now with technology, there are other ways to reach your customers, so people stop buying ad space."

He handed her the notebook. She took it from him and glanced at what he'd written.

"I used to write short stories and poems and stuff. It was silly," Cindy said.

"Why was it silly?" he asked.

She shrugged her shoulders. "I dunno. I guess I didn't want people to tell me my stories were stupid or boring or that my poetry sucked."

"I'm sure they didn't suck or were stupid. Do you still have them? The stories and poems?" She giggled. "Seriously? I dunno, maybe at home in a box in the basement. I haven't thought about it in years."

"Well, maybe someday you'll let me read them. I wrote down all my info. I even provided some references for you to call."

Cindy stood up. "If this works out, we can talk about knocking down the cost of rent. I'll make a few calls and let you know." She paused for a moment, then said, "You'd really want to read my stories and stuff?"

"Yes," Michael said, "I'd really like to read them."

* * *

"So, this will be the stage area?" Anna asked, walking around the dining room of Zoe's restaurant.

"Yes, I thought we could put the mic here, then have all this room for the servers to walk through."

"Good idea," Anna said. "I didn't think of that."

"This is going to be so good, Zoe. The social media campaign Chloe did was amazing. There are people who are already donating! She even set up an account for those who wish to donate now. She's been amazing. You've been amazing."

Zoe watched her as she wandered around the room. "You know, I think the media will be here, too. This place could really use a fresh coat of paint, but who has time for painting?" Zoe said, frowning.

"Oh, it looks great, Zoe. You have a nice place. I like it. I you should add some Mexican food, but I'm biased," Anna joked.

"Preparing Mexican food takes time...well, good Mexican food. It's not my specialty, but I make a mean margarita." She laughed.

"Okay, we're counting down, two weeks from tomorrow," Anna said, sounding excited. "This is going to be a great event! Did you know Chloe set up an online sign-up sheet? When I last checked, it was full. I don't think we'll be able to let people sign up the night of the event. I mean, we can have only so many people up there, right?"

"Right, or we'll be here all night. The show should end around 11 pm. I've got a modified food and bar menu. I'll have a little more staff here, too. They've volunteered to help out. It should be good."

"Great. I know you want to get home. Thanks for seeing me so late. I thought it would be better with no one here." She hugged Zoe and walked towards the door. "See you later!" she said and walked out the door.

Zoe waved to her and locked the door behind her. She walked in the center of the dining room, sat on the floor, crossed her legs, and put her hands on her knees. She took 3 deep breaths and could feel her chest rising and falling with every inhale and exhale. She closed her eyes and began to chant *Om Namah Shivaya*. This was the chant she'd learned before her college days.

One day, when she was about 14, she found her cousin sitting in the basement, cross-legged, chanting. She thought she'd gone crazy. Her cousin explained to her that she was meditating. She put her index finger to her lips and made a shushing sound.

Zoe sat and watched her cousin for several more minutes until she stopped chanting. "What's meditating?" Zoe asked.

"It's a way to connect with the Universe," her cousin replied in a gentle tone. "It helps me stay centered and grounded. I got into it a few years ago. You have to be quiet, I don't want my mom to hear. She thinks it's all mumbo jumbo, but meditation is a good thing, Zoe. You should try it. I can help you."

Zoe cocked her head to one side. "Meditation? What is it? I mean, what do you do?"

Her cousin smiled. "Well, most people sit like me." She gestured for Zoe to sit.

"Now, some people lay down or sit in a chair. The most important thing is that you be comfortable. Okay?" she said. Zoe nodded her head. "You don't have to chant, but I like to.

Some people close their eyes, sit quietly, and try empty their minds of all thoughts. Just let your mind be still. It takes some gettin' used to, but once you continue to do it, it becomes second nature."

Zoe put her hands on her knees and closed her eyes. "Okay, now what were you saying?" Her cousin laughed. "I think you should start with the simple OM chant. So now close your eyes and think or say, 'OM'. Be sure to breathe, too; that's important. Before I start to meditate, I take several deep breaths. In through the nose, then out through the mouth. You try it."

Zoe took several deep breaths in through her nose, then out through her mouth. She felt her body get warm, and she began to relax. She felt a calming wave flow over her.

She then heard her cousin say, "Now when you're ready, go back to normal breathing and start to say or think OM."

Zoe began to say the word over and over again. It was strange because somehow this word helped her relaxed even more.

She wasn't sure how much time had passed, but she heard her cousin say, "That's good for a beginner."

Zoe opened her eyes with great care. "Wow, that was cool," she whispered.

"Yes, meditation is cool, but don't let our parents catch you. They just wouldn't get it."

Zoe sat in the middle of her restaurant, her voice barely

rising above a whisper as she chanted. She smiled as the memory of her cousin flooded her mind. She then took a deep breath, bowed her head, and mouthed the words *thank you.*

Chapter 30

Lily walked down the sidewalk, checking each building number as she passed. She slowed her pace as she approached the office of *Big World*. She stood in front of the door for a moment, and then opened it.

She peered in her head, then her body followed. The main room was quiet and empty. She started to turn and leave when a voice said, "Hi, can I help you?" She spun around to find a tall Asian man smiling at her. He was walking toward her.

"Can I help you?" he said again.

"I'm looking for Tallulah. She told me to meet her here," Lily said, staring at the floor.

"You must be Lily," Michael said. "Come in. Tallulah should be here soon. She went to get coffee."

He extended his hand at Lily. She stared for a moment, then took her time to shake his hand.

"You can sit anywhere you'd like," he said. "That desk over there is Tallulah's. You can sit there if you'd like."

She looked up and walked over to Tallulah's desk, then sat down in one of the chairs. She put her hands in her pocket and kept staring at the floor.

"I can't offer you any coffee yet, but would you like some water?" Michael asked. She shook her head no.

"I'm fine. Thank you," she said.

He walked over to her. "I heard your record. Your voice is amazing."

She looked up at Michael. She thought he looked kind.

"Thank you," she managed to say.

He started to say something else when Tallulah walked in with 4 large coffees. "I'm so sorry I'm late, Lily, but my boss here had to have coffee."

Michael smiled and grabbed one of the cups. "Thank you," he said. "I'll be in my office." With that he turned and walked out of the room.

Tallulah offered Lily some coffee, but she shook her head no. "I want to listen to the record again," she said in a gentle tone.

"Of course," Tallulah said. "I have the player right here."

She reached under her desk and produced the briefcase record player and record. She handed the record to Lily, opened the player, and plugged it in.

"All set. Whenever you're ready," she said.

Lily stared at the record cover. She pulled the record from the jacket and set it on the player. Then, she placed the needle on the record and waited.

As the music filled the room, she sat down and listened. She closed her eyes and lost herself in the moment. It felt as if she had transported herself back in time. She could see herself standing in the small record room, Owen smiling at her, nodding his head to her voice.

Tallulah watched her. She spotted Michael standing in the office doorway, watching. The music had caught his attention, and he listened and watched. She walked over to him.

"See?" she whispered. "She has an amazing voice. She

sounds just like the record."

He nodded and gestured for her to follow him into his office. When she was inside, he closed the door.

"I think I found an apartment," he said.

She frowned. "Really? I was just getting used to having you around."

"Well, it's not definite. The lady's checking my references. I'm hoping to manage the place for her. If I do, she'll knock some off the rent," he said.

"Okay. Well, I'm happy for you, Michael. I really hope it works out. I'll miss you," she said.

"I'm not moving to Egypt, T; just on the other side of town. I'll be able to publish maybe 3 or 4 more issues before the funds dry up. Everything will work out. It has to." He smiled at her.

She walked over to the office door and peered out the window. "She'll be out there all afternoon," she said.

"So, tell me about your story," he said. "When will it be ready for me to read?"

"About that," she said. "So, *You & Me* wants to run it, too. Sharon has offered me the cover."

"No shit?" he said. "T, that's great. But wait, I still get to run it, too, right?"

"Of course," she answered. "I guess Sharon wanted *You & Me* to pick it up as well before someone else does. She said she was going to talk with Sylvia Blass. When I talked to her, she gave me the green light."

"Wow, the cover of a big magazine. I knew you had it in you. I hope your head doesn't get too big to fit through the door." He smirked.

She chuckled. "Yes, I'll be thanking all the little people

when I get my Pulitzer. I'll include you. I'm almost done. You'll be the first person to read it. Sharon wants me to add the open mic into the story, so I thought I'd check with you as well.

"Hey, whatever she runs, I run," he said.

* * *

Chloe sat in her office, her fingers flying over the keyboard, when a light knock sounded at her door.

"Come in," she said, not taking her eyes off the computer.

"Chloe, you got more flowers," her assistant said.

Chloe looked up to see her holding a large bouquet of yellow roses.

"Oh, there are more," her assistant said.

Chloe looked around her office. "Where am I going to put them?"

There were several bouquets of white and yellow roses throughout her office. Stanley had been sending them to her every other day ever since the tour of the shelter.

"Stanley," she said. "Okay, let's figure out where to put them."

Her assistant put the flowers on the desk. "There are 4 more dozen at my desk."

"Take one of them home," Chloe said. "This has gotta stop. See if you can get Mr. Roberts on the phone."

Her assistant nodded and left the room. A few moments later, she buzzed in on the intercom. "Mr. Roberts, line 2."

Chloe cleared her throat, picked up the phone, and pushed the line 2 button. "Hello, Stanley. Thank you for the flowers, again."

"You like them?" he asked.

"Oh, they're beautiful. But Stanley, come on, this must stop. You're going to have my office flying with rumors."

He chuckled. "It's just my way of saying thank you for all your hard work. Nothing more."

"Well, it's gotta stop. Please. "I'm flattered, but Stanley, I told you, I don't date clients," she said in a stern tone.

"I know, I know. I'm saying thank you. I won't send any more flowers. I promise," he said.

"Thank you." She looked around the room. "They are beautiful," she said.

"Like you," he said, then clicked off the phone.

Chapter 31

Carla Avery pulled into the long circular driveway. She came to a stop and put the car in park, then grabbed her briefcase and stepped out of the car. She fumbled for her cell phone as she tried to shut the car door. She shook her head and walked up to the door, rang the bell, and waited.

A young-looking Mexican woman opened the door. "Yes, may I help you?" she asked. "I'm here to see Mrs. Blass," she announced. "I'm Carla Avery."

The young Mexican woman nodded her head and stood aside. Once inside, she spoke again. "Mrs. Blass is in the study. Follow me. I'll show you the way."

Carla looked around the large house. She thought it felt cold and unwelcoming. She followed the woman into a large room and saw Sylvia sitting on a large desk, typing on her laptop. She looked up as they entered the room.

"Ms. Avery, thank you for coming. Come in. Please, sit down and make yourself comfortable.

Can I get you anything? Water? Tea?" Sylvia asked.

Carla walked over to a large, overstuffed couch and sat down. She placed her briefcase on the table and unlatched it.

"I'm here to discuss the trust. I have some information to share with you," she said.

"I understand. You can go, Isabelle," she said to the young maid standing in the doorway. She watched Isabelle shut the door and turned toward Carla. "Thank you for coming out here. I haven't had the strength to leave the house lately," she said.

Carla nodded. A moment of awkward silence passed, then Sylvia stood up and walked over to where Carla was sitting.

Carla spoke, "I've looked into re-establishing the trust. Lily Blass asked about the funds because they weren't given to the Marigold Homeless Shelter. Now, she hasn't retained counsel or demanded answers from the bank, but I'm sure she will. The fact remains that if we establish the trust, we need to expose ourselves to the bank. We could make a large donation to the shelter without revealing our identities."

"I was very rude to you the first time we met," Sylvia said. "I'd spoken to you on the phone before us meeting. Do you remember?"

Carla looked at Sylvia. "Yes, this is true. I'm not sure where you're going with this, Mrs. Blass."

"Well, to be honest, I thought you were white when we spoke. "Needless to say, I was surprised when we met face-to-face," Sylvia said.

Carla's eyebrows raised, and she turned toward Sylvia. She smiled and said, "Mrs. Blass, it's sad you think a well-educated woman who speaks English well is white." Society has imposed unfair stereotypes on Black women. People expect us to be uneducated, brash, forceful, angry, and rude. We're supposed to be less than, single mothers on welfare who are lazy and don't want to work hard. Your remarks only reinforce what I'm saying. I'm a damn good attorney. I've worked hard in school. I come from a stable and loving two-parent home. I topped my class in law school. I've shown my skills to my colleagues, professors, and opponents. Still, I hear comments like, "You sound like a white woman."

Sylvia looked at Carla and said, "I've learned much about myself since my diagnosis. I don't know if the cancer is a blessing or curse. I mean, if I didn't have cancer, if I wasn't dying, I don't know if I would have recognized my own bullshit. It's funny how a thing like the color of their skin can change your attitude about someone before they even speak. I'm an expert at stereotypes, Ms. Avery. I understand what it's like not to like someone because of their skin color. And I also realize the extent of its stupidity. I know there's more to life than skin color. I know we're all connected, somehow. When you're faced with their own mortality, you begin to understand what's important. So, Ms. Avery, I tell you this to express my sincere apologies. You're a very capable attorney, regardless of what you look like. I wanted you to know. I'm trying to right the wrongs with the time I have left."

"Thank you, Mrs. Blass. I'm sorry it took something so drastic to make you change your thinking."

"Yes, me too. I've already made plans to donate to the shelter under the name Lily Blass, my half-sister. I did find her, you know. I had my editor go and meet with her. She doesn't want to meet me, and frankly, I don't blame her. I can't go back and change what happened to her, but I can try and do the right thing now."

Sylvia's words surprised Carla with their ease. "I have these papers for you to sign." She said, handing the forms to Sylvia.

Sylvia didn't even read the forms. She found where her signature belonged and signed.

"Now, I do have something I want to speak with you about,"

Sylvia said. "I've been working on my will, and I want you to handle it."

"I'm not an estate planning attorney," Carla said, putting the forms back into the briefcase.

"You told me you're an exceptionally skilled attorney. Your firm handles all my legal business, and I want you to handle this," Sylvia said.

"Why?" she asked.

"Because you're one of the few people who have ever set me straight. That day in your office, I gained much respect for you, Carla. You didn't take any of my shit. I like that," she said.

"Well, Mrs. Blass, I rarely take shit, as you call it, from anyone. What did you have in mind for your will?"

"I want to donate my estate, money, and all my worldly possessions to my sister, Lilian Blass. I also want to donate to the American Cancer Society, and of course the Marigold Homeless Shelter." She handed Carla a notebook. "It's all written in here. I have no family, or pets for that matter. My only real family is Lily. I've also made smaller provisions for my maids - the ones I fired and an ex-employee named Anna. I fired her as well, not because she wasn't a good employee, but because she spoke Spanish and is Mexican." Carla shot her a disconcerting look.

"Oh, don't look at me like that, Carla. I know how it sounds. I know what people think about me. I know people have called me 'Dragon Lady', 'the Bitch', 'the woman who sold out her mother for headlines'. Anyone who's ever given a damn about me, I've runoff. My friends aren't my friends. Money has brought me a lot of things, but not happiness. I don't think I've even been happy. But giving everything to Lily and others, well, it does make me happy. Funny, because I never would have guessed I'd be saying this."

She paused and smiled. "I've also decided not to have chemo/radiation therapy. I've looked into some holistic treatments and would rather go in that direction. I know we aren't friends, Carla, but I do trust you with my wishes."

Carla nodded. "Okay, Sylvia. Shall we begin?"

Chapter 32

Lily and Tallulah sat in the small cafe. Lily took a drink of her coffee and said, "I want to thank you for the record and the player. I think I wore out the needle." She laughed.

Lily's smile was bright, and she was clear-headed and sober. She pulled out an AA red sobriety coin and put it on the table. "I've been sober for 30 days," she announced.

Tallulah smiled at her. "That's great, Lily. You look good. Do you mind if I record you while we talk?" she asked.

"No. I don't mind. I find it funny that you're so interested in my life," Lily said.

Tallulah pulled out the small recorder and placed it on the table. She pushed the red record button. "After meeting Sharon Eckerson, she told me she wanted to share my story about you and the shelter in You & Me." How do you feel about that?" she asked.

She looked at the recorder, then at Tallulah. "I'm getting better every day. I'm finally okay with accepting who I am. I went to see Owen. It was so good to see him. He put a lot of energy into my career. I plan on paying him back."

"And what about Sylvia?" Tallulah asked.

"I'm not sure how I feel about her. I'm not sure if I'm ready to meet her, but I'm okay with her magazine having my story. At least I know, since you're doing it, it'll be the truth."

"Okay, tell me about Owen and you seeing him again," Tallulah said.

"I haven't seen Owen in years. I used to write him or would call, but then I just stopped. It was so good to see him. I've always felt guilty for the fire to his studio. I mean, they never found out who did it, but we both know. After we were blackballed from the industry, he nearly lost it all. Still, he never spoke an unkind word to me. Never. He was always kind to me. Even to this day. We spent the entire day together, looking at old pictures, remembering the good times and the bad."

She paused and took a drink of her coffee, then picked up the sobriety coin on the table. "I told him I was in a program and going to sing at the open mic. He told me I should have been singing, and maybe he's right. It wasn't the money or fame that captivated me; it was the music."

"So what now, Lily?" Tallulah asked.

"Well, I'm going to stay sober, keep working my program. I have a little money, so I can maybe get a place of my own and a job. Stay off the street," she said.

"What about singing and your career?"

"Career?" Lily chuckled. "I don't have a singing career. I'm going to sing for the shelter. Do you see any producers lined up to sign me? No one knows who I am, and I'm sure no one cares."

Tallulah looked at her. "Well Lily, that may be true today, but once the story breaks, I think you'll be surprised by what happens." The world is different today, especially with social media. Trust me, people will want to hear you sing."

Lily half-smiled and looked at the coin in her hand. "I never had a career; I had a shot at a career."

"Well, you have a week until the open mic. Do you know what you're singing?" Tallulah asked.

"No, not yet. It'll be a surprise," she said, grinning.

"There will be a photographer there, especially for you for the article for *You & Me*."

A look of concern and dread came over her face. "What do you mean, photographer? I don't want my picture taken. Look at me. I'm an old, withered up woman. I don't want my picture taken. I've seen that magazine, it's all models and glamour. I won't do it."

Tallulah sat there, her mouth open just a bit. "Lily –"

Lily held up her hand in protest. "I won't have my picture taken, Tallulah. I won't. It's a national magazine. I won't do it."

"What if we had your makeup and hair done?" Tallulah asked.

Lily raised her eyebrow just a bit. "Look, I appreciate everything you've done for me, but I can't go wasting my money on hair and makeup."

Tallulah perked up. "It won't cost you anything. Let me do this for you."

Lily sighed. "It won't cost me anything?"

"I promise," Tallulah said. "I'll make all the arrangements, but you have to promise to show up."

Lily nodded. "Okay, I'll show up. But if I don't like it, then no pictures, okay?" she said. Tallulah nodded. "Okay."

After Tallulah's interview, she walked Lily to the bus stop. They waited together until the bus arrived. "Lily, please call me tomorrow. I'll have everything set up, okay?"

Lily nodded and stepped on the bus. Tallulah saw the doors close and the bus drive off. Then, she took out her cell phone and called Chloe.

"Wat up, girl!" Chloe shouted into the phone.

"I need a favor. Are you up for Chloe's makeover boot camp?" Tallulah asked.

"Are you gettin' rid of the locs? Fuck yeah, I've got so many styles for your hair. We can do weave or –"

"Chloe, stop, it's not for me. It's for Lily. I told her about *You & Me* bringing in a photographer, and she freaked. I need you to give her one of your extra special, I'm a badass bitch makeovers."

"It's not for you?" Chloe said, sounding disappointed.

"No, for Lily. Wait – what's wrong with the way I look?"

"Well, you hardly wear makeup. Your clothes are off, and while you're pretty, I think we could try something different than the locs," Chloe said.

"Well, I'm sorry, you'll have to work your magic on Lily. Will you do it? I don't think we could do it before the open mic, but we could do it that day," Tallulah said.

"Okay, but we need to do it early. I'm going with Stanley, as his guest," Chloe announced. "What? Wait, I thought you didn't get involved with your clients? Sounds suspect," she said. "Girl, this man was sending me roses every other day. I finally had to call him and tell him to stop."

"No shit. I never get roses," Tallulah said.

"You will. Yes, I'll do Lily's makeover. Maybe I'll get my hands on you, too."

"Not happenin'. Just stick to Lily. I'll set everything up. We can do it at my place."

"Okay. I'll bring the stuff. But remember, it has to be early,"

Chloe said.

"You got it. Thanks, girl," Tallulah said and clicked off the phone.

Lily stepped off the bus and walked a block until she was in front of the bank. She peered inside, cupping her hands around her eyes. She took a step back, took a deep breath, and walked inside. The security guard nodded and smiled at her as she walked past him. No one seemed alerted by her presence this time. She walked up to a teller and asked to speak with Mr. Franklin.

The teller smiled at her and said, "It'll be just a moment. You can have a seat right over there." Lily nodded and took a seat, then watched people come in and out of the bank. She noticed the young woman who stopped her last time. She walked by and smiled. After several moments, Mr. Franklin was standing in front of her.

"Hello, may I help you?" he asked.

"Hello, Mr. Franklin. It's me, Lily Blass."

Mr. Franklin's eyes widened, and he smiled at her. "Ms. Blass, I didn't recognize you. You look wonderful. Please come into my office."

She followed him into his office. He shut the door behind her.

"Please have a seat," he said.

"I'm here about the trust. The money for the shelter."

He pulled out a file from a desk drawer. "Ms. Blass, it would appear someone has gained access to your trust. Someone withdrew the funds from the account without my knowledge. An attorney and my superiors contacted me several weeks ago about the trust. The trust can't be restored, but the attorney has given a check for $500,000. I have the check right here. I would have called you but didn't know how to reach you. This situation is unusual, but if you agree to accept the money, we can drop the entire matter. My instructions were to wait for your response. I understand, Ms. Blass. I'm just the banking manager. I've received instructions from my superiors on how to handle this. I don't know how someone accessed your trust, but the person who took the funds is now returning them, with interest."

He handed a large manila envelope to her. She took the envelope and opened it. Inside was a cashier's check for $500,000, made out to Lillian Blass. She held the check in her hand. Then, she looked up at Mr. Franklin. His anxious face showed he was eager for her response. She looked down at the check again. She took out a folded piece of paper from the envelope, opened it, and read.

Mr. Franklin shifted in his chair. He placed his hands on his desk and scooted his chair closer to the desk. He didn't understand any of this. When he realized the trust wasn't intact, he immediately alerted his superiors at the bank. They told him not to do anything, that they would handle it, then they removed all his access.

One day, a nice looking attorney named Carla Avery came to see him. She gave him the envelope and instructions on what to do if Lily should become angry or want to press charges. She told him the trust wouldn't be re-established, but the monies would be given back with interest. She told him he would be receiving a call from his superiors to confirm. Twenty minutes after she left his office, he got the call.

"Mr. Franklin, I want to donate this entire check to the Marigold Homeless Shelter. I want the donation to be anonymous. As for the trust, I'm not a lawyer, but I'm sure laws were broken...but all that matters is the shelter gets the money. "I want someone to donate it next week, not a day before," she said.

He let out a sigh of relief, ensuring no one noticed. "I'm happy to start the donation to the shelter on your behalf, without revealing your identity. I'll need you to sign the check, then I'll start the process. Will you be needing anything else?" he asked.

She grabbed a pen sitting on his desk, signed the back of the check, and handed it to Mr. Franklin. She stood up and said, "Thank you, Mr. Franklin," then walked out of the office with the manila envelope in hand.

* * *

"I can't believe you got the cover. I'm so proud of you," Marc said, smiling at Tallulah.

She grabbed one of his fries and laughed. "I know, right? One day I'm begging Michael to let me write this story, and the next thing I know, I get the same story for the cover of *You & Me*. It's crazy."

"You did a good thing, Lula," he said.

They both sat on the bench near the foundation where they had their first date. They ate their burger and fries in comfortable silence. She felt at ease with him. He was easy to talk to. It's not that she hadn't dated before, but he wasn't like the others. He had goals and dreams of his own. He was self-motivated and determined. Yet, he had a kind and soft demeanor.

"I told Lily a photographer was comin' to take pictures for

the *You & Me* story. She freaked. I promised her a makeover," she said.

"What kind of makeover?" he asked.

"I called in the big guns: Chloe."

Marc laughed.

"So, I was thinking about doing a li'l somethin' somethin' for the open mic," she announced.

"Really. You're a poet, too?" he joked.

"Maybe," she said.

"What's it called?" he asked.

She thought for a moment. "It actually doesn't have a title." "Can I hear it?" he asked.

"No." She gave him a little shove. "You'll have to wait until the open mic."

"Okay, okay." He laughed. He wrapped his arms around her and pulled her close to him. The smell of her perfume lingered in the air. He breathed it in and exhaled.

"You wanna come see my place?" he asked.

She tried to withhold her excitement. "Yes. Maybe we can watch a movie or something?" she said, trying to sound casual.

"Sure." He stood up and reached for her hand. "Can I read your article before you publish it?" he asked.

She stopped walking and looked at him. "You wanna read it?"

He leaned in and pressed his lips gently against hers. She leaned into his embrace and kissed him back. She could feel a warm sensation in her spine. It started like a small wave, then expanded gradually through her entire body.

He pulled away and said, "I want to read everything you write."

Her eyes were still closed. She puckered her lips and waited with anticipation for him to continue. After a few seconds, she opened her eyes to see him smiling at her.

"Very funny," she said and leaned in and kissed him.

As they started walking, he squeezed her hand. "So, can I read it?" he asked.

"Sure," she said, still under the spell of his kiss.

She felt the warm sensation fade away from her spine, followed by a similar feeling in her stomach. She smiled and squeezed his hand.

Chapter 33

The warm wind passed over the face of Owen Katz. He was sitting outside in his wheelchair, admiring the white, fluffy clouds. Each one changed its shape gradually as they drifted by in the sky.

The visit from Lily had changed him. He became a little nicer to the staff, although they still got on his nerves. He looked forward to her weekly calls. She'd tell him about her program, and he would send words of support and encouragement. It was the medicine he needed.

She'd made him promise he would go sit outside and get some fresh air. He wheeled himself through his room doorway and down the hall to the small terrace. The staff gave him funny looks the first time he did this. He nodded and kept wheeling himself forward to the door.

As he moved past the nurse's station, the doctor noticed him wheeling by. She put down her chart and walked over to him.

"Now, where do you think you're going?" she asked.

"I'm going outside to get some fresh air. It's allowed, ain't it?" he grumbled.

"It's encouraged," she said.

She walked behind the wheelchair, placed her hands on the

chair handles, and began to push. Once outside, she wheeled him next to a table with an umbrella.

"How's this?" she asked.

"This'll do just fine," Owen replied.

She touched him on his shoulder. "I'm glad you're getting around, Owen." She smiled and walked inside.

Soon, he made it a habit to wheel himself out to the terrace every day. He smiled at the nursing staff as he wheeled by. He became less grumpy and more willing to speak to the other residents.

On the day he wheeled himself outside to sit in the sun, he was surprised to hear a woman's voice calling his name. He turned around to find a stylish, white, older woman looking down at him. He looked up at her; she looked familiar, but he couldn't quite remember where he'd seen her.

"Owen Katz?" she said.

"Yes, I'm Owen. Who are you?"

"Can I join you?" she asked.

"It's a free country," he said.

He watched as she pulled over a chair from a nearby table. She placed it next to him and sat down. She laid a small clutch bag in her lap, shifted in her chair, and removed her sunglasses

"Do you know me?" she asked.

"Now, what kind of stupid-ass question is that, lady? No, I don't know you," he said.

She smiled and chuckled. "My name is Sylvia Blass," she said.

Owen squinted his and put his hand underneath this chin. "Well, well, Sylvia Blass. I can see the resemblance with your mother. What do you want? Whatever it is, I ain't interested. Lily told me about you looking for her. She told me everything," he said.

"You've seen Lily?" she asked, sounding surprised.

"Yeah, she came to see me. She told me about you and your private investigator. Now, what do you want?" he grumbled.

She cleared her throat. "Well, you're right, I did hire a private investigator to find her. The information provided to me led me to you. I read about your studio burning all those years ago. I also know that my mother was somehow involved. I guess I wanted to meet you and tell you how sorry I am. I really don't know why I'm here."

He stared at her. "Okay, so you're sorry. What do you want? You want to hurt Lily some more? Is that why you're looking for her? She told me she didn't want to meet you, so why don't you leave her alone?" he said.

"I'm not here for Lily. I'm here to see you," she said.

Owen chuckled. "What the hell do you want with me? Your mother burned down my recording studio and ended my career in the music business. There's nothing you have that I want," he said.

She sighed. "I didn't know what my mother had done until after she died. I was a young girl when she found out my dad had other children, Lily and her brother Clyde. This was kept from me. I didn't know. We didn't have the best relationship, Mr. Katz. When she died, I was given access to her safe in the big house. That's when I found out about Lily and Clyde, my father's will, and you."

"But you did nothing," he said.

"Yes, I did nothing," she said.

She shifted in her chair. "Mr. Katz, I'm dying."

He didn't react to her words; he continued. "Did you

know she even went as far to stop the insurance from paying for the damage? I don't know why she did it, but she did. Amanda Worthington-Blass was a cold, calculating bitch who punished Lily and her family for your father. Lily and Clyde were innocent, but she blamed them anyway."

She nodded her head in agreement. "Yes, I know, Mr. Katz."

He thought for a moment. "Hey, didn't you plaster her death all over the front pages? Yeah, yeah, you sold her out for money and headlines," he said.

She took a deep breath. "Mr. Katz, I want to pay for the damage to your studio. I...I know it doesn't make up for what happened, but I do want to do something."

"After all these years, years of knowing, now you want to give me money?" He chuckled. "Look around, lady. I'm old and tired. I've had to struggle all my life. My wife left me long ago out of embarrassment. My daughter put me in a home as soon as she could. My friends and business associates walked away years ago. What do you think your fucking money is going to do for me now? See, that's the problem with people like you, they think money can make up for past bullshit. Well, I'm here to tell you, your money won't change what happened!" Owen shouted.

"Mr. Katz, please. I just want to –"

"Please what? Take your fucking money so you can feel better? Oh, now you're dying and want to make good? Get the fuck out of here. You're ridiculous. Lily doesn't want anything to do with you, and neither do I. She didn't even take the money your father left. Did you know that? She didn't want it. All Lily wanted to do was sing. That's all. Sing. And your fucking mother used all her money and power to make sure that dream never came true. She killed it, just like that!

Lily could take it, the death of her brother, then her mother. We both know who was responsible, but we couldn't prove it. Lily checked out. She couldn't do it. She lived on the streets for years! Now get the fuck out of here!" he shouted.

She stood up. "Mr. Katz, Owen," she said.

He didn't look at her; turned his head away. She walked in front of him so he would have to look at her.

"I know money can't make up for what happened. I know. But it can help now. I'm leaving you the information for the account I set up for you. Do nothing, but the money is there, in your name, free and clear. Yes, my mother was a bitch, mean and unkind. I've been no better. And yes, maybe it took my impending death to make me see, but at least I do see now. I'm trying to make amends the best way I know how."

She pulled an envelope out of her clutch purse and set it on the table next to him. "Here's the information. Do with it what you like. I am sorry, Mr. Katz."

Sylvia turned and walked back inside the building. He watched her walk away, then looked at the envelope on the table. He picked it up and opened it, and his eyes widened as he read the information. He put the paperback in the envelope and wheeled himself inside.

Chapter 34

Michael looked around the apartment. He put his backpack down on the long coffee table and wandered into the kitchen. Cindy was sitting at the kitchen table, reading through his application.

"Well Michael, everything looks good. You can move in whenever you're ready. Right now, there are two other tenants in the building. Collect their rent, show the empty apartments, and rent them. I'll come on the 5th to collect the rent. I have a folder here where I keep the repair people's information. Now, since you manage the building, I'll take half off the rent. Deal?" she said, looking up at him.

"Deal," he said.

"Good. You're actually doing me a favor. It's hard for me to get over here, so this is great," she said.

"Yeah," he said. "It works for me, too."

"Do you want the furniture?" she asked. "If not, we can put it into storage." He shrugged. "I'll bring my bed and couch. Everything else can stay." "Okay," she said, "I'll have my uncle pick it up tomorrow."

"I guess we're all set. Here are the keys," she said, handing him a set of keys. He took the keys from her and smiled. "Did you bring your poems?"

She smiled with a hint of embarrassment. "Well, I did manage to find one or two." "Great, where are they?" he asked.

She picked up her purse, dug inside, and pulled out two pieces of small paper. She looked at them, then after a moment of hesitation, handed them to him.

"I thought you may have forgotten, and I didn't want to bring it up," she said.

Michael took the pieces of paper and read out loud:

"You inspire me to be the best I could ever be,
Especially on days when I am so low
You have picked me up so many times
Especially on the days when I am so low
You give me strength when I am weak
And never once ask for anything in return
You keep me sane in times of insanity
And never once ask me anything in return."

He looked up to see her staring at him. She had a look of discomfort on her face.

"It's good," he said.

"You think so?" she said, perking up.

"Yes. My friends are having an open mic. You should come read your poem," he said.

She laughed. "Oh no, I can't even believe I let you read it."

"Well, it's good. If you change your mind, it's Friday, at Zoe's Soul Food Kitchen. Show starts at 8 pm. There will be a lot of novice poets. I'm sure you'll be in good company," he said.

Michael handed back the poem. Cindy took it from his hands and said, "You really liked it?"

He nodded. "I have to get going, but I'll move in this

weekend if that's okay," he said.

"Sure," she said, looking down at her poem.

He stood for a moment, watching her. She was studying her poem as if she'd never read it before.

"Well, I'll see you later," he said.

She waved to him but didn't look up and continued to read her poem. He watched her take her time as she sat down, her eyes fixated on the paper. He stood a moment longer, then left the room.

* * *

"We want the partition to be over here," Chloe said, giving directions to the two men holding the large wall.

They nodded and walked the partition to the other side of the restaurant at a leisurely pace. She watched the two men carry the heavy partition and set it down. It was black with white letters and read *Marigold Shelter 1st Annual Open Mic*. In the center was a silhouette of a person standing in front of a microphone. She nodded and walked to the back of the restaurant. There, she found Zoe busy giving directions to her staff.

Zoe looked up at her and mouthed, "Five minutes." Chloe nodded and walked into her office, sat down, and pulled out her cell phone. She checked her messages, scribbled some notes in her notebook, and clicked off the phone.

Zoe rushed into her office. "Tell me again why I wanted to run a restaurant? You know when they say good help is hard to find? Well, it's true," she said, sitting down in a huff in the chair behind her desk.

"You could be working for someone else," Chloe said.

"True, true. So, are we on track for Friday?" Zoe asked.

"Of course. Girl, this is me you're talking to. Did I tell you I'm giving Lily a makeover for her performance?" she said.

"No, how'd that happen? Wait...T?"

"Of course. From what I know, Lily didn't like the idea of *You & Me* sending a photographer." "So, what's the plan?" Zoe asked.

"I'll meet T and Lily at T's place. I need to finish early because I'm coming as Stanley's guest."

"Wait, you're coming with Stanley Roberts?" Zoe said. "Shut the fuck up. You sleeping with him?"

Chloe smiled. "No, girl, and let me tell you something, it's hard. The man sent me flowers every day until I told him to stop. He calls and leaves me the sweetest messages. Girl, he fucking with my emotions, my mojo, my good sense, and my rule to never date clients."

"Well, he is fine. I dunno, Chloe, you may have met your match." "I know. He is fine. I never thought I'd say that about a white boy."

"That's 'grown-ass man', excuse you," Zoe added.

"Okay, white man. He is fine for a white man, but –"

"But what?" Zoe asked. "He's fine, rich, nice, easygoing, smart. I read where he's one of the year's most eligible bachelors."

"I know, I know," Chloe said, sounding distressed. "I cannot date this man. I mean, I could fuck him. Yes, I could... BUT he's a client, so no, no, no," Chloe said.

"Hmm," said Zoe.

"What the fuck does 'hmm' mean?" Chloe asked. "You know what it means," she said, smiling at her. "What should

I do, Zoe?"

"I've never seen you so fucked up over a man before, Chloe. I think you should follow your heart."

"Follow my heart?" Chloe blurted out. "What the fuck, Zoe? Follow my heart?"

She shrugged. "It doesn't matter what I say. You're gonna do you, and I love you for that."

Chloe sighed. "Yeah, you right. Okay, okay, enough about him. Let me show you the backdrop I had delivered. I had them put in the spot we talked about."

"So, what if he makes a move? Whatcha gonna do?" She asked with a sly smile.

"Stop. He's not going to make a move," she said.

"I think you should go for it. I do. I mean, why not? Fuck it, Chloe, he likes you."

Her eyes widened. "Are you serious right now? You? Zoe? Aren't you the same person who told me not to shit where I eat? Not to dip my ink in the company well? Don't grunt where you hunt? Don't buy your honey where you get your money? Wasn't that you?"

Zoe laughed. "Did I say all that? All I'm saying is that for the first time, I approve of your taste in men. He ain't raunchy, or busted, or broke, or ugly, or tired, or trifling. That's like a unicorn for you."

Chloe laughed. She knew she was right. Her taste in men wasn't all the great. She never wanted a boyfriend. Her attitude was to fuck 'em and dump 'em.

"Chloe, your longest relationship was with a pair of earrings. Again, all I'm saying is, he's a nice guy. Very nice. He might be the one." She smirked.

"The one?" she echoed. "What the hell is wrong with you?

Why are giving me all this bad advice?"

"I dunno. Love, maybe," she said.

Chloe rolled her eyes. "It's overrated. I get the same thing from chocolate."

"Okay, okay. Maybe it is bad advice, but there are worse men to end up with, Chloe. I like him. He's down to Earth, funny, kind, and seems to want to help people. I'm just saying, he's a unicorn."

Zoe's comments surprised her. She'd always been the level-headed one. The one who made calculated moves and didn't go out on whims or leap without looking. The two friends sat in silence for a moment until Zoe spoke.

"I think you have to keep an open mind, Chloe. "I respect your rule about clients, but Stanley Roberts might be worth it," she said, raising an eyebrow.

"He is a tall drink of Hennessy," Chloe whispered.

Zoe patted her hand. "Don't worry, everything will work out. It always does."

"For you, Zoe," Chloe said. "Things always work out for you."

Zoe smiled. "Maybe, but I believe the Universe is trying to tell you something. You should listen."

Chloe looked at her and rolled her eyes. "Girl, please."

Zoe chuckled. "Okay, so back to business. Someone asked me who's hosting the mic."

She looked at her. "Hosting?"

"Yeah, you know, someone to introduce people, keep the crowd engaged. Who you got lined up?"

"I thought you and Anna had that covered?" Chloe said.

They both looked at one another.

"Oh shit!" said Zoe. "We don't have a host. I'm not gonna

do it. I've got enough going on in the kitchen."

"Well, I'm not gonna do it. Maybe Anna?" Chloe said.

"Are you kidding? She's been running around like a crazy person. I don't think we can ask her to do it, Chloe," she replied.

They both sat for a moment, then in unison, they said, "T!"

"She's a writer, a poet...she'll do it!" said Chloe. "Besides, she owes me, with the Lily makeover thing."

"That's right, if she says no, then bring on the pleading and guilt." Zoe laughed.

Chapter 35

Owen wheeled himself into the local bank. As he entered, he looked around until he made eye contact with a young woman. She smiled at him and walked over to him.

"May I help you?" she said.

He pulled out an envelope and said, "Yes, I'd like to make a withdrawal, please."

* * *

Lily sat in the small hotel room, playing her record over and over again. She listened to the words and got lost in the music. She'd listened all day and didn't even realize it was evening until her stomach growled. She turned off the player and grabbed her jacket.

She walked down to a small corner store. As she walked in, she passed a large magazine rack and spotted the latest edition of *You & Me* magazine. She picked up the magazine and examined it. She'd known about Sylvia's magazine; she actually never read it.

On the cover was a young, smiling white woman with perfect

teeth. Her blonde hair cascaded over her shoulders in an elegant manner. She was sitting with her hand below her chin. Her sky blue eyes and pale white skin were accented by her blood-red lipstick. The headline read, "*Beautiful you in 30 days!*"

Lily flipped through the pages. Each one showed models, fashion tips, makeup advice, celebrity gossip, and more. She tucked the magazine under her arm and picked up a ham sandwich, small bag of chips, water, and a candy bar. As she passed the cooler full of beer, she made a short stop. She felt her heart race, licked her lips, then kept walking. She paid for her food and drink and left the store.

When she arrived back to the safety of her room, she sat on the bed, reading the magazine and eating her sandwich. She examined each page with great attention, wondering how much of Sylvia was in the magazine.

She'd given up on the idea of beauty a long time ago. She didn't care about her hair or clothes. She didn't read about celebrities or cared who wore it better. She couldn't picture herself in the magazine. All these women were young, beautiful, and white.

She walked into the bathroom and looked at herself in the mirror. She struggled to recognize the reflection staring back at her. Her face was clear and smooth, but she'd aged over the years. She had slight bags underneath her eyes. She noticed crow's feet forming around her eyes and mouth. She smiled, then frowned at her reflection.

She shook her head and returned to the main room. There, she grabbed a small piece of paper from the desk. Then, she dialed the number written on it. She listened to the phone trill in her ear. Finally, on the 3rd trill, a voice came over the phone.

"Hello?"

"Tallulah, it's Lily. I can't do it. "I can't stand in front of all those people knowing my picture will be in this magazine," she said, waving the magazine around.

"Lily, calm down. I promise you'll look great. At least let's try, okay?" she said, trying to sound reassuring.

"I got a copy of the magazine. All the girls are young, beautiful, and white!" she yelled into the phone.

"Lily, I promise you'll be perfect. My girl Chloe is a fashionista. Do you trust me?" she asked.

Lily was pacing back and forth. "I guess I do," she said.

"Please trust me, Lily. You're beautiful. The women in the magazine aren't real. Real beauty comes from within. Lily, you're beautiful. Trust me," she said.

Lily sat on the edge of the bed. She could feel the tears swell up in her eyes. "Tallulah, I'm scared," she whispered. "I'm so fucking scared."

"Lily," she said, "I know you've been through a lot. I know your story...well, most of it. I want to help. Please trust me. I know you're scared. Who isn't? But you have a spark. I see it, and I think others will, too. I promise your pictures will be great. Okay?"

She wiped the tears from her cheeks. "I want a drink," she said, "but I won't. I won't drink."

"Are you okay?"

"Yes, I'm okay. I got scared. I was looking at Sylvia's magazine, and I got scared," Lily replied.

"I understand," Tallulah said. "You promise to meet me tomorrow? My place?"

"Yes, I'll be there," she said and hung up the phone.

She put down the magazine and walked over to the record player. It was sitting on the small desk in the room. She turned it on and gently set the needle on the record. Then, she started singing along, swaying to the music. She picked up the magazine, threw it in a nearby trash can, and continued to sing along.

* * *

Stanley sat in his office chair, reading an older copy of *BW*. He set down the newspaper when Tonya, his assistant, walked into his office.

"You're all set for tomorrow. Chloe sent over your itinerary. She has you speaking with a few reporters and giving a small speech before the event," she said, not looking up.

She waited for his reply, but when there was silence, she looked up from her notepad. Stanley was staring out the window. He leaned back into his large leather chair and folded his hands behind his head.

"Stanley. Stanley, I'm going to need you to focus, please," she said.

He turned around to look at her. "I am focused. I heard you." He turned his chair back around and gazed out the window.

"Are you okay, Stanley?"

"Yeah, yeah, I'm good. I just...well..." He trailed off.

"She doesn't date her clients. Stanley, you're a client," Tonya said, sitting down in the chair in front of the desk. "She probably doesn't want to deal with the office rumors and talk. And then there's the press, your parents, ex-girlfriends. You're a big deal, Stanley. One of the most eligible bachelors.

343

That's a lot for a woman. Personally, I like Chloe," she said.

"Me, too," said Stanley.

She smiled. "Turn around."

She watched as he turned around, taking his time to face her. "Why is this one different?" she asked, peering at him.

He shrugged. "I don't know. She's different. She's never once showed any interest in me. She called me and told me to stop sending flowers, she sends my calls to voicemail, she's beautiful, smart, funny. I usually have no issues with women. Maybe she doesn't like me."

"Wow. You're hooked. I've never seen you like this before. You usually date, then put them in the friends with benefits zone."

He smiled. "Do I?"

"There are some women in the world who are strong and enjoy their independence. They're not looking for someone to take care of them; they're looking for a companion., a partner, and friend. Someone they can enjoy, talk to, laugh with...hell, even cry with."

"I can cry," he said.

She laughed. "If you want my advice, tell Chloe what you want. Some of us want to hear it. Make her believe the rumors and talk won't matter because it shouldn't. Here's your itinerary. Please be ready. The car will pick you up here. Then to Chloe, then to the press conference at the shelter, then the event." She handed him a folder. "Everything you need is in here."

Stanley took the folder and put it down on his desk. "Do you think she won't go out with me because I'm white?" he asked.

Tonya shook her head. "No. Do you want to go out with

her because she's Black?" She waited for him to answer, then said, "I sound stupid, don't I? Well, so do you. I'm leaving for the evening." She looked at him and thought he looked like a wounded puppy. She sighed and sat back down. "Okay, okay, you look too pitiful for me to leave. What can I do to help?" she said.

He perked up. "There's nothing for you to do, Tonya. You asking is more than enough. You're like family to me. Thank you for listening."

"So, you're okay?" she said.

"Yeah, I'm good. I'll figure this out. I always do," he said.

Tonya stood up and smiled at him. "You're a good boss. A pain in the ass, yes, but a good boss. I'm glad you think of me as family." She turned and left the room.

Stanley leaned back in his chair, his mind drifting to Chloe. He liked her. She wasn't like the other women he'd dated. Most of them were around for the money. His mother had often tried to pair him with women who had good breeding and social status. She would say things like "She's well-educated, Stanley. She comes from a fine family. You should call her and go do what young people do." Sometimes she would say, "Her family has connections that could help you and your father. You should call her and go do what young people do." He would nod and kiss her on the cheek.

He knew dating Chloe would present a problem for his mother. She wasn't rich or Ivy League-educated, and she wasn't white. He knew the idea of dating a woman of color would piss her off. He could picture her face when he introduced them. He smiled at the thought of bringing Chloe home to meet the parents.

His father would raise an eyebrow and be cordial. His

mother would huff and pout. She would seethe at him all through dinner, then excuse herself without so much as an explanation. Her silence would be louder than all the screaming in the world, and he was completely prepared to deal with it.

He sighed and said out loud, "None of that matters if she refused to go out with me." He picked up the *Big World* paper in his lap and continued to read.

Chapter 36

When Sylvia arrived back home from her trip to see Owen, exhaustion overwhelmed her. She lay in bed and wasn't feeling well. Her stomach felt as if someone was twisting around her insides. She'd lost weight, and it hurt when she ate or drank. She could bear all this if she wasn't alone. No one to lean on, no one to talk to, no one to cry with, no one.

She propped the big pillows behind her back. Then, she grabbed her cell phone from the nightstand. She scrolled through the numbers until she found Claudia Roberts. She stared at her name, then decided to call her. Claudia answered in an upbeat and joyful tone.

"Hello," she said.

"Claudia, darling, it's Sylvia."

"Sylvia, how are you? I haven't heard from you since the anniversary party. Where have you been?"

She cleared her throat. "I've been busy. I...well...I'm sick."

"Sick? Well, are you in bed? Have you seen a doctor?" Claudia asked.

"Yes. I've seen a doctor," she replied.

"Oh, good. So, I've got so much gossip to fill you in on. I mean, you missed a wonderful party with the Beckers. You know how Francis Becker throws a party. She had the most fabulous food, but the decor was dreadful. Poor dear, she raved all night about her decorator. She has no taste and all the money. Such a shame."

She listened to Claudia go on about the music, food, who attended, what they wore, and who they were with. She laughed with a hint of amusement at her anecdotes about the new maid or how she had to fire the gardener.

"So, are you coming to Spain next month? You know I purchased a new villa, and Jackson is letting me throw a big party. The who's who will be there. You must come, Sylvia," Claudia said

"I don't think I'll be able to make it, Claudia," she said.

"Oh, no. Well, I'll be sure to tell you all about it. If you change your mind, let me know. I must go now. It's been great hearing from you. Ciao."

In that moment, Sylvia realized she had no friends. Not one. She looked down at her phone and scrolled through the names until she came to Monica Dancy. She stared at the name. She remembered the last time she saw her. It was about 2 years ago at a dinner party.

During the party, she found herself alone with Monica. They were both in the restroom. Monica was fixing her hair in the mirror when she walked in. Monica looked at her in the mirror, then continued to fix her hair.

"I really don't know you why bother," Sylvia said. "It won't help." Monica shot her a look. "Really, Monica, why are you here? You don't belong here."

Monica froze, then turned, looked at her, and pierced her lips together. "No one wants me here? You've got that wrong; no one wants you here. Everyone knows what a bitch you are.

348

When exactly did you get your invitation to this party? Or did you just hear about it and assume you were invited? Probably Claudia. She does feel sorry for you. We talk about it all the time. She's the only one who will have anything to do with you, and that's out of pity. Unlike you, Sylvia, I have friends – and unlike you, I don't have to pay people to be around me."

Monica tossed her hair and walked for the door. As she opened it, she said, "Oh, and Sylvia? Fuck you." She quickly walked out of the bathroom, letting the door slam behind her.

She was right, Sylvia thought to herself.

She threw the phone across the room and watched it shatter against the wall.

"Fuck!" she screamed.

For the first time, she understood what Monica had said. She was alone. She felt her eyes swell up with tears.

"I'm tired of fucking crying!" she screamed.

She dragged herself out of bed and made her way to her desk. On the desk sat the black folder Sharon had given her. She placed her hand gently on top of the folder. She decided if Lily wouldn't meet her, she'd go meet Lily.

* * *

"You have to do this, T! We need you to do this," Chloe said into the phone. "Besides, it would be good exposure for your article."

"What the hell do I know about hosting?" she said.

"You're perfect," Chloe said.

"You didn't answer my question."

"Look T, we didn't even think about a host, and when we

did, you were the first person we thought of. Come on, it's a few hours for one night," Zoe said.

Tallulah groaned into the phone. "Oh, okay. But this means I have to be there early, and I have Lily coming here for her makeup and stuff."

"Don't worry, I got you," said Chloe. "I'll meet Lily and make sure she gets to the open mic." "See, it all works out," said Zoe.

"Yeah, right," she said, not sounding happy.

"So, usually the host will kick off the show with something. You got poems and stuff. I know you do," Chloe said.

"Yeah, I got poems and stuff," she said. "I can do anything? Any poem?" "Of course," said Zoe. "It's an open mic."

Tallulah lay on her small sofa, with her legs dangling over one of the sofa arms. They'd asked her to host the open mic, and she wasn't ready. She'd never read her poetry in front of an audience. She got up, walked into her bedroom, and began to rummage through the closet. After several moments, she found what she was looking for: An old large shoebox.

She took the box and placed it on the bed, then took off the lid to reveal all her old journals and notebooks. She'd kept a journal since she was eight but hadn't written anything for the past 5 years. She didn't know why; all she knew was, she didn't feel like writing anymore. "Did I lose my spark?" she said out loud.

In quiet moments—like brushing her teeth, doing laundry, or drinking tea—doubts about her writing skills would sneak in. She'd always wanted to be a writer, and she was, but it wasn't like she'd written the great American novel. She had been plagued all her life by moments of not being good enough or not being accepted. When those moments arose – and they did often – she would push them deep down inside. She forced herself to move forward.

She started going through each journal until she found one from her senior year in high school. She wrote a lot back then. She flipped through the journal. A smile spread across her face when she saw an entry that said, "*Beat Michael again today in chess. He's really obsessed with winning. You'd think he'd be proud because he taught me how to play the game. I don't see what all the fuss is about. Maybe I'll let him win tomorrow. He really is my best friend.*"

She continued to flip through the journal until she found an entry that read, "*You Sound White*".

It wasn't as much a journal entry as it was a poem. She continued to read:

My skin is black
And I offer no apologies
My lips are full
My hair is nappy
My ass is round
My thighs are big
And I offer no apologies
You've held me down
Pushing my head underwater
You laugh at me
Snicker and grin
Because I'm supposed to be less than
I'm educated and smart
I'm gonna leave my mark
On this world
So the words that I speak
And knowledge that I seek

All come to light
But again you try to hold me down
By telling me I sound white
My skin is black
And I offer no apologies
My lips are full
My hair is nappy
My ass is round
My thighs are big
But I know wrong from right
An educated sista
That you can't handle
So you tell me I sound white
You've got me trippin'
Like there's something wrong with me
But I can see, you just mad
'Cause I ain't what you'd thought I'd be
Brown skin white words
And I make no apologies
But people usually fear what they can't understand
Call me an anomaly
My skin is black
My lips are full
My hair is nappy
My ass is round
My thighs are big
And I make no apologies
But people usually fear what they can't understand
Call me an anomaly
Not black enough for blacks
And too black for the whites

All because you say I sound white.

As she read the last sentence, she decided she would open with this poem. It still resonated with her. Even now, as an adult, she heard these same words from both Black and white people.

She remembered on the first day of AP English, a girl in class told her she was trying to sound white. During her interview at a big newspaper, one interviewer made an accidental remark that she sounded white. The guy she dated told her she sounded white. She'd always felt the need to defend her Blackness, but now, in this moment, she didn't care anymore. At the end of the day, she was still Black.

She continued to go through her journals until she found 3 more poems she'd written in college. She read each poem. "Not bad," she said to herself. She put the poems aside and put the box back in the closet.

The apartment was quiet. Michael had moved out, and Tallulah lived alone again. She had gotten used to having him around, but she knew he wouldn't stay long. She heard a knock at the door and walked out of the bedroom and to the front door. She opened it to find a smiling Mrs. Herrera, who held a basket in her hands.

"Hola, Tallulah, are you hungry?"

Chapter 37

"It's my money. I can do whatever I want with it. I can't take it with me, now can I? I guess you'd rather have me give it to you."

Sylvia's voice was low and harsh. She was speaking to her attorney, Mr. Meyers. She put on a good front, but she was getting weaker by the day. She'd forgone all traditional treatment. No chemo, no radiation. She read where those things would make it worse. She'd lose her hair and be sick all the time. She'd rather die than lose her hair.

She sat up tall in the large black chair, took a sip of water from the glass sitting in front of her, and waited for a response.

"Of course it's your money," Mr. Meyers replied. "It's so unlike you, Sylvia, to give your money away. I want to be sure you understand."

"What the fuck does it matter? I won't be here. You'll get your fee. I've always given to charity, and this is no different. I want shelters built in cities that urgently need them. I've provided you with all the instructions. I then want you to give the rest of the money, my estate, jewels, paintings, etc., to my half-sister. She can do whatever she wants with it. I've added an addendum to give a year's salary to my staff. This includes those I fired unfairly and Ms. Gomez, who worked with me at the magazine. Now, I expect you to do everything I've asked. No questions, no debate. I have complete awareness of what I'm doing."

She took another sip of water. She felt as if she was going to vomit. Her stomach churned, and she felt a sharp pain. She inhaled deeply and leaned forward, clutching her stomach.

Mr. Meyer sprung to his feet and walked over to her. "Sylvia, are you okay? Can I do something?" he asked. He was sitting next to her, looking very concerned.

She closed her eyes and leaned back in the chair. "No, no. I'm okay. It's the cancer working its way through my body," she replied. Her voice had no tone, no fight.

He looked perplexed. "Why have you refused treatment, Sylvia? No chemo? It could save your life."

She took a deep breath and closed her eyes. The pain gradually diminished. She inhaled and exhaled a few more times, then opened her eyes with deliberate care.

"Life is a funny thing. Most of us take it for granted. When I was a little girl, I would go with my father. He was tall and strong. My hero. People loved him. He was always helping people. He didn't judge people. My mother was the exact opposite. She judged everyone; it was about social status, money, power. They fought all the time. The yelling and screaming became normal until he died. Then the yelling and screaming stopped. My mother became a different person. It changed her. It changed me. I became like her. Now, years later, I finally get what my father meant. He found happiness in helping others." She leaned into the chair and closed her eyes. "I want to do these things. As far as saving my life, chemo and radiation is something I don't want. Now, is

355

there anything else you need from me?" she said, sounding impatient.

Mr. Meyer stared at her. He couldn't believe what he was hearing. He'd been her attorney for the past 20 years. She was mean, cold, and calculating, especially with her divorce. She took a big part of his fortune. But more than that, she took the one thing he loved most: his magazine. She'd never read it and until the divorce had no interest in his business dealings.

She refused to have children. She viewed children as a burden, something to hold you back. She spent his money and had several affairs. Mr. Meyer didn't get why her ex-husband stayed married. But when she found out he was cheating, she let him have it. She hired the best lawyers money could buy and took him to school. When the smoke cleared, she'd won.

He left the marriage a broken man. She'd used every trick in the book, including having him sign a very one-sided prenup.

He shook his head no and stood up. "I'll have everything drawn up and messengered to your home."

She shook her head and stood up. "Very good. Thank you. By the way, your other attorney, Ms.

Avery, is she available?" Sylvia said.

He examined her with suspicion and said, "Yes, she's in her office." I can send for her if you'd like."

"No, point me in the right direction," she said.

* * *

Tallulah stood in her bathroom, looking in the mirror. She fixed her locs and picked up a brush.

It would be her mic.

"Welcome to the first annual Marigold Shelter Open Mic!" She spoke in a loud voice. "I'm your host, Finesse the Poet."

She stopped and smiled at herself. She'd come up with that name in high school. She never told anyone, but she'd entered a few poetry contests under that name. She didn't win, but she did receive a few honorable mentions.

Tallulah used the name again in college. She wrote for the campus newspaper and submitted poems to the poetry club's newsletter. She never told anyone it was her alter ego.

She cleared her throat, still looking in the mirror. She then held up the hairbrush. "Tonight, we come together to celebrate the art of the spoken word and the soul of the artist. Now, you can speak, sing, or play poetry. So tonight, we welcome the poets who have chosen to share their thoughts with us. Because we're artists and sensitive, keep your negative comments to yourself. This is a stage of love, power, and encouragement.

"Okay," she said, "that sounds pretty fuckin' good!"

She walked into the bedroom and picked up the papers she'd laid on the bed. She read through them and smiled. She was as ready as she was ever going to be.

* * *

Chloe waded through the bags of beauty supplies in her office. She'd gathered every sample she could find over the past several days. If she was going to do Lily's makeup, she wanted to make sure she had options. She sat down at her desk and opened a large bag. Inside were hair rollers, a blow dryer, conditioners, shampoo, hair dye, and a flat iron. She examined everything with great attention, and then placed the bag down next to her desk.

Her assistant walked into the office and glanced around. "Wow, you must be planning to look fabulous tonight!" she said."

Chloe smiled. "Not for me, but for a friend."

Her assistant moved some of the bags sitting in a chair and sat down. She had a smirk on her face. Chloe looked up to see her grinning at her. She shook her head and said, "Okay, April, what's up? You've got a weird look on your face."

"Well, I'm excited for you. Going out with Stanley Roberts! You are so lucky. You know, I read where he's one of the most eligible bachelors. Girls would kill to be you tonight, Chloe!"

Chloe raised an eyebrow. "Well, it's not a date. It's business."

April smiled and said, "Well, date or business, you're lucky. At least you don't talk like those ghetto girls, so if you're interviewed –"

Chloe interrupted her. "Come again? I don't sound like what?"

April could hear the tone change in Chloe's voice. She stuttered a little. "N-n-no, I meant you sound very professional."

"Professional?" Chloe echoed.

"Yeah, I mean, you see, some women on TV, they sound... well..."

"Black?" Chloe answered for her.

"No, I just meant you sound...well..."

As Chloe stared at her, she could feel herself getting angry. She wanted to show her just how "Black" she could be. She could hear Zoe's voice in her head.

Sometimes you have to educate those around you.

She cleared her throat and opened her mouth to speak, but April spoke first. "Chloe, I just meant – "

"I know what you meant, so please stop talking. I put myself through college. I worked two jobs, held down a full class schedule and excelled at all my classes. I was top in my class. I worked here as an intern for 2 years before the company offered me a full-time job. From there, I worked my way up to the senior rep. I sound, as you say, not ghetto. It's sad that an educated Black woman, who uses all her vowels and consonants, is called sounding white. That's what you meant."

She paused. She was trying to stay calm and choose her words with great care. She wanted to convey a message to her young assistant she wouldn't forget.

"My girlfriend Tallulah always mentions that people tell her she sounds white. In the future, I would appreciate it if you think before you speak. Don't label people by how they sound or look, and don't ever tell any woman of color she sounds white."

April looked down at the floor, then raised her eyes to meet Chloe's with a deliberate slowness. "Chloe, I am so sorry. I didn't mean anything by it, really."

Chloe held up her hand. "Remember what I said. If you want to keep working with me, you'll need to change your mindset. If this is too much to ask, I'm sure one of the other seniors could use you, or maybe another firm."

April looked at her and nodded her head. "I'm sorry, Chloe. I love working for you. You're the best boss I've ever had. I didn't mean to offend you."

"I'm not offended; I'm disappointed," Chloe said. Her voice was calm but firm. "Now, I need the social media stats from the shelter campaign."

April nodded. "I'll get them immediately." She stood up and left the office in haste.

Chloe watched her leave and smiled.

Zoe would be so proud of me, she thought to herself.

* * *

Lily sat on the edge of the bed, wrapped only in a towel. She felt nervous and scared. She rocked back and forth, with her arms wrapped around her body. As she rocked, she began to sing in a gentle voice.

I don't feel sorry for you
You say it's never your fault
You're singing that same sad tune
I'm more happy without you
You need to find another home
I'm more happy without you

She stopped rocking and stood up and walked into the bathroom. "I'd better do this now, while I still have the nerve," she said.

She turned on the shower, dropped the towel to the floor, and stepped inside.

Chapter 38

"No, no, no, that goes over here!" Zoe yelled. She was busy mixing a large bowl of sweet potatoes. "The pie tins are in the fridge. Can you grab them?" she yelled.

"Zoe, calm down. Everything will be ready for tonight," Robert said.

He'd been with her since she opened. She had her doubts when she hired him, but he turned out to be a loyal and valuable employee.

She looked at him and sighed. "We've been so busy since all the social media stuff went out. "I'm grateful, but a little overwhelmed," she said, her hand moving quickly as she stirred the pie batter.

"If you stir that any more, it'll turn to liquid." He laughed.

She looked at the bowl and stopped stirring. "Okay, okay. You're better under pressure," she joked.

"I'm going to prep all the sides for tonight. Your pies tins are already out on the counter." He pointed to several pie tins.

"Oh, I didn't see those," she said, her cheeks reddening with embarrassment.

He smiled at her. "Look, go take a break. I got the pies."

She hesitated before putting down the mixing bowl.

"Thanks, Robert. I've been at it since about 5 this morning."

"I know," he said. "Now go sit down somewhere. I got this."

Zoe shook her head, left the kitchen, and went out into the main dining area of the restaurant. It was strange for it to be empty this time of day. She decided to close the restaurant when Anna showed her the number of tickets that sold.

It's going to be very crowded in here, she thought to herself.

A large partition decorated the stage area. The background was black. Silver letters read: MARIGOLD SHELTER 1ST ANNUAL OPEN MIC. The microphone sat in a tall mic stand. On each side of the mic were instruments, a small drum set, and a guitar and bass. This had been Chloe's idea.

"We need to have live musicians to assist the poets," she said during a yoga class. Zoe looked at her. "Okay, don't they like to get paid?"

"Let me handle it," Chloe said while trying to hold her downward-facing dog pose.

And handle it she did. Zoe looked around the room and sat down in the closest chair to the mic stand. "Well," she said, "here we go."

* * *

Lily was completely dressed. She'd purchased a dress from the thrift store. It was solid black, with a V-neck. It was plain looking, no-frills or slits. She tried to find a pair of shoes but could find only a pair of black petal pushers.

She put the dress and shoes in a bag. Then, she walked to the phone and dialed Tallulah. Tallulah answered on the second ring.

"Hello?" Tallulah answered.

"Hi Tallulah, it's me, Lily. I'm coming to your house. I found a dress and some shoes," she said.

"Great. Do you need the address again?" Tallulah asked.

"No, I have it. If I don't like the makeover, no pictures, right?" she asked. Her voice quivered a little.

"Yes, if you don't like the makeover, no pictures," Tallulah replied.

"Okay. Bye."

Lily hung up the phone, took a deep breath, grabbed the bag with her dress and shoes, and left the hotel room.

Chloe honked as she pulled up in front of Tallulah's building. She waited until Tallulah emerged, then waved and jumped out of the car.

"Wow, you weren't playin', were you?" said Tallulah as she looked at all the bags in Chloe's back seat.

"I know this is important to you and Lily, so I brought everything I could find. I even found some clothes she might like. I have shoes, tights, tops, makeup, hair products – the works! You know a bitch a Girl Scout."

"You're my favorite!" Tallulah said, hugging her.

"So where's Lily?" Chloe asked while handing her some bags.

"She called and said she's on her way. I hope she likes whatever you do."

They made their way up to the 2nd floor and into Tallulah's apartment. Tallulah opened the door and let Chloe in, then shut the door behind her.

"So much stuff!" Tallulah said.

"Well, I thought we could do something with you, too," she

said, setting down the bags. "Me? What's wrong with me?"

"Well, not much, but we can do something about your makeup and style those locs." "I also brought something for you to wear," she said with a tone that conveyed certainty.

"I've never been good with makeup, Chloe. You know this."

"I know. So while we wait for Lily, have a seat." She grabbed a kitchen chair and set it in the middle of the small living room. "Let a bitch work her magic."

Lily stepped off the bus and walked to the apartment building. She took a piece of paper from her pocket. She checked the address. She hurriedly placed it back and entered the apartment building. She was walking up the first step when she heard an apartment door open. A small Hispanic woman stuck her head out the door.

"Hola, are you looking for Tallulah?" Mrs. Herrera asked.

Lily nodded.

Mrs. Herrera smiled at her. "Go upstairs, first apartment." Lily nodded and said, "Thank you."

She turned and headed up the steps. When she reached the top, she paused. She looked at the door, gripped her bag a little tighter, took a deep breath, and knocked on the door.

The door swung open, and there stood Chloe. She wore a form-fitting baby blue dress. Her makeup was flawless, and her hair flowed down her back. Taken aback by her beauty, Lily stared and opened her mouth but didn't speak.

"You must be Lily," Chloe said with enthusiasm. "I've heard so much about you. Come in," she said, moving to one side and allowing her entrance into the apartment.

Lily entered a chaotic scene filled with bags, makeup, hair care products, clothes, and shoes. She looked up to see a very different looking Tallulah come out of the bedroom. She gasped as Tallulah spoke.

"Lily, I'm so glad you made it. This is my very good friend Chloe. She's our resident stylist."

"You look so different. I wasn't sure if it was you."

Tallulah laughed. "Yeah, it's me. Chloe thought I could use some highlighting. I'm the hostess tonight."

Tallulah placed her locs on top of her head in a princess style bun. She styled her eyes in a smoky look, adding hints of blue, purple, and gold. Her eyeliner was deep back and outlined her entire eye. She wore fake eyelashes, which caused her to blink rapidly. Her lips were a dark mahogany and accented her eyes. Lily thought she looked beautiful, elegant, like the women she'd seen in *You & Me* magazine.

"You look beautiful," Lily said.

"And so will you," said Chloe. "Now take off your coat and hat. What's in the bag?" "M...m...my shoes and dress," Lily said with a shy tone.

Chloe reached out her hand for the bag. "Can I see?"

Lily shook her head and handed Chloe the bag, then watched her face as she pulled out the dress.

Chloe held it up and said, "This is pretty, but I have something you'll like. If you don't, we can always go with this. Okay?"

She shook her head yes. She liked Chloe. "Okay." She took off her coat and hat and laid them on the sofa.

"Great. Now come sit," Chloe said, patting the kitchen chair.

Lily sat down and took a deep breath. Chloe kneeled in front of her and grabbed her hand. "Lily, it'll be okay. Your beauty is inherent. I'm only here to enhance that beauty. I'm by no means a professional stylist, but I know a li'l something about makeup and clothes. Okay?" Lily shook her head yes and smiled. "Good. Now let's get started. I want to start with your hair. It's so beautiful. Let's keep the natural look and add some curl and some color."

As Chloe stroked her hair with care, she spoke in a way that suggested they were old friends. Tallulah watched her. The way she smiled and made Lily laugh. The way she made Lily feel at ease. She would chime in from time to time but watching Chloe work was a thing of magic. She had a natural flair for style.

She'd tried, several times, to get Tallulah to wear makeup and switch up her wardrobe. After several years, she'd finally backed off, but she hadn't given up. She often gave Tallulah makeup samples. Sometimes, she dragged her to sales at department stores. Tallulah preferred jeans. She was a writer. She worked either in a small office or from home, so why dress up?

She'd also tried a makeover for Zoe, too, and did manage to talk her into getting a weave. Zoe hated every minute of it. She complained so much, Chloe took it out a week later. Zoe preferred her natural twists, organic face products, and flat shoes.

"How are we friends?" Chloe would ask every time she tried to get Zoe to wear a pair of heels.

After a few hours, Chloe had Lily sitting in the kitchen chair, laughing and talking. She'd just finished applying a rust/gold hair dye to her hair. Lily sat in the chair, with a plastic shower cap on her head.

"So now that we have the color in, let's talk about your outfit for tonight," Chloe said excitedly.

Tallulah was sitting at the kitchen table, working on her

article. She was messaging Sharon while Chloe took Lily into the bedroom.

TB: My friend Chloe is doing her makeup, hair, and clothes. Lily was not happy about the photographer

SE: That's great. Your article will be fantastic. I can't wait to read it.

TB: Sylvia is okay with everything?

SE: Yes, I talked to her. It's better we print the story

TB: Okay. Who is the photographer?

SE: I will send you her info. She should be there at 7 pm. I will let her know to look for you

TB: I won't be hard to find. I'm hosting. Last-minute thing

SE: I wish I could see it. Good luck to you and Lily. Bye

TB: Bye

Tallulah closed her laptop. She could hear Chloe giving her expert opinion on Lily's clothes. Her cell phone buzzed. She rushed to click it on.

"What up, Zoe?"

"Busy. Happy, but busy. What time are you coming?" "In a few. I –"

"Come now. I could use your help."

"Okay. I need to change my clothes. You okay?" Tallulah asked.

"I'm good but could use an extra set of hands," Zoe said.

"I got you. See you in a few."

"Thank you. Love you."

Tallulah clicked off the phone, then got up and walked into the bedroom. Lily wore a soft yellow dress. It had a slight V-neck, and the length was above her knee.

"Lily, you look great!" Tallulah exclaimed as she walked into the bedroom.

"I like it, too, not for this event. Too dressy," Chloe said, putting her hand on her hip. She put a finger across her chin and was deep in thought.

"Well, I like it," said Tallulah. "What do you think, Lily?"

Lily turned at looked at herself in the full-length mirror. The dress was pretty. She swayed from side to side, then said, "I think it's beautiful but too fancy for me."

Chloe frowned. "No dress is ever too fancy for you to wear, but I feel you. Remember, you make the dress; the dress doesn't make you. I've got other stuff for us to try."

Lily shook her head and continued to gaze at herself in the mirror.

"Hey, I spoke to Zoe. She needs my help, so I'm leaving now," Tallulah said. "Can you make sure Lily gets to the restaurant?"

"Of course. Take my car. I'm going to have Stanley pick us up here," Chloe said.

"Stanley? Stanley Roberts?!" Tallulah asked.

"Yep. He asked me to go with him. I think of it as work," she answered.

Tallulah shot her a side-eyed look. "Really?"

"Whatever. Lily, let me make a phone call, then we can rinse the color out."

Chloe grabbed Tallulah by the arm and led her out of the bedroom. "It's not a big deal. I'm not dating him."

She reached for her purse and handed Tallulah her keys.

"Okay, you're not dating him. Can I date him? 'Cause he fine," she joked.

Chloe let out a sigh. "He is fine and soooo nice. I do like him, but, well, I don't date clients. Even a rich, fine ass shot of Hennessy like Stanley Roberts. You know my assistant gave me the green light to date him because at least I sound white?"

"What?" Tallulah said, surprised.

"Yes, girl. But that's a few bottles of wine type of story. You'd better get going. You know how Zoe is."

"You owe me wine service, soon," Tallulah said.

She hugged Chloe, grabbed her bag, notebook, and clothes, and darted out the door.

Chloe pulled out her cell phone and dialed Stanley. She felt surprised to get him on the first ring.

"Chloe, I'm so glad you called. What time should I pick you up?"

"Hi Stanley, slight change of plans. I'm going to text you the address. I'm helping out a friend. Is that okay?"

"Of course. Text me. See you around sixish?" he said.

"That'll be great. Thank you."

"Anytime," he said.

She clicked off and texted him the address, then smiled and went back into the bedroom. "Now let's try this one, then we can rinse."

* * *

Tallulah entered through the back door of the restaurant. She felt surprised by the number of people bustling around. She recognized the regular staff but saw a few new faces running around. She spotted Marc, busy mixing a large container of mac and cheese. He was talking and laughing with Robert, Zoe's regular cook, and he didn't notice her come in. Before she could walk over to him, Zoe grabbed her by her arm and dragged her into the office.

369

"I'm so glad you're here, girl. I don't think I've ever been this busy," she exclaimed while sitting down.

"Okay Boss, what do you need?" Tallulah said.

"Well, we're almost done, but I need all the veggies cut for the salad. Can you prep for me? Please...pretty please?" Zoe said, holding her hands in the prayer position.

"You know I hate prepping, but I'll do it," Tallulah answered. "Show me what and where." Zoe stood up and clapped her hands. "Yea! I love you. You're my favorite."

Tallulah shot her a side-eye. "Really? And what about Chloe?" "Oh, she's my favorite, too. Besides, she ain't here."

"I know. She's giving Lily her makeover. When I left, she was dying her hair and finding her something to wear. I swear that the girl missed her calling. She's a fashionista for real."

"She did your makeup, too?" Zoe asked, staring at Tallulah. Tallulah shook her head yes. "You look pretty." Zoe took her face in her hands and turned it from side to side. "Stop blinking so damn much," she said.

"I can't help it. These damn eyelashes. I don't know if they're going to make it to showtime." She laughed.

"Well, you know me, less is more. I like the old face. This is a good face. But I like your real face."

She hugged her friend and led her out into the kitchen. Tallulah made eye contact with Marc as she entered the kitchen. She smiled and started to walk towards him. He waved and met her halfway.

"Hey, you. I haven't seen you for a while. How are you?" he said, hugging her.

She hugged him back. "So much has been going on," she said.

"You look different. Good, really good. I mean, you always

370

looked good, but you look different now. I like it," he said.

"Well, I'm hosting tonight, so Chloe thought I needed to switch up my look."

Marc smiled. His smile was the kind of smile that could have you daydreaming about making babies.

"Well, if you aren't too busy, Ms. Hostess, I'd love to take you out after the show. Maybe get a drink or something?" he said.

"Okay, I'd love that." She could feel herself blushing. She was getting warm all over. He had that effect on her.

Zoe stood there, watching them talk. She sighed and said, "Can we work now?" She threw Tallulah an apron and pointed to a counter full of fresh vegetables. "Get to cutting." She laughed.

Tallulah nodded and looked at Marc. "The boss has spoken," she said.

* * *

Michael sat in his office, going over the latest issue of *BW*. He was in his editor zone when the buzzing of his cell phone interrupted him. He rushed to check and smiled when he saw it was Zoe calling.

"Hey, you," he said.

"Hi, I was checking in. I haven't seen you," she said.

"Yeah, I know. I've been busy working on the last couple of issues. I even dusted off my resume and will start looking for a real job."

She could hear the hurt in his voice. She paused, then said, "Do you want to hang out after the show tonight? I could get some wine."

He smiled and said, "That's the best offer I've had in a long time."

"Good, I thought we could go to my place. After tonight, I need a break from the restaurant." "Okay, I would say my place, but it's pretty cluttered with boxes and stuff."

"No worries. See you later?" she asked.

"Of course. I'll be there around 7 pm."

"Okay, see you soon," she said.

Michael clicked off the phone and put it down. He started at the layout. He drew his eyes to the empty space where Tallulah's article would go. He sighed and went back into editing mode.

Chapter 39

"Here are the revisions you asked for, Sylvia. Are you sure you want to do this?" Mr. Meyer asked.

"Yes, I'm sure."

Sylvia was sitting at her desk in the study. She felt weak and tired. The cancer was spreading through her body. She no longer went into the office; instead, she spoke to Sharon daily by phone. She looked aged and withered. She spoke in whispers.

She placed the pen on the table and reclined in the large overstuffed chair. She turned her head towards Mr. Meyer. "I never thought my attorney would be the one person concerned with my welfare." She let out a quiet chuckle to herself.

He shifted in his chair. "Sylvia, I've known you a long time. Your family for a long time."

He leaned forward and took her hand. "I'm here because I want to be."

She smiled and closed her eyes. "You'll need to notify everyone after I'm dead. I've written precise instructions, and I want them carried out to a T."

He shook his head, then released her hand and stood up. "Of course, Sylvia. I'll see myself out."

She nodded and watched him leave. She stood up, wobbled

slightly, and grabbed the gold cane sitting next to the chair. She started the long walk to her bedroom. She'd moved to the main level of the house due to the long flight of steps that led up to her bedroom. As she started moving, her nurse came in. "Mrs. Blass, please let me help you."

The nurse rushed to her side and helped her walk. "Mrs. Blass, a Claudia Roberts called. She wanted to know if you'd be joining them next week?"

She stopped walking and looked at the nurse. "When she calls back, tell her I have a previous engagement, then tell her to go straight to hell."

* * *

Chloe paced back and forth in the living room. She waited for Lily to come out of the bedroom with a sense of anxiety.

"How's it going in there?" she yelled.

"I'm fine," answered Lily.

The door opened, and Lily stepped into the living room. Chloe's smile stretched across her face. "Oh girl, you look fucking great!"

She was wearing a beautiful gold-colored dress. Her hair was a light rust gold color. Chloe had twisted it into a bun. Her makeup was flawless. Not too much eye shadow or base, but enough to bring out the youngness in her face. She looked 10 years younger.

She stood in the doorway, holding her breath. "Well?" said Chloe.

"Thank you," she managed to say. She was overcome with emotion. She could feel tears swell up in her eyes.

"Don't you dare cry. You'll ruin your makeup. Stop it," Chloe said. Her voice was cracking as she tried to hold her emotions in check.

Lily walked back into the bedroom and stared at herself in the full-length mirror. She smiled as she turned around. Chloe walked in behind her. "You are so fabulous." It's all you," Lily said.

"No, the beauty was already there. I'm an artist; I enhanced the beauty. The natural beauty was already there."

Lily turned and hugged Chloe. "Thank you," she whispered. A tear rolled down her cheek.

"I said no crying," Chloe said as she wiped a tear from Lily's cheek.

They both laughed.

"Okay, now for shoes," Chloe said, looking around the room.

She found a pair of black low heels. They were perfect.

"I didn't know your size, but I think these will fit. Not too high, but not flat either." She handed the shoes to her. "Now put these on. Our ride will be here in 10 minutes."

She sat down and put on the shoes, then stood up and went straight to the mirror. Chloe started to gather clothes, shoes, makeup, and hair care products. She put them all into bags. She had the living room in a mostly clean state when her cell phone buzzed. It was a text from Stanley, letting her know he was outside.

"Come on, Lily. Time to go."

Lily and Chloe walked out of Tallulah's apartment building. Lily gasped when she saw the long black limo.

She looked at Chloe. "A limo?"

Chloe smiled. "Of course."

The driver was holding the door open. He made a small bow as Chloe slid into the limo. Lily followed suit and got inside.

"Ladies, you look beautiful," Stanley said.

"Thank you, Stanley," Chloe said. "I want you to meet Ms. Lily Duke. She'll be singing for us tonight."

He smiled and extended his hand. "It's very nice to meet you, Ms. Duke. I'm Stanley Roberts." She smiled and extended her hand. "Nice to meet you."

He sat back in the seat and turned his attention toward Chloe, who was sitting across from him.

She crossed her legs at the ankle and slightly leaned to one side. He gazed at her.

She is so beautiful, he thought to himself.

"I'm so glad you decided to be my guest tonight," he said. "I was hoping to maybe spend some time with you off the clock. You know, after the show." Lily looked at Chloe, then again at Stanley.

"Stanley, I'm flattered. I am, but you know I don't date my clients," she said.

"I know, but don't think of it as a date, and don't think of me as a client." He grinned.

Lily continued to look back and forth at them.

Chloe smiled. She wanted to jump him right then and there. She wanted to know what it would be like to kiss him. She wanted to know what his arms felt like wrapped around her body. She wanted to make love to him.

Who I am kidding? she thought. *I want to fuck him.*

"Okay, Stanley," she said in a gentle tone. "I'd love to spend some time with you tonight." Stanley smiled and winked at Lily.

The limo pulled in front of Zoe's restaurant. The driver

376

hopped out and opened the car door.

Lily, Chloe, and Stanley emerged from the limo. The driver shut the door behind them.

"No need to come back, Steve," Stanley said.

The trio walked into the restaurant. Anna immediately spotted them and ran over to greet them. "Chloe, Stanley, so good to see you." She paused as she turned to Lily. "Lily...is that you?" Lily smiled and shook her head.

"Oh my God, you look great. I didn't even recognize you," Anna said.

She pointed to Chloe. "She did it."

Anna smiled at Chloe. "Well, I'm next. You look great. I love your hair. The dress. Oh my God, I can't get over it. You're a completely different person." She grabbed Lily by the hand. "I want to hear everything you've been doing."

Chloe and Stanley watched them walk away. "What was that about?" he asked.

"Come on, let's get a seat, and I'll tell you all about it," she said.

The time for the open mic had finally arrived. Tallulah was in Zoe's office, pacing back and forth. She was nervous. She'd never hosted anything in her life, much less a poetry gig. In her hands, she held her poems. She'd tried to memorize them, but her brain just couldn't hold the words.

She stopped pacing and said a small prayer.

"God, please help me do well tonight. I know we don't talk much, but you know me. I'm your girl, Tallulah. I know you got me this on this. Amen."

She walked out of the office and into the kitchen. The kitchen staff was busy chattering and working. She made eye contact with Marc. He smiled and walked toward her.

"Good luck, Lula." He gently kissed her on the lips.

She smiled at him. "Thank you."

As she walked toward the mic, she felt butterflies in her stomach. It was an excitement she hadn't felt before. She looked around the room. The crowd packed the restaurant. She'd never seen so many people in Zoe's place. There were people standing because there were no more seats. As she continued walking, she made eye contact with Chloe, Stanley, Zoe, and Michael. They were sitting at a table in the front row. She smiled at them. They clapped and gave her the thumbs up. She looked at Lily, who was sitting next to them. She thought she looked stunning. She nodded to her and smiled. She could hear the clicking of the *You & Me* photographer's camera as she snapped photos of her walking to the mic. All this made her nervous, but in some strange way, she was calm, too.

She stood in front of the crowd and gazed around, holding her hand above her eyes. Whistles and claps came from the crowd. She took a deep breath and spoke into the mic.

"Hello. Welcome to the 1st annual Marigold Shelter open mic. My name is Finesse da Poet, and I'm your hostess for this evening. Tonight we're here to help raise money for the Marigold Shelter. I'd like to introduce the Director of the Marigold Shelter, Anna Gomez."

Anna stood as the crowd clapped. She walked to up Tallulah and hugged her, then stepped in front of the mic.

"Thank you, everyone. Florence Marigold started the Marigold Shelter 45 years ago. She worked with great dedication to ensure no one was left out in the cold. Marigold Shelter offers shelter, food, clothing, and more to the city's homeless. There are about 7500 homeless people in our city. We need a bigger space due to the growing homeless population. This way, we won't have to turn anyone away. I thank you for your support tonight. Thank you, Zoe, for welcoming us to your lovely restaurant. Also, a big thank you to Mr. Stanley Roberts for his generous donation to our cause. Thank you."

The crowd roared in applause and whistles. Anna made her way back to her seat. Tallulah, once again, stood in front of the crowd.

"Thank you. Ladies and gentlemen, poets, singers, artists, and dreamers, are we ready to get this party started??!!"

The crowd went crazy. The applause was so loud, you couldn't hear yourself think.

"Let's go!" she said. She felt a rush of energy run through her body. "First things first. The rules. This mic is open to anyone who's brave enough to come forth. There will be no booing or bullshit. We're artists and sensitive about our shit. I have the sign-up list and will introduce each artist. We have a great band here behind me. If you need their help, let them know. Y'all good with the rules?"

The crowd clapped and whistled.

"I'm your first poet of the evening. I call this 'You Sound White.'"

She read her poem. The crowd was silent as she moved through each line. Her voice was strong and commanding. She found her rhythm, and the words flowed from her lips. As she spoke, she closed her eyes. The words came to her. When she finished, she bowed her head and took a step back.

The crowd was frantic with applause. She heard whistles and yelps.

Someone said, "I know that's right!" Another one said, "Okay, now!" She thought she heard Chloe say, "That's my bitch, okay!"

379

After a few moments, she stepped back up to the mic and introduced the next poet.

Poets, musicians, and singers all took their moment at the mic. She watched as the crowd smiled, clapped, and laughed. It couldn't have been more perfect. Chloe had come up to her during the show and said, "Who the fuck is Finesse da Poet, and why haven't we met her before?"

The night continued on until it was time for the last artist, Lily Duke. She'd asked to be last, and Tallulah promised her she'd make it happen.

She walked up to the mic and spoke. "I'd like to introduce our last performer of the evening. Please welcome my dear friend, Lily Duke."

Lily took her time standing up before approaching the microphone. She didn't have any music to give the band, but she told them they could play along if they wanted.

She felt a little flushed as she faced the crowd. It was always her dream to be on stage, doing what she loved: Singing. She took a deep breath, closed her eyes, and started singing.

I don't feel sorry for you
You say it isn't your fault
You're always singing that same sad tune
I'm more happy without you
You need to find another home
I'm more happy without you
You say to give you a chance
You say people can change
But it's that same sad tune
I'm more happy without you
You need to leave my happy home
I'm more happy without you

And now that I've moved on
Got you out of my life
You creep back in
Making no sacrifice
And now I've grown strong
So much better that you're gone
I'm ready to move on
I don't feel sorry for you
Singing that same sad tune
I'm more happy without you
You need to find another home
I'm more happy without you

Her voice was sultry and smooth. Her sound mesmerized the crowd. Her voice carried throughout the room. They hung on every note, their anticipation growing for the next. She swayed back and forth. She closed her eyes, and in an instant, she felt young again. Her voice became stronger and bolder. She didn't even notice the sound of the bass moving with her words. When she hit the last note, the last word, the crowd went crazy. They were on their feet, clapping, shouting and yelling. She brought the house down.

She opened her eyes and looked out at the people. They were applauding her. She looked back at the band and smiled. They, too, were clapping.

Tallulah walked over and hugged her. It was then she noticed the photographer snap her picture. She didn't care anymore. She closed her eyes and hugged Tallulah.

Four weeks after the open mic, Tallulah's article was the cover story for *You & Me* magazine. *Big World* had run a similar story the week before. The article created a buzz throughout the industry.

Sylvia Blass revealed to the world that she had a sister who was half-Black. Tallulah shared the story with so much love and care that she found no fault in the article.

She lay in her bed, feeling weak and tired. It was becoming harder to breathe. The magazine was next to her. She'd finished reading the article when her nurse came into the bedroom.

"Sylvia, someone's here to see you," she said in a gentle tone.

"Who?" she asked.

"Mr. Stanley Roberts," the nurse announced.

The announcement surprised her. She struggled to sit up in bed.

"Hand me a mirror and warm cloth," she said.

The nurse followed her instructions. She dabbed her face with the washcloth and gazed at herself in the mirror. She fixed her hair the best she could, then told the nurse to show him in.

He entered the bedroom with caution. He struggled to recognize her from the last time he saw her. He approached the bed with caution, trying to cut any noise. He could hear her ragged breathing as he approached.

"I'm not asleep, Stanley. Come in, come in," she said, breathing heavy.

"Sylvia, I had no idea you were –"

"Dying?" she interrupted.

"I spoke to my mother the other day, and she didn't mention anything," he said.

"No one knew until the article in the magazine came out," she said. "It's the first time I gave Sharon complete control – and look, copies are flying off the shelves."

He smiled. "May I sit down?"

"Of course, sit."

He sat in a chair next to her bed. In his hands, he held a copy of the magazine. He clenched it in his hands. "I'm one of those who bought a copy. The story is really good. I have a deep sense of admiration. I came over here to talk to you about your magazine."

"Oh?" she said.

"Yes. The cover story - Lily Duke - your sister. I met her at a fundraiser for a homeless shelter. I heard her sing. It was something to see and hear."

"So I've been told," she replied.

"Sylvia, I'll admit, I've never read *You & Me* until this issue. Someone told me months ago you may be looking for a buyer."

"You want to buy my little magazine, Stanley?" she said.

"I want to buy and expand. I want to do more stories like this one. I want to change people's lives for the better," he replied, sounding excited.

"I see," she said, her breath coming in rapid gasps. She closed her eyes and took a deep breath.

"Yes. Your magazine, this issue, is exactly what I want to do. I don't want to reinvent the wheel, so I thought I'd approach you about selling. Selling to me."

Sylvia opened her eyes with hesitation and turned toward him. "Stanley, I've spent many years hurting people. I have no real friends or meaningful relationships. I never thought I'd die alone. Actually, I never thought about dying until I found out I was. I've been trying to decide what to do with *You & Me*. I took it from my ex-husband. Not because I wanted it, but because he did. You've given me an idea. If I sell to you, there are some terms you must meet."

He shook his head. "Okay, what terms?"

"You keep Sharon on as editor. This issue you admire so is her brainchild. You want more of that, then keep her on."

He thought a moment, then looked down at the magazine he held in his hands. "You know," he said, not taking his eyes off the magazine, "this issue is good, Sylvia. So different than the others."

"Yes, I know. I read it. All the more reason to keep Sharon. The next thing is this Tallulah Brock. She wrote the article you like so much," she said.

"Yes, I know. I've met her," he said.

"Hire her. She's freelance. Make her a senior writer or whatever, but hire her."

"Anything else?" he asked

Change the name as the final step. Call it whatever you'd like, but not *You & Me*. You can discuss the price with my attorney. That's all. Meet my terms, and the magazine is yours," she said.

He sat for a moment, thinking about her terms. "I'll have my attorney contact yours. I think we can meet your terms."

"Good. Now if there isn't anything else, Stanley, I'm very tired. This was the most excitement I've had in a long time. I need to rest."

She closed her eyes. He sat a moment longer, then stood up. He looked at her as she lay there with her eyes closed. He felt sorry for her. She looked frail, not at all what he remembered from their last meeting.

He turned and left the room. He was eager to get the paperwork done on the magazine. As he walked to his car, he called his attorney and told him what he wanted. His head was spinning with ideas. He couldn't wait to call Chloe.

Chapter 40

“That was great, Lily. Let’s take a break,” the man said from the sound booth. “It sounded great.” Lily shook her head and took off the headphones, then walked out of the small booth and over to Owen. He was sitting in his wheelchair, grinning.

“You look like the cat who ate the canary,” she said with a playful smile to him.

“You sounded great. You’re going to be the latest sensation, Lily,” he said.

Owen had taken the money Sylvia had given him and hired a producer and studio to record Lily’s album. He struggled to find someone to produce her. Then, her performance videos went viral, and offers began pouring in.

She was hesitant, but he told her he would be with her every step of the way. “I’m in a wheelchair Lily; I’m not dead. I won’t let anyone take advantage of us, of you. You’re finally on your way, and no one will stop us this time. I promise,” he said.

They’d decided to work with a small, independent label. Lily’s music would come out in a few months. There were talks of tours, club dates, TV appearances, and concerts. It was all happening so fast. Lily was glad to have Owen with her. He'd always been that shoulder she could lean on.

He rented a small house for the two of them and left the nursing home. He felt as if he had a reason to live. He was alive again. The excitement of Lily's raising success gave him a spark and jolt of life.

On the day You & Me hit the newsstands, Lily and Owen were in the studio. They were recording when the producer said to take a break.

"Why are you grinning like that, Owen? What's going on?" she said.

He handed her a copy of You & Me. She gasped when she saw her face on the cover. She turned and looked and him, then back at the magazine.

"What? This is me!" she said.

He nodded.

"This is me!" she said again

Again, he nodded. She put her hand over her mouth, then turned her head toward him. "This is me!" she said.

"We've already had this conversation, darlin'. I think you should read the story. That Tallulah did you justice. Hell, she even mentioned me," he said.

Lily quickly opened to Tallulah's story. Her eyes darted across the page as she read. There was a picture of her singing at the open mic. She didn't even realize the photographer was taking pictures.

He watched her as she read. He hadn't felt this good in years. He'd even called his daughter and told her he'd moved out of the nursing home. He told her he was back in the music business and not to come around asking for money.

She finished the article. There were tears rolling down her cheeks. "I don't know what to say. I never thought I would ever see my face on the cover of a fashion magazine."

"Well," he said, "We were both due for some good luck. Hell, Lily, I was stuck in a fucking nursing home, and you were living on the street. Look at us now. You singing again, me back in a studio. I may be old, but I ain't dead. We get to live our lives now."

She smiled. The producer walked over to both of them. "Okay, Lily, we're ready. You sound great. I'd like to record the song you did, you know, the one on YouTube."

Lily shook her head. "It doesn't have a title, and I never wrote music for it," she said. "

I think I can help with that."

The producer, Owen, and Lily spent the rest of the day in the studio, recording. She was finally living her dream. She was a singer.

Chapter 41

Michael sat in the small offices at *Big World*. He'd printed his last edition of the small paper. He sat in the middle of the room on the floor. He sold or gave away the desk, chairs, bookcases, phone, and other equipment. The room was empty.

Next to him was a small blue cooler and chess game. He opened it and pulled out a beer, popped off the top, and took a big drink.

Tallulah walked in and smiled when she spotted him on the floor. "Wow, I don't think I've even seen this room empty." She walked over to him and sat down. He handed her a beer. They clicked bottles, and both took a drink.

"Well, Boss, it's been a pleasure working with you. Michael, you're a damn good editor. You've been a good friend to me for a long time. I love you. Cheers."

He smiled. "Thanks, T. I love you, too. You're a damn good reporter. I read your article in *You & Me*. It was good. But what amazed me was the poetry. Who knew Tallulah Brock was Finesse da Poet?"

She blushed a little. "Well, it was something I came up with a long time ago. I never told anyone. I don't really know why. But when they asked me to host, I thought, *Why not?* So voila

– Finesse da Poet."

"Well, I found it impressive," he said. "So, what's next?"

"I should be asking you that," she said.

"Well, I have a couple of interviews set up for next week. One is for an editor for an online paper, and the other is editing for a small publishing company. My rent is paid for a few months. I have a little money in the bank. I'm good, T. I'm really good," he said.

"I'm happy for you, Michael. So...what's up with you and Zoe? Is she your girlfriend?" Her tone was playful. She poked him with her finger.

"Let's just say things are going well. I like her," he said.

"Duh. It's about time," she said.

"So, what are you going to do?" he asked.

"I dunno. I guess keep freelancing. Sharon said we could talk about future stuff, and well, they did pay well for my story. So, I'm good, too."

Michael took a long drink from his beer. "Well, the end of a chapter." He put the empty bottle into the cooler, then handed her set of keys.

"You did good, Michael. You did what most never will. You actually lived your dream. That's huge! *Big World* can always come back online, ya know."

"I know. It's something I'm thinking about," he said.

"Well, don't think too long. You'd do well," she said.

The two friends sat in the empty office, then Michael opened the chess set and set up the board.

"Okay, best out of 3," he said.

She laughed. "Just 3?"

He shook his head, yes, and they both laughed. They played and drank for the rest of the afternoon. Tallulah still beat him by winning 2 out of 3.

Chapter 42

Sylvia Blass took her last breath at 10 am this morning. Her breathing had become labored during the night. She'd become restless and confused. She had hallucinations of her mother and cried out several times during the night. Her nurse had made her as comfortable as possible. There was no family to call or friends to notify. She was alone. The rattle in her lungs had started the night before. She was having a hard time swallowing. Her breathing had become crackling and made a wet noise with every rise and fall of her chest.

The nurse sat beside her, watching her breath slower and slower until her chest fell for the last time. She checked her watch and wrote down the time. She covered her face with a sheet and left the room with caution.

Sylvia Blass was dead.

The next day, Stanley Roberts walked into the offices of *You & Me*. He and Sylvia had signed the deal before her passing. He told her he'd meet her terms and price. He was to take over immediately after she died.

He approached the receptionist and requested to speak with Sharon. The receptionist smiled broadly at him. She buzzed Sharon, and Sharon gave her directions to show Stanley to her office.

Sharon stood as he entered her office. She felt surprised by how good looking he was in person. She shook his hand and asked him to sit down.

"What can I do for you, Mr. Roberts?" she said.

"Well, it's more what I can do for you, Mrs. Eckerson."

"Please, call me Sharon."

"Only if you call me Stanley," he said.

"Okay, Stanley, what can you do for me?" she asked.

"Well, first of all, I like the latest article of *You & Me*. It was good, probably the best one yet. I'm told it was because of you."

She smiled. "Thank you."

"Readers would like a magazine with less fluff and more real-life stuff. Maybe learn about what's going on in the world. What do you think?"

"I would agree," she said.

"Good. As of yesterday, I became sole owner of *You & Me* magazine. Part of my terms were to keep you on as editor-in-chief."

"What?" she said, completely surprised.

"Yes. Sylvia sold it to me. Her terms were to keep you on as editor, hire Tallulah Brock, and change the name," he said. "Now, I know she's freelancing, but we need her full-time. Make her a senior writer or whatever."

"I...I...I don't know what to say. Sylvia never said anything to me," Sharon said.

"Well, say yes, that you'll stay. I was looking at the payroll. You, Sharon, are due for a raise. What you did here was good. Can you do it again?"

"Well, yes, I never..." Her voice trailed off.

"Well, I want us to work together. I'm no editor, Sharon, and I know you're talented. Do you want to be a part of a magazine that tells real stories? Stories they may never get told unless we tell them?"

"Yes, I do," she said.

"Then stay. It's no longer *You & Me*. It's *All of Us*." Sharon looked confused.

"The name of the magazine. I changed the name to *All of Us*. What do you think?"

She smiled. "I like it."

"Great, so get your stuff, we're going to lunch. I'd like to get to know my new editor and pick your brain about ideas."

He smiled at her and stood up, then held out his hand and helped her up.

"Stanley, there's one thing you should know. I'm pregnant. I'd planned on resigning after this issue. I know Sylvia never would have understood me wanting to have kids."

"You're pregnant?" he said. "That's great. He or she will get to know Uncle Stanley."

She smiled at him and grabbed her purse and coat. He smiled back at her.

"Now, what do you feel like eating?"

* * *

Tallulah, Chloe, and Zoe sat in the back of Zoe's restaurant. Zoe had decided to close the restaurant for the day. She'd been working long days ever since the open mic. Her customer volume had tripled, and she needed to hire more staff if she was to keep up with the growth.

The three of them sat at the table. Chloe corked a bottle of wine and was pouring it into the three glasses sitting on the table.

"So Finesse, any plans with Marc?" Chloe asked.

Tallulah smiled. "Maybe. What's up with Stanley? The last time I saw you two, you were leaving together."

Chloe smiled. "Well, I would say a good girl doesn't kiss and tell, but I ain't no girl. I'm a woman."

They all laughed

"Seriously, I like him. He isn't like anyone I've ever met."

"Are you seeing him?" Zoe asked.

Chloe smiled and nodded. "We're taking it slow, but I like how things are going now."

Tallulah smiled. "I'm happy for you. And Michael and Zoe, finally."

"Cheers to motherfuckin' that, and amen," Chloe said. They all lifted their glasses and drank.

"So T, what you gonna do for a job?" Zoe asked.

"Well, I still freelance. Lily's article is getting a lot of buzz. Owen Katz called me and asked me to help him write a book. Is that not crazy? Me writing a book?"

"What's crazy about it?" Zoe said. "You're talented."

"You know your poem, 'You Sound White'? I liked it, Tallulah. I could relate. I think a lot of Black women could relate," Zoe said. "I love how you write. I love how you sound."

"Here here," added Chloe. "Finesse my bitch."

"Thank you. Oh, I love you bitches!" she said.

"You know, for a long time, I never felt like I fit in anywhere. I wrote that one day in high school. This white girl told me I was trying to sound white. I wasn't; I was being me. Then I started seeing a trend. I wasn't the only one. You two have had your experiences, even Michael. So, when you asked me to host, I found it and decided to read it."

"You should publish your stuff, T. I mean Finesse. Seriously," Chloe said.

"Zoe cooks, I'm a fashion and PR genius, and you...well, you write. I could be your literary agent!" Chloe's voice went up in tone from her excitement.

"Well, Chloe, let's talk about it. "Set up a lunch," Tallulah said with a laugh.

"I'm serious, Finesse. I'm going to set up a lunch for next week."

Tallulah stared at her. "You're serious?"

"Yes, my boyfriend owns a publishing house." She winked at her.

Epilogue - One year later

Tallulah stood at the podium. She looked out into the audience and cleared her throat. Next to her was a full blow-up of her book, *Fighting My Way Back: The Lily Blass Story*.

Chloe was serious when she told her to publish. She'd taken her advice and met with Owen Katz. He wanted her to write a book about Lily, and him, too. Lily had agreed as well. Chloe had taken the idea to Stanley, and he never looked back. He loved the idea. She asked Michael to edit the book. She couldn't think of anyone better. He agreed without hesitation. They made a great team.

Stanley offered her a literary contract and advance. She'd agreed to write 4 more books for him. She still managed to freelance from time to time, but her life as a writer had changed. She was becoming known and recognized for her talent.

She was surprised by how many women of color reached out to share their stories. They, too, had been told they sounded white. Zoe had given her the idea to start writing down their stories and compiling them for her next book.

"You have the title," Zoe said. "*You Sound White*."

Lily's career had taken off, and she was on an international tour. Lily Blass was becoming a well-known. The magazine article, a viral YouTube video, and Chloe's PR skills helped a lot.

Sylvia's attorney surprised her when he contacted her about her will. Sylvia had left her a fortune. At first, she was afraid to take the money, but Owen had convinced her of all the good she could do. She donated to the Marigold Shelter in the name of her mother, brother, and sister Sylvia. Anna had decided to name the new shelter the Blass House. Lily also decided to take on the Blass name and released her first record as Lily Blass.

Tallulah had finished reading an excerpt from her book. She smiled as the crowd applauded. As she stepped down from the podium, Marc was smiling at her.

"You sounded great," he said.

"Thanks," she said, smiling back.

"Lunch?" he said.

"Okay," she said.

They held hands as they made their way through the book-store. Outside, a black Town Car was waiting. The name on the side of the car read, "King and Queen Car Service".

Marc opened the passenger door for her, then ran around to the driver's side and hopped in.

"So, where to?" he asked.

"I feel like soul food, comfort food," she said, smiling.

He leaned over and kissed her. She kissed him back.

"I know just the place," he said, then put the car in drive.